Praise for SUE HARRISON and
CRY OF THE WIND

"A MASTER STORYTELLER."
Anna Lee Waldo, author of *Sacajawea*

"ROMANTIC AND DRAMATIC...
An intricate pattern of love and hatred,
lust and betrayal. Harrison's engrossing tale
will appeal to Jean Auel fans."
Booklist

"I WAS HOOKED...
Harrison keeps the tension very high, drawing the reader
in... *Cry of the Wind* is bound to keep you entranced."
Denver Post

"HARRISON BRINGS THE CHARACTERS
VIVIDLY ALIVE
as they struggle to subsist in the Alaska of
eighty centuries ago."
Tampa Tribune

"A GREAT ESCAPE...
Harrison reached out and grabbed me...
I was enthralled."
Traverse City Record-Eagle

"A POWERFUL AND COMPELLING SAGA...
A love story that will challenge your imagination
and stimulate your mind...
Every aspect of this story is exceptional."
Rendezvous

SUE HARRISON

CRY OF THE WIND

AVON BOOKS ◆ NEW YORK

This is a work of fiction. Names, characters, places, and incidents either are the product of the author's imagination or are used fictitiously. Any resemblance to actual events, locales, organizations, or persons, living or dead, is entirely coincidental and beyond the intent of either the author or the publisher.

AVON BOOKS, INC.
An Imprint of HarperCollins*Publishers*
10 East 53rd Street
New York, New York 10022-5299

First Avon Books Paperback Printing: February 2000
First Avon Books Hardcover Printing: December 1998

AVON TRADEMARK REG. U.S. PAT. OFF. AND IN OTHER COUNTRIES, MARCA REGISTRADA, HECHO EN U.S.A.

Printed in the U.S.A.

WCD 10 9 8 7 6 5 4 3 2 1

For our children, in love and joy:
our daughter, Krystal,
our son, Neil, and his bride, Tonya

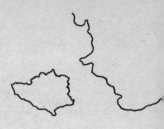

Bering Sea

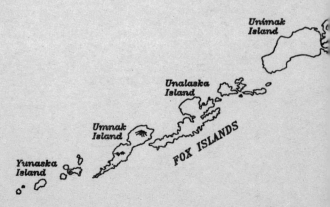

Unimak
Island

Unalaska
Island

Umnak
Island

Yunaska
Island

FOX ISLANDS

Iliamna
Lake

Cousin River
Winter Village

Cousin River
Summer Fish Camp

Near River
Winter Village

Near River
Summer Fish Camp

Walrus
Hunters
Village

Becharof Lake

Alaska Peninsula

First Men
Village

Pacific Ocean

Miles

0   25   50   75   100

Cry of the Wind
I

 # PART ONE

610 B.C.

The old woman looked down at the child. The boy's eyes were shining, alert. She was tired, but how often did a storyteller have the pleasure of passing her tales to a child like this? How often was a Dzuuggi, a child destined to be a storyteller, born to the People? And this one was surely Dzuuggi. She had heard his voice in her dreams even when his mother carried him in her womb.

The old woman had also been chosen Dzuuggi, taught as a child the histories of the River People, but now that knowledge was a burden——so many words to be remembered. Each day as she told the stories to the boy, she felt their weight lift from her, and each day she felt lighter and stronger as though her old bones would straighten, and she would walk once more with firm steps.

She cupped a wooden bowl of willow bark tea in her hands. She raised the tea to her mouth and sipped. The bowl had darkened with age, the wood rich from the many teas it had held, the many stories it had heard.

Be like this bowl, small Dzuuggi, the old woman thought, and she closed her eyes, lifted her head so those thoughts would climb like a prayer. Be like this cup. Hold much, give much, and become rich with what is within you.

"So then, child," she began, "you remember those two storytellers, Aqamdax and Chakliux?"

The boy nodded, whispered the names.

"You do not hear many stories about storytellers; their voices you hear, but only that. So this is something unusual." The old woman paused and stared into the smoke of the hearth fire at the center of her lodge. The wood was still peaked high, a feast for the burning mouth that would finally consume what she had offered. She reached into the smoke, brought a cupped hand to her face as though to pull words from the flames.

"And you remember that Chakliux was from the River People, just like we are?" she asked. "You remember that he was also chosen as Dzuuggi like you?" Though her words were questions, she did not give him time to answer; instead she went on: "And the woman Aqamdax, she was what?"

"Sea Hunter, First Men," the boy said.

The old woman nodded.

"Not River," said the boy.

"Not River, but not so different from us. We share their blood, at least some of us do." She lifted one finger, pressed it to the wrinkles that spread like a fan between her eyes. "You remember Chakliux had a little Sea Hunter blood, though he was River. I told you about his foot."

She pulled off one of her furred lodge boots. The leather sole, softened by wear, dark from hearth fire smoke, had worn thin under her toes. She used one hand to press the side of her foot to the floor.

"Curled on edge, it was," she said, "like an otter's foot when he paddles in the water and his toes were webbed on both feet. Like otter toes." She rubbed her bare foot, rubbed and hummed a tuneless song, then pulled on her boot.

"So now perhaps I will listen," she said, "and you will tell me a little about Chakliux the Dzuuggi."

The boy straightened his shoulders and began to speak in a small, soft voice. The old woman interrupted him. "You think anyone will listen to you if you speak like that?" She pressed her hands into the arch under her rib cage. "From here, your words must come from here." She puffed out her chest with air, and the boy did the same. "Now," she said, and he spoke again, this time much louder.

"Good," said the old woman. "Now I can tell that the words come from your heart."

"When he was a baby," said the boy, "Chakliux was left on the Grandfather Rock to die."

"'Ih?" the old woman said, as if she were listening to an actual storytelling, and the Dzuuggi's words had surprised her. "A Dzuuggi left to die?"

"It is true," the boy said. "His grandfather left him, because of the foot. He did not see it as otter, but only as a curse, and he left Chakliux. But Chakliux did not die. The woman K'os came and found him there. She took him home, and he became her son. But she hated him. She hated everyone else, too, after men took her by force on the Grandfather Rock and killed the spirits of her unborn children. She thought Chakliux was a gift to make up for what had happened.

"When Chakliux grew up, she was jealous of him because he was wise, and because he was chosen to be

Dzuuggi. She even killed his wife and baby."

"They must have driven her from the village after she did that," the old woman said.

The boy leaned toward the old woman and lowered his voice to a whisper. "No, she did it secretly with poison, and so everyone thought they died from sickness."

"You know that she was the one who started the war between the Near River and Cousin River Villages," the old woman said. "Of all the things I have taught you, there is nothing more important than the remembrance of that war. Though it was long ago, much changed because of the fighting. So many of the River People died, and villages that had been strong grew weak."

Her throat sounded full, as if she would cry, but when the boy looked into her eyes, he saw that they were hard and dry. She shook her fist at the hearth fire, and he wondered if the smoke could carry her anger back through the years to those foolish people.

"The Near River and Cousin People fought against each other," she said. "They were related—cousins, the men and women in those two villages—but still they fought."

"Why?" the boy asked.

"No good reason," the old woman told him. "Most fighting starts for no good reason. That is why we have Dzuuggis—to remind us of our foolishness, so we will not do the same things again."

"Chakliux tried to stop the fighting."

"Yes, he did, but they fought anyway."

"And the Near River People won," the boy said.

"Think about that for a moment," said the old woman. "Did anyone truly win? Remember all the lives lost, and the hard winters both villages suffered because so many of their men had died." The old woman sighed and shook her head. She looked at the boy and said, "Tell me about K'os."

"She lived in the Cousin River Village and she tricked the people there," he said. "When she realized that her people were too weak to win the war, she helped the Near River men kill the boys and the strongest women, then she surrendered the rest. But the Near Rivers didn't trust her, so she was made a slave."

"Aaa," said the old woman. "I understand." She sat quietly for a time, then said, "I told you about Aqamdax, how she left her people and came to the River People as wife of the hunter Sok, Chakliux's brother. Sok did not want her and threw her away."

She lifted her finger again and shook it as if in warning. "I will tell you this, child. Sometime you may hear people say since Aqamdax was Sea Hunter, what she did is not important to us. But anyone who tells you that is a fool. You see, each story is like a small fire, giving light and warmth. Why do you think every village has more than one hearth?"

The boy lifted his hands, fingers spread. "With only one," he said, "there would be too much darkness."

"For a child, you are very wise," the old woman told him. "So tell me a little about Aqamdax."

"Chakliux and Aqamdax shared a great love. Chakliux wanted to marry her, but she was sold as a slave to K'os. Later the hunter Night Man bought her to be his wife. Chakliux found out where she was, and when the fighting was over, he went to live with the Cousin River People so he could be near Aqamdax. He married Night Man's sister to be as close to her as possible."

The old woman smiled. "You remember well," she told the boy. She drank a large swallow of her willow tea, then nodded at the water bladder that hung from the lodge poles over their heads. The boy stood and untied the bladder. He handed it to her, and she squeezed water into her cup. She dipped her fingers into the water and sprinkled a few drops over the fire. She drank again, and said, "I think you are ready to learn what happened next. Listen:"

LATE SUMMER
6458 B.C.

TWISTED STALK, WIDOW OF
THE COUSIN RIVER PEOPLE

Sometimes when I wake in the morning, I do not know where I am. How could this place be our village? Where are our hunters, our young women?

The children cry in hunger; the old women no longer greet the day in gladness. Mourning songs fill the air until it is as dark as soot. At night when I close my eyes to sleep, I see our lodges burning. I see the bones of my sons and grandsons dishonored by our enemies.

I remember those days when the Near River and Cousin River Peoples were one, when together we celebrated the great hunters who are grandfathers to both villages.

How did anger make us forget that bond? How did hatred steal into our hearts and capture our souls?

I am afraid for those not yet born. What is our gift to them? The pride of who we are, the joy and beauty of this earth? No, not when we pass down our enmity as heritage, mother to daughter, father to son.

ONE

THE COUSIN RIVER VILLAGE

The old women prepared a separate boiling bag of meat and broth for those three wives in the village who were pregnant: Aqamdax, Star and Red Leaf. Parts of the caribou were taboo for them. The flesh and bones of the neck would cause clumsiness in their unborn children, and the front legs and the meat of the lower jaw and lips must be saved for the old men.

Aqamdax knew her baby was a boy. She hid her laughter when other women told her, since she carried the child low, it was a girl. Did she not hear his whispers, the songs he sang into her dreams? Of course it was a boy. She had known since her fourth moon of pregnancy, when he had first begun moving within her belly.

During the past spring, with only six hunters left in their village after the fighting, the men had been unable to take all the caribou they needed, but at least they had killed enough to stave off their hunger. The women had dried the meat, did not allow one scrap to go to waste. The hides, riddled by the breathing holes of warble fly larvae, were useless for clothing and nearly impossible to scrape, but with their lodges burned and their caches looted, how could the women throw those hides away?

Now at the end of summer, Chakliux and his older

brother Sok had taken a fine, fat caribou bull. For one night, the people pushed away their anger, their helplessness, and celebrated with a feast.

As Aqamdax ate, she hummed songs to her baby, told him to grow strong like the caribou. Some of her singing was in the River tradition of her husband's people. But she had learned most of her songs from her own people, the First Men who lived beside the great North Sea.

The songs kept her mind busy, kept her thoughts on her child and on her husband, away from the hunter Chakliux, honored as Dzuuggi—storyteller—of this village. He was young but wise, given as gift, the people said, from the otters. Who could not see that he carried otter blood, with his left foot bent on edge, his toes webbed?

When everyone had finished eating, and the women had banked the cooking fires into smoke smudges to drive away those night insects that still lingered at the end of summer, then Chakliux and Sok told the story of the hunt.

Aqamdax squatted on her haunches, her legs spread to accommodate her growing belly. She caught sight of her husband, Night Man, watching her, and so was careful not to allow her eyes to linger too long on Chakliux.

Be grateful for Night Man, Aqamdax told herself. Be thankful you are wife and no longer slave. Find joy in the child he has given you, and honor your husband.

She sat with her brother, Ghaden, a boy of five summers, on her right side, Ghaden's stepsister, Yaa, on her left. Both children had lost their parents and had been adopted by Chakliux's wife, Star. But Aqamdax was the one who watched over them, made their clothing, prepared their food. Star had taken them on a whim, like a child who chooses to raise a baby fox. Who could trust her to care for two children?

Yaa snuggled close to Aqamdax, but Ghaden was standing, watching with wide eyes as Sok and Chakliux acted out their hunt.

Chakliux's words carried pictures into her mind, and Aqamdax could see the caribou, the white bands that streaked his sides blending with the lights and shadows of the dwarf birches where he stood; tatters of blood-rich skin hanging from his antlers, the bone-hard tines stained dark as bearberry leaves, autumn red.

Then Star pressed herself between Ghaden and Aqamdax, breaking into that vision of caribou. She tilted her chin up as though to challenge Aqamdax, and pulled Ghaden into her lap.

He struggled against her, and both began to squabble, first in quiet words, then with rising wails. Aqamdax leaned forward, caught her brother's eye and raised her fingers to her mouth in a sign for silence. Ghaden pursed his lips in anger but turned back to watch the men.

Star gave Aqamdax a smug smile, then leaned close to whisper, "In only a few moons I will have two sons." She glanced down at Aqamdax's belly. "At best you will have only one."

Aqamdax closed her eyes to Star's foolishness and did not answer. She could only pity Chakliux's child, asleep in the hard cradle of Star's bones.

In one evening of feasting, the caribou was gone, save for the broth that could still be boiled from skull and ribs. The words and songs of the hunters' stories drifted up until the night air thinned them like smoke, and they floated above the sleeping village, until the people called them back through their dreams.

Aqamdax slept, warm in her hare fur blankets on the women's side of Star's lodge. Beside her, old Long Eyes slept. Long Eyes was Star and Night Man's mother, and since her husband's death seemed more child than woman, as though her spirit had followed her husband into the world of the dead. Often she stayed awake through the night, moaning strange songs, but a full belly had lulled her into sleep. Aqamdax's thoughts grew into pictures, and she was with her husband, Night Man, when Chakliux and Sok brought their caribou into the village. Night Man was scowling, his useless arm bound to his body with strips of caribou hide.

Aqamdax kept her eyes from Chakliux. Night Man was watching her, as he always did when Chakliux was near. She turned her head to look at her husband, smiled and leaned toward him until her hip touched his. There were many small ways to show a husband respect, ways that would not embarrass him in front of other men.

Aqamdax's dreams changed to remembrances of her life as a child, when she had lived with the First Men near the great North Sea. Her father was still alive, and he picked her up, his hands around her waist. Suddenly he was squeezing her, and she could not breathe. She cried for him to stop, then looked down and saw that he was dead, his skin dark, his lips as blue as they had been when he had drowned. She heard her mother wail out in a terrible mourning cry, and her voice was so loud that it woke Aqamdax.

Star and Yaa were beside her.

"You screamed," Yaa said. "What's the matter?"

Aqamdax shook her head, tried to break the last threads that bound her into sleep. "Just a dream," she said, then gasped as the pain took her again, circling her hips and pressing into her bones.

Star drew away, her hands over the small mound that was her baby. "Get her out of here," she told Yaa. "Her child might call mine to come."

Star backed into the far side of the lodge, paying no heed that she walked over her husband's bed to get there.

Chakliux raised up on one elbow, looked first at his wife, then at Aqamdax. "What is wrong?" he asked.

Star pointed rudely with her thumbs. "She, her baby. It is wanting to be born."

Chakliux wrapped a sleeping robe around his shoulders and crept to Night Man. Chakliux shook him until he was awake. "Your wife's child is trying to be born," Chakliux said. "I will go get my aunt."

The pain eased, and Aqamdax was able to speak. "It is early. The baby should not come for more than a moon," she said.

"Go to your birth lodge. I will bring Ligige'," said Chakliux.

"I have no birth lodge."

What woman would prepare her lodge a full moon before delivery? Why tempt a child to come into the world when he is not strong enough to survive?

"Go to Red Leaf's. Hers is ready, is it not?"

Aqamdax nodded. Another pain took her, and she squeezed her eyes shut until it passed. She did not want to go to Red Leaf's lodge, but how could she object? She could not stay here, cursing the men and their weapons, and perhaps Star's unborn baby. Red Leaf had killed Aqamdax's mother and Chakliux's grandfather. She had tried to kill Ghaden. How could Aqamdax use a birth lodge made by a woman whose heart was stained with blood?

With Yaa's help, Aqamdax managed to stumble from the lodge, but just outside the entrance tunnel, she felt the beginning of another pain. She squatted on her haunches, and before the pain tore away her breath, told Yaa to go back and get the cradleboard she had made and the hare furs she had prepared.

Yaa left her, and just as the pain eased, she returned with the cradleboard and furs. She helped Aqamdax to her feet, then they walked to the edge of the village.

When they reached the isolated place where Red Leaf had made her birth lodge, Aqamdax could see it was lit from within. Chakliux must have already brought Ligige' to the lodge, but how could the old woman have started a fire so quickly?

Someone called. Chakliux, Aqamdax thought, and she was surprised. Most men stayed as far as possible from a woman about to deliver a child. A woman's power was great at such times, and even though she meant no harm, that power could destroy a man's hunting luck.

"I cannot find Ligige'," Chakliux said.

The old woman popped her head out of the birth lodge. "Someone else wants me?" she asked. Then, seeing Aqamdax, she frowned. "You, too?"

A pain took her, so Aqamdax could do no more than crouch and brace herself, but she listened as Yaa and Ligige' spoke.

"I have Red Leaf here," Ligige' said. "It will be some time before her baby is born. When did Aqamdax's pains begin?"

"Only a little while ago," Yaa said, "but they are close together, one pain chasing another."

"That happens sometimes when a baby comes early," Ligige' told her. "We cannot have both women in the same lodge. One child's death could curse the other's birth."

Ligige' 's words pierced Aqamdax's heart. How could the woman speak so lightly of the child Aqamdax had grown to love more than her own life?

"Take her to my lodge," Ligige' said. "I will come as soon as I can." She ducked her head back inside, but then she peeked out again. "On your way, wake Day Woman and tell her to come here. She will not want to, but remind her that Red Leaf's child also belongs to her son Sok."

Chakliux saw Yaa leave his mother's lodge, saw his mother walk the path to the birth hut. Aqamdax stopped once, stooped over in pain, then continued to Ligige' 's lodge and slipped inside. Light from the hearth fire soon glowed through the lodge walls, and Chakliux's thoughts turned to his first wife, Gguzaakk.

For a long time after her death, Chakliux could find no reason to live save his duties as Dzuuggi and his desire to keep peace between the Cousin and Near River Peoples, but then he had decided to live in the Near River Village and Aqamdax had come into his life.

She was a storyteller, trained in the traditions of the First Men, and Chakliux had grown to love her, had decided to ask her to be his wife. What could be better than two storytellers living together, learning from one another? But the trader Cen had stolen Aqamdax, taken her to the Cousin River Village and sold her as a slave. Before Chakliux could find where Cen had taken her, Night Man bought Aqamdax as wife, and now Aqamdax labored to deliver Night Man's child.

Chakliux shook his head. Night Man was as foolish as his sister Star. He was worried about whether Aqamdax's child belonged to him. Aqamdax had been forced into other hunters' beds while she was a slave. If the baby was born large and strong, it was not Night Man's, though he would be wise to raise the child as his own. If it was small—a sign it had been born early—it was certainly his child but would probably die.

Chakliux was not wise enough to know which way he should pray—there would be sadness if the child lived or if it died. Instead he prayed for Aqamdax. That she would live. How could he bear to again lose a woman he loved?

Snow-in-her-hair offered Sok a bowl of soup, and he lashed out at her in harsh words. The thin, nearly meatless broth added to his anger. Any wife should be ashamed to offer her husband such poor food. What happened to the caribou belly they had roasted whole, full of the tender summer plants the animal had been eating before Sok and Chakliux had killed it? What happened to the rich broth made from the head? Surely, some of that was left. Who deserved to eat it more than he?

Again he threw harsh words at his wife, but when he saw his son Cries-loud press himself up against the side of the lodge, he was suddenly ashamed of his anger. It was not the broth that tortured his soul but the birth of Red Leaf's child. He would keep the baby if it was healthy, but what about Red Leaf?

She had cost Sok the leadership of the Near River People. Someday, he would have been their chief hunter, and Chakliux had held an honored place as storyteller. Together they would have guided the people, turned them from war toward ways of respect, but Red Leaf had destroyed any chance of that when she killed his grandfather. Now Sok lived in exile, forced, because of what his wife had done, to leave the village of his birth.

Red Leaf was alive now only because she carried Sok's baby. She had claimed that she killed out of love for him, to give him the chance to have his grandfather's place as chief hunter. In that way, perhaps he was nearly as guilty of the killing as Red Leaf. But he would have never wished for his grandfather's death.

During all the moons awaiting this night of birth, Sok had been unable to decide what he should do. Now, without doubt, in the remnants of the Cousin River Village, he was chief hunter. There was little honor in it, but still the people looked to him to provide food. They faced a harsh winter. Their only hope of survival was a successful fall caribou hunt.

If he killed Red Leaf, would her blood keep the animals from giving themselves to his spear? If he did not kill Red Leaf, would his grandfather's need for revenge turn the caribou from the Cousin River hunters?

TWO

Near dawn, Aqamdax's pains stopped. Ligige' had given her tea steeped from balsam poplar root, and the old woman began to hope that the medicine had worked. If Aqamdax could hold the child in her belly for even eight or ten more days, there was a chance that it would live.

After Aqamdax fell asleep, Ligige' crept back through the village to Star's lodge and went inside. She woke Star and told her that Aqamdax's labor had stopped, then saw that both Chakliux and Night Man were awake.

"The child?" Night Man asked.

"The birth pains have stopped."

"Aqamdax?" asked Chakliux.

His voice was a whisper, and Ligige' was not sure whether he spoke only to say her name or if he was asking about her.

"She is strong. It is not Aqamdax I worry about."

Ligige' went then to Red Leaf's birth lodge. The day was brightening, the sky clear and without clouds. She did not bother to call out or scratch at the doorflap. She merely pulled it aside and stooped to enter.

Day Woman looked up and smiled, a baby in her arms. "A daughter," she said. "Fine and strong. She looks like Sok."

The baby's mouth was pursed, and she sucked at her

15

fist. Ligige' squatted on her heels and pulled back the ground squirrel blankets that covered the child. She inspected her arms and legs, hands and feet. She pressed on the baby's belly, chuckled when the dark eyes opened, the mouth puckered in protest.

"She is healthy," Ligige' said. "Red Leaf?"

Day Woman lifted her chin toward the back of the lodge, where Red Leaf lay still and white, eyes closed in sleep. There was a smear of blood on her face, but hare fur blankets were pulled up to her shoulders, and there was no other sign she had just given birth.

"Has Red Leaf fed her yet?"

"No."

"Good. Do not allow her to feed the child until Sok decides what to do. If he kills Red Leaf, we do not need the power of her milk to draw the child into the spirit world."

"A daughter," Sok said and scowled.

Ligige' snorted and tipped the baby so he could see her from where he sat beside the hearth fire. "A daughter is not such a terrible thing," she said. "You have Cries-loud and Carries Much, two strong sons who live here with you, and that other son who is now in the spirit world. But would any of them take care of you when you are old? Someday you'll be glad to have a daughter."

"I am glad to have a daughter," he said, his lips still drawn into a frown. "Here, let me have her."

Ligige' placed the baby into his arms, and he held her awkwardly, a hand's length from his body.

"Your mother says she looks like you."

"Ah, that is not good for a girl," said Sok, but he smiled and clasped the child more tightly so she was snuggled against his chest.

For a time Ligige' said nothing, but finally she knew she must speak. Snow-in-her-hair and her infant son, Carries Much, as well as Red Leaf's son Cries-loud were in the lodge, but she supposed they must be a part of any decision that Sok made.

"Red Leaf has not nursed your daughter yet," Ligige'

said. "Bird Caller has enough milk. Do you want me to take the baby to her?"

Sok handed the child back to Ligige'. When his words came, they were slow and weighted with sorrow. "I must speak to my brother first. For now, take the baby to my mother. Tell her that until I make my decision, the child should have only water."

Red Leaf's baby grew thin on two days of water before Sok finally returned to Ligige', before he told her what must be done. He came in quiet dignity, and Ligige' knew his decision even before he told her, but she waited until the words came from Sok's mouth.

"Chakliux says we need strong women, and my son Cries-loud begs for his mother's life, but I have decided that we risk too much to have her among us."

"So you will drive her from the village?" Ligige' asked, though she knew that was not what Sok had decided.

"She must die," he said.

"I suppose it does no good to tell you that you risk a greater curse by killing her, a woman with the blood power of new birth."

"I will wait until her blood no longer flows."

"That is wise."

Ligige' filled a bowl with ground squirrel stew from her cooking bag. She held it out to Sok, but he shook his head. "You can risk your strength by refusing food?" she asked.

He took the bowl, squatted on his haunches and plunged his fingers into the meat, scooped it into his mouth.

"Has Red Leaf been told?" Ligige' asked.

"No, but she expects as much."

"You will be the one to kill her?"

"Who else? I cannot ask Chakliux. Why should he risk his hunting powers over something my wife did?"

"I will do it for you."

"What if she fights? You are not strong enough."

"She will not expect it from me. I can wait until she is asleep. Or I could use poison."

"Is there something that would take her quickly?"

"There might be."

Sok sat very still for a long time, one hand raised to his forehead, the other cradling his bowl. Ligige' turned her back, pretended to be busy with many things.

"You have heard what will happen to Red Leaf?" Star asked Aqamdax.

"I have heard," Aqamdax told her. She did not want to talk about it, did not want to think about it. It was enough for her to worry about her own child.

Star had avoided Aqamdax since she returned to the lodge, and who could blame her? Aqamdax would have done the same, though perhaps a little less obviously. Why risk your baby for the sake of politeness? But now Star sidled close to her, and Aqamdax knew the conversation was not over.

"I wonder how Sok will kill her. Perhaps he will use a knife just like Red Leaf used to kill—"

"You should not be this close to me," Aqamdax said to the woman, and Star gasped, as though the realization of her child's peril had just come to her.

She scuttled to the other side of the lodge. Aqamdax closed her eyes and stretched, straightened her shoulders. "I will go outside, Sister," she said to Star. "That will be safest."

She was weaving grass mats for the lodge floor. The grass in this place where the River People had chosen to live was not as good as what grew near the First Men villages, but it made sturdy mats. At one time, the women had laughed at her floor mats. Their village had been strong then, and there were caribou skins that could be used to pad floors. Now there were not even enough skins for lodge walls.

Aqamdax squatted on her haunches at the sun side of the lodge. In her own village, she would have found a place away from the wind, but here she had grown to appreciate a windy day. The sound took her back to her own people, to the First Men Village and the noise of the waves.

There, Aqamdax had grown used to the wideness of the sea and horizons that spread to the edge of the earth. The River People's land was cut into small pieces by trees and hills. Some days, during the two years she had been with the River People, she felt closed in, as though she had been made to sit too long in a small place, legs and arms cramped for room.

A shadow fell across her work, and Aqamdax looked up to see the boy Cries-loud, Sok's son. Once, in a time that now seemed very long ago, he and his older brother, that first Carries Much, had been her stepsons. Now, even though she was no longer wife to their father, Cries-loud often came to her with his small boy triumphs, his problems and questions.

He squatted beside her, his legs crossed. Aqamdax smiled a greeting and was not surprised when Cries-loud said, "Star told me my mother is going to die."

Aqamdax wanted to gather the boy into her arms, hold him as she held Ghaden when he was sad or tired, but Cries-loud was not a child. He had eight summers. Soon he would hunt with the men.

"You understand why?" Aqamdax asked.

"I understand."

"You know that this was a difficult decision for your father?"

He nodded. "Star told me it must be done because there is a curse. Do you think all the fighting and all the terrible things that happened to us were because of what my mother did?"

"I am not wise enough to know that, Cries-loud. There were many people besides your mother who did foolish things. I have heard the stories of the dogs that died in the Near River Village. A shaman did that. Surely his powers were greater than your mother's. There was a woman named K'os who lived in this village before you and your father came here. She is gone now, but she was very evil, even had people killed."

"Did someone kill her?"

"No."

"My father says I cannot see my mother. He says I cannot speak to her again."

Aqamdax's eyes filled with tears. What a foolishness, all this killing. Did men not face enough death just in hunting? Did women not do the same in childbirth? Chakliux had worked hard to protect these villages from one another, but it seemed that some spirit of anger and death lingered even yet.

She placed an arm around Cries-loud's shoulders, and he leaned into her. "You should remember the good times with your mother and all the good things she has done. Your new sister will need you to protect her. You are the big brother for her and for Carries Much." When she said Carries Much, she felt Cries-loud shudder and knew he was thinking of his older brother, killed during the fighting.

Then, though Aqamdax had not planned to tell a story, an old River tale came to her. "There was once a wise porcupine and a foolish raven," she began, the words singing from her mouth. She felt Cries-loud relax beside her.

He was too old for a children's story, but he listened as Aqamdax spoke.

THREE

THE NEAR RIVER VILLAGE
K'os leaned over the boiling bag and pretended she did
not hear what Blue Flower was saying. As widow of the
Near River shaman, Blue Flower held a place of respect,
and could make the youngest wives scurry to do her bid-
ding simply by raising her eyes to the sky as though she
had special spirit powers. She claimed to be the healer in
this village, though she knew nothing but a few of the
chants her husband once used.

K'os had seen her set broken bones so poorly that arms
and legs would be crippled forever. Blue Flower seldom
gathered plants for medicine and seemed to know only
the most familiar—willow bark to ease pain, fireweed for
upset stomachs. Even a child knew such things!

K'os had offered to teach Blue Flower about herbs and
plants, but the woman had reacted in horror. Who would
be foolish enough to trust a Cousin River slave?

Though Blue Flower was incompetent as a healer, still
K'os had to admire her for the honored place she had
made for herself. K'os had heard the whispered tales of
how Blue Flower's husband, Wolf-and-Raven, had slyly
killed Near River dogs so when the deaths stopped he
could claim he had successfully driven the evil from their
village. What did Blue Flower have to boast about, being

21

wife to a man like that? He had been caught in his
scheme, caught by an old woman, the one called Ligige'.
Of course, some said Ligige' had had the help of Chakliux.

Chakliux, K'os's own son. He was a greater fool than
Wolf-and-Raven. The Near River People held him in great
esteem. So why had he allowed a man like Fox Barking
to drive him from this village? She had taught him better
than that! With elders as weak as Fox Barking and Sun
Caller, he would have soon secured a place as leader.

Blue Flower lifted a ladle in K'os's direction, whispered
something to the other women. They laughed. K'os turned
her back on them, began a chant of nonsense words. Soon
they were quiet, and K'os began to sing louder. One by
one they left, until K'os was there alone with the few
children who always lingered near the hearths hoping for
handouts.

K'os continued to sing, beckoning the youngest of the
children with a piece of boiled fish, dripping juice from
the soup broth. The child crept forward, and when he had
it in his hand turned and ran. An older boy tried to grab
the fish from him, but K'os called to him, offered him a
chunk of meat. Soon she had given each child something
to eat, and as they stood around her, she began a story,
something she remembered from when she was a child.

She did not like children—their sticky fingers always
reaching to touch or grasp, their whiny voices competing
for attention. But she had watched Aqamdax work her
way from slave to wife in the Cousin River Village, and
Aqamdax had begun with the children. What better way
to win the parents than through their sons and daughters?

Dii shuddered at her husband's touch. She knew she
should be grateful he had chosen her from among the
Cousin girls taken as slaves, but when he called her to his
bed, she had to force herself not to shrink from his groping hands.

He was a lazy man, sleeping long into each morning.
She often asked herself why the Near River People had
selected him as leader of their elders. Even Sun Caller

seemed a better choice. He was shy in speaking out, and the words came from his mouth in broken, stuttering phrases, but there was a wisdom about him that Dii had noticed even the first time he came to her lodge.

Fox Barking lifted the hare fur robe that lay over him, and Dii saw that his penis was swollen, ready for her. At least it would be over quickly, she told herself as she slipped off her long caribou hide shirt and slid in beside him. He grabbed her breasts, and she winced. She would soon be in her moon blood time, and they were tender.

She turned her thoughts to good things, as she always did when she was in her husband's bed. If she allowed her mind to be filled with her sorrows, her husband's groping and thrusting always seemed more painful. She was, after all, second wife of a man who was leader of the elders. She had her own lodge, a good one, and her husband received large shares of whatever meat the hunters brought into the village, so her food cache was nearly full, even before the fall caribou hunts.

The spirits must have taken pity on her for her losses: the death of her mother on their journey to this village; the slaughter of her father, uncle and brothers in the fighting. Yes, they had taken pity, had allowed her to be a slave only a few days before Fox Barking had chosen her. He had introduced her to his first wife, Gull Beak, an old woman whose teeth were worn to the gums, but for all her homeliness Gull Beak had a true heart. She did not ask much of Dii and sewed most of Fox Barking's clothing. Dii hoped Gull Beak would live a long time. Surely Fox Barking would not look on Dii's sewing with favor after having worn Gull Beak's fine clothing for so many years.

Fox Barking groaned, then his body relaxed over hers. He would sleep now, trapping Dii under him unless she was able to pull away.

"I must go to the hearths," she whispered. "It is my turn there."

He mumbled a reply, then rolled to his side so she could leave his bed. She slid out, took a long breath.

"Bring me back something when you return," he told her. "I will be ready to eat."

Dii used the edges of her hands to wipe Fox Barking's sweat from her chest and belly. She pulled on the knee-length pants she wore in summers, then slipped into her boots and parka. The boots had moose hide soles, but the uppers and all of her other clothing were made of caribou hide, everything sewn by her mother the winter before the fighting.

She looked back at Fox Barking. His eyes were closed. The scar that ran from his forehead down over his right eye and to his jaw gathered the skin as though a woman had run a thread through his flesh and pulled it tight. She was glad that Fox Barking did not allow her to eat with him. It would have been difficult for her to swallow her food if she had to look at his face. Of course, there were others in the village who bore scars. Third Tree had only one eye, and Talks-all-night carried the marks of burns she received as a child when her grandmother's lodge caught fire. Those scars, though they were worse than Fox Barking's, did not turn Dii's stomach. But who noticed Third Tree's empty eye once he began telling his jokes? And who noticed Talks-all-night's burns when her gentle spirit made itself known through her kindness?

Dii left her husband and walked to the hearth fires. She was still not accustomed to the closeness of the Near River lodges. In her own village, lodges had been far enough apart so a woman could keep her drying racks close. Here the women set their racks at the edge of the bowl of earth where the village was nestled. They lost dried meat and fish because of this strange practice. Wild animals were more bold in stealing from the edges of a village than they were in braving dogs and people to sneak between lodges. Of course, children kept watch over the racks, usually the boys, those not quite old enough to join the hunting trips. But what wolf, what lynx, was afraid of a boy?

Dii avoided the edges of the village as much as possible. Where else would the warriors' spirits stay, those from both the Cousin and Near River Villages who had been killed in the fighting? Somewhere out there were her father and brothers. She did not want to meet them, nor any of the Cousin men's spirits. Surely they must hate her now that she was wife to one of the Near River elders.

She did not mind taking her turn at the cooking hearths, though it was not like it had been in the Cousin Village, with all the women sharing and laughing. Here the mix of Cousin and Near River was still uncomfortable, but in the past few moons the women had seemed to drift into an arrangement favored by all. The Cousin women, most now wives, came early, started the fires when dawn was only a gray promise of light. Then later, when husbands were beginning to awaken, the Near River women came and the Cousin women left, taking a share of food to their lodges. From then on they took turns. Only in evenings when everyone was hungry did the two groups mingle.

Dii had taken a turn at dawn, and now the Near River women should be at the hearths, but better to be with them than under Fox Barking's sweating body. She lowered her head and determined to say little, giving no one reason to find fault with her. But when she reached the hearths, only the woman K'os was there.

When she had lived in the Cousin River Village, Dii had feared K'os. K'os had been the village healer, and able to help many with her medicines. But who had not heard the stories of men and women—those K'os hated—who died horrible deaths? Some even said she had killed her own son's wife. In the Cousin River Village, Dii had seldom spoken to the woman, tried not to look at her, but here K'os was only a slave.

No one came to her for medicines. No one gave her the honor due a healer. In the Cousin River Village, many men visited her lodge, gave gifts for her favors. K'os was supposed to be old, but her hair was as thick and black as a young woman's, her skin unlined, her eyes large and bright. Even her teeth were strong and unbroken.

K'os raised her head and called out a greeting. Dii could not ignore her. Her mother had taught her that every person deserved to be treated fairly, even slaves.

"Good morning," Dii said. "My husband sent me to get

food." She dipped her ladle into a boiling bag and stirred the contents.

"You are Fox Barking's wife," K'os said.

"Yes," Dii answered, then did not know what else to say. She did not want to boast of being a wife when K'os was still a slave. Finally, she said, "Second wife."

"Ah, yes, there is that other one—Gull Beak. Is that her name?"

Dii nodded.

"She is old, that one," K'os said, then plucked a bit of fish from the bag she was stirring and ate it.

Dii's eyes widened in surprise. Surely slaves were not to eat from the boiling bags without permission, but who was here to stop her? She remembered when K'os herself had owned a slave, the Sea Hunter woman Aqamdax. She remembered how thin and worn Aqamdax had become. Sometimes Dii's mother had given the woman a little food, even though she was a slave, even though she was Sea Hunter.

Dii tried to remember which Near River family owned K'os, but she could not. There were too many families to learn all at once, though she now knew those who were her husband's friends or related to him in some way.

"Does she have any children, this Gull Beak?" K'os asked.

"None living," Dii said. "And she is so old she does not even go to the moon blood lodge anymore."

"So I suppose Fox Barking hopes you will give him a son."

Dii's cheeks suddenly burned red. "Yes," she said quietly.

"I have medicines that will help you conceive."

Dii considered being pregnant. It would not be easy delivering a child in this village, without her mother to help her, but then she reminded herself of the moons during her pregnancy that Fox Barking could not ask her to his bed. That would be worth something. And what about the joy of having someone who truly belonged to her, who carried the blood of her father and mother?

"It would be a good thing to have a baby," Dii said.

K'os nodded. "Sun Girl, that is your name, is it not?"

"I have changed it. I am Dii now. Because no one else in my family is still alive."

"Dii, then," K'os said, and smiled as though amused by what Dii had said.

Dii turned her head away and reminded herself to be wary. Only a fool would trust someone who could smile at another's sorrow.

"Tomorrow, come to the hearths again in the morning," said K'os. "If I am not here, then come the next day. I will bring you something. It does not help everyone—it did not help me—but perhaps it will give you a child."

Dii thanked her, then began to fill the small caribou hide bag she had brought with her. Fox Barking would expect her back soon.

"I am surprised that your husband keeps his first wife, old as she is and unable to give him children," K'os said.

"It is her sewing. She is gifted. He keeps the best parkas for himself and is able to earn much in trade from the others. Animals honor him because of the respect he shows them in his clothing."

"Only for her parkas, then," K'os said, and Dii glanced at her to see if the words were a question, but it seemed as though K'os had forgotten Dii was there, the woman's eyes looking up and out, beyond the tops of the lodges.

FOUR

"So what do you know about the woman called Gull Beak?" K'os asked.

Two Fist, the wife of the man who owned K'os, frowned. K'os held her smile in her mouth. Did Two Fist suspect how often her husband took K'os to his bed? Possibly, but she had caught them only once, the lazy one, coming back from the cooking hearths long before she should have. The woman turned away without answering.

Let her ignore me, K'os thought. There are others to ask. She continued to stir the cooking bag, filled bowls for two hunters, then, when Two Fist pointed with a toe at one of the hearths, she gathered an armload of wood from a pile nearby and carefully added pieces to the fire.

There were five hearth fires in a circle at the center of the village, a fire named for each of the four directions of the wind and another for the sun. She wondered whether there were any hearth fires burning in the Cousin River Village, or if the people had gone to their summer fish camps. They had probably stayed in their winter village. It was close to the Grandfather Lake, and there was good fishing at that lake, summer and winter. Besides, the Near River and Cousin fish camps were less than a day's walk apart. Why chance living so close to those people who had nearly destroyed them?

Even most of the Near River People had chosen to stay in their winter village, though the salmon fishing there was not as good as it was near the mouth of the river. Of course, a fish camp was not truly a village, just a scattering of tents—a few here and a few farther upstream and some beyond those. An easy place for warriors wanting revenge to kill families, one by one. K'os set the last piece of wood into a hearth fire and stood. She brushed her hands together, then began to stir a cooking bag.

"I thought you knew all the women in this village," Two Fist said. "You have been with us almost five moons."

"There are too many to learn so quickly," K'os replied. Of course, she did know most of the men, many of them because they had visited her when she had lived in the Cousin River Village. Women were usually not important to her. Why should they be? Men held the power.

When K'os had first come to the Near River Village, Fox Barking claimed her for himself, and so she had thought her revenge would be easy. She owed him for much more than that long-ago rape and beating, which had left her unable to have children. Her revenge would also be for what he had done to her people in the Cousin River Village. He would die, yes, but it would not be a quick death. As his slave, surely she would have opportunity to slip poison into his food—a little each day until sickness weakened him and his spirit could no longer stand against death.

But though he had kept most of her belongings, he had soon traded her to Black Mouth. Now it would be more difficult to carry out her plans for revenge, but perhaps Gull Beak was the answer.

"Gull Beak stays mostly to herself," Two Fist said. "Her husband is not an easy man to please, and all her children have died. Fox Barking keeps her for the sake of the parkas she makes. She is gifted."

K'os listened as Two Fist continued to speak about the woman, but set her face as though she were bored. Soon, she would visit Gull Beak, but Two Fist did not need to know.

THE COUSIN RIVER VILLAGE

"You understand that I have no choice," Sok said to Red Leaf. The two were alone. He had called her outside the birth lodge and stayed several paces from her as he spoke.

"My daughter is well?" she asked, as though he had told her nothing about her fate. The child had been taken from her three days before.

"Strong, yes. Bird Caller feeds her."

"And Cries-loud?"

"He is good. A fine son."

Red Leaf raised her eyes to his face. It was, he realized, the first time she had looked at him since he found out she killed his grandfather.

"How will I die?"

He was startled by her question, then reflected that if he were in her situation, he would ask the same thing.

"I have not yet decided."

"Before . . . before then," Red Leaf said, "could I see my children one last time?"

Sok looked up into the sky. It was growing dark; stars prickled their way through a light cover of clouds.

"No," he said. "To them you are already dead."

It was nearly night when the boy Cries-loud came to Bird Caller. "My father wants to see his new daughter," he told her.

"I will come as soon as I feed my husband," she said.

"He told me to bring the child."

Bird Caller looked at Sky Watcher. He shrugged. "She's his daughter, not yours. I have told you many times not to forget that."

Bird Caller went to the lodge pole where the baby hung in her cradleboard and untied the thongs that secured the board. She was a good baby, slept well, cried little. Her face was strong-boned like her father's, but she was dark-skinned like Red Leaf.

Bird Caller followed Cries-loud outside the lodge, entrusted the cradleboard to his arms. "Bring her back when she is hungry," she told him. She watched him head toward Sok's lodge, then she turned and went back to her husband, setting a smile on her face before she entered the lodge.

"Do not worry, little wife," Sky Watcher said. He reached for her, pulled her down beside him. "Besides, it will not take me long to put another baby inside you. Then you will have two to help you forget that one we lost."

FIVE

Chakliux rolled quietly from his bedding furs so he would not wake the others in the lodge. He had told Star he would spend the day near the Grandfather Lake spearing salmon at one of the outlet streams. She had wanted to come with him, but he knew she would be a hindrance. He also knew that if he left her, she would be a problem for someone in the village, most likely Aqamdax.

He slipped on his summer leggings, then took his parka and leister, a throwing board and fish darts. He would stop at his mother's lodge. She was an early riser. Perhaps she would be willing to spend the day with Star.

He paused as he pulled aside the doorflap, looked at Aqamdax asleep in her bedding furs, allowed his gaze to linger. She was tall for a woman, and he had heard men in the village criticize her First Men features—a nose too small, a face too round, a greedy mouth, for surely a mouth that wide would talk and eat more than its share. But he saw the remembrance of her smiles, her dark eyes spilling out her joy, her stories filled with wisdom, her laughter with mischief.

She deserved better than Night Man.

Ligige' stirred the hearth coals with a stick and pulled on her parka. In her old age she often seemed cold, and so had taken to sleeping in leggings and a long-sleeved caribou shirt.

Her dreams had been so vivid, they had awakened her. She shivered, unable to forget the scream that had pierced her sleep. It was a man's scream, she was sure, a warrior's cry. Why would she dream such a thing?

Then suddenly her heart was beating too quickly. Had the Near River men decided to make another attack? Didn't they realize there was nothing left for them in this poor village?

She heard voices, then the barking of dogs, so she put on her summer boots and went outside. The hearth fire in Day Woman's lodge was burning, and then the fire in Star's lodge also began to glow. Sok ran past her, and Ligige' called to him.

"What has happened?"

"Our mother," he cried. "Bring your medicines."

Ligige' hurried back into her lodge and grabbed the marten skin that held her plant medicines. By the time she crawled through her entrance tunnel, most of the people in the village had gathered around Day Woman's lodge. Ligige' pushed her way through.

Inside, Sok and Chakliux knelt beside their mother. Star was there also, for once quiet, her eyes large and dark, childlike, as she looked up at Ligige'.

"Someone has killed her," Star whispered.

"No," Sok said. He had lifted Day Woman's head and shoulders to his lap, cradled her like a child. "She is not dead."

Ligige' passed a hand over Day Woman's mouth, felt a gentle stir of air. She pressed the tips of her fingers to the pulse point at the side of Day Woman's neck.

"She is alive," she said. "What happened?"

There were medicines she could give if some spirit had tried to stop Day Woman's heart, and teas to strengthen the body, to fight whatever evil had gotten hold of her.

Chakliux gently drew away the blanket, and Ligige' gasped as she saw the blood.

"A knife, I would guess," Chakliux said.

There were many slashes along the woman's arms, even on her hands.

"She was stabbed in the belly several times," said Chakliux. "Look at her hands. She fought. Her left arm was partially bound when I found her. She must have tried to stop the bleeding herself. I came to tell her where I was going today. I thought I would find her awake, but instead I found this."

He lifted his head to gesture toward Day Woman's sleeping mats. "She must have been attacked when she was asleep. Her bed is full of blood."

"It was not long ago or she would be dead," Ligige' said, then handed a packet of fresh bedstraw plants to Star. "Warm these in a cilt'ogho of water. Leave the plants whole. Do not boil them."

Star took the bedstraw, but only stared at it. In exasperation, Ligige' grabbed the plants from her, flipped aside the inner doorflap. The old woman Twisted Stalk was on her hands and knees in the entrance tunnel. "Here," Ligige' said, handing her the plants. "Warm these in water. Do it now."

She felt the gentle pressure of Chakliux's hand on her arm and knew he was telling her to be calm.

How could she be calm when her medicines were not enough to save Day Woman, and what good were her prayers? She had done little in her life to earn the power she needed to prevail against such terrible injuries. She was like a child, and the knowledge of her helplessness made her angry.

Ligige' looked up at Chakliux, her tears so heavy they were like stones resting against her eyes. "I cannot save her," she told him. But she went back into the lodge, tried to stop what little blood was left in Day Woman's body from leaking out onto the floor.

THE NEAR RIVER VILLAGE
"Gull Beak," K'os called.

It was morning, but not so early that the old woman should still be asleep. Although what did Gull Beak have to do all day except sew? Why not be lazy?

"I brought you wood," K'os called, and dropped the armful of windfall branches beside Gull Beak's lodge. It was a good lodge, well-made, though K'os could see that the caribou hides were beginning to wear at the seams.

K'os picked up a branch and scratched at the lodge walls.

"You, Slave! What do you want?"

She turned and saw Gull Beak walking toward her.

"You think I would still be asleep this late in the day? A wise woman has more to do than sleep."

K'os set her mouth in anger but said nothing. If Gull Beak was so wise, why did she speak to K'os in such a way? Even though K'os was a slave, she had power enough to take Gull Beak's life.

"I came to bring you wood," K'os said in a sweet voice, and lowered her eyes as though she spoke in respect.

Gull Beak stopped at the heap of branches. "Who told you to do this?" she asked. "My husband?"

She was a homely woman, tall and too thin, with large ears, small eyes. Surely her true name was not Gull Beak. Who would choose to name herself for a bird as lazy as a gull? But K'os could understand how she could be given the name by others. Her nose was sharp and long like the bill of a bird, and her voice so loud it carried like a gull's above the sounds of the village.

"No one told me. Even a slave has time to help others."

Gull Beak began to laugh. "But no slave would. I am not stupid. I know how it is with the Cousin River slaves. You do not have enough to eat. The fur on your parka is wearing thin and will not be good enough to get you through the winter. If no one made you do this, then why did you?"

K'os narrowed her eyes. Gull Beak was wiser than she had thought—who would believe a woman with any wisdom at all—would be wife to Fox Barking?

"In my village, I was a healer," K'os told her. "I had everything I wanted. My husband was chief hunter. I even had a slave myself, though I took pity on her and arranged that she should become a wife. I do not want to be a slave forever."

"You do not have to tell me what you were. I know. Everyone knows. We remember your visit to our village and how your husband died in a lodge fire while you were here. How can you hope to become wife when the men saw your husband's bad luck? Do you think any hunter in this village will risk taking you? Most people think Black Mouth is foolish enough to have you as slave."

"Has anything terrible happened to Black Mouth?" K'os asked. "Has his hunting been bad? Have his children grown ill? Is his wife dead? No. His hunting skills have increased, two moons ago his wife delivered a strong son, and each of his children is well."

Gull Beak snorted. "If you are so lucky, why does Black Mouth not marry you himself?"

"Two Fist does not want him to take a second wife."

Gull Beak shrugged. She kept a hearth outside her lodge, as though she were in a fish camp. She picked up several branches, laid them over the coals and tucked in a bit of birchbark she took from a pouch at her waist. Soon flames were licking into the branches. She adjusted a tripod over the fire and hung a cooking bag, crawled into her lodge and came back with a bladder of water. She dumped the water into the bag.

"Stay for a little while," she said to K'os. "The wood has earned you something to eat. I took a fine fat duck yesterday with my bola, and my husband was given some moose. Together they make a good stew."

K'os squatted beside the hearth, but Gull Beak made a rude gesture with her hand and said, "I am not your slave. Do not expect me to do all the work. Take some of the wood you brought and feed the fire. Then tell me why you came."

"In hopes of a good meal," K'os told her as she chose branches from the woodpile.

"You are a woman who thinks further than her belly," Gull Beak said, and K'os smiled. Perhaps she liked Gull Beak.

"Since I was a child, all things have been given to me," K'os said. "Now, life is not easy. What good is a woman who is slave? The first hard winter, she is given to the wind so her food can be eaten by someone else. But I have been trained as a healer, and I have noticed that there is no healer in this village."

"Blue Flower," Gull Beak said. She gave a bowl to K'os, then filled her own and gestured toward the boiling bag. "Do not take too much. My husband will want some later."

K'os had been watching Gull Beak, knew how seldom Fox Barking came to the woman's lodge, but if he had given her moose meat the day before, perhaps he would expect to share some of her stew. She filled her bowl only half full, though she was hungry and her body craved fat.

"Blue Flower is not a healer," K'os said.

Gull Beak flicked her fingers into the wind. "Surely you did not come here just to tell me that."

"I want to be the healer in this village."

Gull Beak laughed. "You think they will trust you, a slave from the Cousin River People? You think they will take your medicines? You could kill as easily as heal."

"That is why I have come to you."

Gull Beak tilted her head, arched an eyebrow.

"What if I taught you the medicines, and you gave them to the people?"

"Why would you do that?"

"With the trade goods you got in exchange, you would buy me from Black Mouth. I would work with you as healer until the people began to trust me. Then perhaps there would be some hunter who wanted me as wife, once he sees I do not carry bad luck."

"How do I know I can trust your medicines? What if you do this only to get revenge?"

"I will take every medicine myself before we give it to anyone."

Gull Beak raised her bowl of meat and ate until the bowl was empty.

When she finished, she smacked her lips in appreciation, then said, "I have food. I have a husband. I am honored in this village for the parkas I make. I do not want to be a healer."

"I have seen your parkas," K'os said. "They are beautiful. It is sad that you do not have a slave. Then you would not have to work so hard to keep traplines and catch salmon. You would have more time to sew."

K'os ate the last of her meat, stood and politely thanked Gull Beak for the food. "I am going now," she said in the traditional River farewell. "Two Fist will be wondering where I am." And as she left, K'os said, "It is good at least that your husband is not a lazy man. It is good that Fox Barking always brings you much meat."

She walked away with a smile on her face.

THE COUSIN RIVER VILLAGE

After Day Woman died, Sok went to Red Leaf's birth lodge. She had killed before. What would stop her from killing again? How better to get revenge than to kill Sok's mother?

He called to her, and when there was no answer, he pulled aside the doorflap, saw Cries-loud alone inside, the boy curled into a tight ball. Sok sighed his relief when, at his touch, his son sprang to his feet.

"She is gone, and she took our sister," Cries-loud said before Sok could speak. "She left during the night. I brought her food and the baby. I don't care what you do to me. I could not let you kill my mother."

Sok closed his eyes. Red Leaf. The woman had caused him more sorrow than anyone should have to bear. She had killed his grandfather, now had stolen his daughter, had probably killed his mother as well. Who else would do such a thing?

Had Red Leaf taken no thought of the curse she had put on the boy, his oldest living son? Sleeping in this lodge, a place drenched in birth blood, could draw away his hunting powers for his whole life. And Sok was here, too, cursing himself, just as his son had been cursed.

"Come with me. We should not be here," he told Cries-loud. He took the boy to Star's lodge, to his brother Chakliux. Who else was wiser? Who would better know what to do?

SIX

THE NEAR RIVER VILLAGE

K'os learned of old Vole's ailment only by good fortune. She was sitting outside Two Fist's lodge splitting a chunk of white whale sinew into strands for thread. Two Fist had bought the sinew from a trader, boasted to the other women of how well-sewn her husband's boots and parka would be, bound at each seam with strong beluga sinew. But she was not the one who had to tease out the stubborn strands, so much more difficult to split for twisting than caribou sinew.

What did it matter? K'os told herself. In payment for her hard work, she had managed to sneak away a bit of lynx fur from a pelt, only a small piece cut from the belly edge, but enough for her needs. She had tucked it away with the other treasures she had already accumulated— the eye of a fresh-killed fox, now dried so it was only a brittle circle, thin as a leaf; the beak from a kingfisher and the breast skin, still feathered, of a flycatcher.

When she heard Vole coming down the path, K'os did not look up from her work. One advantage in being a slave was that most people ignored her. But suddenly Vole began to wail. Holding a hand under her belly, she crouched for a moment in the path, sobbing like a child. K'os continued to sew, and finally two other women came by, helped Vole to her feet and guided her back to her lodge, but not before K'os had heard the old woman's lamentations about blood in her urine, pain and cramps beneath her belly.

Later, when K'os had finished splitting the sinew and Two Fist had sent her to help at the fish weir, she took time to walk past Gull Beak's tent, to stop and call quietly. When Gull Beak came out, K'os leaned close to her and whispered, "Vole is sick."

"Do you have medicine that will help her?"

K'os nodded.

"I will arrange for you to come to my lodge tonight, after the men have eaten."

K'os walked to the Near River and waded into the water. She gritted her teeth against the cold and lowered her small net. She stood still until the fish thought her legs were nothing more than logs. Finally a salmon swam near, and in one quick movement she lifted the net, bringing the fish up from the water, then heaved it to the shore, where boys were waiting with clubs.

She lowered her net again, and to take her mind from the bone-aching cold of the water, began to plan what she would do to the fine parka Gull Beak was making for Fox Barking. She had told K'os that it would have decorations made in sacred symbols. Circles with eagle feathers at his shoulders, so his vision would be clear; beaver ears sewn to each side of the hood to strengthen his hearing; a strip of fishskin just above the hem ruff to protect him from strange spirits when he traveled far from their village. Across the chest she would sew a band of raven beaks she had bought in trade. Each time Fox Barking wore the parka, the beaks would catch the sun and the feathers would dance in the wind.

But when K'os added her amulets and curses, every time he wore that parka, the beaks would cry to the spirits: Here is a man who steals the joy of young women. The eagle feathers would say: Beware of an elder who has built his power on death and lies.

THE COUSIN RIVER VILLAGE

Yaa made herself small in the back corner of Star's lodge

and tried to think only of her sewing. It was not polite to listen to others' conversations, but Ligige' 's words carried loud through the caribou hide walls. And though Chakliux's voice was not as strident, it was a storyteller's voice and, even when he spoke softly, seemed to find its way into a listener's ears. Yaa thought they must be standing outside, at the back of the lodge.

"You are sure?" Chakliux asked, and Yaa could hear the exasperation in Ligige' 's words as she said once more, "I am sure. It was Red Leaf. I saw Ghaden's wounds after she attacked him. I myself helped prepare my own brother's body for death rites after she—" Ligige' 's voice broke, and for a moment Yaa heard nothing. Then again Chakliux spoke.

"Then, she had a reason for killing, as foolish as that reason might have seemed to us. But why would she kill my mother?"

"To escape!" Ligige' said.

"So why go to Day Woman's lodge? Why not just leave the village? If she attacked my mother in her bed, then surely it wasn't because Day Woman was trying to prevent her escape."

"Perhaps there was something in the lodge that Red Leaf wanted," Ligige' said. "Perhaps she went to steal something and Day Woman woke up."

"That could be—"

Their voices were fading and Yaa realized that they must be walking away from the lodge even as they spoke. She set down her sewing and looked over at Long Eyes. The old woman was asleep, muttering long strings of words, too jumbled for Yaa to understand. In her dreaming, Long Eyes flung away her rabbit skin blanket, and Yaa went over to cover her again.

"You are safe," Yaa said, and smoothed back Long Eyes's hair. She crooned a soft song and thought about Red Leaf. How strange that a woman could live among them like an ordinary person and then become a killer. What would make someone do that?

The men had decided not to follow Red Leaf. Why should they? She and her baby were probably already dead. The smell of Red Leaf's birth blood and the milk breath of her baby would draw wolves. Yaa shuddered to think of their deaths under sharp, tearing teeth. And what had that little daughter done to deserve a death like that?

Yaa had seen Bird Caller's tears for that baby, though even Sok had not mourned his little daughter. He told Chakliux he was glad Red Leaf had taken the baby with her. He did not want to raise the girl; she would remind him only of his mother's death.

Yaa counted out the days on her fingers. Three, now, the village had been in mourning. One more day and they would put Day Woman's body on the death scaffolds in the sacred woods. Then her small lodge would be burned. A sad waste of caribou hides, but what else could they do? Not even Ligige' was brave enough to live in a lodge filled with the blood of a death like Day Woman's. What had her life been but sadness? Better to purge the village of that bad luck than to save a few worn caribou skins.

Yaa returned to her sewing and pushed the thoughts of death and killing from her mind. She was making Ghaden a pair of leggings and did not want to stitch sadness or bad luck into the seams. Instead she thought of hawks and lemmings. What better animals to give Ghaden skill and good luck in his hunting?

Aqamdax was careful. She never lifted heavy loads. She walked slowly and kept her thoughts to good things. She sang songs of patience to the son she carried in her belly, and she prayed that he would not be born early. Boy children were weaker than girls, the old women said, with less fat under their skin to keep them alive.

But the second day after Day Woman's mourning had ended, Aqamdax awakened to pain.

She was sitting on her bedding furs, her hands over her belly, when Star woke up and began to scream. "Leave! Leave my lodge! If my baby comes early because of you, I will kill your child!"

Her yelling woke Chakliux. He pulled Star from her bed and walked her outside. Then Night Man also was awake. He rubbed his eyes and asked, "The pains have begun again?"

"They are not strong," Aqamdax told him.

"It is best that you leave."

She waited for him to promise prayers for her safety, for her life and the child's, but he did not. Star had told her that Night Man was afraid the baby did not belong to him, and Aqamdax could see that fear in his eyes.

She had had a moon blood time before she became Night Man's wife, and K'os had not given her to any man after that. The child had to be Night Man's. She had told him that, but he ignored her, as though she had said nothing at all.

Aqamdax gathered her things, birth amulets and supplies for the baby. She had not made a cradle in the tradition of the First Men—a square frame of wood, hung from lodge rafters, that held a hammock where the baby slept—but instead, to please her husband, had fashioned a stiff cradleboard with a spruce wood back and a lacing of rawhide that would hold the baby's head up, as though the child were standing in place.

During the two days after Day Woman's mourning, Aqamdax had made herself a birth shelter of woven mats and willow poles. It was small, but Ligige' had loaned her a scraped caribou skin to wrap around the peak, and Aqamdax had built it under a large white spruce in the hope that the tree would offer a shelter from rain and wind.

As she left Star's lodge, Aqamdax called for Yaa to bring several water bladders and a pouch of dried fish. Yaa scrambled from her bed to follow Aqamdax from the lodge, turned to scold her brother Ghaden when he tried to hold her back.

Biter, Ghaden's dog, followed Yaa, and Ghaden let out another protest, until Night Man glared at him and said, "Act like a man. You are not a baby like the one about to be born."

Then Ghaden was quiet, and when he thought Night Man was not looking, he stuck his thumb in his mouth, drew his head down under a hare fur blanket and pretended to go back to sleep.

When Star and Chakliux returned to the lodge, Star was quiet, and Ghaden, peeking out from his blankets, could see that there was a calmness in her eyes. Even without Yaa in the lodge, it might be a good day.

He got up from his bed, went outside to the edge of the river and relieved himself. He took several fish from one of the drying racks and stuffed them up his parka sleeves. Like all the boys in the village, he would spend part of the day guarding the racks from foxes and ravens who tried to sneak in and steal meat.

At first the guarding had not been difficult. A raised stick, a yell, would drive them away, but with each successful theft, the foxes grew more bold, and now would growl at him when he came close. Squirrel had told Ghaden about a fox that had grabbed the end of his stick and tried to pull it from his hands. Finally, Squirrel's older brother saw what was happening and chased the fox away by throwing stones.

After hearing Squirrel's story, Ghaden had asked Yaa to make him a small pouch. Now he stooped at the riverbank and filled the pouch with stones, then he walked back to the lodge.

He had shared Chakliux's mourning for Day Woman, remembered his own sorrow when his mother, Daes, had died, though that had been long ago. Now he could barely remember her face, mostly just her smile. Each day he repeated in his mind the Sea Hunter words she had taught him so he would not forget them as well. When they were gone, what would be left of her?

Sometimes he spoke to his sister, Aqamdax, about her, but when he did, Aqamdax always looked sad. Someday he would surprise her with his Sea Hunter words, then perhaps she would be happy. He was glad Aqamdax lived in their lodge and didn't belong to K'os anymore. K'os had been mean to Aqamdax, had made her stay out in the entrance tunnel to sleep, even in the middle of winter.

It was better for Aqamdax now that she was wife to Night Man, even though Night Man was usually cross with her, often yelling, though it was Star who almost always caused any problems. What other woman in the village always ruined the clothing she was trying to make or allowed the cooking bag to catch fire? Who else burned the meat she was roasting?

Though Chakliux had given Star enough caribou hides to build a new lodge, and Chakliux, Ghaden and even Night Man had dug a circle into the ground for the lodge, had cut poles and carried stones, Star had yet to begin sewing the lodge cover.

It would be easier to have Star in a different lodge, though Ghaden was not sure if he and Yaa would stay with Night Man and Aqamdax or go with Star and Chakliux. Night Man did not like Chakliux, though Chakliux was a good husband to Star, always giving her small gifts like bird feathers and fox tails.

Ghaden slipped back into the lodge, was quiet as he skirted Long Eyes's bed. The old woman was still asleep. Star was doing something to whatever was in the cooking bag, and soon she left the lodge, perhaps to bring back more food, Ghaden thought, but most likely to wander the village, doing nothing at all.

Ghaden got two bowls of meat, handed one to Night Man, the other to Chakliux. Chakliux raised his eyebrows at Ghaden, lifted the bowl as he did so, but Ghaden shook his head and pulled a fish from his sleeve. Chakliux grinned at him and began to eat.

Ghaden hunkered down in his bed. He wished Yaa would not have taken Biter. He liked to have his dog with him.

At least Red Leaf was gone from the village. Ghaden knew she was the one who had killed his mother. She had also stabbed him, and the places where the knife had cut still ached sometimes, especially when it was cold outside.

He tried not to think of the night it had happened, tried not to remember that it was his fault. He had seen Red Leaf, dressed like a man, like a hunter, and thought that she was his father, the trader Cen. He had run from the safety of their lodge entrance to Red Leaf, and his mother had followed him. If he had stayed with his mother, Red Leaf would have never known they were there, waiting until his mother's sister-wife went to sleep and they could sneak back into the lodge. Why they had to do that each time they visited Cen in his trader's lodge, Ghaden still did not understand, nor did he understand why they did not live with his father. But there were many things in the world he did not understand, things that even Yaa seemed puzzled about.

But now Red Leaf was gone. She would soon die, the people said, living away from the village with a baby to care for. That was too bad, Ghaden reflected. He had wanted her to live until he was a man so he could kill her himself.

Aqamdax squatted at the entrance of the birth lodge. She had built the lodge so the door faced east, to honor the light. Since she left Star's lodge, dawn had spread up over the sky, chasing away the stars, pinching them out one by one. Pain gripped her, and she took long, deep breaths until it passed. The pains were not terrible, not nearly as hard as those that had taken her the first time she went into labor. She was not worried. Ligige' 's tea had stopped her pains before. It would again.

As a child, she had often seen women in the First Men Village walking out labor pains. She smiled as she remembered the whispers among the women and the stern faces of the men, each pretending he did not know a baby was about to be born.

Even here among the River People most women in labor walked to speed their deliveries, but Aqamdax stayed still. It was best if the baby was not yet born, if he waited a few more days.

Soon Yaa brought Ligige', and the old woman began fussing over Aqamdax, ordering Yaa to bring wood, start a fire, fetch water. Ligige' had brought a tripod from her own hearth, and when the flames died down, she set it over the coals. She seemed worried about something, and finally Aqamdax said, "You are well?" Ligige' nodded, and Aqamdax asked, "Is everyone in the village all right?"

"Everyone is all right, but there is some spirit of mischief at work. My dog chewed himself loose last night, and by the time I found him early this morning, my hearth coals had grown cold."

She continued to mutter about dogs and hearth coals. Aqamdax, in her relief, tried to keep her mouth from showing any kind of smile. It was always an embarrassment when a woman's hearth coals went out, especially for an old woman who had no children to watch, who had nothing to tend except her own lodge.

"I would have had this tea ready for you much sooner if all those things had not happened to me."

Aqamdax, bracing herself against another pain, said nothing.

Ligige' stopped to watch her. "The pains are not as bad?" she asked.

"No," Aqamdax said, "and not so close together."

"Good. Perhaps then it will not matter how late I am making this tea."

With a wooden bowl, Ligige' scooped water from the boiling bag, added a piece of balsam poplar root to steep, removed the root and handed the bowl to Aqamdax. "Drink it quickly, before another pain comes."

Aqamdax took a sip. It was too hot, but she drank it anyway. It burned a path to her stomach, and she prayed it would stop her pains.

"You have been walking?" Ligige' asked.

"I thought it was better if I did not."

"Good, stay still. Yaa, go back to your lodge. Get Aqamdax something to keep her hands busy."

"My basket," Aqamdax told Yaa, and the girl ran off.

"It will keep your thoughts away from the baby. Maybe when he realizes no one is thinking about him, he will decide to wait and come out another day."

Yaa ducked into the lodge. Biter had returned with her, and he leaped over Ghaden, making the boy laugh. Night Man and Chakliux were eating. She said nothing to them, waiting, as was polite, for Night Man to ask about his wife. Finally she fetched the basket, walking purposely close to him, but when he spoke he said, "Come back when you can. Long Eyes will soon be awake, and Star is not here."

"Your wife . . ." she began, but Night Man turned his head away.

"How is Aqamdax?" Chakliux finally asked.

Night Man set his mouth into a frown, but Yaa answered, "Ligige' has given her medicine again to stop the baby from coming."

She stood for a moment to see if they had more questions, but neither man spoke, so Yaa told Ghaden to roll his bedding mats and gather firewood. He made a face at her, but she knew he would do what she asked.

"Do not forget Long Eyes," Night Man said as she left the lodge.

Chakliux sat with Night Man, waiting for him to begin prayers or chants. Some husbands even fasted when a wife was in labor, but Night Man did none of these things. Chakliux stayed, thinking Night Man might want someone to talk to. But Night Man acted as though he were alone in the lodge, and Chakliux wondered if he should leave. He wanted to make his own prayers, voice his own chants, a protection for Aqamdax and her child.

He decided to wait until Yaa returned. She could tell him one more time how Aqamdax was doing. Finally the doorflap opened, and Yaa stepped inside. At the same moment, Long Eyes awoke, the old woman peering around the lodge, screeching when she saw Chakliux, then calming again when she noticed Night Man beside him. Night Man helped Yaa get Long Eyes out of bed, told the girl to take her to the woman's place, then bring her back and feed her. Yaa got Long Eyes into a summer parka, laced boots on her feet, then she and Night Man helped the woman outside.

Chakliux could hear Yaa and Night Man speaking but could not decipher their words. When Night Man came back, Chakliux asked him about Aqamdax, but Night Man shrugged.

"Really, I do not care," he said. He dipped his bowl into the cooking bag. "You want more?" he asked, but

Chakliux suddenly found himself unable to eat.

He watched as Night Man lifted the bowl to his lips, swallowed several mouthfuls of meat.

"You do not care," Chakliux said.

Night Man lowered his bowl. "I did not choose her for myself. She is not of our people, but she is not a terrible wife, and so I will keep her. What other woman would have me?" He nodded at his useless arm. "I do not want her to die, but the baby means nothing."

"Even if it is a son?"

"I'm sure it is not mine."

Chakliux felt his face flush, first in disbelief, then in anger. "You think she has slept with another man?"

"Not since she became my wife. But she was a slave before that. K'os made her sleep with men, then took their gifts for herself. The child could belong to some warrior now dead, killed by the Near Rivers in the fighting."

"It would still be yours—a daughter to care for you in your old age, a son to bring meat. . . ."

"What if the true father's spirit comes back to see this child, to watch him grow into a man, and finds that I have claimed him as my own? Do you think he would be glad to see his son raised by a man who laid in his bed and did nothing while the Near Rivers killed everyone and stole our women?"

"I think he would be glad that a man with a good heart is raising his son."

But Night Man said, "If the baby comes early and is strong enough to live, I will know it is not mine."

The tea did not stop the pains. Each one was a little harder, lasted a little longer. Finally Ligige' told Aqamdax to go inside the birth lodge. She helped her lie down on the mats.

Ligige' lifted the summer parka Aqamdax wore, pulled down Aqamdax's short caribou hide pants, then during a pain slid a finger up into the birth canal.

"You might as well go outside and walk," Ligige' said, and helped Aqamdax to her feet. "You have opened at least halfway. I do not think my tea will help now. The baby has decided to come."

THE NEAR RIVER VILLAGE

Gull Beak leaned near as K'os gutted and sliced the salmon, then handed them to Two Fist's young daughter, who hung the split carcasses by the tails from the drying racks.

"The medicine worked," Gull Beak whispered.

K'os's woman's knife, making quick horizontal slices through the thick pink flesh, paused for a moment, then continued as though Gull Beak had said nothing.

"I brought you birdbone beads."

K'os stood, wiped a hand on her caribou hide pants and opened a pouch that hung at her waist. Gull Beak slipped the packet of beads into the pouch, and K'os pulled the drawstring tight.

"Come to me if you hear of others," she told Gull Beak, then squatted again in front of the heap of gleaming fish.

SEVEN

THE COUSIN RIVER VILLAGE

Aqamdax braced herself with the babiche rope. She had tied it to a stout branch of the white spruce that stood over the birth lodge. The rope disappeared through the mat roofing of the lodge, and Aqamdax wished she could follow it outside, away from the pain and the dense air, sharp with the smell of sweat and birth fluids.

She heard Ligige' 's voice telling her to push, to push and to breathe, but the words were far away and difficult for her to understand. Each pain was a wave, and she tried to float above it, as though she were back in that small iqyax with Sok, riding the North Sea when she came as his bride to the River People.

Then suddenly the pain peaked, so hard, so rending that she thought she could not live through it, but then there was another voice, the sudden sound of a baby crying. Hard, angry cries.

"A son," Ligige' called out. "A boy, a hunter."

"Is he big enough? Is he all right?" Aqamdax asked.

"He is small but strong. Listen to him cry." Then Ligige' lifted the child and placed him in Aqamdax's arms. Aqamdax tried to lay back, but Ligige' stopped her. "Wait until the afterbirth has passed," she said, and then called out for Yaa as if she could see through the mat walls and know that the girl was waiting outside.

Yaa crawled into the lodge. "How did you know I was here?" she asked, then, before Ligige' could answer, said, "Boy or girl?"

"Boy," Ligige' told her. "I knew you were there, because if I were you, that's where I would be."

Yaa laughed, and Ligige' lifted her chin toward Aqamdax. "Go sit behind her. Hold her up until the afterbirth comes."

The cord, thick and blue, twisted down from the baby's belly. When it no longer pulsed, Ligige' tied it off at the navel, and then again a hand's length away. She cut it between the ties with the obsidian blade of her birth knife. Then the placenta came in a rush of blood and water, and Ligige' wrapped it in a mat, set it aside to burn later.

"Lay her down," she told Yaa.

Yaa scooted from behind Aqamdax, gently settling her to the mat-covered floor. Ligige' cleaned and covered Aqamdax, then took the baby from her arms and washed him. She wrapped him in the softened hare pelts Aqamdax had prepared for him and handed him back to his mother.

"He is so small that he may not know how to suck. Try him and see."

She watched as Aqamdax rolled to her side, pulled up her shirt and offered the baby her nipple. He turned his head and clamped his mouth over it, began to nurse.

Ligige' chuckled. "Yaa, stay here with her. I have other things to do."

Ligige' left, carrying the afterbirth. When the burning was done, Ligige' returned to the lodge, ducked her head inside.

"They are both asleep," Yaa whispered to her.

"Stay with them until Aqamdax wakes up. Don't you wake her; let her sleep. Then come get me."

Ligige' walked toward the village. It was always good to tell a father about the birth of a son. This child was small, born too early without doubt, but he was strong. He nursed well, and Aqamdax would be a good mother. The child should live, at least until the starving days of late winter. Then who could say? But why think about sorrows that might never come? There would be time enough to mourn later, if the child died.

She scratched at Star's lodge, heard Long Eyes lift her voice in a vague answer. Ligige' crouched to crawl inside and almost ran into Chakliux.

"A son!" Ligige' said, singing out the words.

She saw the pinched look of worry on his face. "Aqamdax?" he asked.

"A strong woman. She will be a good mother."

Chakliux closed his eyes, let out his breath.

"Where is Night Man?"

"Inside." Chakliux stood back, held open the doorflap. He waited until Ligige' was in the lodge, then he moved his lips in a silent prayer of thanksgiving. As he crawled back inside, he heard Night Man's voice raised in anger and so stayed near the entrance, his eyes turned away.

"You are sure the child was born early?" Night Man asked.

Ligige' had squatted beside him, her hands draped over her knees, and Chakliux, glancing quickly at her and then away, noticed that she looked tired. She was, after all, an old woman, and she had been awakened early to tend Aqamdax.

"He is very small," she said, "but strong. Already he is eating."

"You think, then, that he will live?"

"No one can say for sure. He must decide for himself whether he wants to stay in this world. I have seen large babies die and weak ones live, but there is no reason why this child should die."

Night Man grunted, and Ligige' said, "If you want to see him, I will bring him outside to you. Come to the edge of the village."

"No, I will wait until it is time for his mother to leave the birth lodge."

Ligige' shrugged, and Chakliux realized that since Star was not there, perhaps he should offer food.

"Aunt, you are hungry," he said, and fetched a bowl, filled it with broth and meat.

She took the bowl and ate, and to Chakliux's surprise, Long Eyes stood and unhooked a water bladder, offered it to Ligige'. Perhaps a baby in the lodge would bring Long Eyes back to them. At one time, she had been a fine wife to Cloud Finder. It would be a good sign if her spirit decided to return to the village.

Chakliux heard a scuffling in the entrance tunnel, then Yaa was back in the lodge, her eyes dancing.

"I went to your lodge first," she said to Ligige'. "Then I thought you might be here. Aqamdax is awake."

"No problems?" Ligige' asked.

"I don't think so."

Ligige' stood and dipped her bowl into the cooking bag. "Then I will eat a little more before I go back. You have the food Aqamdax set aside for herself?" she asked through a mouthful of meat.

"It is in the cache," Yaa said.

"Get it for me. I will take it to her when I go."

Yaa returned quickly with a woven grass bag. Ligige' set down her empty bowl and opened the bag, pawed through the contents.

"You cannot let a woman who has just given birth eat any fresh meat," she told Yaa. "Smoked fish is good. This"—she pulled out several sticks of dried meat—"is it from last year? Didn't this village lose all last year's meat in the fighting?"

"I gave it to her," Chakliux said. "It is some I brought with me when I left the Near River Village."

"From Near River hunters?" Night Man asked.

"It is seal meat from the First Men. I spent last winter in their village."

Night Man frowned. "You are sure it is not Near River?"

"It is not."

Anger tightened Chakliux's chest, and he turned away. Who did not know a woman needed meat after giving birth? Yet this man would sacrifice his wife's strength over his hatred for the Near River People. He almost reminded Night Man who had begun the fighting, who had struck first, but he did not allow the words to move from his heart to his mouth.

Instead he stood, said, "I must find my wife, tell her that she has a nephew." He left the lodge, glad to get away from Night Man's smoldering anger.

"Is the baby my brother?" Ghaden asked Yaa. He stroked Biter's back with his fingertips, leaving tracks like small valleys in the dog's brown fur.

"Star's baby will be your brother or sister," Yaa told him, "and that makes Aqamdax's baby your cousin." She paused. "Well, no. Aqamdax is your sister, so you are his uncle. At least, I think you are his uncle. And I am kind of an aunt."

Ghaden puffed up his chest. "I will have to take care of him. I will have to show him how to hunt." He went to the weapons area where Night Man and Chakliux kept their spears and throwers, their darts and lances. He had a bola there and a small thrusting lance. The lance was really only a toy, even though the wooden shaft had been sharpened into a point and hardened in fire. But the bola was a true weapon. Chakliux had made it for him and was teaching him how to swing it so he didn't hit himself with the sharp stones. He hadn't got a bird yet, but soon he would. Then he would give the new baby one of the feathers, something Aqamdax could put in his amulet. He picked up his bola, ran his hands from the braided handle to the stones. Each stone was tied securely to the end of one of the bola's rawhide strings.

He wanted to take the weapon over to where Yaa sat, to hold it in his lap and think about the birds he would kill, the praise Yaa and Aqamdax would give him when they added the meat and bones from those birds to their cooking bags, or roasted them on a stick, but Yaa was a girl. She might pull away some of the bola's power. So he hung it again from its wooden hook on one of the lodge poles, then went and sat down beside Biter.

Suddenly the doorflap opened and Star came in. "You are a lazy one," she said to Yaa. "Have you checked the traplines? And you, you could bring wood," she said to Ghaden.

Ghaden knew Yaa was tired from being up early with Aqamdax and helping Ligige', but he was glad to have something to do. It was boring in the lodge. He slipped on his summer boots, then followed Yaa and Biter. He heard Star speak to Night Man while he was still in the entrance tunnel: "She had a son, I am told."

Ghaden stopped for a moment so he could hear Night Man's reply, but he could not make out the mumbled words.

Star's voice lifted in laughter, then Ghaden heard Long Eyes also laugh, the sound like a weak and fading echo.

"You think it is yours?" Star said. "With all the men K'os brought into her lodge, you truly think Aqamdax's son is yours?" Again she laughed.

For some reason the sound made Ghaden shiver.

That evening, after Ligige' had left her for the night, Aqamdax still could not sleep. The joy and wonder of having her own child filled her like laughter.

She ran a finger over her son's cheek. Even in his sleep, he turned toward the touch, opening his mouth, moving his head until he succeeded in getting her fingertip to his lips. He sucked for a moment, then relaxed. She had just fed him, so she knew he was not hungry. A bubble colored by her milk lingered at one corner of his mouth.

Among the Cousin River People, the men were the ones who named the babies. Night Man would give him a River name, but that did not matter. Aqamdax would call him Angax, the First Men word for power. Surely such a name would lend him the strength he needed to survive.

Angax looked like Night Man, even Ligige' had said so. He had Night Man's strong chin and his eyes that tilted down at the sides. Just above his forehead a swirl of black hair turned a small circle, like an eddy at the side of a river; that, too, was Night Man's. Aqamdax had counted her son's fingers and toes, long thin fingers like her own, and she had unwrapped and wrapped him many times. When she nursed him, small pains twisted just below her belly, but Ligige' had called them afterbirth pains, something every woman had, nothing to worry about.

So now for Aqamdax there was only happiness. She had hoped Night Man would come to see the baby but thought perhaps such a thing was against River taboos. They were a strange people, with many things forbidden to both men and women.

Aqamdax had been out of the lodge once to relieve herself, her baby tied to her chest, but mostly she had lain still and watched her son.

It had not been a long labor, Ligige' told her. Many women having first babies went a whole day or more. But Aqamdax had grinned and told Ligige' that it had been long enough.

Before she left, Ligige' had asked to hold the baby, then she had poked and prodded until Angax wrinkled up his face and began to cry. But Ligige' smiled, and to Aqamdax's relief once again pronounced him healthy.

When the old woman left, she had promised to send Yaa, so Aqamdax was not surprised when she heard someone approaching the birth lodge. She eased herself up to sit on the pad of moss and fireweed fluff that caught her afterbirth blood, but when the doorflap was pulled aside, it was Star.

"I have come to see my nephew," Star said.

Aqamdax felt her heart quicken as Star held her hands out for the baby. "He is asleep now," she said, and wished Ligige', even Yaa, were there with her.

She pulled down the front of her shirt, adjusted the loose neck that she had made large enough for the baby when he was tied against her chest.

"See?" she said, showing Star his head.

His eyes were squeezed shut, and he had a tiny fist raised to his mouth.

"It is too dark in here to see him," Star said.

Aqamdax pushed herself slowly to her feet. The first time she stood after giving birth, darkness had begun to close in around her eyes, but since then she had had no problem.

"I will come outside," she told Star. It was nearly evening, but the sun was still up, and she could see the clear blue of the sky through a chink in the lodge wall.

Outside, Aqamdax again pulled down the neck of her shirt. Star patted the baby's head, asked if Aqamdax had named him. She did not tell Star his First Men name. It was better to keep that name as a protection, known only to a few who could be trusted with the knowledge.

"I thought Night Man should name him," she said.

Star shrugged, then she turned to point with her chin toward the village, and said, "Look. My brother wants to see his son. He cannot come too close, you know, but he waits for me to bring the child to him."

Aqamdax wrapped her arms around Angax, bound safe and warm against her skin. Fear flooded her chest, and she could not breathe, then the fear turned to anger, as though she were a wolf mother protecting her pups. How could she give this precious son to Star? Perhaps if Ligige' had come and asked such a thing, she would not mind. . . .

Aqamdax looked past Star to her husband, felt the assurance of his presence. What could happen to a child in such a short distance? How could she be so foolish as to fear her husband's sister?

"Let me wrap the baby so the wind will not take his breath," she told Star, then went back into the birth lodge.

He woke as Aqamdax laced him into his cradleboard, but he did not cry. She looked into his face. For a moment he seemed to study her, and Aqamdax felt how close they were, their souls nearly one. Then she took him outside and gave him to Star.

She watched as Star walked slowly to Night Man, and Aqamdax closed her eyes in relief when she saw Night Man gather the cradleboard into his strong right arm. To her surprise, they turned from her and began to walk into the village. But what did she know about River People customs? Perhaps they were going to show the baby to others.

She wished the people of this village followed the honored ways of her own village. There, when the mother's time of isolation was ended, she carried the baby to her husband's ulax. Then all the village women came, each bringing a gift, and while everyone sat together in a circle, each took a turn holding the baby, whispering blessings—all while the mother and grandmother watched.

"Bring him back to me soon!" Aqamdax called. "He will be hungry."

Star turned and raised one hand to her, then they were gone, hidden by the lodges and lean-tos of the Cousin River Village.

EIGHT

THE NEAR RIVER VILLAGE
Fox Barking stood at the hearth fires and raised his hands
to the sky. He praised the river for the abundance of fish,
reminding the people that only the summer before, few
salmon had come to them. He praised the caribou who
awaited their hunters, and he spoke of the Near River
warriors, those who still lived among them and those who
had been killed in the fighting.

The few Near River families who had spent the summer
at fish camps had returned. Soon the first bands would set
out from the village to hunt fall caribou.

With caches full of dried and smoked fish, it was a
good time to rejoice in full bellies and strong arms, to
feast on salmon and summer berries and to dream of the
promise of caribou. And why not also tell the people he
had chosen a new name, one that was more fitting for the
man who led them?

From this day, he would be Anaay. What name could
be better? Anaay—that which moves. His mind was always moving, planning what would be best for the village.
And who did not know that the River people also gave
that name to the caribou herd as it traveled, spring and
fall? With a name like Anaay there would be no end to
his powers.

The caribou would recognize him as their own, would sing their journeys through his bones, and so he would always know where his people should hunt, no matter which paths the herds chose.

Then who could deny that he deserved his place as leader of the elders? After all, he was still a good hunter, and he had a new young wife to warm his bed at night. Who could forget his first wife's skills with needle and awl? Each of his women had a good lodge. His caches were full. Even Chakliux, with all his stories, and Sok, with his thick arms and strong spear, could not compare to Anaay.

K'os watched from the edge of the crowd as Fox Barking spoke. With each word he puffed out his chest, but his arms and legs were spindly, and there was no way he could increase their size simply by filling himself with air. His belly had grown fat since she came to the village; even the splendor of his caribou hide parka trimmed with beaver and marten fur, even the birdbone beads that adorned his knee-high summer moccasins, could not hide his true shape.

She listened to him praise the Near River People, their strength, their cunning, and with each word she ground her teeth. She longed to scream out her hatred, but why give warning of her intent? Fox Barking would learn soon enough that she was still an enemy to be feared.

Tiring of his proud words, she turned to leave, but then Fox Barking said that he had chosen a new name. Anaay, he said, and K'os's anger dissipated in a flood of mirth. Perhaps she would have to do less than she thought. Even a child would understand that the name boasted of his powers to guide hunters to caribou. Even a child could see that Fox Barking did not have the spiritual strength to do such a thing.

During her life, K'os had heard of only one man who knew the paths of the caribou. He had died when she was still a child, but she remembered him. In humility, he had named himself Koldze' Nihwdelnen, and in truth to his name, he kept nothing for himself. He was thin, and his clothes were old. His wife had died before K'os was born, and he had not married again, but rather went from lodge to lodge, living with one family, then another, and each hunter hoped Koldze' Nihwdelnen would stay with him and so bring luck to his weapons.

How could Fox Barking hope to compare to someone like that? The caribou would sense his greed, and Fox Barking's foolishness would rise up like xos cogh thorns to drive the caribou away.

But though these thoughts were as loud as any of Fox Barking's words, K'os kept them behind clenched teeth, and when he had finished speaking, she made her way in silence through the crowd as they gathered at the village hearths.

She used a stout branch to push a hot stone from the fire, then, with the stick and green willow tongs, carried it to one of the cooking bags. K'os clacked her tongue so the people would get out of her way, and she walked slowly so that if she dropped the stone, she would not step on it.

She turned her head aside and dropped the stone into the cooking bag. The broth splattered and the stone hissed, but it did not shatter. She used her tongs to scoop out a cooled stone, then carried it, dripping fat and broth, back to the fire, where she settled it into the coals.

Squatting with her back to the people, she scraped the broth from the tongs with her fingers and licked them clean. As a slave, she was not allowed food until everyone else, even the smallest child, had eaten. Who could say what would be left? But she had become clever at stealing broth from stirring sticks, fish from drying racks, and meat from children too young to tell anyone what she had done.

She was carrying a rock to another cooking bag when she saw Gull Beak bend close to Fox Barking. The woman had something in her arms, surely a gift, for she had covered it with a grass mat. Several others also noticed what Gull Beak was doing, and soon most of the women and many of the men were watching. Gull Beak opened the mat, laid a parka on Fox Barking's lap. He smiled, crinkling the scar that disfigured his face, then held up the gift so everyone could see.

The parka was made from the skins of powerful animals: beaver and marmot, wolverine. The marmot was a mountain animal. How many trades had it taken Gull Beak to get enough marmot pelts? K'os wondered. The back of the parka and each arm were sewn with shell beads in sacred designs of circles and lines. Black-tipped weasel tails hung from the top seams of the hood, and beaver ears to help Fox Barking's hearing were sewn on each side. A row of raven beaks, shiny with oil, dangled just above the parka's wolverine hem ruff, and as Gull Beak had told K'os, eagle feathers in eye circles hung at each shoulder.

Fox Barking stood and pulled off his old parka, then slipped on the new. "What wife could do better?" he boasted, and one of the young men called out, "So Anaay, what gift do you give in return?"

Fox Barking sputtered a few words, then finally spread his arms wide to encompass the feast and said, "This food, a summer of plenty. The salmon returned to our river. All these things I give."

But K'os saw the narrowing of eyes, heard the angry whispers. How dare Fox Barking claim what everyone had worked hard to do?

Fox Barking's new young wife, Dii, spoke to Gull Beak, then stepped close to her husband, stood on her toes to whisper into his ear. Though K'os was too far away to hear what Dii said, suddenly, as though she had been told, K'os knew. She bit her lips to keep from smiling. When Fox Barking brought K'os to the Near River Village, traded her so quickly to Black Mouth, she thought it would take a long time to gain opportunity for revenge.

So, would Fox Barking do what his wives asked? She waited, hissing a promise as she watched: "If you do not take me now, Fox Barking, it does not matter. I have promised to kill you, and I will."

Then Fox Barking picked up his summer parka, carried it to Black Mouth. He lifted his chin toward K'os. Black Mouth pointed with pursed lips at Fox Barking's boots, but Fox Barking merely laughed. Black Mouth lifted his chin to the necklaces the man wore. Fox Barking removed one, then two, and finally Black Mouth nodded.

"A slave for my wife," Fox Barking announced. "The woman K'os to make her life easy, so she can sew more parkas."

The people laughed, and K'os joined them.

THE COUSIN RIVER VILLAGE

Aqamdax slipped her hands under her shirt and cupped her breasts. Milk seeped between her fingers. She got up again from the soft pad of moss and looked out through the doorflap. The sky was dark. Her stomach twisted, and she clamped her mouth shut over a sudden wave of nausea.

They had been gone too long. What if Night Man had asked Star to bring Angax back to her, and Star, stopping to visit someone, had forgotten the baby? What if she had left him outside? What if he had begun to cry, and Star had become angry?

But surely if something had happened to him, Ligige' or even Yaa would have come to tell her.

She slipped on her summer boots, laced them and went outside. For a time, she merely stood, looking toward the village, hoping to see Night Man or Star. Trees and brush hid some of the lodges from her eyes, but she could see Ligige' 's lodge, lit from the inside with a hearth fire.

If she walked through the trees, careful to stay away from any path one of the hunters might use, perhaps it would do no harm to go to Ligige' 's lodge. She took the most difficult way, through a thick brush of alder saplings. Finally, she was close enough to see the shadow of the woman inside.

She did not want to walk the cleared ground between the lodge and the trees, so first she called, crying out the old woman's name until her throat ached. Ligige' did not come, so Aqamdax walked to the back of the lodge, scratched at the caribou hide cover, then called again.

Ligige' 's voice came to her. "Who are you? Tsaani,

my brother? Little Fox, my sister? Have you come to take me to the world of the dead?"

"Ligige', it is Aqamdax."

Then Ligige' peered around the side of the lodge, her eyes round in surprise.

"Why are you here?" she asked. "You know you might curse our hunters. Is the baby sick?"

Aqamdax backed away from the lodge, and Ligige' followed, using her hands to sweep the ground where Aqamdax had walked.

"I do not have the baby," Aqamdax told Ligige', and Ligige' looked up at her, suddenly still.

"What? Where is he?"

"You did not see him?" Aqamdax said. "Star did not bring him to you?"

"You gave your son to Star?" Ligige' asked, and spoke with such horror that Aqamdax bent double and began to retch.

"So, Husband," Star said, "I have started sewing the caribou hide cover for our lodge." She held up her hands, fingers splayed. "My hands will soon look like an old woman's."

"You are a good wife," Chakliux told her, though in his heart he knew the dishonesty of his words. Any other woman would have had the cover done by now.

There was no scratching at the doorflap, no polite words or clearing of a throat, but suddenly Ligige' was inside the lodge. Pointing one gnarled finger at Star, she asked, "Where is the baby?"

Star patted her belly and smiled.

"No," Ligige' said, "Aqamdax's son."

Star shrugged and bent her head over the caribou hide.

Chakliux stood, looked hard into Ligige' 's eyes. "What has happened?" he asked.

"Aqamdax is at my lodge. She came asking if I had seen her son. She claims Star and Night Man took him."

"You took him?" Chakliux asked his wife, but Star only stuck out her lower lip, like a child pouting, and did not answer.

Chakliux squatted beside her, cupped her chin in his palm and lifted her head. She slapped his hand away.

"How should I know what happened to the baby?" she said. "I didn't do anything to him. Maybe Aqamdax lost him. She's careless like that."

"You know that's not true," Ligige' told Star. "Where is Night Man?"

"You expect me to answer for my brother? It is enough that I take care of those two Near River children."

"So where are they?" Ligige' asked.

"With Sky Watcher and his wife," Star said. "Sky Watcher has promised to show Ghaden—"

Chakliux interrupted her. "Star, did you and Night Man go to Aqamdax and get the baby?"

"Yes," Star said. "What is the problem in that? Night Man is the boy's father. At least Aqamdax says he is."

"So Night Man has the baby?" Ligige' asked.

Star nodded.

"That is good," said Ligige'.

Star dropped her head, but not before Chakliux saw a smirk tighten her lips.

"No, Ligige'," he said to his aunt, "that is not good."

He pulled his parka from its hanging peg and slipped quickly out through the entrance tunnel. He headed toward the hunters' lodge, though since the Near Rivers had burned the village, it was more lean-to than lodge.

Ligige' called him, so he stopped and turned.

"Where are you going?"

"To find Night Man. Go back to Aqamdax," he said. "Stay with her until I bring the baby."

At the hunters' lodge, he interrupted a story old Take More was telling, earned dark looks for his rudeness. He asked them if they knew where Night Man was, but no one had seen him. Then he went to the other lodges in the village, scratching at doorflaps, waiting impatiently until someone answered him. Finally Twisted Stalk said she had seen Night Man carrying something, walking in the direction of the Grandfather Lake. Then, though the sky was dark and his otter foot ached, Chakliux ran.

*　　*　　*

Aqamdax, huddled at the back of Ligige' 's lodge, waited. She kept her fears pressed down and did not allow them to form thoughts in her mind, but her chest felt as though it were weighted with rocks. Why had she allowed Star to take the baby? Why had she trusted the woman? But what else could she have done? Night Man wanted to see his son. She hummed lullabies she had learned as a child from her mother, hoped the songs carried some power to keep her baby safe, even in this land so far from her home.

Then she heard Ligige' call. "Aqamdax, are you here?"

"Aunt, I am behind your lodge. Have you found my son?"

Ligige' did not answer, but instead came to her, and Aqamdax could not hold back a sob when she saw that Ligige' 's arms were empty.

"I was foolish to give him to Star. I should have known. . . ."

Ligige' gathered Aqamdax close, patted her back as though she were a child. "Hush, now. Star does not have him. She says the baby is with Night Man."

Hope lifted some of Aqamdax's pain, and she raised her head, looked first at Ligige', then out into the village. "Where is he?" she asked.

"Star does not know, but Chakliux has promised to find him."

Then Aqamdax saw someone running. Though the darkness was broken only by the light that leaked from each lodge, she could tell it was Chakliux. He disappeared behind a lean-to, then she saw him on the path to the Grandfather Lake.

She pulled away from Ligige', and before the old woman could stop her, Aqamdax ran after him.

NINE

Trees and shrubs tried to hold Chakliux back, but still he ran. Twice he stumbled, his otter foot giving way, but he caught himself with his fingertips, pushed himself up to his feet. By the time he reached the Grandfather Lake, the moon had risen, glazing the water with silver, and Chakliux, his mind clouded with fatigue, saw the silver first as ice.

From the dark spruce woods near the lake came the call of an owl, and Chakliux shuddered at the knowledge of what that call could mean. He allowed himself only a moment to rest, then climbed the hill to the Grandfather Rock. Usually he avoided the rock. He had been left there as a baby, given to the wind by his grandfather Tsaani because of his otter foot. Why come and remind the winds what had been taken from them? Who could say what gift they might demand in exchange?

Now he went, climbed as quickly as he could, sometimes scrambling up the path on all fours. But when he came to the rock, he saw nothing except the moonlight gilding its dark, flat top.

Suddenly it seemed as though a part of the rock had moved. Chakliux's knife came into his hand so quickly that he did not remember removing it from the sheath.

Then he realized that a man had been crouched beside the rock.

"I thought you might come."

Chakliux recognized Night Man's voice.

"Where is your son?" Chakliux asked.

"He is not my son."

Night Man stood, lifted a woven hare fur blanket and draped it over the Grandfather Rock. "You think I would leave him here? I have heard the stories of how you came to us as animal-gift, found here on this rock by K'os. You think when I decided to throw away my wife's son that I would leave him on this rock?

"Because this rock allowed you to live when you were supposed to die, my father and two of my brothers are dead, and I will never again be a hunter." He held out his shriveled arm. "You deny that your spear did this?"

"Where is the baby, Night Man?" Chakliux asked, his words like ice.

Night Man extended his hand back toward the lake. "There, in the water. Drowned."

Anger filled Chakliux like a storm, roared in his ears like the wind. "You think you have killed only a baby, but you have killed the hunter he would have been! You have killed his children, and everyone he would have fed. A village of people die in this one death!" Chakliux stopped, caught his breath. When he spoke again, his voice was quiet. "Ligige' told you he was born early. Aqamdax said the boy was yours."

Night Man spat. "Ligige' is your aunt. She is Near River. Why should I trust her? As for Aqamdax—any woman would lie to save her child."

"You fool! You would tear out your wife's heart because of your own pride. Even if Aqamdax was wrong, even if the child was not yours, you would have taught him, and in that way he would have carried a piece of your spirit. As would his children and grandchildren."

"According to the traditions of our people, I had the right to do what I did."

"If the ways of a people allow evil, then they have begun their own destruction," Chakliux answered.

"You speak of evil when you yourself have killed so many? I will give Aqamdax another child, and this time I will know it is mine."

When Aqamdax came to the Grandfather Lake, she heard nothing but her own ragged breath. Surely she would soon wake to find herself in the birth lodge. Her son would be suckling her breast, his dark hair soft against her skin, his tiny fingers clasped around her thumb. She had never known anything more precious than holding him in her arms. She had never experienced a deeper joy.

She saw in the moonlight that the tops of her moccasins were stained with blood. She had heard of women bleeding to death after childbirth, but if her son was dead, she did not care. She would rather go with him to the spirit world. Who would take care of him if she did not? Perhaps her mother, but who could say? Her mother might not recognize Angax as her grandson. He looked so much like the River People.

When Aqamdax caught her breath, she straightened. She had not passed Chakliux on the path, and so he had to be here. But even with the moonlight, it would be difficult to see him. Perhaps some movement might catch her eye. . . .

Then she heard voices, not the calls of night animals but the sound of men arguing. She walked toward the voices, up the hill toward the Grandfather Rock, and her legs felt as though they would allow her to fall. People sometimes left babies on that rock to die.

Before she reached the rock, she knew the voices belonged to Night Man and Chakliux. Chakliux's voice, though it was raised in anger, gave her strength.

When they saw her, Night Man raised his good hand in a gesture of protection to defend himself from the powers she carried as a woman who had just given birth.

"Where is my son?" she asked him.

For a long time Night Man said nothing, then Aqamdax saw the hare fur blanket in his hands. She ran to him, snatched it away.

"Where is my son!" she screamed. Her fear throbbed

like a pulse through her words. She swept her hands over the rock, sure she would find the child's blood, but she felt only the brittle prick of lichen and the warmth of the stone, still releasing the heat it had gathered during the day.

Then Chakliux's hands were on her shoulders, and she felt his strength. She relaxed, leaned her head back against his chest, but Night Man said, "I gave him to the lake. He is there now, with the water spirits."

The words were like the blade of a knife, cutting through her flesh and into her bones until she could only scream.

She wrenched herself from Chakliux's grasp and ran.

"Do not go after her," said Night Man. "You already cursed yourself by touching her. She still bleeds from the birth."

But Chakliux turned from Night Man and followed Aqamdax down the hill. He found her kneeling on the shore, hands held out toward the lake. He wrapped his arms around her, but she struggled against him.

"My son," she said, and looked out at the water. "There, I see him. He is floating on that wave. If I wait, he will come to me."

"Aqamdax, Aqamdax, he is gone. There is nothing on the water. We must go back to the village. Ligige' has medicine for you, something that will help you regain your strength."

She stood, and Chakliux tucked an arm around her, tried to lead her away, but she broke from him and started out into the water, the blanket trailing from her hands. He went after her, caught her. He expected a struggle, but she allowed him to take her back to shore. Then, turning to him, she smiled and held up a short branch, forked on one end.

"I told you," she said. "Here he is. Look. He is not dead. See."

She knelt and wrapped the branch carefully in the sodden blanket, held it to her breast. Chakliux, tears burning his eyes, gathered her close and walked her back to the village.

 # PART
TWO

The stories had taken them from winter and on through the summer. Each morning and each evening the old woman had told the boy more about Aqamdax and Chakliux. She still had much to tell him, but already the fireweed blossoms had climbed to the tops of their stalks. Soon the leaves would turn, and the people would follow the caribou.

The old woman pushed herself to her feet and crawled out the doorflap of her fishcamp lodge. After tonight, they would have a few days without stories while they walked back to the winter village. She stretched her arms, saw how frail they had become, little more than skin over bones. The long walk would not be easy for her, but then she saw the boy coming, his face bright with a smile, and she knew she would have the strength.

He lifted a hand in greeting, and she welcomed him into her lodge, offering fresh fish that she had roasted outside over the fire. She did not wait for him to finish eating before she began. The stories pressed too hard in her throat, the words scrambling over one another to get to the boy's ears.

"The Near River Village," she said, "K'os and Fox Barking. Listen:"

K'OS, SLAVE OF THE NEAR RIVER PEOPLE:

He names himself Anaay and hopes to call caribou. Fool! It will take more than the power of a name to get the stink of fox out of him.

That night after he bought me for his wives, he took me to Gull Beak's lodge. He told me I would live there, and I was glad for that. Her lodge might as well get used to me, for soon it will be mine. I thought we would spend the night there, Gull Beak and I, but he sent her away.

He brought no gifts, and being slave, I expected none. He took me to Gull Beak's bed and with a knife in his fist, forced me to lie belly down.

"I know your hands," he told me.

So I knew he had not forgotten what they did to me so long ago. He and his friends. Two of those three men have felt my revenge. Fox Barking is next, and he will die more horribly than the others.

Look! What do I see? Ravens rejoice over their feast, taking the eyes first.

Fox Barking, do you understand the riddle?

TEN

THE NEAR RIVER VILLAGE
"Hold her still," K'os said.

The child lay on her side on a mat of caribou hides while her father gripped her legs. K'os had wrapped a round river rock, half the size of her fist, in the furred pelt of a river otter. She lifted the stone in one hand, said to the father, "The pelt is sacred, you see."

He nodded, and K'os placed the stone in the child's armpit, then pushed down on the arm.

The girl's sobbing rose to a shriek as the arm bone slipped back into the shoulder socket.

"You have killed her," Red Leggings, the mother, cried out, but the girl's father spit out a quick reprimand.

"Foolish woman, the arm is back in place. See for yourself."

"She must sit up now," K'os said.

The man lifted his daughter to his lap and watched as K'os bound the upper arm to the girl's body with a band of caribou hide.

"It is done," said K'os. "I will give your wife caribou leaves to heat and lay over the shoulder. They will deaden the pain." She raised her head to look at Red Leggings. "You know how to make tea from willow?"

75

Red Leggings looked away, but her husband said, "She knows."

"Give your daughter willow tea when she complains of pain."

K'os drew out another length of scraped and softened caribou hide from her bag of supplies and fashioned a sling. She lifted her chin toward Red Leggings and said, "Come here. I will show you how to tie it."

Red Leggings crept forward, sniffing as if she were a child, but K'os ignored her red, accusing eyes and wrapped the girl's arm, tied the sling so the knot would not rub at the back of the neck.

She nodded at Gull Beak, and the woman removed a packet of caribou leaves from the medicine bag and handed it to K'os. K'os opened the pack, took a leaf, laid it on her arm, rubbed it against her skin. She was a slave, and she was Cousin River. It would take a long time to earn the people's trust.

"You see?" she said. "It will not hurt her."

But the girl's father looked at Gull Beak and asked, "It is caribou leaf as she said?"

"It is caribou leaf. I was with her when she gathered it," Gull Beak answered.

"Her shoulder will hurt, but in a day or two she should begin to move her arm," said K'os, as though the girl's father had not expressed his doubt, as though Gull Beak were not even in the lodge. "Use the caribou leaves and give her willow tea. Make her wear the band and sling for a few days."

"Blue Flower told me that there are songs that should be sung," Red Leggings said.

K'os shrugged. "Tell Blue Flower to come and sing, but for the rest of today, keep the girl quiet and let her sleep."

As she and Gull Beak left the lodge, K'os said, "So what will you ask them in exchange for our medicine?"

"You think a caribou hide is too much?"

"She is their only daughter. Ask for a hide, and also for that string of seal teeth I saw hanging on a lodge pole.

That will be mine, if you can get it. If not, I will take half the hide."

She glanced from the sides of her eyes to see if Gull Beak would protest, but she did not. After all, the woman's lodge was already full of good things that K'os's skills had brought her: beads and hides and pelts, baskets and even a stone lamp that burned grease, something brought into the village by a trader.

Gull Beak lifted her chin toward the center of the village. "Take a turn at the hearths. If someone needs us, I will come for you. I have beads to sew on the winter boots I am making my husband."

K'os did as Gull Beak told her. Better to take a turn at the hearths than to be put to work in the river gaffing fish or scraping the moose hide Fox Barking had managed to cheat away from some hunter.

The wind was sharp. It cut through the village from the north and carried the smell of winter. The balsam poplar were turning yellow, leaves dropping to color the earth and make a bed for the snow. Two groups from the village had already left to hunt caribou, but Fox Barking stayed. He said he was fasting so he could hear the caribou more clearly. But so far his hunger had not called them into his dreams. Strange how in the lodge of a man who was fasting the stew bags—left full each night—were almost empty by morning.

Fasting or not, Fox Barking must soon decide where they would hunt. Otherwise the caribou would be past them, secure in their winter grounds.

He planned to take K'os and Dii, leave Gull Beak here in the winter village. There was so much to do in preparation for the hunt that K'os had not yet had the opportunity to finish her special gift for Fox Barking. She had to work when Gull Beak was busy somewhere else and would not walk in on her. Could K'os risk Gull Beak's seeing the strips of flycatcher skin, the kingfisher feathers, the fox eye? What about the gull feathers or the bits of grebe neck skin? If a wife could bless a man with her sewing skills, why couldn't a slave curse him with hers?

THE COUSIN RIVER VILLAGE

Night Man raised his left arm and, gritting his teeth, slowly straightened it. Five times he moved it up from his side, splayed his fingers, then lowered it and tightened his hand into a fist.

"Something good has happened here," he finally said.

"As my child grows, so you gain strength," Star replied, and laid her hand on the small mound of her belly.

Aqamdax bent her head over her sewing and pretended not to hear them. She could feel no joy for her husband's returning strength. Perhaps his spirit realized that if Night Man became sick again, Aqamdax would not work for his healing. And what chance would he have with only Star and Long Eyes to care for him?

"Perhaps Aqamdax's son took the pain with him when he died," Star said.

Aqamdax sucked in her breath. Was there no end to Star's foolishness? She stood up, left her sewing in the middle of the floor. It was a boot for Night Man. Let his sister finish it. Aqamdax pulled on her winter parka. It was cold outside, and the ground grew harder with each night's freeze. Two days before, it had snowed, though the sun had melted the snow by noon. She left the lodge without saying where she was going or when she would return. How could she tell them when she did not know herself?

She started toward Ligige' 's lodge, but instead walked to the spruce woods. The trees took the brunt of the wind, and Aqamdax pushed back her parka hood so the ruff just covered her ears. There was a large black boulder midway through the woods, and she walked until she came to it. The rock seemed to have no special powers, nothing to give but also no need to take, especially from someone like Aqamdax, whose sorrow had made her weak.

She squatted on her haunches, facing the path that led back to the village. When had she left the First Men Village? she asked herself. Only two years ago?

What a fool she had been to abandon the old woman Qung and her comfortable ulax. There Aqamdax had learned to be a storyteller, was finally held in honor by the people who had despised her for so long. Surely, if she had been patient, one of the men would have taken her as wife. Surely a First Men husband would not have killed his own son.

Aqamdax's throat ached with unshed tears.

Other women have lost babies, she told herself. Yellow Bird, Ligige' and Twisted Stalk had all come to her, whispered their sorrow, told of babies who had died long ago. Those women now treated her as one of them, bonded through pain as sisters—at least one solace in the midst of her agony.

"It has been long enough," Bird Caller told her only the day before. "Go back to your husband's bed, get the hope of another child."

Bird Caller had missed her last moon blood time, and Aqamdax could see the joy of hope the woman carried within her. But Bird Caller's husband had not killed her first child.

How could Aqamdax go to Night Man's bed? How could she bear to have his hands on her? She lowered her head to her arms and allowed herself to cry. Sometimes the tears helped, though she hid from Star and Night Man. Why show them her weakness? Suddenly there was a strong hand on her shoulder. She gasped and jumped, then saw it was Chakliux.

She blinked away her tears.

"You are all right?" he asked.

She cleared her throat, nodded.

"It's snowing again," he said.

She looked up at the sky, watched the large flakes drop slowly to the ground.

"Night Man sent you to find me?" she asked.

"No. I came here to get away from the village, to have time for my own thoughts."

He squatted beside her, crossed his arms over his upraised knees. He lifted his chin at her parka and said, "Perhaps you could make me one like that."

Aqamdax had cut her parka in the manner of the First Men's birdskin sax, so it was wide enough to pull over her legs when she squatted on her haunches. She pulled it down now, tucked it around her feet.

"It would get in your way when you are hunting," she said, then saw that she had hurt him. "But if you want one . . ."

"If you have time to make it," he said.

"I have time," Aqamdax said. Then, covering her embarrassment with words, she added, "Soon you will leave for the caribou hunt. Night Man has said he will not go. You will hunt with Sok?"

"Perhaps."

He placed an arm around her shoulders, and lifted her left hand, pushed back the sleeve of her parka so he could see the bracelet she wore. It was a sinew bracelet with knots made to look like the face of an otter. He had brought it back from the Walrus People and given it to her the night he came to warn the Cousin People of the Near River attack.

"You still wear it," he said.

She smiled. Her face felt stiff from her tears, but it was good to smile. She tipped her chin toward his side where the whale tooth carved into the whorls of a shell hung from his belt. She had given him the tooth. It had been passed down in the First Men Village, storyteller to storyteller, from a time so ancient even Qung did not know why it was carved in such a way.

He looked into her eyes, and she was suddenly uncomfortable. She began to speak about the snow and the trees. She told Chakliux about the first time she had come through these woods, she and her little brother Ghaden with the trader Cen and Night Man's brother, Tikaani. She told Chakliux about her father and mother, about games she had played as a child.

Even as she spoke some inner voice chided her, saying she had become too much River, trying to fill the world with her words. Had she forgotten the rudeness of interrupting a person's thoughts with needless chatter?

Finally Chakliux said, "Hush, Aqamdax. You do not

need to hide your sorrow when you are with me. Sometimes tears are the best thing."

Then she turned her head into his shoulder, and he held her as she wept.

ELEVEN

THE FOUR RIVERS VILLAGE
The dogs were barking, but dogs often barked. Surely most of the people had left the village to hunt caribou. Snow was falling hard. It covered Red Leaf's tracks, and that was a good thing, but she felt its chill through her parka. Her daughter moved against her chest, and Red Leaf held her breath in fear the baby would begin to cry. She waited, but the child only settled herself more deeply into sleep.

In the gray light of dusk, Red Leaf studied the caches, each a roofed square of logs set high on four legs. She chose the nearest one, lifted the ladder and set it into place. The dogs raised their barking into high-pitched yips. Someone might come out to check, but perhaps they would think it was only a fox, and what could a fox do with all the cache ladders propped against lodges and woodpiles?

She climbed the ladder, unlatched the cache door and looked inside. There were several caribou hide packs stuffed full. Choose well, she told herself, and selected the largest one. She took it, crept down the ladder and hurried away. If the snow did not get too deep, she might be able to reach her lean-to before morning.

She had pitched the lean-to at the base of a fallen

spruce. The roots had taken a large round of sod from the earth, and she used it as a wall against the north wind, overlapping spruce branches and draping a caribou hide to make a shelter. For a time, she was able to trap hares and ptarmigan, but during the last handful of days, her snares had stayed empty, and she had run out of the dried fish she brought with her from the Cousin River Village.

Ah, she had told herself after she finished eating the last piece, it is good the fish is gone. The less I have from that place, the better. But with nothing to put in her belly except a weak tea made of willow, the bark bitter now that winter was so close, she began to dream of going back.

Of course, Sok would kill her if she did. What choice did he have? No matter that she had killed his grandfather to give Sok the honored place of chief hunter in the Near River Village. No matter that she had given him two fine sons. She would die. She felt a brief stirring of anger but pushed it down, pretended it was not there. What else could Sok do? He had to avenge his grandfather's death.

Her daughter moved again, so with each step Red Leaf made small jostling movements. At least she was far enough from any village that if the baby cried no one would hear her. Except the wolves that sometimes followed when she left her shelter. She stopped, strapped the caribou pack to her back, and to keep the baby quiet began to sing a lullaby she had learned from Aqamdax when that Sea Hunter woman had been her sister-wife. At least Sok had had the sense to throw Aqamdax away. She was not a terrible woman, but who could say what curses she brought, coming from the Sea Hunter Village? They did not follow sacred ways.

The wind was increasing, and the snow fell so hard that it hindered Red Leaf's walking. She wished she had brought snowshoes with her when she left the Cousin River Village, but in her hurry, she had forgotten many things. Besides, who would have believed a winter storm would come so early?

At least when she reached the spruce woods, the trees would break the wind. She continued to walk. With the caribou pack strapped to her back and the weight of the baby against her chest, she bent closer to the ground with each step. In time, the wind shifted and blew from the north, and Red Leaf lifted one arm to shield her face. Night had fallen, and she could see nothing.

Suddenly she ran into something, hitting her arm hard enough to draw a quick cry of protest from her lips, then a breath of gratitude.

It was a tree, she was sure. She had reached the spruce woods. In spite of the storm, the snow, the load she was carrying, she had reached the forest. She straightened, felt her daughter lose her grip on her nipple and waited to see if the child would cry. She did not. Perhaps she was asleep.

Red Leaf was a large woman with heavy breasts, even when she was not feeding a baby. Even during these starving days, she had had plenty of milk for her daughter. She was strong, but in the storm, the caribou pack was heavy on her back, and she would be glad to set it down.

Her shelter was not far from the edge of the forest, though she knew she was not on the animal path she had followed from the trees to the village. Still, she would stay just inside the windbreak of alder and willow that grew between spruce and tundra. She would walk to the stream that wandered among the trees, follow it to the bend not far from where the fallen spruce lay.

Red Leaf reached out toward the tree she had run into. Strange that she had missed the underbrush of edge growth, though perhaps the weight of the wet snow had bent the branches low enough for her to walk over them. She shuffled ahead a few steps until she came to the next tree, then suddenly she knew where she was. The knowledge was like a weight that knocked her from her feet, and she sat down in the snow, leaned against the pack on her back.

She had made a large circle in her walking and returned to the Four Rivers food caches.

THE NEAR RIVER VILLAGE

Anaay lay on his bed. Dii watched him from the corners

of her eyes, glancing back now and again to the awl she was using. Twice she had plunged the thing into her fingers, but what was a little blood compared to her husband's work as he sought the caribou, tried to feel the singing of their legs as they walked south to their winter feeding grounds?

She was surprised that he even allowed her to stay in the lodge with him. Surely the caribou would sense her presence—a woman now bleeding from two fingertips—and be frightened from Anaay's calling. But he had asked that she stay, and perhaps it was good that she did. Who would bring Anaay water if she was not here? Who would bring him the urine trough and carry it away so the smell would not offend the caribou?

Three days they had been in the lodge now. Most of the time, Anaay slept, for when else did caribou visit a man but in his dreams? How else did a man hear caribou songs but when his own spirit was quiet and away from his body, living in that world of sleep?

"Ah! Ah! Ah!" Anaay called out, and Dii put down her awl, waited to see if he wanted her to do something, but he said nothing more.

Perhaps in his dreams the caribou were teaching him something. Perhaps now Anaay would know where their hunters should go. Dii wanted to stay and watch, but she decided that there was a chance the caribou would not truly speak to her husband unless she was outside the lodge. She pulled her parka from a peg and crawled out the entrance tunnel. She would stay close enough to the door to hear Anaay if he called her.

She was surprised to see that it was dark. When had the night come? It was strange, but for all Anaay's sleeping, it seemed that Dii could not sleep, as though he had stolen her dreams to give himself more, and she was left to wander in a sleepless world.

"Ah! Ah! Ah!" she heard again, but she did not go back inside.

She squatted on her haunches, making herself small against the cold. Half the sky was starred, the other half dark, clouds moving in from the north, perhaps snow.

Then she heard another sound, something so low and far away that at first she did not hear it with her ears but only in her chest, a rhythm, as though she suddenly had been given another heart to beat alongside her own.

It came as a pattering, like the first drops of rain against a lodge cover, but gradually spread from her chest to her arms and legs. It became thunderous and traveled up her neck until finally even her ears could hear it. Then she knew what it was, and she had to cover her mouth with her hands to hold back a cry of wonder.

She ran inside the lodge, expecting to see her husband awake and preparing to tell the hunters what he had heard, what he now knew. But he was asleep, his mouth hanging open, one arm flung up over his eyes, the other lying on his chest, his hand knotted into a fist.

Of course, she told herself. What else should she expect? She had heard the caribou, had felt the thunder of their hooves, but she did not know where they were, how far from camp, what direction they traveled. There was much more to know, and surely those were the things Anaay was learning as he slept.

THE FOUR RIVERS VILLAGE

Red Leaf wanted to stay where she was. Perhaps, even in the storm, her clothing would keep her warm enough that she could sleep a little while. She had walked so long and so far. The ache of her empty belly had spread to her whole body, so that it did not seem that she was hungry, only sick. Besides, it would take so much effort to unstrap the caribou skin from her back, to open it and get out food.

But how foolish to die here, so close to warm lodges and full caches. Of course, she was not going to die. She would sleep, only that. Just a little sleep. . . .

No! The word was so loud that Red Leaf's eyes opened wide, and she tried to see through the curtain of snow and darkness to discover who had yelled at her.

Finally she realized it was her own voice. Death must be close, she thought.

Leaning forward to grasp one of the cache poles, she

pulled herself up, then staggered again out into the storm. The wind was at her back, as it had been when she started out, as it would be if she walked straight. She began, and this time she counted her steps. After each handful, she stopped to be sure the wind stayed behind her.

She heard a high, thin keening. The wind, she told herself, and took another handful of steps, stopped, checked the direction of the driving snow, walked again, five steps. The keening also continued, until Red Leaf realized it was her daughter. The child had probably not regained her hold on Red Leaf's breast.

She stopped and dropped to her knees, pulled off a caribou hide mitten with her teeth, and held it clamped tightly in her mouth so the wind would not take it. She took her arm from the sleeve of her parka and drew it inside to the warmth where her daughter lay, the child naked save for the moss and ground squirrel skins that were bound between her legs. Red Leaf lifted her breast and guided it to the baby's mouth. She felt the sudden tightness as the baby began to suck and her milk let down.

Red Leaf got her hand and arm back into her parka sleeve, then put on her mitten. She balanced herself on hands and feet and tried to stand. She could not. Panic gripped her. She tried again, but fell, then rolled to her side, the giant pack pinning her to the ground.

She wrapped her arms around her daughter and lay still, allowed the snow to cover her. "Eat well, dear one," she whispered. "Eat long and well."

TWELVE

THE NEAR RIVER VILLAGE

At dawn, the sky was hung with heavy, dark clouds, their bellies so full that Dii could not see the sun. She hurried to the hearths, an east wind tearing at her parka, bringing the smell of snow, sharp tang of winter. She no longer felt the thunder of caribou hooves, and so wondered what Anaay heard as he lay still lost in his dreaming.

She ate quickly so she could go back to him, and when she returned to the lodge, he was awake. He greeted her with a scowl and a harsh demand for water, but her heart quickened in gladness with the knowledge that his dreams had brought him what he sought. When he opened his fur robes to show her his need, for the first time she went to his bed in joy.

THE FOUR RIVERS VILLAGE

Red Leaf awoke to darkness, something too close to her face. She struck out with her arms, flailed wildly until she remembered what she had done. She felt her daughter stir within her parka, and she began to laugh. She had prepared herself for death but had won life. Who could believe such a thing?

The ache of her legs reminded her how hard she had struggled, even after she fell. She had cut the straps that bound the caribou pack to her back, but even without that weight had been unable to get to her feet. Finally, she had lain still, resigned to her death, but her daughter's suckling had reminded her of her own hunger, and she had decided that she, too, should eat. Why die with an empty stomach when a pack of food lay nearby?

She had cut the neat cross-stitches that closed the hide over whatever was inside, had scolded herself for the greediness that had made her take the largest pack. She might have been able to go on if the pack had not been so heavy. Perhaps it had been the pack itself that turned her back toward the village. Perhaps it had decided to stay with those people who had filled it with winter food.

But once she opened it, she could not fault herself for her choice. It was full of fat, the thick hard fat that forms over the haunches of caribou and moose, smaller chunks that come from mountain sheep—a store of fat that would keep a family strong through at least one winter moon, perhaps more.

She chose a piece of sheep fat, bit into it and felt it crumble in her mouth. It tasted of the mountains, of the wind and the sun, and it spread fire from her mouth to her belly, warming her as if she had swallowed coals from a hearth.

She ate until she was no longer hungry, until the warmed fat leaked from her mouth to coat her lips. She softened a chunk in her hands, then rubbed it over her face to soothe the burn left by wind and snow.

While she ate, she had used the stuffed caribou hide as a windbreak. When she finished, she noticed that a drift had formed over her and the hide. Suddenly an idea came, and it was so strange that it nearly made her laugh. She lunged into the snow under her, scooped it out with wide sweeps of her hands. She made the hole as long as the caribou pack and twice as wide.

When she reached the sedges and grass of the tundra, she stopped, and unpacked the hide, piling the slabs of fat neatly at the windward side of the hole, then packed snow over them. She spread the empty caribou hide in the other side of the hole, the opening toward the pile of fat, and crawled inside. Now and again she stuck her arm up through the snow, clearing it away so she would not smother.

Finally she could no longer stay awake. If I die, I die, she told herself. It is what my husband wanted. At least in dying, I will please him.

But now she was awake and alive, perhaps in some spirit world, but she did not think so. Would she still be inside the caribou hide if she had gone to a spirit world? Would her daughter be suckling at her breast?

She raised her arm, broke through the snow easily. A rush of cold air flooded the caribou hide, and a shaft of light. The wind had died. The storm had passed. She decided she would eat first, then repack the caribou hide and carry it to her shelter.

She pried out a wedge of fat. It tasted of spruce—acrid, bitter—so she knew it came from a bull moose in rut. She grimaced but continued to eat. Though not nearly as good as the sweet sheep fat, it would give her the strength she needed to walk back to her shelter.

She was sucking the last of the fat from her fingertips when a small cascade of snow showered in on her. She raised her arm and cleared her airhole, then heard a high-pitched whine, felt the rapid scraping of clawed feet against the hide.

Wolves, she thought, and her heart beat so hard that she could feel the pulse of it at her throat. She unsheathed her sleeve knife.

At least one of them would die before they took her.

THE NEAR RIVER VILLAGE

Dii went to Sun Caller first, then Giving Meat, the two male elders, besides Anaay, who were left in the Near River Village after the fighting. She brought them to the lodge where Anaay waited. He was dressed in his most elaborate parka, wore all his necklaces and amulets. They made a mound around his neck, and with his hood thrown back, his head looked too small for his body, as though it would slip down and become lost in the fur and beads.

He stared for a moment at the two men sitting near his

fire—Sun Caller small but straight, rolling and unrolling a caribou hide mitten in nervous fingers, and Giving Meat, drooling like a child, his eyes wandering as though he did not know where he was—then Anaay told Dii to bring the other hunters as well, even the oldest boys. What he had to say was so important that every man, not just the elders, should be told.

It had taken all her courage to bring the two elders to her lodge. Now to go and get the hunters . . . Why would they listen to her, a woman just recently a slave?

"There are so many hunters, Husband," she said quietly, "and I am new in the village. What if I miss someone? Should I get Gull Beak to help me?"

He frowned at her, and she quickly added, "With two of us, they will come more quickly, and Gull Beak can help me with the food."

He tipped his head up toward the top of the lodge, as though considering her words, then said, "Yes. That is best. Get Gull Beak."

So Dii stopped to get Gull Beak, who put K'os to work filling cooking bags, then they stopped at each hunter's lodge, scratched at the doorflap and called. Most of the men, busy preparing weapons for the caribou hunt, frowned at them, turned their heads away as the women spoke.

But Dii and Gull Beak told each of them what Anaay had said, explained that the caribou had sung their wandering into Anaay's bones and he knew where the Near River men must hunt.

K'os crouched in the entrance tunnel of Gull Beak's lodge and watched the men. Ah, for the power to turn herself into flea or mouse and listen to what Fox Barking had to say. Surely, it was something to do with caribou hunting. What else did the men think of these days? With the freedom Gull Beak now gave her to gather plants and roots, K'os had begun to offer herself to hunters. There were quiet places in woods and willow thickets where wives did not see. Their generosity had allowed her to fill her sewing bag with beads and feathers, shells and teeth.

Lately, though, most of the men had been too busy for her. They must stay away from women, purify themselves for the caribou, they told her. So as she prepared the meat stews that Gull Beak had requested, she added a generous portion of dried yellow violets ground into powder. She wondered how Anaay would explain the men's stomach cramps and diarrhea. Perhaps then they would realize that he did not have the powers he claimed. At least their sickness would delay the start of any hunt, give K'os time to finish her work on Anaay's parka.

For every charm Gull Beak had sewn to seams, on furs and in beads and feathers, K'os had added a curse. Tufts of lynx fur to make Anaay's joints stiff; the barbs from kingfisher feathers sewn with cunning stitches into the seams under each arm to enhance his carelessness; the dried fox eye tacked under the circled eagle feathers to twist Anaay's sight; thin strips of flycatcher skin sewn under the hood ruff to draw a lingering death.

She had yet to slit the beaver ears that Gull Wing had sewn on the parka hood. K'os would make only the tiniest cuts, just wide enough to slip cod ear bones, flat and white, delicate as snowflakes, inside those beaver ears. She would use the finest wisp of sinew to tack each cut closed, then crush each bone as it lay inside its beaver ear. And Anaay's hearing would be brittle and broken.

Perhaps after a few moons, Anaay would realize that his new parka brought him only bad luck, but surely the blame would fall on Gull Beak. Not that K'os had any dispute with Gull Beak. The woman treated her more like a sister-wife than a slave. But she was in the way. How good that she was old. Old people always died during hard winters. At least she would die quickly, a death that Fox Barking would one day envy.

THE FOUR RIVERS VILLAGE
Red Leaf burst up through the snow, stabbing with her knife, screaming. One of the wolves yelped in pain, then Red Leaf heard the surprised voice of a man. She stopped, planted her feet firmly over the pile of snow that had sheltered her and faced him with the knife in her hand.

She moved the blade toward a growl that came from her left, then saw that it was only a dog, gray and black. A slash at the top of the animal's head bubbled blood.

"Tracker!" the man yelled at the animal. "Be still."

The hunter held his hands palms out. "I will not hurt you," he said, and Red Leaf nearly laughed. He stood without a knife. His spear and a fire bow weapon—like the ones the Cousin River People had used against her village—hung on his back. His hood was pulled far forward, shielding his eyes from the sun on the snow, so she could not see his face.

"I thought your dog was a wolf," Red Leaf said. "Get him away from me."

The man lifted his chin at the mound of snow. "You slept there?" he asked.

"The storm caught me. What choice did I have?"

"You are not from the Four Rivers Village."

Red Leaf almost said she was Near River, but there were always those who considered people from one village or another as enemy. Why say something that could be used against her?

"You are Four Rivers?" she asked.

He shrugged. "This winter I am."

"You should see to your dog. The cut still bleeds."

"Head wounds bleed much," he told her, but he walked over to the dog, used his gloved hand to stanch the flow, then wiped the blood on the snow.

"There is somewhere you need to go?" he asked her. "I can help you."

"My lodge is not far," she said. "I can travel by myself."

"You have no snowshoes?"

"When I left my lodge there was no snow," she said, and tried to smile, but her lips stretched and cracked until she could taste blood. "Go wherever it is you are going. I have a few supplies to gather."

She stooped as though to crawl back into her snow cave, but he did not move.

"Someone took food from my cache," he said. "A full caribou hide packed with fat. I am a trader. I need that fat. What I do not eat this winter, I will trade in spring."

She kept her back toward him, but he continued to talk.

"It might surprise you what people will give in those starving moons for a taste of fat. Parkas heavy with embroidery, burial moccasins with beaded soles, such things are not of much value to an empty belly."

She turned her head to look over her shoulder at him. "Then you best go quickly and catch that one who took it."

The dog growled again, and Red Leaf lifted her knife toward him.

"Tracker says you are the one."

"I have nothing except my own supplies." She patted her chest. "A cilt'ogho of coals, some dried fish. You would take that from me?"

"I take only what is mine," he told her, then he shouted at his dog, and before Red Leaf had time to protest, the animal knocked her back into the snow. The trader grasped her knife hand, wrestled away the weapon and held it to her neck until Red Leaf cried out, "Call off your dog and I will give you what I have."

He spoke to the animal, the words in a language Red Leaf did not understand. The dog backed away, but his lips were still drawn back from his teeth. Red Leaf began to roll from her back to hands and knees, but the dog growled again, lunged forward.

"This will not take me long," the trader told her. "But I would lie still if I were you."

He hacked at the crusted snow with a walking stick until he came to the caribou hide. He ran his hands over the lacing.

"It is mine," he said.

"I found it," she told him. "I was battling the storm and I found the hide. It was partially buried in the snow. It made a good shelter, but it is not mine. If it is yours, take it with my gratitude. It served me well."

"What of the fat I had stored inside?"

Red Leaf shrugged. "The hide was empty when I found it."

Again she rolled to her side, tried to stand. Again the

dog growled. "I have no weapons," she said. "Tell your dog—"

"Tracker!"

The dog sat back on his haunches, whined, and Red Leaf stood up, backed away.

"Tracker!" the trader called, and pointed at the snow cave. "Here, dig!"

Red Leaf began to walk. Perhaps the man, in finding his slabs of fat, would not think it worth following her. She hated to lose the knife. She had only one other, and that was a woman's knife with a curved blade. But better to save her life than stay hoping he would return the weapon.

The man called out, but she did not look back, did not slow down. The snow was deep and soft. With each step she sank past her knees, but still she walked. Then she felt a hand grab her hood. She tried to jerk away but could not. She turned to face the trader, and he waved a hand-sized chunk of white fat in her face.

"What of this?"

"Where did you find that?" she asked, trying to act as though she were surprised.

"In the hole you dug."

"I wish I would have known," she said. "I would have feasted during that long storm."

He pushed his parka hood back to his ears, and for the first time, Red Leaf saw him clearly. Her chest squeezed tight in surprise.

He was Cen, the trader who had brought the Sea Hunter woman Daes to the Near River Village. Though Daes had given birth to the boy Ghaden several moons after Cen had left her at their village, most of the Near River women thought he was Ghaden's father.

Cen's face had changed since the last time she had seen him. His nose was crooked, and a scar drew up one side of his mouth, but Red Leaf knew he was Cen. Did she not see his face most nights in her dreams, the man accused of what she had done? But how could Cen be alive? Surely he had died from the beating he received when the people thought he had killed Sok's grandfather Tsaani, and also Daes.

"I did not take it. I found it," she said again.

"What were you doing out in the storm?" he asked.

"My husband is a trader of sorts," she said, mumbling the first thing that came to her mind. How could she tell him her name? He might have already heard that she was the one who killed Daes and Tsaani. If he had cared for the woman, he would want revenge. Even if he had not, surely he would kill her for the wounds his son Ghaden had suffered, and for his own injuries.

"Your husband is a trader?" he asked, speaking slowly. "Where is he now?"

"He is lazy. He stayed in our lodge, and I went out to check my traplines. The storm caught me before I could get back."

"I have never known a trader who was lazy."

"Then you must not know my husband," Red Leaf said. She turned and started to trudge away, but called back over her shoulder, "I am sorry about the caribou pack being stolen from your cache. It is good I found it for you."

She continued to walk, hoping he would stay with his pack, but suddenly his hands were on her shoulders. She lost her balance and fell backward into the snow. Cen knelt beside her, loosened the drawstring at her hood and pulled it back from her face. He stared at her but finally shook his head and said, "I see too many women in my trading."

Red Leaf, realizing he did not recognize her, tried not to show her relief.

"I know you took my caribou pack and the fat I had stored. My dog caught your scent on the cache and brought me to you."

Red Leaf laughed. "What dog could do that?"

"This dog can." Cen tilted his head as he looked at her. "I thought you would be a man. The pack is heavy."

"I did not take it," Red Leaf said again.

But Cen continued as though she had said nothing at all. "You are a big woman, though. Strong." He pulled her to her feet, then pushed up one of her parka sleeves, looked at her arm. "You haven't eaten much lately. Who are you?"

Why not tell him a good story? Red Leaf thought, and she began to speak, spinning out lies. "For some years," she said, "until I was almost a woman, I lived in the Near River Village. Then my father died and my mother married a man who did some trading with the Near River and Cousin Villages. That is how we lived. One day he brought a man for me to marry. I became a wife then and had a baby. A daughter."

She stopped and realized that Cen was looking at her again, his eyes squinted, and she hoped that her mention of the Near River Village did not suddenly remind him of who she was.

"So you are going back now to your husband?" he asked.

"No."

"Why not?"

"He did not want a daughter. He decided to give her to his sister who lives north on the Great River. She has many sons but needs a daughter to care for her in her old age. I have run away so I can keep my baby."

Suddenly the child let out a cry, and Red Leaf loosened the drawstring at the neck of her parka so Cen could see the baby.

"Where do you live?" he asked.

"There is a spruce forest less than a day's walk from here. I made a shelter in the roots of a fallen tree."

"What is your name?"

Fear twisted itself into her belly, and she could feel her hands tremble. He did not remember her face, but what if he knew her name? Her daughter seemed to sense Red Leaf's fear and again cried out, this time in loud, long wails, so that Red Leaf crooned to the child and fussed getting her to accept a breast. She moved slowly, rocking her body and humming a lullaby, all the time thinking of names.

"Gheli," she finally said.

"Gheli?"

"Yes, my name is Gheli." Let him think she had been named that, by father or uncle, in honor of what she was. Would a woman named Gheli—good, true—steal from a cache? Would she kill?

"Gheli," Cen said, and lifted an arm toward the snow cave. "Repack my caribou hide."

She considered refusing, but he had her knife. How could she fight him? Besides, she might have a chance to slip a piece of fat into her parka sleeve.

She walked back to the pack, pulled it from the snow, then beat it with her hands to loosen the ice that had formed from her breath, crusting the inside. She repacked each piece of fat, watching Cen from the corners of her eyes, twice pushing fat up the sleeve of her parka. When she finished, she dragged the pack to him.

"The lacing is cut," she said.

Cen pulled a coil of babiche from under his parka and used it to bind the bag, nodding when Red Leaf stooped to help him. She thought he would tell her to carry the hide, but he heaved it to his own back and began to follow his trail through the snow toward the Four Rivers Village.

Red Leaf watched for a time, then started in the opposite direction. She had gone only a few steps when she heard him call.

"Gheli!" he said. "I have a warm lodge, and I need a wife."

She turned and looked at him. It would be a dangerous thing to have Cen as husband. Someday he would find out who she was and what she had done, but what chance did she have living alone, with no food? Perhaps she could stay with him long enough to set aside meat and hides, cache them away from the village, so she could survive if she had to leave quickly.

She made her way toward him. His snowshoes packed the snow so Red Leaf's feet did not sink so far with each step. And so they walked, Cen, Gheli and the dog, Tracker, to the Four Rivers Village.

THIRTEEN

THE NEAR RIVER VILLAGE

Dii hung the boiling bag from a lodge pole. It was heavy, full of fat and meat from the moose two hunters had taken several days before. She gathered an armful of wooden bowls and filled them. She offered the first to her husband, Anaay, but he waved it away. She gave it instead to Sun Caller, then set another beside Giving Meat. Giving Meat tipped the bowl over, then began to eat the stew with his fingers, scooping it from the floor, smearing it on his face. Dii looked away, pretended not to see. It was like that for an elder sometimes, and only a fool would ridicule. Who could say? She herself might someday be the same way.

Gull Beak and K'os came to the lodge carrying more cooking bags. They hung them near the door and began to help Dii. Anaay stood, and Dii watched her husband in pride, her eyes caressing the new parka he wore, her hands remembering the warmth of his skin when she had joined him in his bed that morning.

She felt a glow in her belly and wondered if they had begun a child this day. She had been drinking the tea made from raspberry leaves K'os gave her. It would, K'os promised, strengthen her womb. What a wondrous child she and Anaay would have, conceived while the sound of caribou still shook his parents' bones.

Anaay began to speak, and his voice filled the lodge. "I have dreamed caribou songs," he said.

Several of the youngest hunters lowered their bowls and lifted their voices in a quick hunting chant, a cry that made Dii shiver in joy. She had not wanted to come to this village, had not wanted to belong to Anaay. Life had been easier living with her mother and father, with her brothers and uncle. But now she was a wife, and what more could she ask than to be the wife of Anaay, a man who dreamed caribou?

"I called the animals, and they come to us. We must leave our village and prepare to meet them."

As Anaay spoke, the men continued to eat, and soon the meat stew was gone. Gull Beak nodded toward the entrance tunnel so Dii knew the woman wanted her to go to the hearths and get more food. Dii had hoped to be in the lodge when Anaay explained where the caribou were. Like Anaay, she carried the knowledge in her bones, and it quivered inside her, needing to be told.

But Gull Beak was first wife, and Dii must do as she asked. Sighing, she left the lodge. If she hurried, perhaps she would not miss much of what her husband had to say.

K'os watched in satisfaction as each of the men ate the stew. This night they would get little sleep. She tucked her laughter inside her mouth and passed a water bladder to one of the younger hunters. She had pleasured him twice during the past moon, before preparations had begun for the caribou hunt. He was named River Ice Dancer, and he was a young man full of himself. During their coupling, he had pretended he knew what he was doing, but his touch was rough and his attempts to enter her were fumbling and unsure. K'os blinked her eyes at him, and he puffed out his chest.

Little boy, I have had nearly every man in this lodge, K'os thought. But she smiled at him and let him believe in his own importance.

Dii came back with a boiling bag of hare meat and ptarmigan. Gull Wing took the bag from her as she crawled into the lodge, but few hunters asked for more food. Most were intent on what Anaay was saying. Bowls, some still partially full, lay forgotten on the floor.

Anaay chanted a song that his dreams had brought him, and the words came to Dii in the rhythm of caribou hooves. Then he was suddenly quiet, and everyone in the lodge waited, hands still, eyes watching.

Finally he said, "This I have heard in my caribou dreams. Three days we travel north, then two days toward the east."

The men let out their breath, and the noise was like a sigh, the sound of water rushing over sand. The old hunters began to sing, and the young hunters joined them.

Anaay lifted his eyes to his wives and K'os, at the back of the lodge. He frowned and motioned for them to leave. There were plans and chants a woman should not hear.

When they went outside, Dii stood in the lee of her lodge, watched Gull Beak and K'os walk away. Gull Beak was a thin, awkward woman. Her bones seemed too large for her skin, but K'os walked gracefully, her furred parka moving with her as though she were an animal in its own pelt.

Dii wanted to stay close to the lodge, to see if Anaay's voice carried through the caribou hide walls, but what wife would risk cursing her husband in such a way? Instead, she walked to a rock she had found at the river side of the village. It was a sheltered place, open to sun but shut away from the wind by trees that grew on either side. She climbed to the top, drew her knees up under her chin.

Three days north, her husband had said, and two days toward the sun. She had felt the hooves of the caribou. She had even heard the clicking of their joints—a sacred rhythm The People had learned and imitated with their hoof rattlers and drums. And by morning, she had known the sound came from the west, and it was close, not nearly a five-day walk.

She held her mind still for a time, scarcely taking a breath, waiting to see if she would hear them again, those caribou. But her head was filled with the sounds of the village, women's voices, children playing, and the noise of the Near River as it flowed between its banks.

But, of course, Anaay was right. How foolish to think she would hear the caribou. She was a woman, and not even from this village. No wonder she had heard all things wrong.

THE COUSIN RIVER VILLAGE

"If the day is good," Chakliux said, "we will go tomorrow."

Aqamdax shivered when she heard the words, though she had known as much before he spoke.

She and Chakliux were sitting together at the place they had come to call Black Rock. Almost every day they found time to meet there. Sometimes they discussed the problems of their village; sometimes they followed the First Men custom and sat in silence.

"How many will go?" Aqamdax asked.

"Those of us who are hunters: Sok and I, Sky Watcher, Take More and Man Laughing. Sok will bring Cries-loud and Snow-in-her-hair. Sky Watcher will bring Bird Caller. Star has said she does not want to go, so Ligige' will come."

"It will be a hard trip for Ligige'."

"She is strong, and she has a good dog."

"Night Man says we will stay."

"I know. I asked him if I might take you, since Star does not want to leave her mother."

Aqamdax caught her breath. "You asked if you could take me?"

Chakliux lowered his head, combed his fingers through the fur ruff at the bottom of his parka. "I told him I would not expect the rights of hunting partner."

Aqamdax felt her cheeks burn. Hunting partners sometimes shared wives, especially on long trips when one wife went along to help butcher and the other stayed behind to watch over children too young or elders too weak to go.

Aqamdax waited to see if Chakliux would say anything else, but he did not. She closed her eyes and let herself imagine what it would be like to follow Chakliux to the caribou. She had never been on a caribou hunt, but when she had lived in the Near River Village, the women had told her of the long days of walking, of building rock and brush fences to direct the animals to an enclosure where the men would kill them with strong birch-shafted spears. Then the butchering would begin, and the packing of meat.

Sometimes, if they were far from the village and the weather was warm so fresh meat would not freeze, they would stay where they were. The men would make racks, and the women would slice the meat thin to dry, but usually nights were cold enough to freeze the meat, and they would return to the village, laden with heavy packs.

Each hunter owned a caribou hide lean-to. Aqamdax thought of herself sleeping in such a shelter with Chakliux, a fire at the open side to hold in their warmth. She imagined him next to her in the night, and felt the dangerous need that had driven her to many men's beds when she had lived in the First Men Village.

That was after her father drowned and her mother ran away with the River trader Cen. Aqamdax had had no one, and only when she was warm and close in a hunter's arms could she feel safe.

After Qung took her in, taught her to tell stories, the emptiness left her, had not returned even when Sok tried to trade her to the Walrus shaman, even when he threw her away. During all the moons she had lived among the Cousin River People, first as a slave, then as a wife, the emptiness had not returned. But now, with her baby dead and her hatred for Night Man growing, she felt as though her heart had become small, leaving a great empty space in her chest.

Suddenly she was afraid to be alone with Chakliux. "I am going now," she told him, but then leaned close to whisper. "I wish I could go with you. I wish you were Night Man's hunting partner."

THE NEAR RIVER VILLAGE
That night the hunters woke with pains that twisted from belly to anus. They called first for Blue Flower, who sang

her songs. When her singing did not stop their pain, they asked for Gull Beak and K'os, who gave them teas of salmonberry root. But Dii slept without knowing what had happened.

Anaay, anxious to tell the men of his dreams, had eaten after everyone left, and by then only the hare and ptarmigan stew from the village hearths remained. He grumbled some, scolded Dii for not saving a portion of the moose meat for him. Didn't she remember that moose stew was his favorite? What kind of wife was she to forget such a thing?

In the morning, Dii went early to the cooking hearths. She hoped other women would be there, would tell of the hunting plans their men had made. She thought she would probably go with Anaay, but he was old, and as leader of the elders, he was sure to receive a share of the meat. Perhaps he would stay in the winter village and let others do his hunting for him.

To her surprise, the hearths were deserted, the coals still banked from the night before. Were all the wives helping their husbands pack food and supplies? Would they leave even yet this day?

Dii gathered armfuls of wood, then carefully pushed back the ashes of the eastern hearth. With one of the willow tongs, she exposed the coals, then sprinkled on handfuls of clubgrass fluff, encouraged the flames with her breath. One by one, she started each of the five hearth fires, and hung several of the empty cooking bags she had brought from her lodge on the tripods.

"Those are not from last night?"

Dii looked up. It was Gull Beak. Her eyes were circled with dark rings, and her hair hung in strands that had loosened from her braids.

"Yes," Dii said.

"You ate from it?"

"Only the ptarmigan and hare stew," she answered.

"Were you sick?"

"No. Were you?"

"I did not eat until I was back in my own lodge, but all the men who ate at your lodge were sick. K'os and I and Blue Flower were awake all night giving teas to soothe bellies. You did not know?"

"I slept."

"Anaay was not sick?" Gull Beak asked.

"He ate only ptarmigan and hare," Dii told her, "though he was angry all the moose meat was gone."

Gull Beak shook her head. "He should be grateful," she said. "I'm going to bed. If Anaay wants me, tell him I am busy. Scrape out the cooking bags and rinse them before putting more meat in."

After Gull Beak left, several other women came to the hearths, one of them—mother to the young man called River Ice Dancer—called to her.

"So you, too, were awake all night with a sick husband?" she asked.

"Anaay was not sick," Dii said.

The woman frowned. "Perhaps he is used to your poor cooking. I have heard that Cousin women are worthless in preparing food."

Though usually Dii said nothing when the Near River women taunted her, this time she did not ignore the insult. "The food came from Gull Beak's lodge," she told them.

But as she walked away, she wondered what had brought the sickness. Perhaps in taking the moose, the Near River hunters had broken some taboo. Or maybe it was in punishment for what the Near Rivers had done to the Cousin River Village. No, she decided. How could such a small punishment be given for burning an entire village?

FOURTEEN

THE FOUR RIVERS VILLAGE

Red Leaf had expected a trader's lean-to, so when Cen tied Tracker outside the large, well-made lodge, questions bubbled from her mouth.

"You live here?" she asked.

When he did not answer, she decided he had only borrowed Tracker to help him find the caribou hide, and now he was returning the dog to its owner.

"So Tracker is not your dog," she said.

Again he did not answer, and so she began to speak of what had occupied her mind during the walk to the village. "You said you needed a woman. What happened to your wife?"

Finally, when he had the dog tied and fed, Cen turned to Red Leaf and said, "Gheli, you are a woman of too much mouth. Be quiet. If you watch and listen you will learn all you need to know, and because of your silence, people will think you are wise."

He turned his back on her and walked toward the food caches. Did he expect her to follow? How should she know what he wanted her to do when he would not answer her questions? Suddenly, she was angry. He had asked her to come with him. She could have walked to her own shelter. By night, she would have been there, but here she was in this strange village with a man who would kill her when he heard her true name.

Cen stopped, looked back at her, then lifted his chin toward the lodge. "Go inside," he told her.

She crawled into the entrance tunnel, stopped to scratch at the inner doorflap. There was no answer, so she went inside. The lodge was large, beautifully made. The caribou hide lining stretched up almost to the smoke hole and was decorated with dark and light circles of caribou hide in a pattern that reminded Red Leaf of clouds. The floor was covered with grass mats, woven much like those Aqamdax made. At the center of the lodge, the floor had been dug down more than a hand's length into the bare earth and lined with rock and sand for a hearth.

Red Leaf stirred the ashes, but there was no spark of life. She debated with herself whether or not to start a fire. What if this was not Cen's lodge? What would the woman who owned it think if she came in to find a stranger had begun a fire in her hearth?

Perhaps she would be glad for a warm lodge, Red Leaf told herself, and reached into her parka for the cilt'ogho that held the coal she had brought from her own shelter.

She thought it might be dead, she had been away so long, though she had fed it another knot of wood. She dumped the coal and ashes into the hearth, smiled to see the faint spark of red at the center of one of the knots. She coaxed the fire with clubgrass fluff and curls of birchbark until she had flames, then she added wood.

When the fire was strong, Red Leaf pulled her daughter from the warmth of her parka. The child wailed in the sudden chill of the lodge.

"Hush, be still," Red Leaf crooned to her.

She threw the baby's moss swaddling into the fire and wiped her clean, then padded her ground squirrel wrappings with fresh moss from a small bag of supplies tied to the belt that held up Red Leaf's leggings. She placed the baby again under her parka, fastened the binding that held her secure under Red Leaf's breasts.

When the child began nursing, Red Leaf went outside, filled a boiling bag with clean snow. In the lodge, she hung the bag from a tripod set over the firepit. She found several empty water bladders and softened them by rolling each between her palms so they would be ready to fill when the snow melted.

Finally she heard someone in the entrance tunnel, and she stood, her mouth full of words in explanation of why she was here and what she was doing.

It was Cen. He nodded at the fire and handed her a fishskin bag filled with smoked salmon. The smell of it made Red Leaf's stomach roll.

"Eat," he said, then held out his hand.

She gave him a piece of fish and took one for herself, then ate so quickly that her belly still felt empty when she was done. She checked the snow in the boiling bag. It had melted. She filled a water bladder, gave it to Cen, then went out for more snow. When she returned he was leaning against a woven willow backrest.

"The stream on the north side of the village is a good place to get water," he told her. "The women keep it open most of the winter. It empties into a small lake not far from here."

"The women will not care if I get water there?"

He shrugged. "I am not a woman. What can I tell you? Let me see your daughter."

Red Leaf was surprised at his interest, but she pulled the baby from her breast, slipped the child from under her parka and held her so Cen could see. The child's eyes were closed, but her mouth was pursed and moved as though she still nursed.

"You have named her?"

"No."

"I should name her now that I am her father," Cen said.

Red Leaf tried not to show her surprise. Already he considered himself father? "She needs a name," Red Leaf agreed.

"There was a woman I once knew, a good woman," Cen told her. "Her name needs to be remembered." He looked at the child, narrowed his eyes as if to judge how well that name would fit her. "Yes," he finally said. "She is Daes."

THE COUSIN RIVER VILLAGE

The wind woke Aqamdax, and she lay listening as it pressed against the walls, searching for a way to get inside. Did it know that they were a lodge of only women and children? Chakliux and Night Man were spending the night with the other men in the village. Their hunters' lodge had been destroyed in the fighting, and now they had only a crude lean-to, but as Chakliux had said, their songs were still sacred, and their stories still good to hear.

Aqamdax raised herself on her elbows. Star's mouth was open in sleep, and Long Eyes lay still. Ghaden and Yaa were curled together with the dog Biter. Aqamdax lay back down, but her chest was heavy with the knowledge that Chakliux would leave the next day. She clasped her sleeping robes in both hands, held tight, forced her thoughts away from the emptiness of her belly, the ache of her breasts. How could she live with both Chakliux and her son gone?

Soon her husband would take her into his bed. She wondered each night if he would call her, but some men waited two, three moons after the birth of a child before feeling safe from any blood power their wives might carry. She tried not to think of his hands on her, and instead saw her belly again swell with a baby. This time, she would never let the child out of her arms. She would run away, like Red Leaf had run away, rather than take the chance that Night Man would kill it.

Her muscles seemed to tense and jump under her skin, and she turned on her sleeping mats, one way, then the other. Finally, she slipped from her bed, grabbed her parka and boots, and went out into the night.

She had expected the air to be cold—a light snow had fallen only the day before—but the wind had changed and now blew from the south, bringing warmth like a remembrance of summer. She put on her parka and boots, then walked quickly through the village, found the path that led into the spruce woods.

A foolish place to go alone in the night, Aqamdax told herself. There were wolves. Perhaps a lynx. But still she walked, frightened at what she was doing but directed by the emptiness that had opened again within her chest.

What difference if they killed her, those wolves? That lynx? At least she would be with her son, with her mother and father. Perhaps she would walk forever, past the woods, on into the tundra until death in one way or another found her.

She pushed away the faces that came to her mind: Ghaden, Yaa, Chakliux, Ligige'. Ligige' was old, so she did not have many more summers to live. And Ghaden and Yaa had each other. But Aqamdax could find no excuse for leaving Chakliux.

When she came to Black Rock, she was suddenly tired. She climbed up on it, tucked her parka around her feet and lowered her head to her raised knees. It is a good night to be outside, Aqamdax told herself, and looked up at the stars, tried to keep her thoughts from her sorrow.

Chakliux left the hunters' lodge. The others were asleep, but since Night Man had killed Aqamdax's son, Chakliux hated to be in the same lodge with him. His breath seemed to poison the air, and his dreams battled against Chakliux's dreams, disturbing his sleep. Chakliux worried that such enmity would take away the men's hunting luck, so finally he left, took his frustrations into the night, where the winds would pull them away.

He carried his sleeping robe with him, the woven hare fur blanket that Red Leaf had given him when he first lived with the Near River People. It was cunningly made, that robe, with twists and loops that held in a man's heat, even on the coldest nights, but who could say? Perhaps those same twists and loops were a net catching Night Man's dreams and directing them to Chakliux. Or perhaps the blanket held Chakliux's anger, so that even though it felt light, it was heavy with his need for revenge. How could he leave it in the hunters' lodge, where it might steal away hunting skills—the accuracy of a spear, the strength of a bow?

He walked toward Black Rock. It was a good place, that rock. The thought of it calmed him. That he found Aqamdax there, even in the night, did not seem strange.

He boosted himself up beside her, felt her tremble, and realized that she was crying.

He wrapped an arm around her, and she leaned against him. Though they spoke no words, his anger seeped away, and Aqamdax was quiet, so only their breath moved between them.

THE NEAR RIVER VILLAGE

The night before the caribou hunters left the village, Anaay awoke Dii and pushed himself into her bed. She was surprised. Surely a man about to go on a caribou hunt should not carry the smell of a woman with him.

As a girl, she had heard the stories women told at hearth fires, words passed behind hands. They spoke of the men's need for women after the caribou were killed, when there was no longer a chance of losing hunting luck.

The women, exhausted from butchering, often did not share their men's joy in coupling, but only endured, grateful that at least they could lie down during this chore, and glad to know that the men would sleep quickly and soundly afterwards.

Dii's mother had chided the women when they complained about their men's desires. Who were the ones to risk their lives so the people could have meat? Who were the ones to work hardest in killing those caribou? Not the women.

Be grateful, she had told Dii, when your husband wants you. Be glad that you are able to bring joy to his life.

So Dii did not allow herself to worry about Anaay's choice as he came to her bed. Instead she closed her eyes and remembered him as he spoke to the hunters, remembered the honor he earned by dreaming caribou. And she did not let herself think of her own dreams, the singing that had come to her bones as warm and strong as a south wind.

FIFTEEN

THE COUSIN RIVER VILLAGE

Aqamdax moved against him, and Chakliux felt the prickling of the calluses on her palms as she stroked his arms and chest. His hands found their way under her parka, and he did not stop himself until he was holding her breasts, the nipples rising firm and hard under his fingertips. Then he pulled away, apologizing for what he had done.

"No, Chakliux, do not stop," Aqamdax begged. "I need you to hold me. I need . . ."

He gathered her close, as if she were a child, stroked her hair, pressed his cheek against hers, and made himself content with only that. Even in his years with Gguzaakk, in the joys they had shared as husband and wife, he had never wanted a woman as much as he wanted Aqamdax, but to take her now, in this place, hiding from her husband and his wife, with his need fed by anger . . .

Tomorrow he would leave for the caribou hunt. How could he expect animals to give themselves if he did not have the strength of will to do what was right? How could he expect animals to honor him if he brought dishonor to his wife and his wife's brother? And how could he expect Aqamdax to stop him?

When they had both lived in the Near River Village, they had been friends. He had shared the joys and sorrows of his own life, and she had shared hers. He knew that in the First Men Village, she had taken many men into her bed, but only to fill the emptiness of her life.

Perhaps her need now was not truly for him but only to forget her loss.

"Chakliux," she whispered, "please, I want to be your wife. I don't want to live with Night Man. I will throw him away and stay with you. I do not care if you keep Star. I will be second wife."

She cupped her hands at the sides of his face, and though, in the darkness, he could not see her eyes, he knew from her voice that she was crying.

"I will give you a son. Many sons."

"Aqamdax," he said, and clasped her wrists, pulled her hands to his chest. "Be still, be quiet and listen. When the hunt is over, and we have taken the caribou we need for winter, then you can throw away Night Man and I will take you as wife. In the spring, if you want, we will leave this village. If you would rather live with your own people, we will go there. Whatever you want we will do, but not until we have taken the meat we need to live through the winter."

She was quiet then. Quickly she raised one hand to his face, then just as quickly drew it away. She slipped down from the rock. "Hunt safely; hunt well," she said.

Later, in Star's lodge, Aqamdax lay in her bedding furs and remembered the promises so many people had made to her: Day Breaker, that First Men hunter who had pledged to take her as wife; her mother, who had said she would return but never did; Night Man, who had promised her sons and instead . . .

Why trust Chakliux? some voice whispered to her from the darkness. Why trust anyone? But how could she allow herself to doubt? During those few quick moments she had been in Chakliux's arms, the pain of her loss had diminished, and she had almost felt alive again.

She clasped her amulet, felt the hard lump that was a piece of the stick she had brought back from the Grandfather Lake the night her son had died.

Though she had no memory of doing so, Chakliux had told her that she waded out into the lake and brought back this stick, had wrapped it like a baby. She kept it with her for three days before she realized what it was.

She remembered that realization, seeing the stick in a hare fur blanket, screaming at the knowledge that her baby was dead. She was in her birth lodge, still bleeding and unable to live in the village, but Ligige' had been with her. . . .

Until tonight she had not cared if she was alive or dead. The pain she carried was so much greater than anything her eyes saw, her ears heard. But now Chakliux had given her hope. He would become her husband. They would have to endure the separation of the caribou hunt. During that time she would remain wife to Night Man, and pray each day that he would not ask her into his bed.

Her thoughts were interrupted by Biter's growl.

She and Star were on their feet almost at the same time, then Ghaden and Yaa as well. Ghaden ran to the weapons corner, was grabbing his spear when Night Man thrust aside the inner doorflap and came into the lodge.

He gave no greeting, only blinked until in the hearth coals' light he was able to fix his eyes on Star.

"Sister, I have decided to go with them," he told her. "I have one good arm. That is enough to throw a spear."

Only a moon before, if Aqamdax had heard her husband say such words, she would have rejoiced that his strength was returning, but tonight it meant nothing to her until he said, "Wife, you will go with me."

Then she looked down quickly, so he would not see the joy in her eyes and know the reason she was glad.

THE NEAR RIVER VILLAGE

By midmorning the men were ready to leave. They carried their weapons—throwing boards and spears, lances. Some of the young hunters had made fire bow weapons, but others grumbled that such weapons would hurt their luck. Had the young men forgotten that the Cousin River hunters had used bows against them? What about old Blue Jay? He had been the one who brought the weapon to their village long ago, had hung it on his lodge wall to give him luck. Hadn't he and his wife, his lodge and everything in it perished in a fire?

There was too much talking, too many complaints and accusations. Anaay lifted himself to his toes, thrust his walking stick toward the sky.

"Listen, hunters," he called out. When the men were finally quiet, he glared at those who carried fire bow weapons. "Young men always look for something new," Anaay said. "Let them use the weapon and see for themselves that caribou will honor only spears."

Anaay rolled his shoulders against the ache of his back. He should have returned to his own bed last night rather than stay with Dii. Actually, he should have spent the night with Gull Beak, but it was difficult to want her wrinkles and dry bones when Dii was near.

When they returned with their caribou, he would spend his first night in the village with Gull Beak. That should satisfy her. He looked back, saw that Dii and K'os had taken their places on either side of his three dogs. The women were loaded down with packs of food and bedding. He, like the other hunters, carried nothing but his weapons, though that alone was enough.

Anaay was not sure how to begin this walk. He needed sacred words, a prayer, a chant, but nothing came to him. He cried out to Sun Caller and several of the others. "You are ready?"

There was a mumbling among the men, then someone explained that they were waiting for the boy River Ice Dancer.

When River Ice Dancer finally joined them, Anaay noticed that he took a place close to K'os, that he could not keep his eyes from her. Anaay knew the feeling. If any woman could rouse a man, K'os could. Even her walking sent Anaay's thoughts to what she kept between her legs, but who could trust her? He should have left her with the Cousin Rivers.

K'os claimed to be a healer, and it was true that her medicines had helped people in this village, but Anaay reminded everyone to treat her cures with caution.

His own powers were greater than hers, he had no doubt. If they were not, then why was she his slave? But still, he was careful. He could not risk his life foolishly. What would his people do without him? They would have chosen Chakliux, a cripple, to lead them, and Sok would have been chief hunter. What would happen to a village led by men like that? Soon everyone would be weak and cursed.

Finally, as the people's restlessness showed itself in raised voices and barking dogs, Anaay again lifted his walking stick and shouted, "Let us go. Carry sacred thoughts that honor the caribou."

The people were suddenly quiet, as though they expected him to say more. He considered a riddle, but realized it might remind them of Chakliux, the one who had taught them how to make riddles. Instead, he told how the singing had come into his dreams, how he had fasted and sung chants. As he spoke he felt himself grow large, as though those around him were only children.

Then he saw that the women were shifting from foot to foot, moving their shoulders and heads under the straps and tumplines of their heavy packs. Men started to finger their weapons, check boots and adjust parka hoods. How could they expect to have a successful hunt when they could not even spend a short time considering sacred ways?

In disgust, Anaay turned his back on them and began to walk.

SIXTEEN

THE COUSIN RIVER PEOPLE

Star whined continuously, slowing their progress, but Chakliux could feel nothing but happiness. Though she came as Night Man's wife, Aqamdax was with them.

Chakliux kept his eyes from her and his thoughts framed in chants that would honor the caribou, but still the gladness was there, lifting him with each step so that even his otter foot did not get tired as he walked.

"Husband, I need to rest," Star said, running up from the group of wives to join him as he walked with the hunters.

Sky Watcher frowned at her, jerked his head back toward the women. "You should not walk with us," he told her, but Star curled her lip at him and continued to cling to Chakliux.

"Wife," Chakliux said, "I told you not to come on this hunting trip. I told you to stay with your mother and Ligige'. I will take you back now. If we walk until night, we will arrive at the village in time to sleep in your lodge, and tomorrow or the next day I will catch up with the others."

"I do not want to go back, I want only to stop. We have walked enough for one day." She pitched her voice into a high thin wail that seemed to catch in Chakliux's back teeth and spread pain up into his head.

"Stop if you want to stop, but the rest of us will go on. You have come on a hunt before. You know we do not rest until night."

Star stomped away from him, then began to complain to the other women. They ignored her. Though Chakliux's baby was only yet a small mound in her belly, Star had the lightest pack of all. Even the girl Yaa was carrying more.

Chakliux returned to caribou chants, but not before allowing his eyes to fall for a moment on Aqamdax. She was watching him, and smiled when she saw him look at her.

Then he prayed that the caribou would be plentiful, that the hunt would go well and quickly, and soon he could claim Aqamdax as wife.

THE NEAR RIVER PEOPLE

They had walked only four days when they came upon the signs of another camp. K'os sucked in her cheeks to keep from smiling. It was a Cousin River camp. They had made their fire close to the river and held down the edges of their lean-tos with mounds of dirt.

She saw the scowl on Fox Barking's face, heard him sputter out curses. Had he thought the Cousin People would no longer follow the caribou? Did he assume he could easily claim their hunting territory?

She had wondered when he told the people of dreaming caribou that he did not realize the animals he spoke about, three days north, two east, were those hunted by the Cousin men. Did he think the Near Rivers would be welcome? Did he think the Cousin women who traveled with his hunters as slaves and wives would not long to rejoin their own people? Fool! Perhaps the curse charms she had sewn into his parka were already beginning to work. She had been able to add the last of them the night before they left.

"It is a Cousin camp," Dii said to her, and K'os was so deep in her thoughts that she jumped at the words.

Dii repeated what she had said, then added, "You think Anaay knows this?"

"He should. What hunter would not?"

"He is Near River. He might not recognize the things we do."

K'os shrugged. "Have you been on a caribou hunt before?" she asked.

"Twice, with my—" She stopped.

K'os raised her eyebrows to show she understood. It was taboo to mention the dead, and Dii was wise to hold in her words, especially since her husband was so foolish and powerless.

"Then you know the way from here to the caribou crossing."

Dii nodded. "Should I say something to Anaay?"

"If I were you, I would not," K'os answered.

"But what if he does not know?"

"Let his slave tell him," K'os said. "Better that a young wife not lose face."

She saw the gratitude in Dii's eyes and allowed herself to smile at the girl. Let her think K'os did this out of kindness. Gratitude was a heavy debt.

Anaay cut into Sun Caller's words. The man's stuttering made Anaay's head ache.

"You think this was a Cousin camp?" Anaay said. "They do not have enough hunters to even leave their village. Do they think the caribou will respect them after what they did this past year, the fighting they began, the defeat they suffered at our hands?"

"I . . . I d-do not know any-anything ab-b-bout that, only that this camp is C-Cousin."

"He is right."

The voice, K'os's voice, made Anaay jump to his feet. "You think I would take the word of a slave?" he said.

K'os pushed back her parka hood, then squatted on her haunches at the remains of a camp hearth. When she spoke, it was to Sun Caller and to River Ice Dancer and the other men gathered with them.

"Look," she said. "See how the rocks are piled in a

circle here, two hands high. That is something the Cousin People do. And see . . ." She pointed. "Look at this hole here. They sharpen the ends of their tripod sticks. The Near Rivers do not."

"So, perhaps they are Four Rivers or Caribou People," Anaay said.

She smirked, and Anaay reached out to slap her, but she jumped up and away so that he lost his balance and nearly fell into the ashes. Several hunters turned their heads. Anaay did not let himself think of the smiles they were hiding.

"Do what you want," K'os said. "It means nothing to me, but I would not be surprised if the Cousin hunters, however few of them remain, follow their custom and hunt at the Caribou River."

"A-a-a river hunt," Sun Caller explained to the younger hunters. "Wh-when I was a y-young man, we joined them on this hunt for a y-year. Th-there was too much disagreement over the sharing of meat, s-s-so we did not hunt with them again."

K'os lifted her chin at Anaay. "You think the singing you heard was from the animals that the Cousin hunt each year?" she asked him.

Anaay slitted his eyes, spoke to her through his teeth. "Go back to the women. Even my wife has more sense than to speak when hunters decide what to do. You are slave. Do not forget that."

"Perhaps it's time she was sold to another," River Ice Dancer said, but Anaay ignored his impertinence. He was little more than a boy. Let him try to control a woman like K'os.

She walked away, swinging her hips, and the hunters' eyes followed her until she was lost in the group of women who huddled near dogs and packs.

"So perhaps Anaay should do more dreaming," one of the hunters said. "We do not need to spend strength and weapons on Cousin men. Even if there are only a few of them, I do not want to fight. My wife is here, and my oldest son."

"There are those of us who have Cousin wives," said

First Eagle, one of the youngest hunters. "How do we know they will not join their people and fight against us from within our own camp?"

"You whine so much, I think you are a woman," Anaay told him, snarling the words. "We usually hunt with fences and a corral to direct the animals to our weapons. The Cousin use water to slow the caribou, and their women stand in the river so the dead animals will float to them. We have not had much experience hunting this way, but perhaps the songs came to me because this year we are supposed to hunt a river crossing. Leave me alone and I will think about this. Make camp here, and give me time to pray."

He walked away from them all. Left them without looking back. Why listen to their grumbling? Had they heard the singing? Did they know more about caribou than he did?

When he was out of sight of the camp, away from the noise of the women, he removed his weapons from their scabbards and set them on the ground. He squatted beside them, rested his right hand on his throwing board and spear, then closed his eyes and began to sing. It was a song that had once belonged to the old man Tsaani.

Tsaani had given it to his grandson Sok, so it did not belong to Anaay, but Sok no longer lived with the Near River People. He would not know Anaay was using it. And surely Tsaani would not mind. Perhaps he would prefer that Anaay use it. After all, it was Sok's wife who killed Tsaani, and Anaay had told the people who the killer was. Tsaani owed him for that, at least a song.

Anaay tried to remember back to the night of his caribou dreaming. He had seen the caribou, had heard the clicking of their passage, a sound like stones rattling against stones. He had felt the ground shake, and when he awoke, he had had his face turned to the northeast wall of the lodge. What else did he need besides that? If his dreams had told him to travel north and east, then that is what he must do.

He thought again of what Sun Caller had told him about the river hunt. Sun Caller did not seem to remember that

Anaay had broken his arm that autumn and so had not been there.

While the other men were hunting, Anaay had stayed in the village and earned himself Gull Beak as wife. She had been second wife to a man who was away on the caribou hunt, and by the time her husband had returned to the winter village, Anaay was already living in Gull Beak's lodge. So how could he regret missing that hunt? There were other ways to learn how to kill caribou at river crossings.

Surely K'os had been on river hunts, but he could not let her know that he had never taken caribou in such a way. K'os was a woman who would use such knowledge to get revenge. He could not allow himself to forget that time long ago when she had killed his brother Gull Wing with only a sleeve knife. Of course, Gull Wing deserved the death he got. It had been his idea to rape K'os, though she was just a girl. Anaay and Sleeps Long had only watched at first, and if Gull Wing had not goaded them, they would never have done such a thing.

He closed his eyes for a moment and remembered that day at the Grandfather Rock. He had sunk himself into K'os's soft flesh, felt her struggle against him as he thrust. What should she expect? She had flirted with the three men when they ate in her mother's lodge, then followed them from the village. Did she think they were made of stone?

He had believed they killed her, she had lain still for so long, her parka stuffed into her mouth and pulled up over her head. Then, to his horror, she had moved, sliding so quickly from the rock to thrust her knife into Gull Wing's heart that no one had been able to stop her. It was fitting revenge for Gull Wing's death that K'os was now Anaay's slave. But Anaay could not allow himself to forget for even a day what K'os had done.

He started another song, then thought of his new wife, Dii. Perhaps, though she was young, she had traveled with the Cousin People on river crossing hunts.

*   *   *

"He wants you," K'os told her.

Dii looked into K'os's face, tried to read her thoughts, but K'os's eyes were so dark—as though no light came into them—that Dii wondered how K'os could see.

"My husband?" Dii asked.

"Yes, Fox Barking, your husband."

Dii shuddered at the disrespect in K'os's words. Of all the people in the Near River Village, K'os was the only one who did not give Anaay the honor of his new name. But had she not always been a woman of disrespect? Dii remembered the Cousin wives whispering about K'os as they tended hearth fires. Even now, though K'os was a slave, the women, both Cousin and Near River, gossiped about her.

She went with men into the forest and returned with gifts a slave could earn only in one way, but that was of no concern to Dii as long as her sister-wife, Gull Beak, and her husband did not care.

Of course, K'os was angry that Anaay kept her as a slave rather than making her a wife. Perhaps she held Anaay responsible for the defeat of the Cousin People, but even then, she should respect the name itself. It alluded to the power of caribou dreaming, and who did not know that every name also had its own spirit, apart from the spirit of the person who used it?

"Where is Anaay?" she asked K'os, saying the name loudly and with a lift of her chin. At least K'os should know that Dii honored her husband.

K'os shrugged, but as she walked away, Dii saw her twist her head only for the blink of an eye toward the river. When K'os was out of sight, Dii stood on tiptoe, scanning the growth of brush that marked the river's course.

At first she did not see him. He wore his new parka, and the browns and golds of the furs blended into the stones and frost-killed grasses. Then as though her eyes suddenly cleared, she saw the outline of his hair, dark as a shadow. He was sitting on a large rock that was balanced, it seemed, on the rubble of stones and driftwood that spread up from the water. When he saw her, he called out, but she could not hear his words. The river was noisy as it rushed over the gravel of its bed.

She drew close, and he set his feet against the ground, pushed back. The rock he was sitting on moved.

"Look! What do I see?" he said to her, and it was good to hear the beginning of a riddle. The Near Rivers were not riddle tellers like the Cousin People.

"It claims power but has no strength except its size."

Dii raised her eyebrows at him and smiled. It was a poor riddle, with no difficulty to it. Of course, he meant the rock. It must have been flung to the banks during the spring breakup, but the smaller stones under it kept it away from the strength of the earth. If it could not touch the earth, how could it be strong? But she did not want to insult her husband, so her first guess was the river.

"The river?" he said, and laughed until Dii's cheeks reddened with embarrassment. "I thought the Cousin People were good at riddles."

Then Dii allowed her anger to speak for her, and she said, "We are. The answer is the rock you sit on."

He set his mouth into a pout, studied her for a moment, then without referring to the riddle motioned her to squat beside the rock. There was no firm footing on the rounded stones, and to look at him she had to kink her neck, but she reminded herself that he was her husband, a caribou dreamer, and so she ignored the ache of her feet, curled as they were to help keep her balance, and listened to what he had to say.

He began by talking about the days when he was a boy, and then told her of his first kill. He spoke of the first woman he had taken to his bed. It was not something she particularly wanted to hear, and her thoughts drifted to other things, to the repairs she must do on garments, a seam ripped, a boot sole growing thin. Not for the first time, she wished Gull Beak had come on this hunting trip.

K'os could take their turn at the hearth, and would also do much of the work on the tents and making camp, but she would not sew. When Dii asked her, K'os held out her hands in protest, showing the twisted fingers, the swollen joints that she claimed would not allow her to hold awl or needle. For truly, though K'os had the face and body of a young woman, she had the gnarled, bent hands of an elder.

When they had lived in the Cousin Village, K'os still sewed, and a man who received one of her parkas wore it in pride, for she did work as fine as any—even more beautiful than Gull Beak's.

Dii had tried to get her to sew Anaay a parka, had even given her furs and strips of caribou intestine hung out in freezing weather so the intestine turned a pure and beautiful white. But though K'os promised to try, so far Dii had seen no results. She hated to ask for the fur and gut back. Why discourage the woman? Better for Dii to be grateful for her own strong hands.

Suddenly, Dii realized that Anaay had stopped talking and was looking at her as though he expected an answer. Her eyes widened in distress, and she blurted out the first thing that came to her: "I really do not know."

"You don't remember the first time you went on a caribou hunt?" he asked, his voice rising so his last words were nearly a shout.

Dii drew in a quick breath and answered, "What I meant was I do not remember exactly how many summers I had."

She expected her husband to scold her in indignation, but instead his voice was soft, wheedling. "You are my favorite wife, you know," he told her. "Not only of you and Gull Beak, but of the wives I have thrown away."

She was not sure if the words were meant as compliment or warning. He had thrown away wives. Be careful. Do not waste your husband's words by daydreaming when he speaks to you. When she was first his wife, she would have welcomed being thrown away, even driven from the village. At least then she could have tried to return to her own people.

"It is only that I want to know more about you," Anaay continued. "Since we are now hunting caribou, I thought it would be good to speak about those times you have been on a hunt."

Dii started with the preparations made, but saw the impatience in Anaay's eyes, and so described the routes they took. He leaned forward then, asked questions, nodded his head as he listened.

He grew impatient again when she told him that she knew only what the women did: catching dead animals that floated with the buoyancy of their thick-haired hides, then butchering and hauling. Finally he waved one hand at her as though to push her away, and when she remained where she was, he shouted, "Go get me food! Any good wife could see that I am hungry!"

So she left, glad to stretch out her legs and set her feet on flat ground. Then she was ashamed of herself for her disrespect. He was her husband and the leader of his people, but as she looked back, saw him sitting on the rock, she thought again of his riddle and wondered if the true answer was not the rock but Anaay himself. Though he spoke of power and took the highest place among the Near Rivers, there were times when he seemed to have no power at all, when someone might only push him and he would go tumbling down like a rock resting on pebbles.

SEVENTEEN

THE COUSIN RIVER PEOPLE

For three days after they set their hunting tents beside the Caribou River, the people saw no sign of caribou. They sent out boys as scouts and waited, the men boisterous, the women fretful, fear and hope battling within their minds.

Sok and Chakliux were the first to see Sok's son, Cries-loud, run into the camp. The boy was breathing so hard that at first he could do nothing except crouch with hands on knees. But when he raised his head, the smile on his face let them know what he had come to tell them.

"Where?" Sok asked. Then he grinned at Chakliux and said, "This river hunting. It is new to me."

"It is easier," Chakliux told him.

Sok gave him a quick shove and laughed as he said, "For you, Otter, for you. Born to water as you were."

It was a compliment, and Chakliux clapped a hand to his nephew's shoulder. His brother had raised good sons.

"They are coming," Cries-loud said again, as though to remind his father that he had more to tell.

"Where was the sun when you began to run?" Sok asked, and lifted his head as Cries-loud pointed to the peak of the sky, then traced his hand down midway to where the sun was now.

A long run, Chakliux thought, and for a moment felt a twinge of envy quickly replaced by pride for the strength of his nephew's legs.

Sok looked over his son's head at Chakliux. "Tomorrow?"

"The caribou should be here by evening."

"Black Stick and the other boys are still watching the herd?" Sok asked Cries-loud.

"Yes. He or his brother will come if they change direction."

"Good. Go have your mother . . ." he began, then his face darkened. "Go have Snow-in-her-hair give you something to eat, then you and Ghaden cross the river. Stop at the second ridge. The trees there are tall. Climb up so you can see out over the land, and when you spot the caribou, one of you come back and tell us."

Chakliux watched the boy walk away. His caribou hide leggings were wet from crossing the river. "Get new leggings," he called after his nephew, and Cries-loud turned, lifted a hand in reply.

Chakliux hurried to his lean-to. He hoped Star was not there. She would protest against Ghaden's being a lookout, but who was better at climbing trees than Ghaden?

He found the boy outside the tent, braiding four strands of babiche into a long cord. Biter lay on the ground beside him, his head up as he watched the activity of those in tents nearby. The braid was tight and even, and as Chakliux crouched beside Ghaden, he praised him for his work.

"It's for Biter," Ghaden explained, and laid a hand on the dog's back. "He chewed through the other one."

"Dogs will do that," Chakliux said.

"Yes, but he is a good dog. Better than any other in this camp."

"Don't tell that to Sok. He thinks Black Nose is the best."

"Hah! He's wrong."

Ghaden kept his eyes on the braid, continued to twist the babiche.

"How long until you finish?" Chakliux finally asked.

"A while."

"Do you remember the hand signals Sok and I have taught you?"

"For hunting?"

"For hunting."

"I remember."

"What if I asked you to go with Cries-loud and watch for caribou?"

Ghaden jerked his head up, stared into Chakliux's eyes.

"Really?"

"Would I ask if I did not want you to go?"

"When?"

"When you finish the braid."

Ghaden threw it down. "It's done."

Ghaden almost asked if he could take Biter, but then realized that such a foolish question might cost him the opportunity to go. So after he prepared a pack of supplies, he sat beside the dog and crooned his condolences. There were times in his life when he had wished he were a dog, free from chores and able to sleep when he wanted, but now he could feel only sympathy that Biter had to stay in camp and listen to the women talk.

Yaa saw him sitting with Biter and hunkered down beside them.

"The women say you are going to be a watcher."

Ghaden puffed out his chest and nodded his head. His mouth tried to make a smile, but he remembered how solemn the men were when they talked about their hunting, so he kept his lips in a grim line.

"Where are you going? Do you know yet?"

He almost told her, but then he reminded himself that it might be too sacred for a girl to hear. "It's something only men should know," he said.

"Then why did they tell you?" Yaa asked. "You're not a man."

He had no answer for that, only a quick burn of anger. He leaned close and punched his fist into her arm.

"Ah! So you think that's the way men act?" Yaa asked him.

"Only with their sisters."

Yaa began to sputter out a retort, but then she started to laugh, which made Ghaden even more angry.

"They would not ask me if they didn't think I was a man, or at least almost a man!" he shouted.

She began a chant, a song of ridicule girls sometimes sang, and he began his own song, a hunting chant. He raised his voice to cover hers, then Yaa also sang louder. Finally a shadow fell across them, and Ghaden looked up to see Night Man.

Night Man lifted his chin at Yaa. "She is a girl," he said. "I would expect her to act this way." He did not look into Ghaden's eyes, but rather over his head, as though Ghaden were nothing more than a baby in a cradleboard. "I expect better of you."

Ghaden lowered his head, and Yaa shot him a haughty look of anger.

"Niece, go do your own work, and do not let me catch you taunting your brother again. I do not want this caribou hunt to fail because of one small and foolish girl."

Yaa crept away, and Ghaden felt the corners of his mouth twitch into a smile. Then Night Man said, "You, Nephew, it is worse for you. Do not curse your hunting luck with foolish squabbling. When a woman argues with you, walk away."

Ghaden lowered his head, stroked Biter's back.

"Get your pack. Cries-loud waits for you at Sok's tent."

Ghaden jumped to his feet and ran to the tent. Cries-loud was there, standing so he could look out toward the ridges beyond the camp. Chakliux and Sok were beside him. "Second ridge," Chakliux said. "Stay in the group of trees near the middle. Choose one of the tallest so Ghaden can see well."

He turned and saw Ghaden. "You heard what I told Cries-loud?" he asked.

"Yes."

"Good. Climb as high as you can." He handed Ghaden a babiche rope. "Use this to tie yourself to the tree when you have found the best place to sit. When you see something, call down to Cries-loud. He will run and tell us."

Ghaden felt a surge of pride at Chakliux's words. He

would be the one who first saw the caribou. "Do I wait until they pass, or do I tell Cries-loud as soon as I've seen them?"

"Call out as soon as you see them, but Cries-loud will wait until you can tell whether they are heading upriver or downriver from our camp."

Ghaden nodded. It would be exciting to be the one who came to the village with the news of caribou, but Cries-loud was the fastest runner among the boys, and Ghaden was the best climber.

"Go then," Sok said. "Be strong. Be wise."

"Ready?" Cries-loud asked.

Ghaden heaved his pack to his shoulder.

"This is for you," Sok said, and leaned close to slip a long, narrow packet into Ghaden's hand.

It was wrapped in a thin strip of caribou hide, and Ghaden knew it was a knife. He looked up at Sok in happy disbelief.

"Well," Sok said, "it will do you no good wrapped like that."

Ghaden pulled away the caribou hide. The scabbard was laced with ties that would secure the weapon to his arm. He took out the knife and drew in his breath. The chert blade was about the length of his little finger. It was knapped to a fine sharpness and bound to a caribou antler handle.

He opened his mouth to thank Sok but had no words. Sok bent and tied the scabbard above Ghaden's left wrist, then said in a gruff voice, "Do not be so slow about your leaving. The caribou will be upon us before you are ready."

Ghaden fell into step beside Cries-loud, and Cries-loud grinned at him, lifted his sleeve to show Ghaden that he, too, had a new knife. Ghaden had never imagined such happiness. What was better than being a man? What was greater than being a hunter?

Suddenly, slicing into his joy, he heard the keening cry of a woman, and looked back to see Star running toward him, calling out his name and crying curses on her brother and husband.

"Run!" he said to Cries-loud, but they were already at the river, and Cries-loud was trying to see past the water-glare of the sun to the sandbar that meant shallow passage.

Ghaden started in, heard Cries-loud yell, "Not there. It's too deep."

Suddenly Ghaden took a step into nothingness, felt the river bottom fall away. He opened his mouth to cry out, but water flooded into his nose and down into his lungs. He finally touched bottom, kicked hard with his legs and pushed himself up. He choked and sputtered, spitting out water. He drew in a quick breath, but the weight of his pack and wet parka pulled him down again. He fought against the current, held his breath until his lungs would not allow him to do anything but inhale. He gulped in water as the river carried him downstream.

His thoughts slowed, and he opened his eyes. He tried to push himself back to the surface, but his legs were like chunks of wood, numbed by the cold. He slammed into a rock, and the current wrapped him around it. He lifted his head, coughed up water, drew in a breath, then was sucked down again. He clasped the rock, dug his fingers into the slime that covered it. The river pulled, and he felt one of his nails tear away. Still he clung. He lifted his head again, but this time inhaled water. His throat and lungs burned. Darkness claimed him, pushing in from the edges of his vision until he could see nothing.

Then Ghaden closed his eyes, slept.

EIGHTEEN

When Aqamdax heard Star's wails, she did not stop her sewing. Star was always upset about something.

Then other women were screaming, and above their cries, Aqamdax heard the calls for help. She ran to the edge of the camp, saw Chakliux in the river and Sok with his arms around Star. The woman was fighting him, biting, scratching and kicking.

"Someone take her!" Sok yelled.

Aqamdax stepped forward, grabbed Star from behind, her arms around Star's thickening waist. Sok pulled free and ran after Chakliux. Star kicked Aqamdax and struggled to turn her head, baring her teeth as though she would bite. Then Sky Watcher also had his arms around the woman. Finally Bird Caller brought a hare fur blanket, threw it over Star's head.

"Let her go," Sky Watcher told Aqamdax, and when Aqamdax loosed her grip, Sky Watcher pushed Star to the ground and sat on her.

Twisted Stalk lifted a cry of mourning, and Aqamdax looked up to see Chakliux walking toward them. He was carrying Ghaden, the boy with arms and legs hanging limp.

Sok was beside them, and as they passed Sky Watcher and Star, he muttered, "She should be dead, that one. If she has cost this boy his life, I will gladly kill her myself."

Aqamdax watched in numbness, as though she saw all things in a dream. She heard the questions of those around her. What had happened? What had Star done? She felt hands on her arms, but she brushed them away. She had just lost her son. Would she now lose her brother?

"It's my fault," Yaa whispered, and clasped Aqamdax's arm, clung there.

"Hush, be still. You did nothing."

"I teased him. I told him he was not a man."

The people had gathered outside Chakliux's lean-to. The women sat close to the opening, while the men moved about, some lifting a hand to shade their eyes and look out over the river.

With Ligige' back at the winter village, the old woman Twisted Stalk was the closest they had to a healer. She was inside with Ghaden, Sok, and Chakliux. Snow-in-her-hair had taken Star to Twisted Stalk's lean-to, had given her a tea of dog fennel leaves to calm her.

"They say he is still alive," Bird Caller said.

But another woman shook her head.

Alive, Yaa thought, and repeated the word in her mind, holding it there as if it were an amulet with the power to protect Ghaden from death.

"I promised his mother that I would be a good sister to him," she told Aqamdax. "I promised that, but . . ."

Aqamdax slipped an arm around her and rocked as though Yaa were a baby. "Sh-h-h, hush, be still. Every brother and sister fight."

Then Chakliux was beside them. He motioned for Aqamdax to follow him, and ignored Night Man when he scowled. "Yaa, you also," he said.

Yaa crowded into the tent behind Aqamdax. The skin around Ghaden's eyes and mouth seemed almost blue, but he did not look dead. They had taken his wet clothing off, and he had one bare arm flung up over the blanket.

"He is asleep?" Aqamdax asked.

"I do not think so," Chakliux answered her. "We cannot wake him."

Yaa sucked in her breath. There were water spirits, she knew. They lived in lakes and rivers. Had one of them stolen Ghaden's soul? Would he be like Long Eyes, walking around but knowing nothing?

Suddenly the strength went from her legs, and she dropped to the floor beside Ghaden, reached out and stroked his forehead. His skin was hot, but when she touched her own face, she felt the same heat and realized her fingers were cold from her fear.

Night Man peeked into the tent, looked down at Ghaden, but said nothing. He set a hand on Aqamdax's shoulder, and when Chakliux asked her to stay with Ghaden, Night Man protested.

Sok cut him off with quick, sharp words, and Night Man stalked away with steps that pounded into the earth.

"I will stay with him, too," Yaa said in a quiet voice.

"I have something else for you to do," Sok told her. "Come with me."

She followed him to his tent, sure that he would scold her for the fight with Ghaden. She told herself with each step that she deserved his anger, but when they got to the tent, he handed her a pack and said, "There is smoked fish inside. Dry boots and leggings. You need to get yourself a water bladder. Do you have a knife?"

"A woman's knife."

"Take that, and change your boots and leggings as soon as you get across the river."

Yaa's fear of being scolded suddenly turned into horror. "You are sending me away?" she asked in a small voice.

She saw the surprise on Sok's face. Then he said, "You are going with Cries-loud to watch for caribou. The other boys are with the herd, and we cannot spare one of our hunters. Our elders cannot run fast or climb well. You are the only one among the women who has not had a moon blood time." He stopped, looked down at her. "You have not, nae?"

"I have not," she said, her voice a whisper.

He handed her a length of babiche rope, showed her how to tie it around her waist and then to the tree so she was secure in the branches. He gave her a handful of stones, told her to roll them in her palms so the pain from their sharp edges would keep her awake during the night.

"Watch yourself," he said to her. "Do nothing that might curse. Do not even speak. You and Cries-loud decide on signals, perhaps a clap of hands or a whistle, to let him know what you see. We do not want the caribou to hear a girl's voice. Stay in the tree after the caribou have passed until someone comes for you."

He reached to the top of the lean-to, untied a water bladder. "Here, take this," he said to her. "Wait now for Cries-loud."

He left the lean-to, and Yaa sank to her knees. She whispered a chant she had learned as a child, something for a woman to sing when she is worried or tired.

"Mother, help me," she said, and waited to see if she would feel her mother's spirit near, but there was nothing.

"Father," she whispered, and allowed herself to remember her father's face. He had endured much sorrow in his last illness. His favorite wife, Ghaden's mother, had died, and Ghaden had been badly injured. But in his sorrow, he had still watched over his young daughter, had taken Yaa's tears into his own eyes so she was strong enough to bear her sadness.

Like a warm cloak wrapped over her shoulders, she felt her father's strength. Though she could see the disgust in Cries-loud's face when he came to get her, that strength did not leave. Yaa's steps were firm against the earth, and she did not falter in the swift current of the river.

When they finally came to the stand of spruce, Cries-loud selected the tallest. Yaa climbed up, using the limbs like a food cache ladder, until she was in the top of the tree.

There were no caribou, but she could see her people's hunting camp. The river was a wide shining band against the gold and red of the autumn tundra. To her right and left were other trees, some nearly as tall as the one she was in, but most much smaller, and though she knew the strongest branches of a tree grow on the leeward side, away from the wind, it seemed as though each was reaching to the west for the last light of the day.

She tied the babiche rope around her waist and around the tree, got out the stones Sok had given her and held them in her left hand. She waited and watched until the sun was gone, and then in the darkness, she listened, for sometimes caribou walk even in the night, and she knew she would hear the clicking of their legs, the thunder of their hooves.

She took in great breaths of air, testing to see if there was some smell of caribou, and she stretched her eyes wide, so she could see better in the starlight. When she began to grow sleepy, she squeezed her left hand into a tight fist until the stones bit into her flesh and the pain kept her awake.

Aqamdax sat beside Ghaden during the night, one hand on his chest to assure herself that he still breathed. Sometime in that long darkness, Biter crept into the tent and lay beside the boy, nudging Ghaden now and again with his nose. When the first gray light of morning came, Chakliux joined them. He sat close to Aqamdax, and his warmth was a comfort.

Aqamdax knew he had been praying, and she started to get up, whispered she would bring him food and water, but he said, "I need you here more than I need water or food," he said.

"Where is Star?" she whispered.

"With Twisted Stalk."

Aqamdax was squatting in the manner of the First Men, her feet flat against the ground, her knees upraised. She felt Chakliux's fingers gently rub her neck, then the tent flap was thrown back and someone grabbed Aqamdax's arm, pulled her roughly to her feet. She looked up to see Night Man. Star stood behind him, her fingers in her mouth as though she were a child.

"Your husband is here," Night Man said to Star, and pushed her into the tent.

The woman began to wail, and Aqamdax tried to break Night Man's grasp, but he only tightened his hold. "I allow you to stay with your brother, and what do I find? You are with another man." He grasped the knotted otter bracelet on her wrist, twisted until he managed to pull it from her hand.

"You think I do not know where you got this?" he asked her. "You think I do not know why you wear it?"

Star's wails stopped, and Chakliux came from the tent. "Let Aqamdax go," he said to Night Man.

"You would tell a husband what to do with his wife?" Night Man asked, but he released Aqamdax's arm, threw down the otter bracelet and ground it into the mud with his foot.

"Women are killed for betraying their husbands," Night Man said.

"She has not betrayed you."

"The son she bore. You think I do not know he was yours? He is dead to avenge the deaths of my father and brothers. But this one"—he lifted his head toward Aqamdax—"as long as she is mine, she will do as I say."

"You have the right to throw him away." The voice came from behind her, and Aqamdax jumped. It was Sok, and Aqamdax was surprised that he would stand up for her.

"I have done none of the things he accuses me of, but I cannot throw him away," she said. "I will not risk the loss of caribou to our men's spears. Why chance a curse on any hunter in this camp?"

She turned, started toward Night Man's lean-to, but looked back long enough to say to Sok, "Do not let your brother follow me. Make him stay here with Ghaden."

When they came to the tent, Night Man forced Aqamdax inside. He pulled off her clothing, and then his own, pushed open her legs, stroked himself for a moment and entered her. Aqamdax lay still, blocked from her mind all thoughts of what was happening, and prayed that she would not conceive.

NINETEEN

Yaa pried open her left hand, dropped the stones into her pack and slowly straightened her fingers. Her palm was crusted with blood. Though the sun had not yet risen, the eastern sky was nearly light, but she could still see stars to the west.

She heard Cries-loud whistle, and she used the signal he had told her, slapping her hand three times against her pack, to tell him that she saw no caribou.

She pulled out her water bladder and took one sip. Who could say how long she would be up in this tree? She would have to stretch her water out as best she could. She looked again toward the north, then east and west. Sometimes a herd split while crossing lakes or rivers and came from several directions at once.

She pulled a piece of dried caribou meat from her pack, held it up so the smell of the meat would drift toward any spirits that might be near. "This," she hummed beneath her breath. "This. We need caribou, then we will send you the good smell of smoking fires and drying meat."

Chakliux held Star in his arms, rocking her as though she were a baby. Finally he began to tell a story that mothers and fathers tell their children. He felt her relax, and her head fell heavily against his shoulder. He eased her to the floor mats beside Ghaden and covered her with a hare fur blanket. He noticed that her belly had begun to round, and he could not help but lay a hand on it, remembering his first wife, Gguzaakk, and their tiny son.

How many moons was Star into her pregnancy? Three, four? As her husband he should know, but it was not something he often thought about. How would he care for both Star and the baby? Would Star do something foolish to injure the child? At least he would have Yaa to help, but what would Star do when Chakliux took Aqamdax as wife? And now Ghaden . . .

Then, as though the boy heard Chakliux's thoughts, he began to mumble. Biter jumped up and licked Ghaden's face. Chakliux reached out to hold the dog back, but stopped when he saw Ghaden turn his head away from Biter's tongue.

"Biter!" Ghaden called out, then Star was awake, her eyes wide with hope.

Chakliux lifted his fingers to his mouth, tapped them lightly against his lips to request her silence. Ghaden had not yet opened his eyes. Star clamped both hands over her mouth, then the doorflap was pulled aside and Aqamdax crept in. She had rescued the otter bracelet from the mud, and it dangled from her fingers. Chakliux glanced at her, saw the hardness in her eyes, and knew what Night Man had done. But he tilted his head toward Ghaden, lifted his eyebrows, reached for her wrist and pulled her down beside him.

Aqamdax opened her mouth to speak, but Star reached over to press a hand against her lips. Suddenly in the silence Biter barked, a noise sharp enough that Star covered her ears. Ghaden opened his eyes.

"Biter, you dog turd," he mumbled, then Star began to laugh, and Aqamdax started to cry.

"Yaa shouldn't be up there. She's a girl," Ghaden said, his voice pitched into a whine. "I feel good. I can go over there. I'll be more careful in the river."

"Your mother does not want you to go," Chakliux told him.

"Star is not my mother," Ghaden said. "Yaa's my mother. They made her my mother when we lived in the Near River Village."

Chakliux was smoothing a birchwood spear shaft with the edge of a burin stone.

"Look! What do I see?" Chakliux said. "He cries if the ravens take a share of his kill, and he claims that the foxes steal what is his."

Ghaden thrust out his lip. "Wolverine," he muttered.

Chakliux used the riddle often when Ghaden was upset about something. Wolverines were selfish in their kills. They hid what they could not eat, left it to rot in their musky urine, and seldom came back to find it. Was he being selfish in wanting to be a watcher for the caribou? He was old enough, and Yaa had girl things to do.

"Later today, if the caribou have not yet come, then I will take you to the tree. Yaa will be ready to come home by then anyway. She will need to sleep before watching during another night."

"What about Star?"

"We will have Aqamdax keep her busy so she will not know until you are too far away for her to come after you."

"Here," Aqamdax said, "remember that you promised long ago to teach me how to make fishskin baskets. I scraped the skins like you showed me. Now, how do I sew them?"

Star straightened her shoulders in importance, took the fishskins and needle from Aqamdax's hands. Aqamdax sat so her back was to the river and Star's tent was between them and the banks. For a time Star sewed, head down over her work, but then several other women who were working outside stood and began to look toward the river, hands on hips.

Aqamdax was frustrated with herself for not telling them what she hoped to do. She hovered over Star, distracted her with many questions, but finally Star lifted her head and saw the women.

She stood. Aqamdax tried to draw her back down, but

Star pulled away and went to stand with the others. Aq-amdax followed, hoping she would have the strength to hold Star back. She placed a hand lightly on Star's shoulder, looked out to see Ghaden and Chakliux midway across the river.

"There, see," Star said to Aqamdax. "Ghaden is going anyway. You should not have tried to stop him the last time. It caused too many problems."

One of the other women looked at Star in surprise, opened her mouth to say something, but Aqamdax caught her eye, signaled the woman to remain silent.

"You are right, Star," Aqamdax said. "But sometimes it is hard to let boys become men."

A movement at the far edge of the horizon caught Yaa's eye. The last time she thought she had seen something, it was no more than the wind blowing. It was difficult to stay awake, and she did not know if she could keep her eyes open through another night. What did boys do? Surely there was something better than sharp stones. She squinted and watched, moved her head to clear her vision. She kept watching until finally she was sure that she saw something. Not a herd of caribou, but something alone, perhaps one of the wolves that always kept pace with a herd, running at the edges, circling ahead and back, always watching for an animal weak in some way.

She remembered her father's stories of wolves, how they worked together as a pack, sometimes making the herd run so calves would be left behind, an easy kill. She wondered if wolves were the ones who had taught men to hunt together, rather than each man going out alone, working by himself.

Chakliux would probably know if wolves had been their teachers. She felt her thoughts drift toward stories he had told, and then she remembered Aqamdax's stories, First Men tales, so different from those of the River People.

Yaa's eyelids were heavy, and her eyes stung. She blinked to wash away some of the burn. Then she was sitting with a group of her friends, Green Stripe and Best

Fist, Blue Necklace—girls she had known in the Near River Village. Ghaden was with them, healthy and strong, and they were all in the branches of the tree.

Yaa began to giggle. Where had they come from? How had they found her here? Then she gasped and jerked herself awake. She had been dreaming!

She stuck her little finger into her mouth and bit until she tasted blood. The pain cleared her mind, and she looked out again through the tree branches toward the horizon. At first she saw nothing but tundra, then she caught movement again.

No, not wolf, she thought, and watched until she knew it was a man. She whistled to Cries-loud, waited and, receiving no response, whistled again. Finally she heard him call, "Caribou?"

She knew by the hoarseness of his voice that he had been asleep, but she was watcher, not Cries-loud, and perhaps he had different rules to follow.

She slapped her pack three times. No, not caribou.

"Wolf?" he called to her.

She had no signal for wolf, so again slapped her pack three times. Maybe he would realize she meant no.

"Wolf?" he asked again, and again she slapped three times.

"Moose?"

Three slaps.

"What then?"

Yaa could hear the aggravation in his voice.

"Chakliux?"

Three slaps.

He asked no more questions, though Yaa waited, then suddenly he was beside her, his head sticking up through the spruce branches.

"Are you sick? What's the matter?"

She leaned close to him and whispered so any caribou nearby would not hear her voice. "A man, walking."

"Where?" Cries-loud asked, and pulled himself up to sit beside her. He looked out toward the river, toward the Cousin People's hunting camp, but Yaa shook her head and pointed east. Cries-loud watched the man for a long time, then said, "I don't know him. He's not from our village."

Yaa looked again, noticed the quick way the hunter slapped his hands against his sides, how he tilted his head, lifted his chin. Suddenly she knew who it was.

She covered her mouth with her hands, and Cries-loud looked at her in surprise. "You know who it is?" he asked.

"A Near River boy," she said, forgetting to whisper.

Cries-loud shook his head at her and laid fingers against his mouth. She crinkled her face into a frown.

"Near River?" Cries-loud said. "You're sure? They don't hunt here."

"You know him," Yaa whispered. "River Ice Dancer." She leaned closer to whisper. "Remember? I broke his nose once."

Cries-loud smiled his crooked grin. "I'd forgotten," he said.

Yaa balled her hand into a fist and faked a punch to the center of Cries-loud's face. He flinched and raised his eyebrows at her, and she had to clamp her teeth together to keep from laughing.

"I have to tell my father about him," Cries-loud said to her. "If you see caribou, you will have to come down yourself and run to tell the people, but leave as soon as you see the first animals, and run fast, so they do not see you."

He started down the tree, then stopped, looked up at Yaa. "Since we had to have a girl watcher," Cries-loud said, "I'm glad it's you."

It was as fine a compliment as Yaa had ever received, and she covered her face to hide her blush. When she finally pulled her hands away, Cries-loud was halfway down the tree.

THE NEAR RIVER CAMP

K'os saw Anaay outside Dii's tent. He was doing nothing, did not even have a weapon in his hands. She walked over and squatted beside him. He looked at her with surprise, and she saw the derision in his eyes.

"You do not have enough work to do?" he asked.

"I have fed your dogs and cleaned your leggings. You have eaten, and there is a water bladder at your side. The traplines your wife and I set were empty this morning. We wait for the caribou. Have you had any more dreams? Have you called them to us?"

Her insolence was like splinters under his skin. How dare she speak to him in such a way? She was a slave, and he was leader of the whole Near River Village. All these people were here because he had brought them to this place. She was nothing except a woman who fed dogs and warmed the beds of those men he chose for her.

He owed her no answer, but anger forced words from his throat. "I have called the caribou, and they are coming. I have sent our youngest hunters to watch for them. Soon all the women's knives will be busy."

K'os stood and looked down at him. She curled her lips into a sneer. "Do not tell me you called the caribou. I am Cousin River. We passed the rock markers set in place by the Cousin River grandfathers. They guide our hunters, and they guide the caribou. You are stealing meat from the Cousin People. You think I do not know that? If you have the power to call caribou, then why are we here rather than in some new place?"

Anaay clasped the walking stick that lay on the ground beside him. He lashed it toward K'os, but her feet were nimble, and she only laughed at him, dancing away as he cursed her with words and thoughts.

THE COUSIN PEOPLE CAMP

Cries-loud met Chakliux and Ghaden as they came from the river.

"Caribou?" Chakliux asked, but Cries-loud did not answer. Instead he bent down to clasp Ghaden's shoulders.

"You are alive!" he shouted, then, as though he had only just heard Chakliux, he said, "No, no caribou, but Yaa saw a man. She says it is someone from the Near River Village. A boy called River Ice Dancer."

Chakliux filled his cheeks with air and blew it out in a quick, angry breath. "She is sure?" he asked.

Cries-loud nodded.

"He is a problem we do not need," Chakliux said. "Did she see any other Near River hunters?"

"No."

"Perhaps they have tired of the boy's foolish ways and made him leave the village. Or perhaps the Near Rivers think their victory has given them the right to hunt our river."

Chakliux tilted his head to look up at the sky. If the Near River hunters planned to take their caribou, then there was little hope the Cousin People would survive the winter. Perhaps by luck they could move quickly enough to find another herd, but that was unlikely. They could not even be sure the caribou would come to them here, though the animals had crossed within a half day's walk of this place as long as Chakliux could remember. Perhaps the Near Rivers knew this also. The Cousin women they had taken as slaves and wives might have told them how to hunt at a river crossing.

K'os lived with the Near Rivers now. A woman who would kill her own grandson would have no trouble betraying her people if it meant her belly would be full. And how could they hope to fight the Near Rivers with only five healthy men in the Cousin River camp?

"Go back and tell your father," Chakliux told Cries-loud. "Eat and sleep. Then, if the caribou have not yet come, return to the tree."

He watched until Cries-loud was safely across the river, then walked with Ghaden toward the dark shadows of the spruce tree ridge.

TWENTY

Yaa heard someone climbing and was surprised that Cries-loud had returned so quickly. When Chakliux popped up beside her in the tree, she gasped.

"I brought Ghaden to watch so you could go back to camp and get some sleep," he said.

When Chakliux said Ghaden's name, Yaa nearly spoke out loud, and remembered just as she opened her mouth that she was supposed to whisper. "He's not hurt?"

"He is fine, but I don't want to leave him here watching overnight. Go back and sleep, then return before the sun sets. I will stay with him. Go down and tell him to climb up, but first, where is this Near River hunter Cries-loud told us about?"

Yaa pointed with her chin toward River Ice Dancer. He was close enough now that she could make out several spears slung over his shoulder.

"You are sure it is River Ice Dancer?" Chakliux asked.

"Look," Yaa whispered. "See how he walks with his head up like that? See the way he moves his arms?"

"He's alone?" Chakliux asked.

Yaa nodded.

"Go down and send Ghaden up."

She untied herself and fastened her pack to her back. When she was nearly to the ground, she saw Ghaden.

Tears spilled from her eyes, and she knew he would be disgusted with her. She shimmied down the trunk, turning her face away until her feet were on the ground and she could rub her cheeks dry with the heels of her hands. Then she pointed up, but said nothing.

Ghaden looked pale, though his eyes were clear.

"Cries-loud told us about River Ice Dancer," he said to her.

Yaa leaned close to whisper, "Go up and see what you think."

"You're going to the camp?"

"To sleep. I'll return tonight if the caribou have not come."

She boosted him to the first limbs, and when he caught hold, released her grip. He looked down, gave her a grin, then was gone, hidden by the thick branches of the tree.

Sok left camp as soon as Cries-loud told him about River Ice Dancer. He did not bother to take a pack, only picked up his spear and ran to the river. He waded across and began calling when he reached the second ridge. He pushed through the alder brush that edged the growth of spruce, then heard Chakliux's voice. He followed it to the tree where Chakliux and Ghaden were watching.

Sok climbed up, took several deep breaths before he could get out his questions. "You're sure it's River Ice Dancer? Are there others?"

Ghaden extended his arm to point. "There. Look."

Sok watched for a time, then said, "Yes, it's him."

"I haven't seen any others," Chakliux said. "You think he's a scout?"

"Ghaden, did he own a dog?" Sok asked.

"A big black one," Ghaden answered. "Mean."

"He would have his dog if he was on a trading trip, and his pack would be larger."

They watched as River Ice Dancer topped a treeless ridge, looked for a time toward the river, then broke into an easy lope, returning the way he had come.

"They sent him to find the river," Chakliux said.

Sok patted the knife bound to his left arm. "They'll

have a fight if they think they can take our camp and hunt our caribou."

Chakliux tried to clear his mind of the images that came to him. Men dying. Women weeping over the dead. The acrid smell of lodges burning. But the destruction had been greater than that. When it came time for the warriors to find their places in the spirit world, what would they do? For surely their souls were maimed by their hatred.

At dusk, Yaa and Cries-loud returned. Yaa climbed to her perch in the tree, whispered greetings to Chakliux and Ghaden, and watched as they climbed down. Though she had slept most of the afternoon, she still found it difficult to stay awake once the sun set. Her eyes kept closing until finally she bit the insides of her cheeks, used the taste of her own blood to keep away the dreams that crowded themselves under her eyelids.

The moon had not yet risen, and the stars seemed dim. It is the worst part of the night, she told herself, and thought of the caribou that would come, the days the women would spend cutting meat from the bones, slicing it thin to dry in smoky fires, eating some raw, still warm and rich with blood.

Perhaps, since she had been one of the watchers, Chakliux would allow her to have a few caribou teeth for a necklace. She thought of the warm parkas the women would make from the hides, the boot uppers from the leg skins. She made herself name the Cousin boys who had gone out to search for caribou—Squirrel, Caribou Tail and Black Stick—and wondered if River Ice Dancer was doing the same for the Near River People.

She knew that Chakliux was concerned to see River Ice Dancer near the Cousin hunting camp, but perhaps he had come on his own. He was like that. He did what he wanted and would not take the blame if his choices caused problems. Besides, why would the Near Rivers hunt caribou at a river crossing? They had never hunted rivers before.

Yaa hoped River Ice Dancer had not been kicked out of the Near River Village. If he had been, he would probably come to them, ask to join the Cousin People. How could they refuse him? He was strong, and they needed more hunters.

She would tell them not to take him in—perhaps Chakliux would listen to her, and certainly Sok knew what a problem River Ice Dancer could be.

A sound interrupted her thoughts. It was not caribou, but rather a wind combing the branches of her tree. The needles whispered, spoke to her in riddles:

Listen. What do you hear?

Then she heard the thunder of hooves, not in her ears but through her hands as she gripped the tree. Their walking was a pulse, as though she felt the earth's heart beating.

The moon had risen and was a large yellow circle at the edge of the sky, still not high enough to give much light. But even so she saw the caribou, the white of their necks, the wide stripes that glazed their sides. They were a river, flowing light and dark over the tundra, and she heard their song: the clatter of antlers and leg joints, as though they were dancers, keeping rhythm to sacred chants.

Yaa pursed her lips and made a long, clear whistle. She smiled when she heard Cries-loud call out: "Caribou! Caribou! Caribou!"

TWENTY-ONE

Chakliux first felt the tremor of the earth in his otter foot, and then he heard Cries-loud calling as the boy ran into camp.

"Caribou! Caribou coming! Caribou!"

"Where?" Chakliux asked, and heard his question echoed by Sok and Night Man and several of the women.

"West, they are coming from the west and are turning south. Some have already begun to swim."

Then the hunters were running, each of them grabbing spears and lances and heading upriver, telling the women to gather at that place downriver where the water was shallow and the river wide, the current slow.

The women also were running, slinging ropes over their shoulders and grabbing packs filled with butchering knives and burins.

In the moonlight, Chakliux could see the caribou were a mixed herd led by a large cow, a calf at her side. They swam with heads and chests high in the water, their short tails held straight up. That first cow and her calf were allowed to go through, to feel no spear. For if they killed the leader, how would the caribou know where to come the next year? Who would take them to the Cousin People's camp?

But other cows followed her, then the bulls. The hunters stood on the banks, a few venturing into shallow water. Chakliux's first animal was a cow. She was old, with one broken antler. Chakliux's spear—thrust at her exposed back—severed her spine, and her hollow-haired hide kept her afloat as the current took her downriver to where the women waited.

The caribou that gained the opposite shore did not look back, but scrambled up the bank and went on, as though nothing were happening, as though this river were like every other river they crossed.

Chakliux's second caribou was a young bull, good for meat and hide. The animal, in avoiding one of the other hunters, struck out swimming toward Chakliux. Chakliux stood still, held his spear ready to thrust. When the bull saw him, its eyes rolled white and it began to turn, offering Chakliux an easy strike to the spine at the base of the neck. The hit was solid, but Chakliux's spear point wedged between two vertebrae. He pulled hard against the birch shaft, lost his balance and slipped into the river. The current pushed him into the caribou carcasses that were now floating downstream, but then his otter foot found a submerged log, caught and held until Chakliux could regain his footing. He waded into the shallows, pulled another spear from those he had slung on his back, and waited to make another kill.

During the crossing he took three handfuls of cows, several calves and two young bulls before the large bulls passed him. Their hides, scarred from years of fighting, were good mostly for tents and lodge skins. They were close to the rut, and their need for cows would sour their meat. Chakliux killed only two, then the herd was past. It had been a good hunt, with no one hurt and many caribou taken.

Then suddenly Sok was laughing, clapping his hands to his knees, then the others, too, laughed, and though Chakliux knew their laughter showed their joy, as Dzuuggi, he realized that they must also show their gratitude. He lifted his voice in an ancient song of praise known to men in both Cousin and Near River Villages.

The hunters joined him: Sky Watcher, whose spear

hand was wrapped and dripped blood; Cries-loud, now after this hunt a man rather than boy. Sok, Night Man, Take More and Man Laughing, each hunter with his own story to tell.

Sky Watcher had dragged the first cow taken ashore, and now they beckoned Chakliux forward. He praised the caribou for its meat, then helped Take More remove the heart and liver, give out equal portions.

As the hunters ate, their boasting words left them, and they gave honor in silence. Chakliux took his share, and as the blood soaked into his hands, the meat, warm in his mouth, lifted the cold and weariness of the hunt from his body.

Aqamdax waited with the women, downriver from the crossing and the camp. They had chosen a wide section of sandbars where the current slowed, women standing on each bank. She stayed close to Star, so she could be sure the woman did not do anything foolish. Yaa had not yet joined them, and Aqamdax knew Sok had told her to remain in the watcher's tree until the caribou had passed. It was good she was taking so long, Aqamdax thought. That meant a large herd, not just a few animals straggling at the edge of a group passing a half day's walk to the east or west.

"The best thing about caribou is they float," Twisted Stalk explained to Aqamdax, the old woman chewing at her words as though she were eating while she talked. "That is something to think about since this is your first hunt."

Twisted Stalk took a scrap of haired caribou hide to the edge of the river and threw it out into the current. It bobbed along at the surface until the water swept it out of their sight.

"They are land animals, you see," Twisted Stalk said. "When they are in the river, the water spirits want them out. They bring too much smell of grass and earth with them, so the river floats them up and keeps them high. That way they can see their way to land."

Then several women called out. Aqamdax saw what

they saw, the carcasses of caribou floating down to them, their blood coloring the water. Most of the animals were cows. Aqamdax watched as Hollow Cup and Twisted Stalk waded out into the waist-deep river, wrapped a rope around a cow's spindly antlers, then pulled her to land. Then other women on that side of the river helped them until they had heaved the carcass away from the grip of the water.

Star grabbed Aqamdax's arm, and Aqamdax saw a caribou coming toward them. They each caught an antler and between them pulled the animal to shore. Aqamdax heard Twisted Stalk call to her. Another caribou was floating down their side of the river, and one after that. Aqamdax took the first, and she felt the river lift her from her feet as she caught the animal. It was a large bull, full-necked, the dark portions of its fur nearly black in the moonlight. As she dragged it toward the shore, she saw that other women were wading into the water, then she looked back to see that the river was full of caribou, floating like a raft that stretched bank to bank.

Already she was tired, cold from the river, but still her heart lifted, and she felt like singing. With so much meat, they would have an easier winter. What had Chakliux told her? Fifty caribou for each hunter during a year, some taken in spring hunts, others in the fall, in order to have enough for food and lodges, clothing and oil.

She dragged her caribou ashore and went out for another, choosing to go to the middle of the river, since she was young and strong. And with each caribou she caught, the song of thanksgiving grew in her heart. And with that another song: Wife to Chakliux! Wife to Chakliux!

Yaa watched until the last of the caribou had passed the ridge, then she waited a little while longer. She did not want to curse anyone's hunting luck or drive the caribou back the way they had come, but finally she untied herself from the tree and took one last look.

It was dawn now, the sun working its way up the sky. Yaa grasped the limb she was sitting on and hoisted herself down, then she saw something move out on the tundra. She sighed. Probably a few more caribou straggling in the wake of the main herd. She boosted herself back to her perch. She was tired of the tree and wanted to be a part of the excitement of the butchering, but if more caribou were coming, she would wait as Sok had told her.

She lifted a hand to shield her eyes, squinted, then realized they were not caribou but hunters. A group of three coming from the northwest. Near River? What was he doing out there? Once the Cousin People had killed the caribou did the Near Rivers plan to come in and steal the meat?

That would not be good. The Near Rivers knew this place was claimed by the Cousin People. Forever the caribou had crossed this river, sometimes in large herds, sometimes only a few, but they had always crossed, and the Cousin People had always hunted them here. At least that was what Star had told her. Would there be more fighting?

She pressed her cheek against the tree trunk. The cool pungent smell of black spruce calmed her, but she could still hear her own breath, harsh in her throat, as if she had been running. Finally she heard faint cries and she could see that the hunters had raised their spears toward the ridge, toward the tall trees at the center of that ridge. Did they know she was here? How could they?

Then Yaa realized that they were too small to be River hunters. They were boys, and the middle one walked with a limp. Hadn't Squirrel twisted his ankle only a few days before they left camp? And there was his brother Black Stick beside him.

Because she was a girl, Sok had not been able to tell her the signals watchers used. But she had listened back in the camp, though she pretended to be busy with women things, each time he taught Ghaden.

She closed her eyes and thought for a moment, trying to remember the sign for caribou. A stick or spear raised to the sky three times. Yes. She watched, and her eyes ached with the intensity of trying to see something so distant.

Then she was sure she saw the sign, sure each boy was

waving a stick, slinging it three times toward the sky. But what should she do? There was no one with her to carry the news, and the boys were still a long way off. Besides, when they came to camp they would find it empty, and how would they know which way the people had gone?

She climbed down the tree and ran toward the river.

Star, the only woman not bent over a caribou carcass, was the first to see Yaa. Star lifted her voice in a wail so much like a mourning cry that it startled the others.

"What?" Aqamdax said, and Star pointed toward Yaa.

"Yaa! You are all right?" Aqamdax yelled.

"The boys!" Yaa called. "The boys! Squirrel! Black Stick! Caribou Tail!" Her words were broken by her breathlessness, and Aqamdax could tell she had run a long way.

Aqamdax went out to meet her, clasped her shoulders and said, "Don't try to talk. Take a long breath. Take another. There. Now what has happened?"

"I was . . . I was in the tree . . . waiting like Chakliux told me to . . . then I saw Squirrel and Black Stick and Caribou Tail. . . . They gave the signal for caribou. They were so far away and Cries-loud had already left to help the men, so I came myself and . . ."

"Caribou? She said caribou are coming? *More* caribou?" It was Twisted Stalk, and soon the other women were also crowded close.

"We need to tell Chakliux," Star said, and for once Aqamdax agreed with her.

"Should Yaa go?" Bird Caller asked.

"She is the only one among us who is old enough to go alone and yet has not known moon blood."

"There will be a curse," Star cried.

"Do not speak of curses," Twisted Stalk said. She looked at the other women, then back at the dead caribou they had taken from the river. "Does anyone have a hide off yet?"

"We do," said Hollow Cup.

"Bring it."

She and her sister Yellow Bird brought the hide, folded flesh side in.

"Open it," Twisted Stalk told them. "Now wrap it around her."

Yaa shuddered as the women laid the hide over her shoulders. It had not yet been scraped even the first time, and was thick with fat and severed blood vessels.

"There. Now the river will think she is caribou, and she will not curse anything," Twisted Stalk said.

"We should make a chant," Star suggested, and the women looked at one another, unsure of what to sing.

"Aqamdax," Twisted Stalk said. "You are storyteller. Make a chant."

The first songs that came to her mind were those she had learned in her own village, but would words used by the First Men be good for caribou? Probably not. Then she remembered something Chakliux had taught her, a thanksgiving chant River People used.

It was only a child's song, but she sang it anyway, and soon the other women joined her. What is better than thankfulness? What carries more power than praise?

As she sang, Aqamdax noticed that Yaa was shaking. Not with cold, no, the caribou hide would quickly pull away the chill of Yaa's river crossing. Most likely in nervousness, that she must travel alone to the men's killing grounds.

So when the chant was finished and Yaa started out, walking and running, going as quickly as she could with the heavy caribou hide weighing her down, Aqamdax began another chant, one that she sang only in her mind, a song of strength and courage for her small sister as she carried the good news of caribou.

TWENTY-TWO

Yaa trembled under the weight of the caribou hide, but she made herself run. What was a pounding heart and tired legs compared to a winter belly full of caribou meat? She pushed her way through the brushy banks, once nearly lost the caribou hide when greedy willow branches reached out to grab it from her, but she clasped the hide, twisted her body and got away.

She remembered a story she once heard Chakliux tell, about a man who had been able to become a tree. She wondered if that willow was the man, and she wondered if he would curse her for her selfishness in keeping the hide.

"It is not mine to give you," she whispered, and hoped the wind would take her words back to where that tree-man stood, his feet woven into the soil.

Finally she came to a place where the river bent and flowed from the north, then turned back again to flow from east to west. The willows and alder were flattened, each branch showing the white of fresh breaks. Caribou tracks scarred the earth. As the river straightened, the brush thinned and she saw the men, heard their voices, their laughter.

There was smoke. She could smell it, and the aroma of cooking meat. Then she heard the exclamation of a high-pitched boy's voice. Ghaden, she was sure. She stopped where she was and waited. Let the men come to her, but she lowered the hide so they could see her face.

Ghaden yelled her name and screamed out some foolishness about a caribou eating her. Then Night Man, Chakliux and Sok were beside her, all asking questions. Yaa was not sure whom to answer first, so she waited until Chakliux held up one hand, and the men were silent.

"Why did you come?" he asked, and his voice was hard, angry, so that Yaa knew she had risked much in coming to this sacred place.

"The women sent me," she said.

"Why?" Night Man asked, and his voice was even more terrible than Chakliux's.

Suddenly the weight of the caribou hide, the heat and smell of it were like rocks set on her shoulders, and her legs collapsed under her. Then Sok's hands were standing her up again, but no one took the hide, and she had to concentrate so hard not to fall that she barely had strength to speak.

"Caribou, m-more caribou," she stammered out.

Suddenly all the hunters were crowded around her, and their interest seemed to lend power to her voice. "I saw Squirrel and Black Stick and Caribou Tail coming. I saw them from the tree where I was watching. They were waving their walking sticks three times up in the air. That's the sign for caribou, nae?"

Then she was unsure. After all, no one had taught her the signs. She had only overheard what Ghaden was learning. Perhaps she was wrong and everything she had told the women was foolishness. What would the men do to her?

"That is the sign," Ghaden said, pushing his way between Sok and Chakliux.

He looked into her face and then slipped under the hide with her, lifted some of its weight to his own shoulders.

The men were talking, trying to decide whether to go back to the village or to stay where they were.

"Did the boys make any signal as to which direction

the caribou were coming?" the hunter named Sky Watcher asked.

"No."

"You know the signs?" Sok asked.

Yaa dropped her eyes. "Only a few."

"A walking stick held high and swept in one direction or another. Did they make such a sign?"

Yaa closed her eyes and tried to see the boys again as they came. "They were running," she said. "They put their sticks up in the air, made three swings down and forward, toward the camp." She opened her eyes and looked at Sok.

"We should go to the women, tell them what to expect," said Sky Watcher.

"I am the slowest," Chakliux said. "I will stay and take care of what is here. Ghaden can help me."

Then all the men were busy, each gathering weapons and supplies. They had left the dogs with the women, even Biter, so Yaa waited to see if Chakliux wanted her to help carry any of the supplies the other hunters left.

She squatted down, pulled the hide over her hair and watched until Ghaden tugged at Chakliux's arm, lifted his chin in her direction. She saw Chakliux's surprise.

"I thought you had left," he called to her. "Return to the women. There are things here you should not see."

Yaa sighed, stood and hauled the hide up around her shoulders as best she could. At least this time she did not have to run.

Aqamdax worked quickly, cutting meat, retouching or exchanging her knife blade when it dulled, then cutting again. With each animal, she slit the belly first, removed liver, heart and kidneys, then the skirt of fat that covered the intestines. The stomach, roasted whole, full of the sedges and grasses eaten by the caribou, was a feast in itself, and the intestines, cleaned and scraped, made good carrying tubes for drinking water or to store a mix of fat, meat and dried berries. The women would boil the heads into a rich soup and cook the bones for marrow fat.

The heavy straps of sinew along the backbone made

the best thread, and the women would save bones and antlers for tools and weapons, cooking utensils, scrapers, needles and awls. The hooves were good for glue and dance rattlers, the teeth for ornaments. It was a useful animal, the caribou, though Aqamdax did not think its fat was as good as sea lion fat, its teeth as beautiful as seal teeth.

Star had wandered off, leaving Aqamdax and Twisted Stalk to work without her. Twisted Stalk had begun to mutter angrily under her tongue, words of disgust about Star, but Aqamdax acted as though she did not hear them. She was already Star's sister through marriage, and soon would be her sister-wife. She did not want to add to the problem by criticizing the woman, though everyone knew Star was lazy.

Then suddenly the dogs were barking and the men were coming, all but Take More running. Night Man came to Aqamdax, told her Yaa had found them, that the caribou were coming toward the camp. The women continued to work, though Star began to wail about Chakliux. Where was he? Had he been hurt? Was he killed in the hunt? And where also was her son Ghaden?

Night Man called to his sister, told her that Chakliux was coming, and Ghaden as well. Aqamdax kept her head lowered, tried not to let her relief show in her eyes.

Twisted Stalk chanted a quick praise song, then said, "Your husband, Night Man, he is good to you. I know you grieve for your son, but sometimes women do not understand the ways of men."

And though her anger at Night Man pushed words of disdain into her mouth, Aqamdax kept her teeth clamped tight and said nothing at all as her knife sliced and cut.

The boys said the caribou came from the north, a large herd of so many animals they could not see the end of it, even from the tallest trees. The caribou split around the spruce ridges and those that went east did not cross the river, but instead followed it east. The group that went west of the ridges stopped at the bank just upriver from the Cousin People's camp and stayed there. A few animals began to cross but came back, then they all lay down, chewing old grass they coughed up from their stomachs.

It was as though they knew the people needed time to prepare for them, Twisted Stalk said, and men and women worked together, butchering caribou and packing dogs, even floating some of the meat upstream, wrapped in the haired hides, to the hunting camp. Once everyone was at the camp, the women worked all night, taking short breaks to sleep, then cutting and cutting, grateful that the men were there to retouch knife blades and help with the heavy hides.

In the morning, when the caribou seemed ready to move, the women cached whatever meat was not yet on drying racks, and were grateful that the days were cold enough so the raw meat would keep.

The boys and Yaa were left to tend the drying fires and guard the meat from wolves and scavengers, and the women again walked downriver to catch those caribou that gave themselves to the men's spears.

THE NEAR RIVER CAMP

River Ice Dancer straggled into camp long after the other young men had returned. Anaay spoke to him in disgust, asked what had kept him so long. Had he found a woman somewhere out there on the tundra?

Anaay expected an angry retort, but River Ice Dancer only shrugged and said, "I see you do not want to know what I have to tell you."

He went to Sun Caller. The old man was sitting outside his tent using a hammerstone and antler tine to break slices of chert from a core stone.

"The other watchers," River Ice Dancer asked, "did they see caribou?"

Sun Caller shook his head. "None, and no s-sign of them."

River Ice Dancer puffed out his chest. "I did," he said. "A herd crossed the river where the Cousin men hunt."

Anaay had followed River Ice Dancer to Sun Caller's lean-to, and now, as though he had given no insult, he asked, "And are the Cousin hunters there?"

"They are, and they took many caribou."

"Those are the ones I heard in my dreaming."

Least Weasel, one of Sun Caller's sons, joined them, listened to Anaay and said, "If they are the caribou you heard, then all your fasting and prayers did us little good. Or were you praying for the Cousin People rather than us? For years the Cousin have hunted that river, and we have chosen to hunt the tundra. Why have you brought us here? So we could watch others get their caribou while ours pass in some other place?"

Anaay, sputtering his outrage at Least Weasel's insolence, began to defend his caribou dreams, but River Ice Dancer interrupted to say, "The second herd was much larger."

"What herd?" Least Weasel asked.

"The one that followed the first. They came half a day later, split to go around a ridge. Some went west and others east. I found a tall tree on that ridge and climbed it. From there I could make out the Cousin camp on the other side of the river. It looked as though they had chosen to follow those that went west, though the greatest number of caribou went east."

"Those caribou that honor the sun will also honor our hunters," Anaay said, his words loud and strong above the voices of the men. "Our spears will take many. Go now and prepare to hunt. We leave as soon as River Ice Dancer has a chance to rest and eat. He will show us the way, and we will take caribou."

He went into his tent and did not listen to those men who lifted their voices to ask who among them knew how to hunt caribou in rivers. How could they hunt without the help of brush fences to direct the animals to their spears? How could they hunt in water? Wouldn't the river carry them away?

TWENTY-THREE

THE COUSIN RIVER CAMP

Aqamdax wrapped herself in bedding furs and closed her eyes. She could never remember being so tired. The second hunt had brought in twice as many caribou as the first. When the killing was finished, the men had joined the women, floated and carried the prepared meat to the main camp, but the women stayed at the butchering site, removing hides, gutting carcasses, slicing off bits of the raw meat to eat as they worked so they did not have to stop except to change or sharpen knives.

At the end of the second day, the men came once more and helped take the rest of the meat back to camp. Again, they decided to float it upstream in hides, though when Take More lost a whole hide filled with boned meat, the women in their tiredness screamed out their fury.

The meat was a gift to the river, Sok told them, and Take More was wise rather than clumsy. Most of the women decided Sok was right, but Twisted Stalk continued to grumble. She had been the one to butcher that meat, and the hide had been particularly fine, with broad white bands down the sides of the animal. She had planned to use it for a parka that winter.

A few newly killed caribou always escaped the women's hands to float downstream, Twisted Stalk said.

Wasn't that enough? How greedy was this river?

She complained until all the women hurried past her, eyes averted. Aqamdax hummed apologies under her breath, hoping whatever the river did to Twisted Stalk for her insolence, the curse would not spread to others in the camp.

Finally Chakliux had to remind Twisted Stalk that worse things might happen if she continued her complaints. Then they walked in silence, loaded with meat, most women too tired to talk, too tired even to offer thanksgiving chants for meat that would keep them living through another winter.

THE NEAR RIVER PEOPLE

Dii rejoiced to travel again toward the Caribou River, but a part of her grieved as she remembered her mother and father, her brothers and uncle. Only the year before, they had been alive. Only the year before, she and her friends had no concerns but the small problems that came to all girls. She and her cousin Awl had giggled behind splayed fingers about the hunters who led them. Now most of those hunters were dead, and her friends were wives or slaves to Near River men.

Dii reminded herself that she could not complain about how Anaay treated her. Her cousin Awl was also fortunate in her new husband.

Dii looked ahead to where Anaay walked. Besides his walking stick, he carried only weapons, as did most of the men, while the women carried heavy loads. At least Anaay had three strong dogs, and they helped much.

K'os was wise with dogs. She had suggested that they split the load between two travois and allow one dog to carry only a light pack, then switch the dogs, giving each a time to rest.

"Too bad Gull Beak did not come," Dii had joked to K'os. "Then Anaay's women could also take turns in carrying light and heavy loads."

She thought the comment would make K'os laugh, but K'os only lifted her chin and slitted her eyes as though she were angry.

They walked a day and into a night before setting up camp. The young men sent out as scouts had found a good ridge, dry and with a line of trees to break the wind.

Anaay chose several hunters to go on ahead, to seek those caribou that River Ice Dancer had seen. The men and women who remained in camp stayed in separate tents. Why chance that a wife would ruin her husband's hunting luck? Perhaps even the breath from her throat would do that. Who could risk such a thing?

By morning, the scouts had returned. The caribou were close, they said, only a half day's walk, even less. Dii, sure that the men would tell the women to walk downriver of the herd while they walked east, repacked the dogs' travois and her own pack and set them outside the camp, toward the west.

But Anaay said they would all go together, traveling east to stop the herd's progress, then scouts would circle and force the caribou toward them, make the animals cross the river.

Dii saw the eyes of the Cousin women open wide in surprise, heard their whispers.

How would the caribou react when they saw women with the hunters? What greater insult could be given? And when the animals were killed in the water, who would catch them if the women were upstream with the men?

"I could speak to my husband," Dii said to K'os, but K'os shook her head.

"You think he would listen? You think any of these men will listen? Are we the hunters?"

Dii saw the burden of that knowledge in each Cousin woman's eyes, and as they broke camp, they worked in silence.

Twice during that half-day walk, Dii tried to approach Anaay, to tell him what she knew about river hunting, but each time other men turned her away. Finally she called out, crying her husband's name. Anaay looked back at her, and when she raised her hands in supplication, he strode to where she stood among the women. In relief, Dii began to explain that the women must be downstream, out of sight of the men during the hunt, but when she ventured to look up into Anaay's face, she saw that his cheeks were red in anger, the scar that ran from brow to jaw as stark as snow.

He raised his walking stick, and she ducked, but he caught her across the shoulders. Her pack took the brunt of the blow, and the force of it knocked her to the ground. He slashed the stick against her arms and legs until finally she curled herself into a ball, her pack like the hard shell of a clam, protecting the soft flesh beneath. When his anger was spent, Anaay walked away, and Dii slowly pushed herself to her feet. She took her place again beside K'os, tried to make her aching legs keep up with K'os's long strides.

"Why do you try to help him?" K'os asked. "He is a fool. Let him stay a fool. It is best for us to keep our mouths shut, to stand back and let others take the punishment that Fox Barking's wisdom will bring them."

That evening Dii and K'os set their tent apart from the others. K'os brought stones to make a separate hearth, and none of the other wives came near.

In the night, the singing again found Dii's bones. In her dreams, she heard the caribou, knew they were close. When the thunder of their passing shook her awake, she scrambled from her bed and woke up K'os. They had slept in parkas, leggings and boots, so did not have to dress before they crawled outside. To the east, the sky was lightening with the promise of sun, but to the west Dii saw a moving darkness. Caribou.

Men called from the river. Kills had been made, but other hunters milled in confusion in the dark of early morning. Dii listened until she heard Anaay's voice telling the women to move downstream.

How did Anaay expect them to get around the herd? Dii wondered. They could not walk through.

Then Dii saw that the Near River women carried peeled willow sticks, and some had white hare fur blankets. Men came with weapons, stood beside their wives, watched as the women waved the blankets, raised the sticks, forced the caribou at the edges of the herd to turn in toward the center of the group.

Suddenly one of the women was screaming, crying out for her small daughter. Then, as though the caribou had caught the woman's panic, they turned from the river and ran toward the camp.

K'os cut their dogs loose, then she and Dii left everything and ran. They stumbled over tussocks, filling hands with xos cogh spines, but they got up, ran again.

A large caribou bull came so close that Dii was sure it would trample her. He ran with his head up, eyes rimmed with white, foam flying from his mouth. Dii thrust out her arms, tightened her muscles, and pushed with all her strength. He pressed against her, and she felt her legs begin to give way, then suddenly he was past, cows with calves following in his wake, their breath like smoke in the darkness.

It is a dream, Dii told herself, but still she ran. In her heavy parka she began to sweat, though the air was cold enough to cloud her breath, frost her brows and lashes. Her braids twisted loose, and her hair was pushed into her face by the edges of her parka hood. Her lungs ached, and her legs grew tired, but she ran.

The sky was light with dawn when she realized that the thunder was behind her.

She stopped, fell to her knees. When she could breathe again, she noticed K'os, sitting on the ground some distance back.

"K'os!" Dii called, and though K'os did not answer, she lifted one arm, then let it drop, as though even that was too much for the strength she had left.

Dii looked down at her feet. They were bleeding through her boots, coloring the tundra plants, but the cold of the ground had numbed their pain, so first she began to pull the xos cogh spines from her hands.

THE COUSIN RIVER CAMP
Ghaden tried to push Biter out of the tent. He had been fed too much, that dog, and now was so lazy he did not want to do anything but sleep.

"Biter," Ghaden said in a loud whisper, "it's our turn to watch the meat. Get out!"

Biter rolled to his back, but when Ghaden stepped over him, the dog got up, shook himself and followed Ghaden to the river. They stopped at a shallow place where sand had made a gradual slope from bank to riverbed. Ghaden yanked up his leggings and waded in, leaned over to drink, then splashed his face with water.

He turned toward the bushes to urinate, but then saw something floating just beyond his reach. Had someone killed a caribou this morning? He thought all the men were in the camp. Perhaps a herd had crossed far upriver and wolves had killed one, lost it in the current. He waded out until he was able to catch the carcass, but it was heavier than he had thought, and it started to carry him downstream.

Biter began to bark, and Ghaden yelled for Chakliux and Sok, then for the boys he was supposed to relieve at the drying racks.

Black Stick came running down the bank, told him to let go, but Ghaden could not touch bottom, and hanging on to the caribou, at least he floated.

"Get Chakliux!" Ghaden said. "Get Sok!"

As Black Stick ran back toward the camp, Ghaden felt his arms grow weak with fear. What if Black Stick did not return in time? His hands were already numb. Then suddenly Biter was with him in the river. Ghaden let go of the caribou and lunged for the thick fur at the scruff of Biter's neck.

Black Stick screamed out his words so quickly that Chakliux had to make him start again.

"Ghaden," Black Stick panted, and Chakliux's heart froze.

The boy pointed toward the river. "He's there, in the river. There was a caribou floating—"

But Chakliux did not wait for whatever else Black Stick had to say. He ran to the river, swam out toward the carcass. The cold water bit into his chest, tried to chew its way to his heart.

I am otter, Chakliux told himself. I am otter. The cold cannot stop me. His arms and legs grew stiff, but he managed to reach out, grab the caribou. Ghaden was not there.

"Ghaden!" he screamed. "Ghaden!" Then he heard voices from the shore, looked up to see Sok, Sky Watcher and Black Stick on the bank. Ghaden, his hair and clothing dripping water, was with them, Biter at his side.

Chakliux kept his grip on the caribou, maneuvered it so he was pushing the carcass, and kicked his way to shallow water. Sky Watcher pulled the caribou ashore.

Sok helped Chakliux to his feet, but Sky Watcher leaned over the carcass and pointed at a foreshaft protruding from the caribou's neck. He pursed his lips at the markings and said, "Near River."

TWENTY-FOUR

THE NEAR RIVER CAMP

Anaay cupped his hands over his ears to shut out the sounds of mourning songs. Could any man expect to lead such fools? How had those women happened to place themselves between the men and the animals? They had cursed the hunting as soon as the caribou caught their smell. And which foolish mother—Red Leggings, was it?—had allowed her four-year-old daughter to stay with her? Did the woman think the child was big enough to catch a dead caribou?

But had the men been much better? Most came into the river with only one spear, and when that was cast they had no weapons but the short blades of their knives. As soon as the first woman was hurt, then her husband stopped hunting and tried to get to her, driving the caribou away from the other hunters.

Anaay raised his walking stick and stood at the center of what was left of their camp. He lifted his voice in a chant of protection, but as his mouth sang, his mind formed other words: Fools! Fools!

Dii smoothed Awl's hair. Awl coughed, then tried to smile.

"K'os says your ribs are broken, only that," Dii said.

Where was First Eagle? If he were here, Awl would feel better. But what if he were one of those killed? Dii was not sure how many men had died. Only a few, she thought. More women and children had lost their lives, but among the Cousin women, only Stay Small had been killed, crushed between two caribou while trying to help First Eagle's sister Red Leggings. And what good had it done? The sister was dead, and also her little daughter.

Blue Flower stopped and squatted beside Dii. The woman claimed to be a healer, but K'os said she knew less about medicines than a child.

"You should get her off the wet ground," Blue Flower said, and pointed with her chin at the water oozing from the mud.

Dii had known the place was not a good campsite, but how could she say that when Anaay was the one who chose it? On each side of the camp, the ground made a long, shallow slope that cupped toward the river. Didn't Anaay realize that the slope made a natural walkway for the caribou?

Dii looked up at Blue Flower. "Would you please go get First Eagle?" she asked. The woman frowned, and Dii changed her request. "You are healer. Will you stay here with Awl while I get her husband? He will help me move her."

"K'os has looked at her?" Blue Flower asked.

"Yes."

"What does she say?"

"Broken ribs."

"That is not terrible. There are worse injuries. First Eagle is busy with others. Is she spitting blood?"

"No."

Blue Flower shrugged. "I have more important things to do than look for a Cousin woman's husband, but if I see First Eagle I will tell him to come."

As Blue Flower walked away, Dii called after her. "Have you seen my husband?"

Blue Flower snorted. "You do not hear his chants?"

The noise of mourning, the cries of pain, seemed to funnel down the sloped ground to where Dii sat, but she listened carefully and finally heard Anaay's voice. He was singing a prayer song she had not heard before; he was asking for power, protection. For himself, not others.

"Anaay, see what your foolishness has cost us," Dii whispered, filled with the same revulsion she had known when she first came to him as wife.

He had put them in the caribou's path, so that when the animals panicked, they turned and overran the camp. He had not asked for advice though he knew nothing about river crossing hunts. Besides, this river was claimed by the Cousin People. Why did Anaay think he could hunt here?

What good were his prayer chants if they were sung in selfishness? Did a man ever get so powerful that taboos could be forgotten? Did a people ever prosper once they had forsaken ways of honor and respect?

THE COUSIN RIVER CAMP

Yaa crouched on the leeward side of Chakliux's tent. Her arms ached from wrists to shoulders, and her fingers felt as though they were still knotted around her scraping burin. The excitement of having so much meat in the camp had faded, and now she could think only of the hard work left to do. They had had a celebration feast, but the true feast, with dances and storytelling, would not come until they were back at the winter village. There were many days of scraping and cutting, walking and carrying before then.

The sky was gray and cold. She closed her eyes against it, let herself drift toward sleep. Star had put her to work scraping hides. It was only the first scraping, and most hides had been skinned so well that there was little to do, but why take the chance that small pieces of fat would soak their way through to the hair, stealing the hide's strength, or that blood would rot it?

Each woman used a caribou leg bone scraper, one end of the bone sliced diagonally and notched into tiny teeth, drawing the tool toward herself, counterbraced against her forearms with a leather strap.

Yaa, her arms still too small to use a caribou bone tool

well, worked with a burin scraper she could hold in her
fist, best for ragged edges and holes that pierced the hides,
those places too easily caught by leg bone scrapers.

Yaa had lost count of how many hides she had done
that day, finishing the edges after Star or Aqamdax had
scraped the rest. Enough to go through all her burins.
Night Man had some ready, Star told her, and had sent
her to get them. But surely it wouldn't hurt if she took a
short rest. How could Star complain? None of the women
rested more than she did.

Yaa heard someone walk up and stop beside her. She
sighed. It was probably Star, ready to scold. She opened
her eyes only enough to see through the lashes. Cries-
loud was standing in front of her.

She began to greet him, but her words got tangled in
her throat and came out as a squeak. He flopped down
beside her, grinned. "You don't have to help anymore?"
he asked.

"I'm just resting. They sent me to Night Man to get
more scrapers."

"You tired?"

She nodded. "Yes. But there's a lot more hides left to
do, and after that the leg skins . . ." She glanced at Cries-
loud from the corners of her eyes. She didn't want him
to think she was complaining. "I'm glad, though," she
said quickly. "It's good to have this meat and all these
hides."

"It is good," he said. "The winter won't be so hard."
He lifted his head to look out past the tents of their camp.
He was quiet a long time before he said, "Sometimes I
think if I watch long enough, I'll see her."

Yaa's throat tightened. He was talking about his
mother, Red Leaf. A part of her wondered how he could
still care. Red Leaf had killed Daes and the elder Tsaani,
then Day Woman, Cries-loud's own grandmother. But
there was a part of Yaa that understood. She knew what
it was to lose a mother.

"She did bad things," Cries-loud said, "and I know I'm
not supposed to talk about her. My father says she is dead,
and our sister."

"How can he expect you to forget her?" Yaa said. "She was a good mother to you and to your brother."

"I miss her—and my friends at the Near River Village," he said.

"Me, too." Yaa's words were almost a whisper. She usually didn't let herself think of the Near River Village. There was too much sadness in those thoughts, and perhaps some chance for curses.

"She didn't kill my grandmother," Cries-loud said.

Yaa didn't know what to say, so she picked up a stick lying on the ground, poked a design into the mud.

"The night my mother left, I brought my baby sister to her, and I watched so she could sneak away in the darkness. I even walked with her a long ways out on the tundra. She didn't do anything to my grandmother. She never went near her lodge."

Yaa frowned. "She might have come back. Later."

"Why would she? She got away. If she came back, someone might see her. Besides, she liked my grandmother."

"Have you talked to your father about this?"

"He won't listen."

Yaa drew circles in the dirt. Finally Cries-loud leaned close, gave her a small stone. "I found this," he said. "You can have it."

It was white, translucent, like a little chunk of the moon somehow fallen to earth. She looked up to thank him, but he was already on his feet, walking away. She closed her hand around the stone, felt herself blush. What did it mean when a boy gave you something? She wished her friend Best Fist were here. It would be a good secret to share, this gift. Yaa stood up, slipped the stone into the amulet pouch she wore at her neck. Suddenly she wasn't tired anymore. She ran to Night Man's tent, got the burins and brought them back to Star.

Star scolded her for taking so long, but Yaa didn't care. She hummed a quiet song, her thoughts on Cries-loud. She finished scraping the edges of a hide, folded it flesh side in, rolled it and took another from Star's pile. She draped the hide over her scraping log, dipped her hand in water and rubbed the edges, then as she worked allowed herself to remember Red Leaf.

Cries-loud looked much like her, large and strong. Red Leaf could do hides more quickly than anyone in the village, but though Yaa could remember good things about the woman, she felt no compassion for her. Two good people were dead because of Red Leaf's selfishness.

And perhaps Day Woman. Though Cries-loud had said . . .

Then Yaa caught her breath, shivered though she was not cold. If Red Leaf did not kill Day Woman, who did?

TWENTY-FIVE

All day the Cousin men stayed at the river, watching.
They kept the women and boys away, did not tell them
what they had found. They had argued over the first caribou. The Near Rivers had killed it. Should they give it
to their women to butcher? Would that break some taboo?

"They took our meat, raided our caches," Night Man
said, narrowing his eyes at Sok, spitting out his words in
anger. "Why should we be concerned about taking their
meat?"

When the other men agreed, Chakliux put aside his un-
easiness, helped carry the animal to the women, but that
had been before they found the Near River body, a hunter
Sok and Chakliux knew as Muskrat Singer. During the
rest of that day, the river brought them seven caribou, two
hunters and a young woman, all dead.

That night, they told their women, and at the beginning
of the next day, even before sunrise, Chakliux and Sok,
Sky Watcher and Take More loaded the bodies on a travois, took turns pulling it upriver to find the Near River
camp. Each of the men carried weapons, but Chakliux
expected no fight.

When they approached the camp, they were almost ignored. Most of the people were gathered around the injured or the dead. One old woman tended a boiling bag,

but Chakliux saw no other food being prepared. One tent was still standing; the others were only trampled mounds of hides and broken sticks.

Fox Barking came to them. His parka was stained with blood, his face and hands smeared with dirt. He lifted a walking stick toward the clear sky of the east, toward the round ball of the sun, and said, "You have come to see our defeat? Look, even the sun pulls away the clouds and watches us."

"We have come to offer help," Take More said. "We have food, if you need it, and we have brought these bodies with us."

Fox Barking stepped past them, lifted the blankets that covered the bodies on the travois. Then he called out, "No Teeth, your son is dead. Black Mouth, here is your wife."

Mourning cries pierced the air, and Near River women gathered around the travois. Fox Barking began a chant, something Chakliux had once heard his grandfather Tsaani sing. In disgust, he turned toward the river. The earth was wet, and mud swirled into the water from the softened banks.

"And you also have our caribou, the ones we killed?" Fox Barking called after him, the harsh words interrupting his chants. "You brought us our dead, but not our meat. You intend to keep that?"

"Come and get it yourselves. We will not haul it for you," Sok said.

Fox Barking lifted his lip in a sneer. "So you both decided to live with the Cousin People, or what is left of them," he said to Sok and Chakliux. He smiled at Sok. "It does not surprise me that Chakliux would choose to do so, but you have known a better way. The stink of their camp does not bother you?"

Sok turned his back on the man, as though he did not hear his taunts.

"And your wife, Red Leaf? Did you let her live or did you kill her? And the child, was it boy or girl? Or did you wait to find out?"

Sok turned, and as he turned he brought his arm up, slapped Fox Barking hard across the face. Fox Barking lifted his walking stick, but Sok grabbed it and broke it across his knee. He stalked away, called back to Chakliux, "You deal with him. I will see you in camp."

"Go with Sok," Chakliux said quietly to Sky Watcher and Take More.

Take More made a vulgar gesture at Fox Barking, then hurried to catch up to Sok, but Sky Watcher shook his head. "I will stay. You do not need to be alone here with these people."

"Your brother is a fool," Fox Barking said, rubbing the side of his jaw. "But I do not have to tell you that."

"We have your meat," said Chakliux. "If you need it, send some of your women to get it. Do not come yourself and do not send your men."

THE NEAR RIVER PEOPLE

They spent four days in mourning. Most of the men had wanted to return to the winter village and from there go out in twos and threes to hunt what caribou or moose they could find. Anaay insisted that they stay where they were, and most stayed, but Black Mouth took his dead wife and left, though Anaay told him the wolves would smell death, steal the body before Black Mouth could get back to the village.

Later, in the privacy of his tent, Dii saw her husband dance a curse against Black Mouth, and she shuddered to think what would happen to the man, alone with his dead wife on that long trail to the winter village.

Others wanted to go. Dii could see the wanting in their eyes. Several families—those who had not lost anyone— stayed two days into the mourning, then they also left. Anaay was right about the wolves, many said. It was best to burn the dead bodies after the mourning. Was that not a custom that their grandfathers' grandfathers had followed? Then bones could be cleaned and taken with them to the winter village. At least they could do that.

Dii was one of the women chosen to stay awake the night of the burning, to guard the bones and ashes from wolves and ravens, from spirits who would smell the smoke and think there was a gift for them in the people's fires. She trembled when she thought ahead to that night, and she protected herself with amulets and every chant and prayer she knew. She did not eat anything the day before—none of the fish the men were catching from the river, none of the ptarmigan K'os took in her traps. Why flavor her breath with the taste of meat? Spirits drawn by the smell of burning flesh did not need to be reminded that they could no longer eat.

She wished Blue Flower's husband, the Near River shaman, had not been killed in the fighting. If they had a shaman, he would probably be the one to guard those burning bodies, and she could stay safe in the camp.

Anaay had lit the fire when it was still light, but by night, he and the hunters with him had gathered on the farthest side of the camp, a good way upriver from the byre. Anaay sent her with a curt nod of his head and only one word, "Go," as though even in speaking to her, he took risk. Six women were chosen. All but one were Cousin, and the truth of that smoldered in Dii's breast.

"We are wives now, not slaves," Green Bird said as their husbands sent them off. "Wives have the same value whether Cousin or Near River."

But the other women laughed at her. Light Hair, the one Near River wife, laughed the hardest.

"Even if you give your husband two handfuls of children, all strong sons, you will not have the value of a Near River wife," she said. Then, though she, too, had been condemned to watch the bone fire, she held her head high and looked at them from haughty eyes.

Two women had babies under their parkas, but the children belonged to their Cousin husbands. The other three, Dii among them, had no children, and Dii had had her moon blood time during their journey to the Caribou River, and so knew she had not conceived during those nights of caribou singing.

They walked in the darkness, stumbling over tussocks and uneven ground. The men had given them torches, but said not to light them until they reached the fire. Too much light might give spirits a path back to the camp.

Dii had pulled the hood of her parka tight around her

face, kept her mouth closed, pinched her nose shut, releasing her nostrils only when she had to breathe. Why give those spirits that live in the night more ways to enter her body?

One of the other women, Owl Catcher, leaned close to Dii, asked, "What about K'os? Why didn't Anaay send her instead of you?"

Dii had wondered the same thing, had felt the hurt of her husband's choice, but she only said, "Who can trust K'os? Would you want her here with us?"

Owl Catcher did not answer, so Dii knew she had given the right response to a question asked spitefully. At the fire, though repulsed by the sound and smell of burning bodies, Dii felt her empty belly twist at the reminder of fat and meat. Then suddenly she had to turn from the heat and light of the flames, stumble into the darkness to retch.

She rejoined the others, trembled at the change the fire had made in their faces; brows, noses and cheeks threw shadows that distorted eyes and mouths, as though the passage through darkness had been a birthing into some other world.

Dii looked away, then went to the brush pile the men had heaped some distance from the fire. She brought back branches, began to feed them into the flames. Then one by one the others did the same, until finally Light Hair called out that two should go together, one holding a lit torch to keep spirits and animals away. Dii trembled again, realizing her foolishness in going alone into the darkness, her eyes dimmed by looking into the light of the flames.

When each woman had brought back wood, they sat in silence. Dii, Light Hair and Owl Catcher were on the far side of the fire. The other three women—Cut Ear, her cousin Green Bird and Willow Leaf—huddled together on the camp side.

Earlier that day, Dii had overheard Anaay tell the men how the fire should be made, that each body should be placed on a separate layer of branches one on top of the other. But Sun Caller, a man who usually agreed with all Anaay suggested, had told them in a stuttering speech that there were too many bodies for that. The fire would burn away the bottom branches and the top layers would topple.

"Have you forgotten how many died?" he had asked them, then answered his own question. "Two handfuls in all, not counting Two Fist, taken by her husband.

"And what about the women? Can they be burned with the men?"

Dii was not sure what had been decided, but the fire looked wide enough for three bodies to lie side by side, and she had felt some comfort in knowing someone besides Anaay was making choices for the camp.

If she and the other women kept the fire going all night, then by tomorrow they could dig out the bones and perhaps start back to the winter village. Though they were camped here on Cousin hunting grounds, it no longer seemed Cousin. At this river her people had always known more joy than sadness. Now she would remember only the terror, the stink of burning bodies, the sorrow and the mourning songs.

Above the snapping of the fire, one of the women on the other side of the flames began to speak. The voice was different, as though it belonged to none of them, but the words were familiar, and it seemed the woman spoke Dii's own thoughts.

"We could leave and go to the Cousin camp. We could be there before the Near River men know we are gone."

The words swirled up with the flames, became the smoke, and it seemed that Dii breathed them into her chest. They shimmered there like sun on water, cutting the darkness.

Back with her own people. Back in her own winter village.

Her mother and father and brothers would not be there, but Sky Watcher had been one of those who brought the dead to Anaay. Perhaps he would take her as second wife. She would even be wife to old Take More, though his first wife was a woman of sharp tongue and harsh ways.

From the corners of her eyes, Dii glanced at Light Hair. The Near River woman's face was harsh in the firelight, her mouth pulled down in a frown. But she was the first to answer.

"If I were you," she said, "I would go. This is not good, this hunting camp, and the winter will be long."

Her words were no surprise. If some of the Cousin River wives left, there would be more food for those who remained. What had they taken, five, six caribou? That was hardly enough to feed the hunting camp during the journey back to the winter village. They would bring nothing for the caches except the hides, and what were six caribou hides among so many?

"How will we know the way?" one of the other women asked.

"They are camped on this river," said Owl Catcher. "All we have to do is follow it to their tents."

"What if they do not want us?" asked Cut Ear.

"That is foolish. We are their daughters. Their sisters. Would you turn them away if they had been taken?"

"What if they have already left for the winter village?"

"We know the way to the Cousin River Village. That is not so difficult."

"I will go," Cut Ear said.

"I also," said Green Bird.

"Dii?" Owl Catcher asked.

Dii's heart leapt in hope. But how could she leave Anaay? "What about our husbands?" she asked.

"Throw them away," Owl Catcher said. "They do not care much for us if they sent us to watch these bones burning."

"Awl is here with her husband, and she is hurt. I should not leave her."

"Do what you want," Owl Catcher said. "I am going." She dipped her torch into the fire to renew its flame, then she, Green Bird, Cut Ear and Willow Leaf left, walked away from the death fire.

Dii stood and watched them until the light of Owl Catcher's torch was only a tiny star in the darkness. When she sat down again, she felt an emptiness in her chest, as though a part of her had gone with them and she carried only half her soul.

TWENTY-SIX

THE COUSIN RIVER CAMP

Chakliux saw the women come out of the brush at the east side of the camp. It was just past midday, and at first he thought nothing of their appearance. They were Cut Ear and Willow Leaf, Green Bird. He had grown up with them.

But then Chakliux realized that the three had been among the group of women and girls K'os took with her to the Near River Village. Following the three younger women was Owl Catcher, one of the women taken as a slave during the revenge raid.

Others in the camp looked up, for a moment continued their work, then screamed out their joy. They left boiling bags and drying racks, ran to the four women, opened arms to welcome them.

But Chakliux and Sok went for weapons and stood ready. These four were slaves or perhaps Near River wives. Who could tell where their loyalties would lie?

Sky Watcher left the camp, took a dog with him, but Chakliux did not relax his vigilance even when Sky Watcher returned to report that the women had not been followed.

The Cousin men met at Chakliux's tent, discussed what should be done. If the women's story was true, and it seemed that it was, they had slipped away in the night. If their husbands decided to come for them, they would arrive soon, unless they planned an attack. Then perhaps they would wait a day or so, preparing weapons, making prayers.

Either way, it was best to leave soon. Most of the butchering was done. The frosts were harder each night, and the ground stayed frozen well past midday so it would not be as difficult to walk the tundra, even with heavy packs and travois.

They called Twisted Stalk, told her the women must prepare to move. The men made ready their weapons, watched, guarded.

Twisted Stalk carried the men's message to the wives, and though Aqamdax was glad they would soon be back in the winter village, she understood why the other women grumbled their discontent. They were not waiting to throw away a husband. They were not rejoicing in the hope of becoming wife to a man as good as Chakliux. They wanted two, three more days to finish what they were doing before they had to pack.

Much was done already. All the organ meats—those not eaten—had been boiled and chopped, stuffed into cleaned intestines with dried berries brought from the winter village, then sealed with melted fat. The bellies, too, were done. Most had been roasted whole, and Aqamdax could still remember the sour and sweet taste of each slice, the juice running over her fingers and down her arms as she ate. Other bellies had been scraped out to use as storage containers. Bladders had been emptied, blown up and dried to use for water.

The women saved all the windpipes, scraped them inside and out, washed them and filled them with old grass. If frozen until dry, they turned white and soft, good to decorate parkas and boots. Aqamdax would sew the gut and windpipes she could claim into waterproof chigdax, a kind of parka worn by the First Men. Though the other women scoffed at her when she made them, she was the one to laugh when their furred parkas soaked up the rain and she remained dry. She had made a chigdax for Ghaden and another for Night Man, though he would not wear it.

All the hides had been removed from the caribou carcasses, the sinew taken from along the spines and hung to dry. It amazed Aqamdax how quickly the Cousin women did such things, working together over the large, heavy carcasses.

The first days after the caribou were taken, the women had boiled the heads. What was better than the soft meat of cheeks and the sweet taste of the fat around the eyes? Now they were fleshing hides, though with the cold weather, they could fold and roll those that remained, take them back to the winter camp, without worry they would rot. A few of the women were still slicing meat, but the bones had all been boiled to render out the oil and marrow.

A day or two to finish the hides, that would be best, but Aqamdax understood Chakliux's need to move. She more than any of the women rejoiced that Owl Catcher and the others had been able to return to their village. She knew what it was to long for home. But what if their Near River husbands tried to take them back?

Owl Catcher, in coming to the camp, had traded a living husband for one killed months before during the fighting.

"I am a widow now," she said, "though yesterday I was a wife. But how much better to claim a spirit-husband who was Cousin than a living man who is Near River. Do not expect to see me mourn. During all those moons I lived with the Near Rivers, that was when I sang my mourning songs."

She and the other women, though they had walked all night, worked to help pack and load. Aqamdax caught their excitement, and her hands seemed to work even more quickly.

Only once since her son was born had Night Man taken her into his bed, and she had had a moon blood time since then. Surely, during their traveling, he would stay with the men, guarding the camp, and the next child that grew under her heart would belong to Chakliux.

Their marriage would not come without difficulty. Night Man would be angry when she threw him away. But since her son's death how many women had raised a hand to her ear, leaned close to whisper their anger, their sympathy?

As they worked, Owl Catcher made jokes about her Near River husband, and soon they were all laughing. Then suddenly above the babble, Aqamdax heard Star's cry: "No, no! It is not good that these slave women have come back."

Aqamdax left the others and found Star. She was outside Chakliux's tent, arguing with the boy Black Stick.

"What do you know?" Black Stick yelled, his feelings so intense that spittle flew from his mouth as he spoke. "Green Bird is our sister. We thought she might be dead. What if one of your dead brothers had returned? Would you tell him you did not want him here?"

"You want another fight with the Near River warriors?" Star said. "We have only six men left to us. You have forgotten that?"

The women left their work and gathered near Chakliux's lean-to.

"Are the Near Rivers trying to get the women back?" Aqamdax heard Little Mouse ask.

Then Twisted Stalk raised her voice, said, "What good does it do to fight among ourselves? We must be ready to move tomorrow morning. We have meat to pack, dogs to feed, travois to fill. What good will it do to worry about the Near Rivers? Will it make our work lighter?"

But several women lifted their voices into mourning songs and huddled together as if the Near Rivers had already attacked.

"This is foolishness!" Twisted Stalk said to them, and she stomped away, muttering that at least *she* would be ready to leave, that her tent and meat would be packed, that her dog would be fed and fit to haul a travois in the morning.

Star crouched on her haunches, and several others

squatted beside her. Aqamdax knew what it was to be afraid, but what good did fear bring? She went to the women, spoke a riddle.

"Look! What do I see?" she said, and repeated the words until she had their attention. "They come in anger and have no sympathy for our tears."

"The Near Rivers, they come in anger," Star said, her voice like a child's.

"No," said Aqamdax. "Our own men come in anger when they realize we are not ready to travel. You think they will have sympathy for our tears?"

"Who are you to tell us this?" Little Mouse asked. "You were Near River before you came to us and Sea Hunter before that. It seems that no village wants you. Why should we listen to you?"

Several of the others also made insults, and Aqamdax turned away. What good would it do to force their eyes open if they still refused to see?

Then, to her surprise, she heard Star say, "Aqamdax is right. We are foolish to sit here crying when there is something we can do to help ourselves."

She prodded Little Mouse until the woman stood up. Soon they were busy, sorting meat, dismantling drying racks. And Aqamdax hoped that the work would lift the fear from their hearts.

TWENTY-SEVEN

THE NEAR RIVER CAMP

Anaay clasped his hands together, gritted his teeth. He wanted to reach out and thrust Sun Caller aside. Though Sun Caller was repeating what Anaay had told him to say—that it was foolish to fight so quickly after such a disastrous hunt—his stuttering stretched and distorted the words until even a careful listener lost patience.

Best to interrupt before some other hunter does, Anaay told himself, but before he could get to his feet, Many Words stood. He slashed the air with one hand as though to clear away Sun Caller's broken speech.

The Cousin woman Owl Catcher had been Many Words's second wife. She was a slow, witless woman, and Anaay had thought Many Words would be glad she was gone. There was a shortage of men in the Near River Village. Why not be rid of Owl Catcher and choose one of the young girls?

But now as Many Words spoke, Anaay realized that the man wanted to go after Owl Catcher and bring her back by force if necessary, even take on any brothers or cousins who wanted to fight him.

"B-b-better to go with gifts and s-s-soft words," Sun Caller said, and Anaay took the opportunity of Sun Caller's interruption to remind the men of how incompetent the Cousin River women were. They spent their time weeping over dead husbands and fathers and sons. They made boots in the wrong way, so that the lacing rubbed sores into a man's feet, and their hare fur blankets were not nearly thick enough.

"So why worry about those women who left us?" Anaay said. "There are only four of them, and they are not worth much."

The four husbands raised voices in protest, but Anaay shouted out, "You should have kept them as slaves, then they would belong to you and you could go after them. As wives, they have the right to throw you away."

The angry words died. How could the men deny what Anaay said? The women were wives. Each had the rights of a wife.

"They are not worth fighting for," said Third Tree.

Anaay raised his voice to agree, then added, "We have a choice now. We can go after them, fight, perhaps die, or we can return to the winter village, divide ourselves into hunting groups and get the meat we need for winter."

"I ch-choose to hunt," Sun Caller said.

But Many Words cried out, "You think we cannot win? They have no more than six or eight men."

"They have Sok and Chakliux now," said First Eagle.

Many Words spit. "What are they? Two men disgraced, gone to live with their enemies. We should have killed them when they were in our camp."

"They were good enough to return our dead."

"If we fight the Cousins, we could have their caribou and their women," said Many Words.

"You would be willing to die for that?" First Eagle asked.

"I do not plan to die."

"S-some will d-d-die. That is w-war," Sun Caller said quietly.

They continued to squabble. Their words battered against Anaay's ears, but he did not speak until he heard the first whispers of young men sitting near him, blaming Anaay and his vision of caribou for their problems. Then

Anaay stood, pointed rude fingers at those who were whining.

"You and you," he said, "and you, Many Words, go fight. Plan well, for the Cousin People are not fools. But remember, to them the women are daughters and sisters. To us they are merely wives. Go, all of you, and fight, but think of those killed in the last battle, and then decide which of you will die for this new foolishness.

"And as you fight, Sun Caller and I will take our women and dogs and return to the winter village."

Sun Caller stood, and in a surprisingly clear voice said, "It is not the time to fight. It is the time to hunt."

Then he and Anaay went to what remained of their tents, and one by one, the other men also left.

"You could have gone with those four women," K'os said to Dii. "Why did you stay?"

Dii shook her head. "I am wife. I needed to stay with my husband."

"Those women, all of them, had better husbands than yours. Fox Barking is an old man, worthless."

Dii opened her mouth to defend Anaay, but K'os started to laugh. "He has you in his bed most nights, yet your belly does not swell with child. He led us here to the Caribou River, and though he had never hunted at a river crossing would not listen to any of us who know how it is done." She turned her head toward the place where the men had gathered, where they had argued for most of the morning. "My second husband, you knew him, did he lead our men in such a way? Did he ever allow such arguing?"

Dii thought back to those days when Ground Beater was chief hunter of the Cousin River People. It seemed strange that once K'os had been married to the most important man of their village, that she had been mother to the Dzuuggi, Chakliux. But though Dii had been little more than a child, she had heard the whispers about K'os. That she misused her powers as healer, that she had welcomed many men to her bed. How could Ground Beater have been a better leader than Anaay when he tolerated a wife like that? But why say such a thing to K'os when perhaps the memories of those days were the only joy in her life?

K'os shrugged, flipped her hands in the air. "Each woman sees something special in her husband. Since you have decided to stay with Fox Barking, it is best you think he is a good man. Listen, come with me. There are things you should know about your husband, things I have told no one, ever, but now I will tell you."

K'os led her to the brush at the edge of the river, where the many branches would catch and hold their words so others would not hear. She licked her lips and hunkered down on her haunches, and for the first time, Dii thought she saw some nervousness in the woman.

"Once, long ago, when I was still a girl and had not yet become anyone's wife, Fox Barking and two Near River hunters came to our village. My father, in politeness, brought them to our lodge, gave them food and a place to stay for the night. The next day, the men left to return to their winter village. My mother asked me to go to the Grandfather Lake and get spruce root. Those men followed me. . . ." K'os paused, and Dii looked up, met her eyes, saw a wildness there that made her wish she could close her ears to K'os's next words.

"I was bent over digging roots, offering a gift of thanksgiving to the spruce trees, when two of those men attacked me. Fox Barking was not with them. They forced me . . . they forced me . . . ."

K'os's voice caught, and she shielded her eyes with one hand. Her words were quiet when she finally continued. "But Fox Barking came then, and he killed one of them. The other . . . I do not know what he did to him, but the man ran away. Then Fox Barking helped me back to my mother's lodge.

"Everyone thinks I show disrespect when I do not call him by his new name, but now you see that I call him Fox Barking to honor that memory of what he did for me so long ago."

She lifted her chin, and Dii saw that her eyes were dry and hard. Had she imagined the sob that had broken K'os's words?

"But I found a good husband and forgot about Fox Barking until he bought me from Black Mouth. Then I knew that he remembered also. He saw I was not happy as slave, and I began to hope that he would take me as third wife, but he is leader of his village and does not have time for many wives. Besides, how many children can I give him? I am nearly old. It is better that he has you.

"But I do not like living with Gull Beak. Her words are as sharp as her name. Now that I see the men have not followed our women, I have decided that I, too, will go back to the Cousin People. Especially since I know my son Chakliux has decided to live among them. But I do not want to leave this camp without doing something for Fox Barking and for you."

She reached into the otter skin bag that hung at her waist and pulled out a packet bound with red string. "This you can make into a tea to strengthen Fox Barking's seed. He is an old man, and old men sometimes do not give babies as readily as they did when they were young. Soon you will find yourself full of your husband's child."

"How do I use it?" Dii asked, taking the packet.

"Once a day—just a small amount, what you can fit on a fingertip—mix it into boiling water and wait until it is cool."

"Should I take it in morning or evening? Which is better?"

"No," K'os said quickly. "You do not take it. It is for Fox Barking. In evening, before he sleeps, is best, but anytime, once each day, will work. You should probably not tell him what it is for. Old men are sometimes foolish when it comes to things such as this."

"Thank you," Dii said quietly. She reached for K'os's hand, but K'os stood, backed away smiling. "I will leave tonight, so I have much to do."

"Stay safe," Dii said.

"I am always safe," K'os answered.

K'os left in darkness, slipping away from the fires of the camp, ignoring Dii's whispered blessing as she left. It was good to get away from the woman and from her stupid husband. K'os kept low to the ground, and when she came to the place where the men kept their dogs, she spoke softly and ran a hand over each tether until she found the one she had knotted earlier in the day when she had brought the dogs' food.

The animal belonged to Sun Caller and was one of the golden-eyed dogs she and Ground Beater had brought to the Near River winter village. Like all golden-eyes he was a good dog, broad of chest and thick-furred, with good temperament. Though she and Ground Beater had given the Near Rivers golden-eyed dogs, there were still few of them in the village.

They knew little about breeding, these Near River men. Golden-eyes bred true only with other golden-eyes, or sometimes with a dog that had a father or mother that was golden-eyed. The Near Rivers did not isolate the female golden-eyes when they were in heat, and allowed loyalties to brothers or cousins to determine which male dogs were used in breeding. If they could not appreciate the gift she had given them, then why not take it back?

She cut the dog's tether and coaxed him to follow her from the village. Her welcome at the Cousin camp would be mixed, she was sure. The women would be worried about their husbands, but they would be glad for her medicines, and surely the men would be pleased to see a golden-eyed dog returned.

When she was far enough from the camp, she stopped and took one of the packs from her own back and strapped it to the dog's, then gave him a thin piece of dried caribou. She did not like to walk at night, but what choice did she have?

She glanced back over her shoulder at the dim light from the Near Rivers' hearth fires. Even as foolish as they were, it was difficult for her to leave them. She had wanted to watch the parka she had cursed work its destruction on Fox Barking. But perhaps she had already seen enough. What was worse than that caribou hunt? Besides, bad luck spreads to those who stay too close. At least with the powdered baneberry leaves she had given

Dii, her revenge on Fox Barking would be complete. Sad that she would not be there to see it, but each night as she lay in her bed, she would imagine it. That was almost as good.

Now it was time to be with Chakliux. The wife and son she had taken from him were only a beginning. She owed him even more than what Fox Barking would suffer.

TWENTY-EIGHT

THE COUSIN RIVER CAMP

In groups of two or three, the women straggled in at dawn, two handfuls of them, plus sons and daughters, for none had left their children behind when Near River husbands told them they must come on the hunting trip. Which one of them would trust a child to Near River women?

By the time eight more women were in the camp, Chakliux called the men together. They decided it would be foolish to leave their camp now. With all these women coming to them, the Near River husbands would follow. Better to prepare themselves for attack. Better to be ready to fight where they were than to be caught strung out on the trail back to their winter village.

They moved the camp away from the brush of the riverbank, and Chakliux had the boys cut willow and alder trees that could be piled into a fence and used to shelter a man throwing a spear or drawing a bow. The women unpacked the bladders, heart sacks and caribou bellies they had prepared as containers and filled them with extra water in case the attack lasted a long time. Brush from the cut trees was heaped high around all sides of the camp to act as a barrier against arrows and spears. Twisted Stalk was given the task of keeping a hearth fire burning day and night, and bags of food ready for those who got hungry, hot water for any who might need medicines.

Then they waited.

The last woman to come to them was K'os, followed by a large golden-eyed dog.

"A trap!" Sky Watcher called out. "Do not trust her."

But K'os tilted her head back and laughed. "You think I give up my hate so easily? You think I would fight for the Near Rivers after what they have done to us? They kept me as slave."

"It's true," Owl Catcher said. "She was slave to the one you know as Fox Barking."

"Why did you bring the dog?" Sky Watcher asked.

"I'm an old woman. You expect me to carry my own pack?"

Sky Watcher looked at Chakliux. "She's your mother. You tell us what we should do."

Chakliux glanced at Sok.

"I do not know her," Sok said. "It is your decision."

"She gave me medicine for my head once," Willow Leaf said, rubbing a hand through the thick thatch of her hair. "She can help if any of us are wounded."

Chakliux lifted his chin at Twisted Stalk, and also at Bird Caller, Sky Watcher's wife. "You two, you will watch her. If she gives medicines, make her taste them first herself."

Twisted Stalk began to grumble, but Chakliux called to K'os, "For now, you can join us."

"A strange camp you have," K'os said as she led the dog through brush, between packs and tents.

"A sacred camp," Chakliux replied, "made for protection."

"And you give your allegiance so easily," K'os said to him, then looked at the people gathered. "None of you care that in the last fighting Chakliux sided with the Near Rivers? None of you think he is the dangerous one? You are all afraid of me, I who have been slave and treated by the Near Rivers worse than they treat their dogs."

"You complain for nothing," Cut Ear replied. "For a slave you did not live so terribly." She turned her back on K'os.

"If it were not for me, you could all well be dead," K'os answered. "You would have stayed in the village and fought, and probably been killed, burned up in the lodges."

"Few died, K'os," Sok said. "But that is because your son gave warning of the attack."

K'os whirled on the man. "And you, Sok," she said, "you think I do not know who you are? I knew your father long ago. I pray you are not like him."

Sok strode to K'os, raised a hand as though to strike her, but then only grabbed the hood of her parka and dragged her to the hearth fire, flung her to the ground at Twisted Stalk's feet.

"If she causes any problems," he said to Twisted Stalk, "call me. I will kill her."

They sent Cries-loud, Ghaden and Black Stick upstream to hide in the river brush, to watch for the Near River men.

Ghaden was the first to see them coming. A few carried packs, but most were laden only with weapons. His mouth was suddenly so dry he could not call out to the other boys, so he scurried to where he thought Cries-loud would be waiting, but he was not there.

Ghaden's heart was pounding so hard he could feel its beat in his ears, at the back of his wrists and knees. He would have to make his way to the camp alone.

He crept through the brush as quietly as he could. Sweat ran into his eyes, making them tear. When he was nearly to the camp, he sneaked out to the perimeter of the trees, where brush gave way to tundra. If he ran his fastest, he could give some kind of warning before the Near Rivers were close enough to throw their spears.

He took two deep breaths, then burst into the open. The sun was bright that day, and the ground had softened. Twice he misjudged his step and sank to his knees in the red tundra moss which grows thick over small rivulets. He tripped on a tussock of grass, pushed himself to his feet, then heard someone behind him.

Cries-loud? He stopped, looked back. No, one of the

Near River men. Ghaden ran so hard his breath rattled in his throat. Pain cut in from his side, but he did not stop. When the camp's brush fence was close, he lifted his voice to cry out.

"The Near Rivers! The Near Rivers!"

Then a hand clamped down over his shoulder, stopped him so quickly that he fell. Ghaden landed sitting down, and he began to kick. The hunter leaned over him, grabbed his feet and held him upside down. Ghaden looked up and saw that the one who had him was River Ice Dancer.

Suddenly Ghaden wasn't nearly as afraid. River Ice Dancer was older and bigger, but he was still more boy than man. Who could forget that Yaa had smashed River Ice Dancer's nose? Ghaden thrust with his right leg, managed to break River Ice Dancer's hold and kick him in the face. The boy roared, threw Ghaden to the ground, and sat on him. He drew a knife and held it just under Ghaden's chin.

"I might change your mouth for you," he said. "Or perhaps cut out your eyes. . . ."

Then a shadow fell over them. It was a Near River hunter. Ghaden had seen him before but could not remember his name.

The hunter prodded River Ice Dancer with one toe. "We have come to get our women back, not to kill children. Let him up."

River Ice Dancer rubbed his chin. "He kicked me."

The hunter grabbed River Ice Dancer by one arm and heaved him off Ghaden. Ghaden took a long breath and stood up, backed away.

"I'm First Eagle," the other man said. "You are Ghaden, nae?"

Ghaden nodded.

"You live with the Cousin People now?"

"Yes."

"I saw you with your sister during the fighting. When we came to the Cousin River Village. You remember?"

Ghaden didn't know if the man was asking whether he remembered him or the fighting, so he did not answer.

Who could forget the fighting? But how could he remember one man among many? There had been too much smoke, too much fear.

"We will fight you again," Ghaden said. "You did not kill all of us then, and you will not kill all of us now."

"Ah, little man, you remind me of your father. I remember the finger he offered to the spirits in exchange for your life."

His father? Summer Face, the old man who had died? His father had cut off a finger so Ghaden could live? When Ghaden was staying in the shaman's lodge, recovering from the knife wound, his father had died. No one had told him how, and Ghaden had not wondered much about the death. His father had been old. But if his father sacrificed a finger for him, would that have made him die? Did men, weakened by age, die of such things?

He felt his eyes fill with tears, and angrily raised an arm to dash them away.

"You do not need to be afraid," First Eagle said, and there was a softness in his voice that surprised Ghaden. "We have come to get our wives. That is all."

Ghaden swallowed down his fear, willed away his tears. "If they do not want to go with you," he said in a quiet voice, "Sok and Chakliux will not make them."

An old man joined them, then more Near River hunters. Ghaden had seen them all before. The old man was Fox Barking. He was a lazy one and often rude, but now he seemed to be telling the others what to do.

They began to talk. Most were angry, but First Eagle seemed only sad. No one was looking at Ghaden. He dropped to hands and knees and crawled out between their legs. Fox Barking caught him by his parka hood and lifted him up.

"Stay here!" Fox Barking said. "Do you think you are Cousin River now? Have you forgotten that you once lived with us?"

He set Ghaden down and thumped the dull end of his spear against Ghaden's back. Ghaden slumped down, sat on his haunches until the men were ready to continue toward the camp. Most had argued against fighting, but others joked about killing the rest of the Cousin River People, being rid of them once and for all.

When they started walking, Fox Barking kept one hand twisted into Ghaden's parka hood. Ghaden loosened the drawstring, but Fox Barking merely tightened his grip until Ghaden felt as though someone were choking him, but still he found enough air to say, "My sister, Yaa, is there in the Cousin camp."

"Who?" Fox Barking asked.

"Yaa, my sister." Ghaden tried to turn his head to see if Fox Barking understood, but the man's grip was too tight. "She is not Cousin. Do not kill her."

Chakliux had asked three of the newly returned Cousin women to stay near the brush fence and call out if they saw one of the boys sent as watchers. A foolish decision, Chakliux told himself when the first woman screamed that she had seen Near River hunters. The other two began to cry, one falling to the ground and sobbing so hard that all the Cousin men came running from one of the tents, spears in their hands.

"They have attacked?" Sok asked.

Chakliux blew out his breath in disgust and tilted his head toward the three women. "No, but they saw something."

"Probably a ground squirrel," Take More said.

"No," said Sok. "Look. Near River men."

The Near River men walked openly, without trying to hide themselves or their weapons. As they drew close, Fox Barking pushed his way from the center of the group, and Chakliux could see he had Ghaden.

"Ghaden," Sok said, lifting his chin toward the boy. "But what about Cries-loud and Black Stick?"

"Say nothing," Chakliux told him. "The women do not need to worry about their sons."

Then he heard the sharp intake of a breath, saw that Black Stick's mother was peering over a low spot in the fence. Chakliux waited for an explosion of tears and mourning cries, but she straightened, held her head high, as though she herself were a warrior, and stood waiting, one hand clasping the woman's knife that hung from a sheath around her neck.

The Near River men stopped a few paces from the brush fence, and Fox Barking called out, "You see, I have one of your boys. He says he's a Cousin warrior, though he tells me that his sister is Near River."

Ghaden heard the ridicule in the man's voice, and he struggled against Fox Barking's hold, but the man twisted his fist more tightly into the hood so that Ghaden could scarcely breathe.

"You have our wives?"

Chakliux looked at Sok, and Sok said, "Speak for us."

Sky Watcher nodded his agreement, but Night Man averted his eyes.

"Each woman here is sister or mother, daughter or cousin," Chakliux said. "None is wife."

The Near River hunter Many Words stepped forward, raised a throwing lance over his head. "You lie, Chakliux," he said. "I thought Dzuuggi were forbidden to lie. My wife, Owl Catcher, is there with you."

"Any man who calls my brother a liar is a fool," Sok said.

Many Words continued his insults, but Chakliux cut him off. "The women in this camp are here by choice. Are Near River women no longer allowed to throw away their husbands?"

"There is one who is not wife but slave," Fox Barking said. "Perhaps she has not told you that."

"Which one?" Chakliux asked, though he knew.

"The woman K'os."

"We are lucky that only K'os is slave," Chakliux told the Cousin men. "I thought there might be more."

"You see," Fox Barking called, "I have found a small slave of my own."

He lifted Ghaden by his parka hood. The boy flailed out with feet and fists, finally landing a kick that made Fox Barking drop him. Ghaden scrambled to his feet and ran toward the brush fence. Fox Barking drew back his spear and threw it, butt first. It slammed into the center of Ghaden's back. He cried out and fell to the ground.

Several Cousin men raised voices in anger, but Fox Barking merely smiled, and the scar that marked his face drew one side of his lips high to show his teeth.

Then Chakliux heard a scream, and before he could stop her, Star had torn her way through the brush fence. Aqamdax went after her, knelt with her beside Ghaden. Then Chakliux, too, began to break through the fence, but Sok caught him by the shoulders, shouted at him until Chakliux was still.

"They might not harm a woman," Sok said, "but you . . ."

"Would the Near Rivers have survived the first Cousin attack if I had not told them what to do?" Chakliux asked. "Each man out there owes me his life. You know that."

"I know that," Sok said, "but anger makes a man forget his debts. And his honor."

Sok gestured toward Sky Watcher and Man Laughing, Take More and Night Man. Each stood ready, spears and throwing boards in their hands.

Then Chakliux and Sok also lifted their weapons. Chakliux took in deep breaths to keep his hands from shaking as he set the notched end of a spear into the chip of ivory that held it in place on his spear thrower.

Aqamdax raised her head, looked at Fox Barking. He was a coward, full of fear and of hatred, angry with those who showed wisdom or courage and disdaining any he considered weaker than himself. She could feel the reassuring beat of Ghaden's heart under the tips of her fingers. Fox Barking's spear had knocked the wind from the boy. She prayed it had not broken his spine. She leaned down, saw Ghaden's eyelids flicker.

"You are all right?" she asked.

Star had been screaming since she saw Ghaden fall, cursing Fox Barking and the Near River men. But Aqamdax was able to capture one of her hands, to hold her fingers to a pulse point at the side of Ghaden's neck. The woman's eyes widened, and she stopped screaming, though tears still coursed down her face.

"He is not dead. He is not even hurt," Fox Barking

said. "But do not try to take him. I caught him. He is my slave—to do with as I wish."

"You would enslave a boy from your own village?" Aqamdax asked. She looked into his face, then in insult cut her eyes quickly away. "This man leads you?" Aqamdax said to the other River hunters. "I was with your people only a few moons, but still I remember that he often stayed home when others were hunting. I remember that his second wife's lodge was falling apart, yet he could not keep his eyes or hands from the young girls." She shook her head. "And he leads you?"

Fox Barking pulled a short, thrusting lance from the sheath slung on his back.

Aqamdax wondered if he would risk killing her. Who was she to speak in such a way to hunters? Why should they listen to a woman, especially one who did not even carry River blood? But she knew Fox Barking was a coward. Surely he would realize that Cousin men had spears ready. She waited for his ridicule, his insults, but when he spoke, he said, "I am Anaay, Caribou Singer. I lead these people. Our village is large and strong. We defeated the Cousin warriors. What are they to you? We heard you were only a slave here."

"It is true, I came as slave, but now I am wife, and as wife I have chosen to stay. This boy does not belong to you, as slave or by his choice. He is Cousin."

"He was Near River before he was Cousin, and that is something you cannot change."

"He is my brother by blood, through our mother, who was killed in your village. If he cannot be Cousin because first he was Near River, then it must be true that he cannot be Near River because first he was Sea Hunter."

Fox Barking's eyes narrowed, and his face reddened. "He knows nothing of Sea Hunters. How can he be something he has never seen? You are foolish—"

One of the other Near River men interrupted, speaking softly so that Aqamdax could make out only a few words, but Star whispered, "He tells Fox Barking that there are more important things to think about than Ghaden."

Aqamdax nodded, leaned down to ask Ghaden if he

could move. "I'm not hurt," he said, and Aqamdax could hear the impatience in his voice. "I'm sorry I got caught."

He raised himself to hands and knees, arched his back then got to his feet. When Fox Barking saw him, he let out a roar.

"We are going back inside our camp," Aqamdax said.

"Prove that he is Sea Hunter!" Fox Barking demanded. "If he is, I will let him go!"

Aqamdax caught her lip in her teeth. How could she prove such a thing?

Ghaden turned to Fox Barking and, holding himself very straight, said, *"Tutxakuxtxin hi? Unangax uting."*

Aqamdax covered her mouth in surprise. Who had taught Ghaden First Men words? Their mother?

"What did he say?" Fox Barking asked.

"He speaks the language of our people, the First Men," Aqamdax answered. "The ones you call Sea Hunters. He asks, 'Can you hear?' Then he tells you he is of the First Men."

Fox Barking stood with his mouth open in surprise, and Aqamdax pushed Ghaden ahead of her through the brush fence. She did not see Star pick up Fox Barking's spear, but looked back as she heard the man cry out. It was a beautiful spear, the birch shaft fletched with dark feathers and capped with a walrus ivory foreshaft, a heavy chert point. It was banded in the black and white of a Near River weapon but also carried Fox Barking's ownership marks of blue and yellow.

Star raised her head and looked into Fox Barking's eyes. She drew the chert point across her arm, smiled as she cursed the spear with woman's blood.

TWENTY-NINE

After arguments and discussion, the Cousin River men finally agreed that the Near Rivers could speak to those women who had been their wives. They met just outside the brush fence, and Chakliux or Sok stood beside each of the women, pressing a hand to sheathed knives hung at their waists when any man tried to force a woman to come with him.

Three wives decided to go back with their husbands. Each of those women had no close family members still alive among the Cousin River People, and one was pregnant with her Near River husband's child. The other women chose to stay, and to Chakliux's surprise, one of the Near River men, First Eagle, asked permission to join his wife, Awl, in the Cousin camp.

Night Man and Sky Watcher voiced their disagreement, but Sok said First Eagle was a good hunter and praised him for his courage. Awl was his first wife, a niece to Twisted Stalk. They could not doubt that she was a strong woman. She had managed the walk to the Cousin camp in spite of broken ribs.

Besides, Sok said, they needed another hunter in their village, many more hunters. Chakliux, Man Laughing and Take More agreed with Sok, and so First Eagle was allowed to stay. Then there was only Fox Barking and his demands to have K'os returned to him as slave.

"She is not wife," he called out.

Who could disagree? And who among the Cousin River People truly wanted K'os back with them?

"She is your mother, you must decide," Sok told Chakliux.

"I will speak to him," K'os said. "I'm not afraid. I will tell him I belong to my son, Chakliux."

Chakliux looked down at K'os, at her beautiful face. A man who only glanced at that face, and at K'os's lithe body, would believe she was young, but when a man looked into her eyes could he think she was anything but evil?

She pushed back her parka hood, pulled her hair out of the pins that held it in place behind her head. Glistening black, it fell past her waist, as shining as obsidian. She looked over her shoulder at the men standing around Chakliux.

"Perhaps there is one here who would be my husband," she said. Sok laughed, and Sky Watcher shook his head, but Take More narrowed his eyes, seemed to consider her offer.

"There are few among us who want to die as your husbands have died," Chakliux said.

Take More's eyes widened, and Chakliux hoped he was remembering the stories of Name Giver's slow death, the disease that seemed to eat his belly until he could do nothing but vomit blood. And who would want to burn as Ground Beater had in a stranger's lodge?

Then Take More, too, turned away, and the softness in K'os's face turned to hatred.

"You, Chakliux," she snarled, "I cannot believe I call you son! Any other man would have arranged to buy his mother's freedom. Have you forgotten that you owe me your life?"

"That debt was paid by Gguzaakk and our son," Chakliux told her, his words bitter and edged with grief.

He thought he saw a flicker of fear in K'os's eyes, but it left so quickly he was not sure. Could she be afraid of Gguzaakk's spirit? Did she feel Gguzaakk's presence, as he sometimes did? Or was she truly afraid that he would not stand with her against Fox Barking and the Near River men?

"We go now," he said, grasping a spear in his left hand. He lifted his chin toward the dog K'os had brought with her, told her to bring him.

When she opened her mouth to protest, Chakliux said, "You are afraid I will offer a trade for the dog and not you?"

Then K'os was quiet and followed him from the camp, through the brush fence to the Near River men.

Anaay tensed when he saw Chakliux. His best spear lay tainted on the ground, and though he had others, it was not good for a man to fight without his strongest weapon. K'os followed Chakliux leading the golden-eyed dog she had stolen.

A riddle came to his mind, and Anaay laughed at his own cunning.

"Look! What do I see?" he called. "Three dogs." He frowned when Chakliux showed no reaction to the insult. Then he said, "You have brought her back to me. Or perhaps you want to buy her for yourself." He laughed, long, hard. "What do you offer?" he finally said. "She is worth a caribou just for a night in your bed."

"I would give that for her," River Ice Dancer said.

Anaay flicked his fingers at him in insult.

"Of course, being her son," Anaay said to Chakliux, "you have probably not enjoyed her that way." But he stuck his tongue into his cheek, implying otherwise. Several of the Near River men laughed.

"I do not want her," Chakliux said.

K'os screamed out a curse.

Chakliux said, "Two caribou for the dog."

"No," Anaay answered.

But Least Weasel stepped forward. He was a tall, thin man, his face like a hawk's face, with small round eyes and a hooked nose. He looked down at Anaay, pushed past him to Chakliux. "The dog is my father's," he said. "We did not have a good hunt this year, Chakliux. I will take three caribou for him, with the hides."

"Our women have already butchered and boned the caribou. I will give you the meat of three, the intestines of one, stuffed with fat and dried berries, plus two hides."

"And two bladders, scraped for use as water carriers."

"Done," Chakliux said.

He left K'os, went back through the brush fence, then he, Sok and Sky Watcher came out carrying the meat and hides he had promised. When he brought the last of the meat, Anaay stepped forward and took K'os's arm, began to pull her away.

K'os spit at Chakliux and hissed, "I wish I had left you on the Grandfather Rock. You need to be dead."

Then Chakliux said, "The same price for K'os that I gave for the dog."

Anaay looked at Chakliux, then at K'os. Suddenly in the dark centers of her eyes he saw himself again as a young man lying between her legs, thrusting into her until the blood flowed. He released his clasp on her arm so quickly that she nearly fell.

"I will take the caribou," he said.

When Chakliux returned with K'os, the men in the camp would not look at him. Even Sok turned away, muttering insults about women like K'os.

"Go help Aqamdax," Chakliux told K'os. "There is much to do." He turned his back on her, stood looking out through the brush fence as the Near River men left carrying the meat Chakliux had given.

"Do you have any men or women injured?" K'os asked, standing beside him. Then she drew in her breath, pointed at movement in the alders near the river.

Chakliux squinted, then one corner of his mouth lifted in a smile as Cries-loud and Black Stick darted through the hole in the brush fence. He called out for Snow-in-her-hair and Black Stick's mother. They greeted the boys with tears.

"In this camp today," Chakliux told K'os, "you will help the women."

"I am your mother. Do not consider yourself my owner," K'os said.

"My mother is dead," Chakliux replied. "Today, you are slave and will help the women. Tomorrow, you are free. You will leave us in the morning." Chakliux clasped the front of her parka, gripped tightly. "For Gguzaakk, for my son, I should have killed you long ago. Take the freedom I give you and be grateful."

He released his grip on her, and she hissed out, "You have given me death!"

"I know you better than that, K'os," he said. He lifted his chin toward a storage lean-to beside his tent. "You can clean that out. It is shelter enough for one night. In the morning, you will leave."

She turned her back on him, and he took the golden-eyed dog, tied it at the side of his lean-to, then he went from tent to tent, looking at all the dogs in the camp. At Sok's lean-to, he stopped, stood for a moment considering. He jumped when Sok, who had come up to stand behind him, began to speak.

"You gave them too much," Sok said.

"It is a good dog," Chakliux said.

"Not for the dog. For K'os."

"There are some debts that take much to repay."

"I do not want her here. Bad luck follows her."

"She will be gone by tomorrow."

Sok nodded his approval, and Chakliux pointed with his chin toward one of Sok's dogs, a black male with a white belly and chest, large head, small ears.

"That dog," Chakliux asked. "Would you take a golden-eye for him?"

K'os complained and grumbled as she worked, and though the others ignored her, Yaa found herself watching. She remembered when Aqamdax was K'os's slave, how wicked K'os had been. When Cries-loud convinced Yaa that Red Leaf did not kill Day Woman, Yaa's first thought had been of K'os. Surely she was a woman evil enough to kill. But when Red Leaf died, K'os had been slave, and truly she looked like a slave, her parka ragged and thin, her face gaunt. What slave would escape to kill, then return to her master?

So K'os could not be the killer, but if it was not her, then it must be someone who lived in the Cousin River Village. Yaa shivered and clasped her woman's knife, the only weapon she had, and wished she was a boy with a long-bladed hunters' knife to protect herself and Ghaden.

THIRTY

K'os waited until the darkest part of the night. She knew the cycle of the moon, that it would hide its face until nearly dawn. She would have to walk carefully in the darkness, but with the dog it would not be difficult. She had worked the day before, as Chakliux had ordered her, at first in anger but then in glee, as she realized the women were so busy they would not notice the meat she stole.

With the many caribou they had killed, the Cousin River People would live through this winter. But there would come a year when the caribou were not so plentiful, and then what would they do, with so few men to hunt and so many women to feed?

Of course, some of the old ones would die this winter. They always did. And there were always other deaths, unexpected.

When she was a slave in the Near River Village, K'os had asked about Gull Beak's sister-wife, Day Woman. Where was she? Had she died?

Gull Beak had said Day Woman decided to leave the village with her sons Sok and Chakliux. It was best. The woman was a problem, Gull Beak told her. Always crying, always worrying. K'os had expected to see Day Woman here. She was old, but not too old to help with a caribou hunt.

K'os had whispered her questions to Aqamdax, had claimed concern for Day Woman out of friendship, but Aqamdax knew her too well, smiled in scorn and told K'os not to mention the woman's name. She was dead.

"Sickness or accident?" K'os had asked.

"Sickness," Aqamdax had finally answered, but her hesitation told K'os there was something Aqamdax had chosen not to tell.

"Long Eyes?" K'os had asked.

"Back in the winter village with Ligige'," Aqamdax replied.

"Ligige'?"

"Aunt to Sok and Chakliux," Aqamdax said. "From the Near River Village."

"So, she, too, came with my son?"

"Yes."

K'os had nodded toward Snow-in-her-hair. "That one also."

"Yes, as Sok's wife."

"He had another wife, as I recall, though I have forgotten her name," K'os said.

"Let it stay forgotten," said Aqamdax. "She is dead."

"Accident or sickness?" K'os again asked.

This time without hesitation, Aqamdax answered, "Sickness."

In the darkness, K'os crept from the storage lean-to, her pack in her hands. She took the hare fur blanket Star had loaned her for the night. She had laughed to discover that Chakliux had taken Star as wife, offered sympathy for Aqamdax's dead baby, but held a spiteful joy in her heart when Star told her what Night Man had done.

"Young babies often die," K'os had told Star, and looked down at Star's belly.

Star had crossed her hands over her stomach and hurried away. K'os would have liked to stay, to see the child that Star would give Chakliux. This one she would most likely allow to live, even if it was a boy. Chakliux might find more anguish in watching his son raised by a woman like Star than in losing the boy as an infant.

K'os went to the makeshift storage caches, to those that held the best meat, and filled her packs. Then she returned to her lean-to, took the water bladders, rolled the bedding mats and crept to where Chakliux had tied the dogs. There were four, and she approached them cautiously, offered pieces of meat to keep them quiet. She knew he had put the golden-eye nearest the tent door. In the darkness she groped for the dog's tether, cut it and led the animal out to the brush fence. She was stopped there by one of the boys stationed as watcher.

"I am Chakliux's mother," she told him. "You know me, K'os."

"He said you were leaving tomorrow."

"I am leaving now," she said, and slipped out through the brush fence before he asked any questions about the dog.

She had counted paces from the fence the day before. Eight from where she had stood with Fox Barking. The other distance she had measured only with her eyes. She took three long steps, stooped down and groped the ground, moved slowly closer to the brush fence. Finally she found Fox Barking's fine birch-shafted spear, chuckled in satisfaction.

She turned it point up, spoke a curse against Fox Barking, then another against Chakliux. Those two men, between them, had ruined her life, had robbed her of all good things. But already poor stupid Dii would have begun giving Fox Barking K'os's poison. As for Chakliux, she would find something better. He had already done a fine job of cursing himself, taking a wife like Star.

K'os pulled the dog with her into the river. The cold water bit at her legs, and the current tried to sweep her from her feet, but she held tightly to the dog, allowed him to float her through the deepest parts. When they got to the other side, K'os changed into dry boots and gave the dog time to lick his feet and legs, then she looked up at the sky, set her course by the tail of stars the River People had named for the Cet'aeni, those tailed enemies who lived in trees, and she started toward the Four Rivers Village.

Chakliux was awakened by Star's screech, but he merely rubbed his eyes, stretched. Then she was beside him, shaking him, pulling him from his blankets.

"Your mother . . . your mother . . . your mother . . ."

Chakliux reached up and placed his fingers over her lips. "Be quiet. My mother is gone, I know. And she took one of the dogs."

Star raised her eyebrows at him in surprise. "The golden-eye," she said.

"No. Sok has the golden-eye. I traded the dog for one of his."

"You knew your mother would go? She told you?"

"I have lived long enough with her to know she would do such a thing, and that she would take the dog and steal some meat."

"And you let her?"

"What is best, to have her here with us or to lose a little meat and Sok's old dog?"

Slowly Star smiled, but then she thrust her bottom lip out into a pout. "I wanted her to stay long enough to make me a fine parka. I thought she might if you gave her the pelts." She tilted her head up and closed her eyes. "I wanted fox fur and lynx with strips of black from the leg skins of swans. I wanted shell beads and flicker beaks for luck. So who will make it now?"

Chakliux's stomach twisted at the thought of Star's being mother to his children. Would their sons or daughters be like her, with minds so bent and foolish? He pushed her away from his bed, and in doing so saw that his fingernails were rimmed with blood from the butchering. He remembered the nights he had touched Star as wife, and it suddenly seemed that the blood was her blood, a curse on all he did, pulling away his power and protection.

He flexed his fingers, and they were stiff, as if the blood had spread from his nails to his hands. And then it was the blood of all the men, Cousin and River, killed in the fighting.

He had told himself that he had done what he could, but was that really true? Had he worked hard enough for peace? Or had he allowed anger and impatience to weaken his prayers?

There had been moons when he was merely content to be a hunter, not Dzuuggi, not leader. And there had been that long winter when he went in search of Aqamdax, traveled all the way to the First Men, thinking she had escaped to that faraway place, when she had only been taken as a slave to the Cousin River Village.

"You will find someone to make my parka?" Star asked him.

He frowned at her, shook his head to clear his thoughts, then he lost all patience, answered curtly. "Do as all women do. Make it yourself."

He pulled on boots, leggings and parka, then left the tent, strode quickly away so she would not catch up with him. He walked past Sok's tent to assure himself that the golden-eyed dog was there. He was, sitting alert and watching the activity of the camp while Sok's other dogs slept. Then Chakliux went to the river.

Frost whitened the ground, making the grass brittle under his feet. The few dark leaves that remained on the alders rattled in the wind, fluttered like a caribou's ragged spring coat. But each of Chakliux's steps released the clean, pungent smell the earth takes on before winter.

He took off his boots, waded into a shallow sandy pool, breaking through the skin of ice that webbed the surface. He scrubbed his hands together under the water until the blood was gone from his nails and his skin was bright red from the cold. He looked into the river. It had been dark with silt after the hunt, stained with caribou blood. Now it ran clear, and Chakliux could see the rounded cobbles that covered the riverbed, gold and brown.

The part of him that was otter longed to swim, to feel the pull of the current and the clean rush of the water. He stepped back to the shore, took off his leggings and parka, sliced into the water with a shallow dive, skimmed the bottom. The cold pressed against his chest, reached for his heart with strong grasping fingers, numbed his body to everything but the power the river held within itself even now, as it prepared to rest, dark and silent under winter ice.

THIRTY-ONE

K'os stopped, took the pack from her back and set it on a raised tussock. The sun was up over the horizon, and it was a relief to be walking in light. She slipped down her pants, lifted her parka and spread her legs to urinate. The dog raised his leg against a tussock, and K'os laughed.

He looked up at her, and she gasped, bent closer. She grabbed his muzzle, lifted his head. The dog had dark brown eyes, and the fur circling his mouth was sprinkled with gray. He growled at her, and she cuffed him. He drew his teeth back, and she lifted Fox Barking's spear. He cowered, his back legs trembling, tail tucked. K'os ground her teeth and screamed out her anger, slammed the butt end of the spear into the earth.

Then suddenly she tilted back her head and laughed. Why not appreciate Chakliux's trick? After all, who had taught him devious ways?

She squatted on her heels, studied the dog, thinking. She was strong enough to carry the dog's packs as well as her own, but was she willing to give up the protection a dog offered?

Against what? she asked herself. If he had been the young golden-eye, that was one thing, but this animal? A good dog would have leaped to attack when she threatened him with a spear.

How far could she walk until he would no longer find his way back to the camp? Perhaps another half day. It was at least a three-day walk yet to the Four Rivers Village. If the animal could help her carry part of the load even a short way, she would take advantage of that.

She dug through her river otter medicine skin and found the packet she had bound with red-dyed sinew tied in four double knots. She pulled out a raven's feather she had been saving and broke off several strands of her hair, then twisted them around the center of the feather.

"Look, what do I see?" she said aloud, holding the feather across her eyes, "Darkness, even in sunlight." The dog whined at her words.

THE COUSIN RIVER CAMP

The dog came to them three days later. Squirrel brought him into camp. He was limping, his paws filled with xos cogh thorns. An amulet was bound around his neck: a raven's feather tied with long strands of dark hair.

Chakliux burned the amulet outside camp, then he buried the ashes. Even K'os's power was less than fire, less than earth. He pulled the spines from the dog's paws and rubbed plantain mixed with caribou fat into the wounds. Throughout that day, the dog drank much water, ate grasses, vomited bile.

After the dog defecated a loose, bloody stool, Twisted Stalk fed him a tea of yellow dock and washed his feet in water filled with shredded willow bark, but the animal only grew weaker. Chakliux took him outside camp, sat with him, lifted prayers, sang chants, something he had never done for a dog. When the animal finally died, Chakliux burned the body as he had burned the amulet, then buried the ashes deep in the earth.

He prayed and fasted a day and a night before returning to camp, then washed himself in the river. But though he did all these things, fear pressed into his heart. He answered questions in rudeness and could not stay away from the brush fence, as though he was waiting for the Near Rivers to attack. When his hands were busy packing meat and repairing weapons, his eyes were on the people, watching them, wondering if the dog had brought some illness as a part of K'os's revenge.

THE NEAR RIVER CAMP

For three days after the Near River men returned to their caribou camp, Anaay sent hunters out to search for game. He ordered the women to begin packing for the journey back to the winter village, then went into his tent, told Dii to keep the people away.

She brought him water and stew made with the delicate head meat of the few caribou they had managed to salvage from the hunt. He ate, but when she turned her eyes toward his bed, offering the comfort of her body, he refused her.

She scolded herself for her relief and tried to keep her thoughts away from those Cousin women who had left them. Awl and her husband had shamed the whole camp when they decided to stay with the Cousin River People. Most of the other women had also stayed, and their husbands had returned without them. With fewer Cousin in the camp, the Near River women were more blatant with their insults.

That night, sleeping alone in the tent she had once shared with K'os, Dii again dreamed of caribou. She woke in panic, sure they were about to trample their lean-tos. She crawled from the tent, lifted her eyes to the moon. It was no longer full, but gave light enough for her to pick out each tent and hearth. She stood and realized that the ground was not shaking. There was silence, save for the occasional call of a night animal.

Then she knew that the shaking had again been in her bones and that the caribou were east of the camp, a day's walk.

"You are foolish," she whispered. "Caribou do not sing to women."

But still she could hear them above the silence of the night. The clicking of their legs was loud in her ears, the soft thunder of their hooves, the grunts of the bulls, soon to be in rut. When she shut her eyes, she could see them.

For a long time under the moon, she knelt at the center of the camp and watched caribou.

THE FOUR RIVERS VILLAGE

Red Leaf saw the woman coming into camp, and at first thought she was a hunter, so boldly did she walk, head up, with a fine spear in one hand, a large pack on her back. She was alone. What woman walked alone any distance? And she was tall, taller than most women. But when she drew close, Red Leaf could not mistake the face.

It was K'os, the Cousin River woman. Red Leaf had pitied her when she lost her husband in a fire during their visit to the Near River winter village. But they had made a poor choice in staying with the old woman Song. Elders could be careless with fires, and Song had kept a Sea Hunter lamp burning in her lodge. What foolishness!

So what was K'os doing here? She was one of those taken captive to the Near River Village. Hadn't Aqamdax told her that? Then surely K'os would have heard what Red Leaf had done. Red Leaf turned away before the woman saw her face. Her chest felt as though someone were standing on it, and she could not breathe.

Now what choice did she have? Cen and the hunters would probably be gone until the next full moon. Perhaps beyond that. She would have to leave the village before then, but at least she would have time to pack food and warm clothing.

For a moment she saw her son Cries-loud's face, his tears when she left the Cousin River Village. Her throat tightened. Two sons lost to her, and now a second husband.

Then she heard K'os call, a greeting strangers used with one another, something more appropriate from man to man.

Red Leaf did not turn. Instead she quickened her steps, walked toward Cen's lodge. Though the snow that had almost cost her life had long ago melted, the ground was frozen hard under her feet, so that each of her steps jarred her bones.

Then a hand was on her shoulder, and she heard K'os say, "You did not hear my greeting?"

Red Leaf stopped but did not turn, kept her head down.

"Are the men hunting?" K'os asked.

"Yes, they hunt," Red Leaf said quietly.

K'os rudely tilted her head down to try to look into Red Leaf's face, and Red Leaf hoped the tunnel of her parka hood made shadows enough to distort her features.

"Is there an elder I might speak to? Someone who would be willing to give me shelter?" K'os asked. "Though the people in this village do not know me, they knew a brother of mine who lived here long ago. He and his wife are both dead now, I was told, but he was a fine hunter. Someone will remember him."

Red Leaf pointed toward a lodge at the center of the village, then, with head still down, walked around K'os. She did not let herself breathe until she crawled into the entrance tunnel of Cen's lodge.

THE COUSIN RIVER CAMP

Aqamdax watched Chakliux pace, and it seemed as though his nervousness seeped into her hands, making her fingers clumsy. She and Star were working together, cutting long strips of lacing from a caribou hide.

The excitement of the successful hunt had passed, and the men were bored, a few going out to look for moose or caribou, usually coming back with nothing more than a few white-fronted geese.

Women were tired; even the boys who had come on the hunt were growing whiny. Their small squabbles escalated into arguments between mothers, and sometimes even the uncles or fathers became involved. The people needed to know when they would move back to the winter village. Already two families had left, hauling away their shares of the meat and hides.

Aqamdax and Star finished their cutting, and Star began to pester Bird Caller and Owl Catcher, who were scraping a caribou hide. Aqamdax saw Chakliux slip outside through the brush fence. Night Man was sitting with Man Laughing, their heads bent over a game of throwing sticks. Night Man was losing; Aqamdax could tell by the scowl on his face. She left the pile of lacing and walked to the edge of the camp, trying to keep tents and people between herself and her husband. Then she wondered why she bothered. She did not care what he thought, and it was apparent he had no concern for her, gambling away their food and hides to Man Laughing.

She slipped through the opening in the brush fence, told herself that she had not come to talk to Chakliux, only to escape the noise and people of the camp.

She did not see Chakliux, was disgusted with herself at her disappointment, but a movement at the edge of the river drew her eyes. She walked that way, her breath catching at each step until she was sure it was him, not wolf or bear. He crouched in a growth of willow, their long thin leaves yellowed by the frost and too brittle now to gather and store in oil for winter food. She slipped through the trees, squatted beside him as she had done so often when they both lived in the Near River Village, when they had shared stories and were learning one another's languages.

He was sitting on a rock, slightly higher than she was, and the cool, pale sun of autumn lit his face so it was nearly without shadow. The wind blew his hair back from his forehead, pulled strands from the dark braids.

She smiled, but he did not return that smile. "We will leave soon for the winter village?" she asked him.

He did not answer, and she felt the familiar unrest that had plagued her when she was a girl, as though her muscles fought against her skin. She wanted him to talk to her, to tell her why he had not even looked at her these past few days. Now that the caribou hunt was over, now that they would soon return to winter camp, did he regret his promise to take her as wife? Did he think there would be too many problems with Night Man and Star? Had he said he wanted her as wife only to help her through her wild grief at the death of her son?

The emptiness of that grief still lived with her, woke her in the night with dreams of Angax floating away across the Grandfather Lake. She closed her eyes against the burn of tears, pushed back her parka hood, and allowed herself to think only of the warmth of the sun. Soon enough that warmth would be gone. Already the ground under her feet was cold, warning that winter was close, but why think so far ahead? No one, not even the strongest hunter, could be sure of living through any winter.

She relaxed, content to be beside Chakliux, and when sleep had almost claimed her, she heard his voice, soft and deep, whisper, "What do I see? The winter grows old and in anger sends the wind."

She opened her eyes and turned her head to look at him.

"The winter is not yet here," she said.

He smiled at her, but it was a sad smile. "It's not a riddle about winter," he told her. "It's about my mother."

"What does it mean?" Aqamdax asked.

"It means that when she cannot control what is happening to her, she becomes angry and tries to bring destruction to anyone near."

"You think she has stayed close, then, or perhaps walked back to our winter village?"

Chakliux shook his head. "If she was close, she would have done more than send the dog back to us. He had walked a long way. Of course, he was old and might have gotten lost."

"But the Cousin People hunt here every year, do they not?" Aqamdax asked. "The dog had been here before."

"Yes."

"You think, then, that she cursed us?"

"The amulet was some kind of curse."

"But Sok told us that you burned it and buried the ashes. How could she be stronger than that? If she has so much power, why did she stay slave to Fox Barking? If she has so much power, why did she leave when you told her to leave? Why did she take the old dog and not the golden-eye?"

Chakliux smiled again, and this time the smile lighted his eyes. He reached over to smooth back Aqamdax's hair. "Why do I worry about her when I will soon have the wife I have wanted for so long?" he said.

At his words, Aqamdax had to blink back tears. Then once more they sat in silence, but Aqamdax's thoughts were no longer dark visions of sorrow and death.

THIRTY-TWO

THE FOUR RIVERS VILLAGE
The old man called himself Tree Climber, a foolish name
for someone who scarcely had the strength to sit upright.
His eyes were rheumy and looked sore. That was a good
thing, K'os thought; a healer could do something about
that. She felt the resentment of the old man's wife. The
woman had offered K'os nothing, not even water, until
her husband scolded her, made an insult that included her
brother and dogs.

K'os had pulled off both inner and outer parkas as soon
as she came into the lodge. She laid them over her lap,
tucked her hands under their warm fur. She saw the
woman—Sand Fly, her husband called her—smile at her
gnarled hands, and K'os hated her for that. But Tree
Climber's eyes had stayed on the round, dark-nippled
mounds that were K'os's breasts, peaking over the furred
parkas.

Neither Tree Climber nor Sand Fly asked the questions
that most would have asked: Why did she travel alone?
Where was her husband? Her village?

People had to be careful if a woman alone came to their
lodge. What if she was an outcast, driven from a village
for doing some terrible thing? But then, too, she might be
an animal-woman, sometimes human, sometimes not.

Who would choose to insult someone like that? Who would refuse to give her food or water, a safe place to stay?

It had been a long time since K'os had enjoyed the warmth of a winter lodge, a long time since she had eaten a bowl of hot food. Tree Climber, old as he was, deserved some politeness, even if his wife was rude. So, though he did not ask questions, K'os said, "You heard of the fighting between the Cousin and Near River Villages?"

"The trader Cen lives here now," Tree Climber said. "He told us."

In her surprise, K'os almost forgot what she had been going to say. Cen! She had thought he was dead. Then he had not been killed in the fighting. Coward! He must have deserted the Cousin River warriors when he saw they had no chance for victory against the Near Rivers.

"You know Cen?" the old man asked, and leaned forward, looking into her face through the smoke of the hearth fire that burned between them.

K'os almost told him she did not, but then realized she had to tell the truth. If Cen was in the village, then he would certainly tell the people that he knew her. "Yes, I know him, but I am surprised to know he lives here. I had been told he was dead."

"He's lived here through the summer," the old man said, "though he was away some, trading. Now he is hunting caribou with other men from our village. They have been gone nearly a moon."

"No," his wife said, correcting him. "Only since the full moon." Then she asked K'os, "Are you Near River or Cousin?"

"Cousin, taken as slave to the Near River," K'os told her, and saw the glee in the old woman's eyes.

"They did not treat me well, as you can see," K'os said, raising her hands.

The old woman covered her mouth as though she had not already noticed K'os's hands, had not rejoiced in their deformity. "They do not hurt as much as you might think," K'os said. "I can sew and do all things a woman must do." She kept her voice sweet, did not allow anger to leak into her words, but she slid her eyes toward the old man, raised her brows.

"So why are you here alone?" Sand Fly asked, leaning forward, speaking loudly, as though to draw K'os's eyes from her husband.

"The Near River men decided they would hunt the Caribou River this fall."

"What about the Cousin River People?" Tree Climber asked. "That is where they hunt, nae?"

K'os lifted her shoulders in a shrug. "What could they do? Most of their hunters are dead. They took what caribou they could and returned to their winter village. But one night, while the Near Rivers were still at their caribou camp, I escaped. I do not want to be a slave. I will make some man a good wife. That is why I'm in this village."

"To find a husband?" the old woman said, and began to laugh. "What woman finds her own husband?"

K'os ignored her laughter and looked into the old man's face. "Your eyes bother you?" she asked.

He looked down, and K'os knew he was embarrassed.

"I am a healer," she said softly. "Allow me to stay in this lodge until your hunters return. I will do what I can for you. Besides . . ." She got up and pulled her heavy packs from the entrance tunnel, where she had left them. She untied the largest, took out several sticks of caribou meat. "I did not leave the Near River hunters without helping myself to their drying racks."

Tree Climber arched his eyebrows at his wife, but she turned her back to him. He looked at K'os, at the meat in her hands. "You are welcome in my wife's lodge," he told her.

Red Leaf pulled a caribou belly from the back of the cache. It was full of birds, bank swallows packed whole in oil. They would be good to take with her. Cen had much fish in his cache, and some frozen moose meat, several loops of intestines filled with fat and dried berries. She would take those and the pack she had stolen the first time she raided his cache.

Cen would be angry, but how could she live on dried

fish all winter? They did not have enough fat to keep her warm in the cold. Her belly would be full, but her arms and legs would shrivel, her teeth grow loose in her head. Perhaps, though, she could make a camp beside a lake that had blackfish. Enough blackfish would keep anyone alive, good as they were, so full of oil that they could be burned for fuel as well as eaten. But she could not be sure of finding them.

Besides, with his share from the caribou hunt, Cen should have more than enough fat to get him through the winter, even some left to trade in the spring.

It would have been so much better if she could have spent the winter here. Why had K'os chosen this village?

When Red Leaf had lived in the Cousin River Village waiting for her daughter's birth, she had heard Aqamdax mention K'os now and again. Aqamdax had nothing good to say about the woman. Of course, she had been K'os's slave. What slave loves her master?

Red Leaf could not help but admire K'os's strength. When Ground Beater, K'os's husband, had died in the fire that burned Song's lodge, she had made no accusations, even gave gifts to people in the village for helping her with the mourning.

Red Leaf carried her supplies to the entrance tunnel, where they would remain cold. Cen had left one of his dogs, an old bitch who would probably be eaten during the winter. Red Leaf would take her to carry some of the packs. The most important thing would be to leave the village before K'os saw her and realized who she was. Surely she would tell Cen what Red Leaf had done. Though Cen might allow her to leave with some of his food and his old and worthless dog, without doubt he would come after her if he knew she was the one who had killed Daes.

THE COUSIN RIVER CAMP

Aqamdax ran her fingers lightly over Chakliux's hands. The touch startled him out of his thoughts, out of the darkness that had seemed to swallow him since K'os had left their camp.

"I must go back," she said, leaning close to whisper the words.

"No," he answered, then realized the foolishness of his protest. She belonged to another man, and this was a hunting camp. There was work enough here for three villages of women. But in this quiet place beside the river, hidden by the willow, the stillness seemed to hold him, and he wanted Aqamdax to stay.

"I must," she said, and pushed herself to her knees. He reached for her, intended to hold her only for a moment, to whisper again his promise that he would take her as his wife.

Her parka hood was thrust back, and her hair lay in a thick shining river over one shoulder. He cupped the back of her head, and she leaned forward to press her face against his neck.

"When I have you as wife . . ." he said, and teased her ear with his tongue.

Then her hands were under his parka, cold against his skin. He pushed up her parka, raised his hands to the soft mounds that were her breasts. They held each other, hands stroking, for a long time, then Chakliux took off his parka, laid it on the ground. Aqamdax lay back against the fur, did not protest when he pulled her parka off over her head and filled his eyes with the sight of her. He slipped off his leggings and lay over her, the heat of her body searing his belly, the wind chilling his back.

We should not do this, he thought. If the Dzuuggi could not control his passion, how could he expect to teach others? But with Aqamdax warm under his hands, whispering her love . . .

You are hunter, he told himself, then heard the same words from another voice, perhaps that of his father Ground Beater or of Star's father, Cloud Finder. What animal honors a man who takes another's wife?

Chakliux pressed his hands against the ground, pushed himself away from her. There would be another place for this. A time when they would not have to hide from others.

He looked down at Aqamdax, saw that she was crying.

"Without you, I would have died," she said. "I would have gone on to be with my son."

Chakliux again gathered her into his arms. How could he leave her? What was one more curse against his hunting? How could taking this woman be any worse than having K'os as mother?

He took her gently, as if he was the first man she had known, and when they moved together in the rhythm of their need, he whispered to her in her own language, and she spoke in the River tongue, their words binding them with promises and hope.

THE FOUR RIVERS VILLAGE

That night in Sand Fly's lodge, K'os lay awake staring into the darkness. When she heard Sand Fly's first snores, she considered going to Tree Climber's bed. But he was so old, perhaps he could no longer enjoy a woman. Then each time he looked at her, she would be a reminder of what he had lost. Better to stay where she was, to make her eyes large when he spoke, to give sly smiles when his wife was not looking. Those things would be safer.

Sand Fly had taken her to the women's place, showed her the women's moon blood lodge and pointed out their cache. She had named the important people of the village. There was a shaman, and a chief hunter, First Spear, who had many wives. There was an old woman who considered herself a healer but was not, Sand Fly confided.

"Before I was a slave, I was a healer," K'os reminded the woman, and again asked permission to make medicine for Tree Climber.

Sand Fly blinked round stupid eyes at her, as though considering the request, then went on naming the owners of each lodge. K'os hid her disgust, but to her surprise, when they returned to Sand Fly's lodge, the old woman told her husband that K'os would make medicine for him.

The remainder of that day, K'os had made eye rinses and teas, then salves for Sand Fly's joints and a tonic for her belly. They ate a good meal of fish stew, and K'os settled them into their beds as though they were children.

Even after Tree Climber added his snores to his wife's,

K'os could not sleep. Her legs ached. The days of walking had been difficult. Twice it had snowed and melted, making the mosses and grass slippery. Soon snow would come and stay. Sand Fly said the Four Rivers Village had had a storm nearly a moon earlier, but that snow, too, after several days had melted. It was a strange year. The winter might be severe, all the more reason for her to live in this village until she decided how best to take revenge on a son who had no pity on his mother.

By now, he probably thought she was food for wolves, that her bones were being scattered by foxes and ravens. He would learn differently.

Chakliux and Sok had been blessed with caribou, those two. Fox Barking might have driven them from the Near River Village, but he could not destroy their abilities to lead.

How many men could take a group as decimated as the Cousin River People and, in only a few moons, give them the strength and confidence they needed to take all those caribou? They were still without enough hunters. A poor caribou hunt next year or the year after would cost them their lives. But what village—even the strongest—did not live from winter to winter, praying for hunting luck?

And how many men could take a strong village like the Near Rivers and lead it to destruction as Fox Barking had?

Her thoughts drifted to Sok. She would like to have that one in her bed. He was large and strong, his body thick with muscle. There was much similarity in face between Sok and Chakliux. They both had gull wing brows, large noses, high cheekbones. They were handsome men, and though Chakliux was smaller, the lithe lines of his body were not unpleasant, and his arms were nearly as thick as Sok's. Of course, he had the otter foot. She smiled, remembering that Snow-in-her-hair had refused to accept him as husband because of that foot. Foolish woman!

K'os did not know Sok well, but the fact that he would take Snow-in-her-hair as wife did not say much for his wisdom. She was a beautiful woman, but small and full of complaints. Even one day in the Cousin hunting camp had been enough to tell K'os that. What if Snow's son grew up to be like her?

K'os had seen a boy in that camp who looked much like Sok and had assumed he was the son of Sok's other wife. What was her name?

Red Leaf, yes. K'os had heard stories in the Near River Village. Red Leaf had killed the old man named Tsaani, Chakliux's grandfather. She had also killed the Sea Hunter woman who was Aqamdax's mother.

A pity Red Leaf was dead. A woman who had cost Sok and Chakliux their places in the Near River Village would be a woman worth knowing. Gull Beak had told K'os that Red Leaf had been pregnant. K'os wondered if they had waited until the baby was born or if they had killed two, taking Red Leaf before her delivery.

A cramp tightened the muscles of K'os's right leg. She crawled from her bed and stood.

Sand Fly stirred, raised up on one elbow. "You are all right?" she asked.

"A cramp in my leg. I walked too far in escaping the Near River People," she said, then asked, "Would it bother you if I stirred the coals and made a tea?"

"You have medicine that helps muscle cramps?"

"Yes."

"Make me some, too."

K'os hid a sigh of irritation. She stirred the coals, added birchbark and a few sticks of wood until the fire came to life. While they waited for a boiling bag of water to heat, the old woman babbled, telling one story and another of the people who lived in the village, people K'os did not know and did not care about.

When the water neared boiling, K'os took a packet of crampbark out of her medicine bag, scattered a few shreds into the bottom of two wooden drinking cups, then ladled out the hot water, poured each cup half full. Sand Fly raised the cup to her lips, but K'os held up one hand.

"Wait. It should cool first."

Then she squatted again beside the woman, closed her eyes on Sand Fly's babbling. Finally K'os raised the cup to her lips, inhaled the pungent smell, took a sip. The warmth spread through her, into her arms and legs.

"Good," the old woman said. "Yes, good. You will have to make some of this for Cen."

"Yes, I will."

K'os smiled. She had had better lovers, but Cen was not terrible. Perhaps she should be his wife. She would enjoy going with him on some of his trading trips, especially those to the Cousin River Village. Of course, he might be reluctant to return to that village. Especially since he had not fought with the Cousin men as he had promised. Perhaps he was due revenge for that, but perhaps not. It would be worthwhile to hear his side of the story. Yes, she would have a good life as wife to a trader. First choice of the goods he brought back from his journeys. A chance to visit many villages, find new medicines. And, of course, her revenge on Chakliux. It would be that much easier if she—

Sand Fly's words broke into K'os's thoughts. Was she saying something about Cen's wife? He had taken a wife? Well, why not? If a man wanted to stay in a village, he needed a wife to keep his lodge for him, to watch over his caches. He had wanted K'os for his wife in the Cousin River Village, and she would have agreed if it had not been for Tikaani, and then Sky Watcher. . . .

"He has a wife?" she asked, interrupting the old woman's ramblings.

"Who?" Sand Fly asked, and K'os realized that she was probably already speaking about someone else.

"Cen, the trader."

"Oh, yes."

"One of the daughters of this village?"

The old woman chuckled. "There were many mothers who had eyes set on him. White Lake was so angry when he brought his new woman to camp that she scolded him in front of everyone. And Fern—"

"So this woman is from another village?"

"Who?"

"Cen's wife," K'os said, her patience slipping away.

"The Near River Village, she claims, but then only as

a child. Fern has a brother who lives there with his wife, and she says he has never mentioned anyone by her name. Of course, men do not usually talk about women. Their thoughts are more often on hunting—"

"What is her name?"

"Gheli."

K'os did not know her. A wife, that was not a good thing. Of course, K'os could be a second wife, or perhaps find a young hunter who had no wife. Young men were easy to control, but there was so much freedom in being wife to a trader, and with Cen's son, Ghaden, at the Cousin River Village, surely there would be some way they could plan together to get the boy back and allow K'os her revenge. But this wife was a problem.

For now, then, perhaps the best thing was to become wife to a young hunter, K'os decided. And if he got in the way, he could always die.

Of course, first the people in the village had to accept her, not an easy thing, with her an outsider. But there was her dead brother. . . .

"I had a brother who lived here in this village," K'os said, interrupting whatever Sand Fly was talking about.

K'os could see the surprise in Sand Fly's eyes.

"He lives here?" she asked.

"He used to. He died, and his wife." K'os took a knife from a scabbard at her waist. "He made me this," she said, and handed it to Sand Fly, watched as the old woman turned the blade in her hands. She rubbed her fingers against the caribou hide that wrapped the handle and said, "It is old, this knife, but I seem to remember a man who made knives like this one—he came to us from the Cousin River Village. You would trade it?"

"Not this one," K'os told her.

Trade it? No. Without that knife, she would have been dead long ago. Killed by Fox Barking and his brother—Chakliux's true father—Gull Wing, and that stupid one, Sleeps Long. Surely, without that knife, she would lose all her luck. "The knife is all I have to remind me of my brother. I cannot trade it, but perhaps when they see it, the men of this village will remember him and allow me to stay here."

Sand Fly handed the knife back and nodded. "I think you might be right," she said.

K'os pushed the knife into its scabbard, then took a sip of the tea. It made her relax, and she sat, nearly asleep, as Sand Fly continued to babble.

But finally Sand Fly's words slowed, her eyelids drooped, and she asked, "You think it is time for sleep now?"

"Yes, time for sleep," K'os said. She banked the coals, then guided Sand Fly toward her bed.

"You are a good woman," Sand Fly said to K'os. "It is too bad that other one came. Cen should have you as wife." She squinted and looked up into K'os's face. "Maybe he will throw her away when he sees you. You are prettier. Gheli is a quiet one, and not too friendly. What man wants a wife like that? She probably isn't too friendly in his bed, either." Sand Fly cackled, and K'os forced herself to join her laughter. "Of course, she sews well, that one. You should see the parkas she makes for Cen and the blankets she has for her baby."

"Already, they have a baby?"

"She came with the baby. A girl, though, but big and strong like her mother. But those parkas . . . I wish I had one myself."

K'os pressed a hand against the old woman's mouth. "Hush now, Aunt. Your husband is sleeping, and you should be also."

She helped the woman into her bedding furs, covered her, then lay down in her own bed.

A wife . . . Gheli. Under her breath, K'os cursed the woman and her daughter. At least it was a daughter, that child. The wife could sew. Well, K'os had yet to see any woman who was more gifted with awl and needle than she was, not even Gull Beak . . . not even Red Leaf.

K'os sat up in her bed. Red Leaf. The first woman she had met in the village. She was tall and wide like Red Leaf. She had carried a baby under her parka, the garment cut large through the neck and shoulders. And that parka . . .

She remembered admiring Red Leaf's parkas during that brief time she had spent in the Near River Village the winter before the fighting.

K'os crawled from her bed, shook Sand Fly awake. Sand Fly looked at her, blinked as though trying to remember who she was.

"Tree Climber is sick?" she finally asked.

"No. He is asleep."

"Why do you wake me?"

"I . . . I was afraid I had made your tea too strong. You slept so quickly, but I see you are fine."

Sand Fly patted K'os's hand. "Yes, I am fine," she answered. "You should make yourself some tea for your hands, you know. It might help." Sand Fly closed her eyes. "Some tea, some kind of tea," she mumbled. "I wish I knew of some kind . . . I wish . . ."

"Aunt," K'os asked, pinching the woman's arm to bring her back from her babbling, "did Cen's wife go with him on the caribou hunt or is she still here in the village?"

Sand Fly's eyes fluttered open. "Cen's wife? Cen's wife? Oh, she is here. He wouldn't let her go, you know. With the baby. She is here. I can take you to her. Tomorrow, we will visit her." Sand Fly's eyes closed, and she slept.

THIRTY-THREE

THE COUSIN RIVER CAMP

Chakliux crept into his lean-to, saw with a rise of irritation that Star had not unrolled his bedding furs. His lean-to and Star's faced one another, their open sides nearly meeting around a small warming hearth. Ghaden and Biter were already asleep in the back of the lean-to. Chakliux peered through the smoke haze of the fire, thought he could see Star and Yaa both asleep, Star in front, closest to the hearth, Yaa behind her.

Chakliux had returned to camp well before dark, but he had sat on the leeward side of his lean-to, his hands working over a spear shaft, until the sun set. His thoughts, strong and shining, had been on Aqamdax, and he had to keep his mouth shut against songs that would betray his joy.

When darkness settled over their camp, Sky Watcher came, asked Chakliux to join the men, tell hunting stories from years past. Chakliux went to the men, raised his eyes toward the night and offered a silent prayer. Then he settled himself on a pad of caribou hide and began a litany of stories.

He had told those same stories many times before, but this night his tongue was thick, his words slow and clumsy. The men grew restless, and finally he asked Sok to tell tales from the Near River People. Take More began to grumble, but Sok stopped his complaints with the assurance that he would tell only stories of that time when the Cousin and Near River were one people.

When Sok finished, each man returned to his own tent. The sky was black—no stars, no moon—and Chakliux found his way by the light from hearth coals that glowed red at each lean-to. He looked up, wondered if those grandfathers Sok had spoken about had somehow closed up the holes that let men see the light of the spirit world. If Chakliux had brought a curse on himself, that was something he deserved, and he would bear it in exchange for his time with Aqamdax, but what if he had cursed other men? What if his storytelling from now on was always slow and cumbersome? And what if Aqamdax carried that same curse?

He unrolled his bedding, lay down for a time but could not sleep. He went outside, sat in the darkness and watched Aqamdax's tent. He asked himself why he should carry any guilt. Night Man had killed Aqamdax's son— a healthy child. Surely that was worse than anything Chakliux had done.

Perhaps he should tell Aqamdax to throw Night Man away even before they began their journey back to the winter village. But what if the Near River men were waiting for them, planning an attack? It would be difficult enough for the few Cousin hunters to defend themselves and their women without enmity between Chakliux and Night Man.

Better to wait. He tried to lift prayers to those spirits that lived in the earth and sky and water but was not sure if they could help a man who had cursed himself by breaking the promises of a marriage bond. How could caribou spirits help? How could otter? Did bear spirits understand such things? Could they forgive? What about the spirits of those who were Dzuuggi before him? Would they understand or condemn?

Aqamdax lay still when Night Man came into his lean-to. She would not go to him, even if he demanded. How could she bear his hands after knowing the joy of Chakliux's touch? She wished she had left Night Man before the hunt. How could that have brought a curse? Caribou were good mothers. They kept their calves close and defended them against wolves. They would have no difficulty understanding a woman who did not want to lose another child. Surely they would not expect her to keep a husband like Night Man.

"Aqamdax," Night Man said.

Aqamdax felt her chest tighten, and it seemed as though her heart slowed almost to stopping. "You are hungry?" she asked in a small voice.

He made a harsh sound that was nearly a laugh. "Hungry, yes," he said. "Not for food."

Aqamdax lay very still, said nothing, and Night Man moved as though to come to her bed.

"No, stay there," Aqamdax said. "I will come to you. Lay down. Let me rub your back."

She waited for his answer, holding her breath. He groaned, rolled over. "Be careful. My shoulder was worse today."

He did much for having little strength in his left arm, Aqamdax thought, and knew she had to give grudging respect for that. Sok had worked with him, helped him relearn the use of spear and thrower, even without the balance of a strong left arm and shoulder. He could not throw his spears as fast as another man, but at least he could again consider himself a hunter.

She lay a hand on his shoulder. It was hot. The wound seemed to keep the fever of its illness within itself, but for two moons now there had been no sign of drainage from the scar, and the lumps under his arm seemed a little smaller.

Aqamdax moved her hands to his back, kneaded the muscles. She felt as though the touch of Night Man's skin soiled her. It was one thing to show concern for his wound, something much different to give him pleasure.

"I have caribou leaves we can heat as a poultice for your shoulder," she said.

He snorted. "You are worse than a mother."

Aqamdax got up, felt her way into the darkness at the back of her tent, groped into one of her packs until she found a short-bladed knife, two ground squirrel hides and a cilt'ogho of caribou leaves. She picked up another cilt'ogho, much similar to the first, and held them toward the hearth so he could see them both.

"I have two here, but it is too dark for me to tell which one has the caribou leaves. Perhaps the moon has risen and will give enough light to show me."

"There is no moon," he said, and began to complain, but she crawled out of the tent before his complaints turned to demands. She looked toward Chakliux's lean-to, was sure she saw him sitting outside, his back to Star's warming hearth. She pulled up the sleeve of her parka and she cut her forearm, watched the blood well. She wiped the wound with a ground squirrel hide, and tucked the bloody hide between her legs, then went back inside the lean-to, knelt beside Night Man.

"It is good I went outside," she told him. "The hearth light showed me that I have begun my bleeding. I must leave. This container is full of caribou leaves if you want them."

She set the cilt'ogho beside him and went to her bed, rolled several blankets, picked up a pack of supplies.

"It is too soon," Night Man said. "Your last bleeding was at the full moon."

"It is like that for a woman who has just given birth," Aqamdax replied. "Especially when the baby dies and she does not have another child to take her milk."

He followed her from the lean-to, stood beside the warming fire. His eyes were dark slits.

"I ask you into my bed, and you suddenly discover you are bleeding," Night Man said.

"I will come to your bed if you want," Aqamdax told him. She set down her pack and lifted her parka, pulled the bloody hide from between her legs, held it up with two fingers so he could see the stains. "I am not the one who will be cursed."

Night Man muttered an insult, then went back into the tent.

Aqamdax walked through the camp to the small tiki-yaasde, a tent set aside for women in moon blood. Chakliux had told her that they would leave for the winter village in a day or so, and because she claimed to be bleeding, she would have to walk behind the others, make a separate camp at night. It was something the women spoke about with dread, that separation for bleeding, or worse, giving birth when traveling, but it was better than having Night Man in her bed.

THE NEAR RIVER PEOPLE

Dii's eyes were on Blue Flower's back as the woman trudged in front of her. Blue Flower was a good one to follow, knew how to pick her way through the tundra bog. They had begun in early morning, but now at midday the sun had softened the ground. At least it was not cold enough to freeze wet feet, but Dii wished for a night of deep cold that would harden the tundra, ice the marshy ponds and small rivulets that wound their way through the moss and tussocks.

Anaay sent hunters ahead of the people and to each side. The men returned to camp each night after the women had set up the lean-tos. Dii knew they would see no caribou. It was strange, that knowing, and she had finally come to the place where she no longer questioned herself. The caribou were a day's walk east, the herd moving south just as the Near River People moved south.

She had told no one except K'os about hearing caribou songs, and she knew that even K'os had not truly believed her. She missed K'os. The woman's words were often sharp and disdainful, and she was one to give insults as quickly as others made greetings, but she had much knowledge of plants and medicines. During the journey to the hunting river, she had filled the long walk with explanations of which plants were useful and when to take them from the earth, how to make roots or leaves or flowers into medicines, even dyes.

K'os spoke quickly and sometimes under her breath, as though what she said was more to help herself than Dii, but Dii had stayed close, listened carefully, and each night repeated in her mind what K'os had said. Now, as she followed Blue Flower, she watched for plants, saw many that were familiar, remembered how to use them.

They made camp that night on a small rise crowded with willow, alder and resin birch. Except for demands for food and the repair of his clothing, Anaay had ignored her during much of the hunting trip. This night he was more gentle, and she was not surprised when he pulled her into his lean-to even before most of the people had left the cooking fire. He took her quickly, not even pushing up her parka. After he rolled away from her, she tried to straighten his clothing, lifted bedding furs over him.

He grunted at her, then said, "I have decided we will not yet return to the winter village."

Dii felt her heart drop. Even the Near River Village would seem good after this hunting trip. She was ready to spend her days setting out traplines, learning sewing skills from Gull Beak, gathering those few plants that K'os had said could still be taken before snow covered them. Soon she would give Anaay K'os's medicine, then perhaps she would have the good fortune of giving birth in the summer, when babies had the best chance to grow strong.

"Why?" Dii asked. "The women need to get back. We must be ready for winter."

"You are foolish enough to ask why?" Anaay demanded. He sat up in his bed. "How can we return? We do not have enough meat. The Cousin River People cursed us."

A sudden thrust of anger filled Dii's mouth with insults about Anaay's choice to hunt at another people's river, but what wife would venture to say such things to a husband?

"For the last two nights I have dreamed of caribou," Anaay said.

Dii's hopes rose. Perhaps he knew the caribou walked close to them, people and caribou, like rivers running parallel courses.

But then he said, "They are west of us, a day's walk, perhaps two. That is all."

It was true that the Near River People told stories each

year of a herd of caribou that claimed the land close to the sea, walking the shores, each track like two curved moons in the gray and yellow sands.

Anaay spoke then of the herds he had dreamed, of bulls and cows, of calves that shadowed their mothers as they followed the shores to that land where the Sea Hunters made their villages.

Dii had heard the Sea Hunter woman Aqamdax speak of caribou. Perhaps Anaay was right, but there was a fearful knowing in her mind that he was not.

The dark of the tent gave her courage. It was always easier to speak when others could not see your face. So in quiet words she began, first describing her dreams, so her husband would know that she spoke not as a child but as someone who had experienced the same knowing he had been given.

"Their hooves come into my dreams," she said, "and I feel them shake the earth—sometimes, even when I am awake. Once, I thought they were outside my tent, that they were coming upon us again as they did beside the river. I hear them, and I know where they are. You are probably right, Husband, that there is a herd near the sea. But there is also one passing less than a day's walk to the east, a herd so large they are like a river over the tundra. Send out one of your men. A man alone, a good runner, could see them and be back by night if he left in earliest morning. Then we would not have so far to walk and—"

The blow came from the dark, so she had no time to prepare herself. Her first thought was of wolf or bear, attacking through the thin walls of Anaay's tent, and she cried out in fear, calling Anaay to help her. But then she realized that it was Anaay's fist in her belly, his voice raised in anger, and he cursed her for her foolishness, for believing that she, a woman, would be given caribou songs.

When the blows stopped and Anaay's shouts died away, Dii could only lie still. She breathed in quick, shallow breaths against ribs that ached, and tried not to choke on the blood that ran down her throat. But even as she lay there, she could hear the caribou, feel the pulse of their hooves.

The rhythm of their walking lasted through the night, soothed her like a lullaby, and finally wrapped her into caribou dreams.

THIRTY-FOUR

THE FOUR RIVERS VILLAGE

Red Leaf sat back on her heels and sighed. It was such a warm lodge, and Cen was a good husband, better than Sok in many ways. Red Leaf felt the sting of tears, but she blinked them away. She did not have time for pity.

"We are better off than when we left the Cousin River Village," she said, and looked across the lodge at the baby in her cradleboard. The child's dark eyes were round and wise. "Do not worry, Little Daughter," Red Leaf told her. "We will have a good winter, you and I."

She closed the flap of the large pack she planned to carry. She had filled it with dried and smoked fish from Cen's cache, with the belly of bank swallows, chunks of hardened fat.

She had decided to return first to her own small camp a day's walk from the village. At first the people of the village would simply think she had gone out to check her traplines, then, as the days passed, that she had left as she had come. Perhaps her leaving would add to those whispered rumors that she was an animal-woman, ground squirrel or wolverine, looking for a snug winter den.

She would stay a few days at her old shelter in the spruce forest, take those things she had left there that might be of use to her, then she would go upriver. If she was lucky, she would find a place before the snow came. Already this year summer and autumn had been unusually warm. That was good for now, but a warm fall often meant more snow in winter, so she must find a secure place to make a camp, perhaps near a lake where she could fish through the ice.

She went to the back of the lodge, the area where Cen kept his supplies. She was careful not to touch his weapons. Why leave him a curse? He had been good to her. She found a double pack sewn to a band that would fit over a dog's back. It looked sturdy, though she knew Cen would have taken his best packs with him on the hunt.

Red Leaf held the pack up to the light that came in through the smoke hole. The packs were made of caribou hide, soaked and scraped only enough to take off hair and flesh, then bent into shape, allowed to dry stiff and hard. They did not stink with rot or mildew, but one of the lacings was broken. She pulled out her sewing supplies, found a roll of rawhide, cut a length and softened the end in her mouth, twisted it until it was pointed and would fit through awl holes.

Though sewing gave her great pleasure, she did not enjoy repair work, especially on packs, but she told herself there were many things worse than fixing a seam, and began working.

She thought of the parka she had made for Cen. He had taken it with him on the hunt—a sign of respect to the animals. For what caribou would not give itself to a hunter whose wife was as skilled as Red Leaf?

For Sok, she had sewn a sun motif on each parka and many of his boots, but Cen's name brought to her mind the colors of the tundra, grays and golds, dark shadows that put the grasses in high relief. So she had made the back of Cen's parka in two pieces, each cut into long sharp fingers like blades of grass. The blades coming from the bottom half of the parka were dark, fashioned from mink skins, nearly black. The top half of the parka was fox fur, reds and golds, and she had trimmed the fur until it was the same length as the mink, those two pieces intersecting, the fingers sewn into one another as though the mink were grass, dark in shadow at the approach of night, standing in contrast to a sunset sky.

When she gave Cen the parka, he had taken her to his bed, caressed her as though she were a young girl, a delight to a man's eyes. And she had known then that Cen understood something Sok never had—what she could never be with face or body, she was with the skill of her hands.

Again, she knew the burn of tears. Two strong husbands, and now she had lost both. She sighed, set her lips in a hard line and backstitched the rawhide lacing to hold it in place.

She heard someone scratch at the side of her entrance tunnel. Quickly she set aside the pack she had filled, draped a caribou hide over it, piled fishskin baskets in front of it. The clutter of Cen's lodge had bothered her when she first came, but now she was grateful.

She pulled aside the inner doorflap, called out a welcome. She expected to see old Brown Foot and his wife. The two, living from the generosity of others, came often to Cen's lodge, where they knew they could always get a bowl of soup or stew. Red Leaf went to the cooking bag. In her hurry to pack, she had done nothing with the boiling bag but to stir it once, dip herself a bowl of food and keep working. She should have filled her water bladders. Most were empty, but she was afraid to risk going out more than necessary. She had taken advantage of the dim light of sunrise to carry food in from the cache and to feed the dog.

She scraped the bottom of the boiling bag to get several chunks of meat, softened by long days of cooking, but then looked up to see that it was not Brown Foot but Sand Fly who had come.

Red Leaf raised her eyebrows in greeting, said, "Sit down by the fire. It is cold today." She was about to ask if the old woman wanted food but then saw that Sand Fly was not alone, and the words died in her mouth.

"I have brought a friend," Sand Fly said, and held one hand out toward the Cousin River woman K'os.

THE NEAR RIVER HUNTING CAMP
If anything, Dii's pain was worse, especially her back. She had cleaned the blood from her face, but during the night more must have crusted around her nose and mouth.

Anaay took one look at her, refused the bowl of food she held out to him and left the tent, glancing back over his shoulder to say, "Go wash yourself. You will curse us all."

She pulled her parka hood forward so the ruff hid her face and walked in slow steps to one of the small ponds that dotted the tundra. She broke the ice webbed over the water and crouched to splash her face. As water dripped from her fingers, she saw her reflection in the pond, her nose swollen to twice its size, her eyes ringed with black, a cut on one cheekbone, her bottom lip thick and crusted with blood.

The water felt good, and she drank some, hoping the cold would reach her bones and deaden the pain.

She turned and looked back at the camp. How foolish she had been to stay when she could now be with her own people. Had the Cousin hunters returned to their winter village yet or would they still be downriver, butchering caribou and scraping hides? If she left now, she would reach their camp in only a few days.

She held her breath at the thought of leaving the Near Rivers, of going on her own. But what if the Cousin People had left? And what if Anaay came after her? If he had beaten her for the mention of a dream, what would he do if he caught her after she ran away?

Dii walked back through camp to her tent. Women who came close to greet her looked quickly away when they saw her face and did not stop to talk.

Later that morning, Anaay told the people his dream of caribou singing, how they must travel west toward the sea, how their traveling would not only bring them close to the caribou but also to their winter village. And when the women began taking down their tattered tents, Anaay came over to help Dii, did most of the lifting and hard work, so that Dii, even through split and swollen lips, made herself smile at him.

THE COUSIN RIVER CAMP

Aqamdax hoisted the pack to her back and secured the chest and belly straps—a tumpline around her forehead to help carry the heavy load of meat. Even the men carried large packs, and all but two dogs pulled travois.

She stayed at the back of the group. A woman who had spent the night in the moon blood lodge did not walk close to men, but in traveling the rules were not as strict as in the winter village, so she spoke to other women, laughed at the antics of the boys and helped Bird Caller when one of Sky Watcher's dogs got tangled in his harness and threatened to overturn his travois.

Even under the weight of the pack, her heart sang. Though she was careful to do all that was proper for Night Man and took care of his dogs, now that they were walking, she could not keep herself from watching Chakliux. Once he stopped and looked back at the women. When he saw her, he let his eyes linger, and she did not look away.

Snow began to fall at midday. There was little wind, and soon the snow had made a white layer over the ground so that all things looked alike. What dogs and children could walk across, men and women could not. They stepped into boggy places where red moss grew, unable to see the color that would warn them of water beneath.

Aqamdax watched carefully, trying to choose the best path, following the footprints that had not filled with water, but finally, she, too, fell through, felt water seep in through the seams of her boots. For a time her feet burned with the cold, then they ached, but finally it seemed as though she walked on stumps of wood, her body ending at her ankles.

Finally Chakliux pointed out a high ridge the men knew from other hunting trips and told the women to make camp. The village was only five, six days' walk, and if it took a little longer, why worry? They had meat—more than they had hoped. The butchering had gone well, and they had won back some of their women from the Near Rivers.

He smiled at the Near River hunter, First Eagle, and said, "We have a strong man who has joined us to add his skills to ours. Why walk when our feet are wet? There are trees on that ridge, willow and birch. We will make fires, dry our feet, eat and rest."

He lifted his head until he saw Aqamdax, called her name. She lowered her eyes in embarrassment that he should seek her out so openly. Then she saw Night Man's scowl and held her head high. If this was the time, if Chakliux wanted her to throw Night Man away, then she would not be ashamed.

But Chakliux said, "Aqamdax, perhaps you have stories you could tell us this night."

It had been a long time since the Cousin women had allowed themselves the pleasure of a storytelling evening. The River People did not gather together to listen to stories as often as the First Men did. Usually the men and boys met in the hunters' lodge and shared hunting stories, and grandmothers and aunts told girls the stories passed down to teach wisdom and respect.

"There are many stories that need telling," Aqamdax answered, her words loud, nearly boisterous. "Too many for one storyteller. Perhaps someone else, a Dzuuggi among us, will also have tales to share."

She knew her words carried a teasing sound, but in the joy of the moment, she did not realize her foolishness until Night Man came to her and, careful to stand an arm's length away, said, "You do not bleed, do you? You only told me that so you would not have to share my bed."

"I do not yet know all the customs of your Cousin River People," Aqamdax said. "I will not share stories if some blood curse will come of it. Ask Chakliux for me. Tell him I bleed."

"I do not need to ask Chakliux," Night Man said. "I am your husband and I tell you. You cannot be that close to the men. Stay in the moon blood tent. Listen to Chakliux's stories from there. Listen and remember that he is the one who killed my brothers. He killed many of the warriors from this village. And though he denies it, I believe he also killed my father. Listen and remember.

"Or you might decide that you are not bleeding, that you can spend the evening telling your stories. They say you are good, though I have heard only those silly things you tell Yaa and Ghaden. Show me how good your stories are, then come to my tent and sleep in my bed."

In anger Aqamdax answered him, in disrespect she looked into his eyes. "I will stay in the moon blood lodge," she told him. "I will stay there and listen to Chakliux's stories, and I will remember that you are a man who killed your own son."

She turned her back on him and walked away.

THIRTY-FIVE

"I saw you outside when Aqamdax left my tent," Night Man said, his face pushed close to Chakliux's. "And I have seen you watching her. How strange that you did not notice where she went. She is in moon blood time. Why do you think she walked behind us today and not with the other women? She cannot tell stories tonight."

Chakliux was surprised at his own disappointment. It had been a long time since he and Aqamdax had shared a storytelling. He knew she had left Night Man's tent but doubted that she was in moon blood. If that was the way she had chosen to avoid sleeping in her husband's bed, then he was glad for her choice.

"I have enough stories to fill an evening," Chakliux answered, refusing to return Night Man's insults. "Sok and Sky Watcher are good at reliving hunts. Perhaps the people would like to listen to them as well."

"There are many stories that should be told," Night Man said. "Perhaps we should remember what happened to our men during the fighting with the Near Rivers."

"It is best forgotten," Chakliux told him.

Night Man shrugged and turned his back. As he walked away, he said, "See you do not forget one thing, Otter Foot. Aqamdax is my wife."

THE FOUR RIVERS VILLAGE

"I think we have met before," K'os said, and nodded her head in greeting.

"I hate to think I have so poor a memory," Red Leaf said. "So perhaps we have not." She murmured several compliments as though soft words about K'os's face and clothing could blind the woman's eyes to truth.

"You are Red Leaf from the Near River Village," K'os said.

Red Leaf ignored her, but inclined her head toward the boiling bag, and when Sand Fly raised her eyebrows in agreement, she gave them bowls of meat and broth. They sat down on padded mats, and Red Leaf scooped out meat for herself. She knew she could not eat, but she wrapped her hands around the bowl and the warmth calmed her.

"As a girl, I lived in the Near River Village," Red Leaf said. "Perhaps you remember me from that time. I have a cousin there. Some say we look alike. My name is Gheli. My husband was a trader." She turned and looked at her baby in the cradleboard. "He filled my belly with a daughter, then did not want her. With winter approaching, the child and I were starving, so I set a small camp near this village, hoping I could find someone who needed a wife. Cen took me and my daughter as well."

"You are fortunate," K'os said. She raised the bowl to her mouth and looked at Red Leaf over the rim as she ate. When she finished, she wiped the corners of her lips with her fingertips. "This other woman, Red Leaf, I cannot truly remember the story, but there was some reason she and her husband left the village."

"K'os was a slave at the Near River Village," Sand Fly said.

Red Leaf had heard that K'os was among the women who went to the Near River Village, but she opened her mouth as though in surprise, then asked, "Then someone here in this village bought you from them?"

K'os's smile turned cold. "I escaped. I am here as you were, looking for a husband. If there is no man in need of a wife, then I will ask the elders to allow me to live here with some family until I have enough caribou hides to make my own lodge."

"You hunt?" Red Leaf asked.

K'os laughed. "I am a healer. There is always some need for a healer in a village as large as this one."

"Perhaps Cen could use a second wife," Sand Fly said.

"I am sure, if I was your sister-wife," K'os said slowly, her eyes on Red Leaf's face, "that I would never again mistake you for the woman Red Leaf."

"It would be good to have a sister-wife," Red Leaf said softly. "It is lonely in this lodge when my husband is away."

Sand Fly chortled, showing a gap between her front teeth. "But stay with us until Cen returns," she said to K'os, laying a veined hand on K'os's wrist.

Red Leaf noticed that K'os flinched under Sand Fly's fingers, but who would not? The old woman was too forward in her touching, in her meddling.

"Yes. It is a decision that Cen must make," Red Leaf told K'os.

"Men are like that," Sand Fly said. "They do not like women to tell them what to do."

K'os's eyes glittered, dark as obsidian. "Until then, Gheli, I call you sister in my heart, and I will carry the hope that Cen chooses to take a second wife."

THE COUSIN RIVER PEOPLE

Chakliux began the stories with that tale, nearly as old as the earth, of the raven and the porcupine. He told of the race between them, and how the porcupine, though much slower, used his wisdom to win. Then he changed his stories to those of lynx and wolf, bear and fox, but though his words seemed to catch the interest of the boys, the men began to talk among themselves, and Chakliux felt as if the stories went from his mouth and fell to the earth so quickly that they did not even reach the ears of those nearest him.

Finally he spoke to the men, using a loud voice of celebration, and asked if anyone wanted to tell a hunting story. They were in a camp, without their best clothing and sacred objects, so the stories could not be acted out in the parts of bear and hunter, caribou and wolf. But still, there were new tales to be made from the joy of this year's hunt, and there were always old stories worth repeating.

None of the men stood, and Chakliux called out to Sok, reminded him of the bear hunt they had made with their grandfather, but Sok shook his head slowly, and Chakliux suddenly knew that that story was one Sok could never tell again, not when it was Red Leaf who had taken their grandfather's life.

"Sky Watcher, you have stories. What about that dead caribou that nearly floated you with it downriver?"

That brought smiles, and Sky Watcher told the story, laughing as he spoke. Hunters had drowned in such a way, but how better to rise above fear than with laughter? The story made the people forget their tiredness, and Chakliux could feel their excitement pushing against him.

That lift of joy was one of the things he loved most about storytelling. He began a tale of his own, something passed down from their grandfathers' grandfathers about those warriors who came from the north and tried to destroy the River People. Joining together from their small camps and villages along the rivers, The People had defeated those ancient enemies, but again, it seemed as though Chakliux's words did not reach the Cousin People's ears. He wondered if the recent fighting was still too close in their minds. How could they celebrate past victories when they still mourned a defeat?

He wished Aqamdax was able to tell her stories. With the voices she could draw from her throat—a different sound for each person or animal that spoke—she would be able to hold the attention of the hunters as well as the youngest child.

Finally he decided to tell the people that the storytelling would continue when they celebrated their hunt with a feast at the winter village.

But as the last words of his story came from his mouth, Take More spoke out, his voice belligerent. "We have a Near River hunter here among us," he said, and he turned toward First Eagle. "Perhaps he has stories to tell. How many of our young men did you kill? Perhaps my sister's son."

Then the women began to murmur, but Night Man stood up, looked down at Take More. "You forget who started the fighting," he said. "If we condemn the Near Rivers, then we must also condemn ourselves."

For all the resentment Chakliux held against the man, he could now feel only gratitude, but then Night Man held a hand out toward Chakliux. "A riddle, Otter Foot," he said.

Even though the night had settled around them, even though the fire cast as much shadow as light, Chakliux could see the malice in Night Man's eyes, and so he answered, "We have far to walk tomorrow, and heavy loads. It is time for stories to end and riddles to wait."

Chakliux walked away from the fire, back toward his lean-to. The men and boys left the storytelling circle. The women banked the fire and also went to their lean-tos. Chakliux had told Star to set their tents at the edge of the camp, had explained that he must be able to watch for wolves and, as Dzuuggi, use his prayers to protect the camp. But in truth, he wanted to be close to the moon blood lodge, to be able to help Aqamdax if some animal came to her as she stayed alone.

He saw now that she had made a fire outside the lean-to, and he was glad for the warmth and protection of those flames, but still he wished she was his wife, safe in his tent, lying close to his side each night.

"Look! What do I see?"

Chakliux turned. Night Man was behind him, his eyes also fixed on the moon blood lodge.

"They hide in the willow and think no one knows."

THIRTY-SIX

At first light Chakliux left the tent, walked out with his weapons. Star was asleep, and so he had awakened Yaa, whispered that he was going out to be sure the camp was safe. He did not mention the Near River hunters, but knew by Yaa's round eyes that she understood. He took Biter with him, and together they circled the camp.

Biter lifted his nose several times, testing the wind, but he did not bark. When in his circling Chakliux came to the moon blood tent, he pursed his lips into a thin whistle. Biter whined, and Chakliux laid a hand over the dog's muzzle, then Aqamdax crawled outside.

"We are safe," she said when she saw him.

"We?" Chakliux asked.

"Awl joined me last night."

Chakliux looked back toward the camp, saw no movement between the tents. He squatted on his haunches and gestured to Aqamdax with one hand. She crawled from the lean-to, shivering, her arms wrapped around her shoulders. He reached forward to pull up her parka hood, then dropped his hand without touching her. She flipped up her hood, pushing her hair into her face. Her trill of laughter made him smile.

"Five days?" she asked.

He knew her question was more about when he would

258

take her as wife than how much longer to the winter village. "Perhaps six," he said. "Be careful. I will not talk to you again until we get there. Someone saw us in the willow and told Night Man."

Fear widened her eyes.

"Stay in the moon blood tent at night. Call for me if he threatens you." He handed her a knife, a hunter's knife, long-bladed. "He killed your son. Do not let him take you."

"Chakliux," she said, and he could hear the tears under her words, "you have other knives? He is more likely to kill you."

He patted the sheath strapped to his strong leg, then loosened the neck opening of his parka, let her see the knife inside. He stood, lifted his chin toward Biter. "He is a good dog. He will help me watch."

"Keep him close to you, then," Aqamdax said.

"No, I brought him for you."

"He is Ghaden's dog. . . ."

"You think Ghaden will be upset?" He smiled at her, shook his head. "I must go. Be safe."

He returned to his own tent, to Star, still sleeping, and to Yaa and Ghaden. He helped them pack their supplies, then sent them off while he woke Star. That way he was the only one to take her abuse for disturbing the dreams she claimed would strengthen their baby.

Aqamdax and Awl walked on either side of Biter and led their husbands' dogs, each pulling a travois. At midday, the snow returned, harder and faster than the day before. The wind followed, winter in its breath, and they walked with fur ruffs pulled forward to cover their faces, only their eyes peering out through the tunnels of their parka hoods. The snow was wet, and they had to stop often to break balls of ice from the dogs' feet.

Aqamdax wondered if they would stop as early that day as they had the day before, but Chakliux kept them going, and she knew it was because of her. She wondered who had seen them and why that one had told Night Man. Did she have enemies among the women in the camp? Star resented her, but Star, had she seen them, would have fallen upon them herself, most likely with knife in hand.

They crossed several shallow streams. Aqamdax wore her seal flipper boots, had made sure that Ghaden and Yaa also wore theirs. Though she and Awl walked last in the line of people, Awl's husband often came back to see that they kept up with the others, and at the streams both he and Sok remained behind until everyone had crossed.

During that day of walking, her pack heavy on her back, Aqamdax did not see Chakliux. Late in the afternoon Sok told the women they would walk until the sun set. Aqamdax heard their groans, Star's shrill cry of disagreement, but Aqamdax was glad. The farther they walked, the sooner they would arrive at the winter village.

By the time the sky began darkening in the east, the snow was no more than a few scattered flakes.

"We will stop soon," Awl said, her cheeks dimpling as she added, "Many nights when I lived as slave to the Near Rivers, I dreamed of our winter village."

"You know the Near River men burned the lodges after you and the others left?" Aqamdax asked.

"Yes. The Near River Men boasted of it."

"K'os was not foolish, taking all of you to the Near Rivers as she did."

Awl shook her head as though to disagree. "During that first moon in the Near River Village, I would have gladly lived in ashes to be back with my own people. Do you feel that way about your Sea Hunters?"

"I miss them, and I miss the sea," Aqamdax said. "But I have no family there except for one I call aunt, a storyteller now very old, named Qung. For her, I would go back, except for my brother, Ghaden, and his sister Yaa, and—" Then she stopped herself, for she had nearly named Chakliux. She pretended to adjust the shoulder straps that held her pack, then said, "You see, I have family here among the Cousin River People."

"I lost my father in the fighting," Awl said, "and two summers ago my mother died, and her new baby, but I have Hollow Cup, who is my aunt, and also Night Man and Star. Their grandmother was sister to my grandfather."

"You have your husband," Aqamdax said.

Awl was quiet for a time, and because her hood was pulled forward over her face, Aqamdax could not tell if the woman was glad or angry. But when Awl finally spoke, her voice was tight, as though she spoke through tears.

"I could not believe he chose to come with me. Because of him, I almost did not leave. Even when I came into the Cousin hunting camp, my heart felt torn, and I knew a part of my spirit had stayed with him. You think the men will accept him?"

"Anyone who is not a fool. Besides, Sok and Chakliux are here. They fought with the Near Rivers."

"But Chakliux was raised in the Cousin River Village, and Sok is his brother."

"That's true. But Chakliux told me that there are often marriages between the Cousin and the Near Rivers."

"Not so much as there were—"

Awl's words were interrupted by shouts. Aqamdax stopped, caught hold of Biter's packs to keep him beside her. At first she thought the people cried out only to celebrate a decision to make camp for the night, but then Aqamdax saw Yaa running back to them.

"Near River?" she called to Yaa.

"No, it's Star," Yaa said, and gasped for breath. "Chakliux decided we would cross the river ahead, make camp on the high bank at the other side. He was helping the women across, he and First Eagle. They went one at a time, but Star would not wait her turn."

"The river took her?" Aqamdax asked.

"No, she had already crossed and was climbing the steep bank. It's gravel and slippery, and at the top are balsam poplars. Twisted Stalk said the trees were insulted by Star's rudeness because she pushed ahead of the elders, but Hollow Cup says the river wants her spirit in exchange for Ghaden, since he did not drown at the caribou camp."

"She fell?" Aqamdax asked, shaking her head against Yaa's many words, her foolish explanations.

"A limb from the trees fell." Yaa raised one hand, tapped the back of her head. "Hit her here. She slid into the river, but Chakliux pulled her out. Someone said she was dead."

Aqamdax unstrapped her pack, but Awl grabbed the back of her parka. "You cannot go," she said. "There are enough curses at work here without the power of our moon blood to add problems. Wait and see if Night Man calls you."

Aqamdax could not stop the trembling in her hands. She squatted on her haunches beside Biter and buried her face in the thick fur of his neck. She began a soft song for Star, for Chakliux's baby that grew in Star's belly.

THE FOUR RIVERS VILLAGE
The men shouted out greetings as they came into the village, and Cen was glad he had chosen to hunt caribou this fall rather than make a trading trip. What hunter risked trading meat or fish left from summer until he knew how many caribou he would bring in for his family? And during the fall hunts who was in the winter villages? Only the old women. Who was in the fish camps? No one. It was good, then, to hunt, and to return with full packs to a warm lodge and a strong wife.

The women met them with trilled songs of celebration, and Cen's eyes scanned the faces, hidden by parka hoods and a gentle fall of snow. Finally he saw Gheli, the bulge in her parka that was their daughter.

He wanted to hold her, strong and large, in his arms. He looked forward to a winter in their lodge. Perhaps he would take a dog or two downriver to the Cousin Village with the hope of finding Ghaden, see if they would trade a small boy for the meat that might allow them to live until spring.

He should have gone before now, but he knew the Cousin men would resent him since he had chosen not to fight against the Near Rivers. In truth, what else could he have done? The first Near River man they had killed— even before the attack—was the shaman. How could Cen have stayed to fight after they cursed themselves like that?

They would forgive him when he brought them meat in the starving moons of winter. Until then Cen would spend warm nights with his wife, play silly games with the little daughter he had claimed as his own.

He waited with the hunters until the women finished their songs, then he went to Gheli, saw the smile on her face. The Four River men were more open with their wives than the hunters in many villages, and so Cen pulled her into an embrace.

She pushed back her parka hood, and he saw his daughter's round face, dark like her mother's. She frowned at him, but when he tickled her cheek, she smiled, crinkling her eyes into little half-moons.

"Cen, it is good you are back."

The voice, a woman's voice, did not belong to Gheli, and Cen felt the chill of it in his bones. K'os.

She stood beside Gheli, a hand on Gheli's shoulder. She had pushed her parka hood back to her ears, and her face was as perfect and beautiful as he remembered it, her hair glistening with flakes of new snow.

He stared and could not look away, saw her as she was when she visited his dreams, warm and lithe under his hands. Then he remembered her also with Sky Watcher and with Tikaani, with all the other men she had pleasured, even when she was wife to Ground Beater. Better to be content with a good wife than always worried over a woman like K'os.

He glanced at Gheli, thought to see anger or jealousy, but she was smiling.

"You know K'os?" he asked her.

"We are friends," Gheli told him.

"Friends?" he said, surprised that anyone would consider K'os a friend.

"I thought you were dead," K'os said. "All of us in the Cousin Village thought so, even your little son, Ghaden."

Cen's heart squeezed in his chest at the mention of Ghaden's name. "He is safe, my son?" he asked, and saw the gleam of triumph in K'os's eyes. She was a trader, better than men who had spent their lives trading.

She shrugged her shoulders.

"You have come to this village with your husband?" he asked, turning the conversation away from his son.

"She needs a husband," Gheli said. "She is content to be second wife if the man is a good hunter."

It was a conversation that should not be spoken in the middle of a village, amidst shouts and songs of celebration, but Cen saw the earnestness in Gheli's eyes and knew that in some way K'os had managed to win her loyalty.

He put his arm around his wife's waist, pressed his lips to her ear, whispered, "I am ready to spend time in my wife's lodge."

He looked at K'os, then said, "You see that man over there?" He lifted his chin toward a young man, tall and thin. "He is Eagle Catcher. He needs a wife."

Then, before K'os could answer, Cen pulled Gheli through the crowd of people and took her to their lodge, left K'os standing in the snow.

THE COUSIN RIVER PEOPLE

When Chakliux first reached Star, he thought she was dead. She was face down, her upper body in the river. His otter foot slipped on the gravel bank, and he slid until his feet were in the water and he was sitting beside her. He caught hold of her shoulders, pulled her to his lap. First Eagle and Man Laughing picked her up and carried her to the top of the bank. Chakliux followed them, and when they set her down, he knelt beside her, pressed his fingers against her neck. He felt no pulse. Her skin was cold, her lips blue.

"Star!" he called to her. "Star! If you die, your baby also dies." He looked up as he said the words, as though to convince her spirit to return to her body.

She lay still, and he could see no sign that she breathed. He pressed an ear against her breast, listened for a heartbeat, but the noise of the river was too loud. He looked at the faces around him, gestured toward Twisted Stalk, heard her murmur about the greed of the river, taking a soul in exchange for caribou.

Perhaps she was right, but what good was the woman

if her words only added to the river's power? Who else in the camp knew anything about medicines? They had no shaman to call back Star's spirit.

Again he leaned over his wife, whispered about their baby, and prayed that his words would draw her back. Suddenly she coughed, her body jerking in spasms.

"Her spirit, it tries to return," Twisted Stalk said.

Star coughed again, and Chakliux thought he could hear the noise of the river in her lungs. Perhaps if they could get that water out, her spirit would have the space it needed and would go back into her body.

"You know some medicine to clear her lungs?" he asked Twisted Stalk.

The old woman shook her head.

Then Chakliux saw Yaa, her small face pinched and white. "Get Aqamdax," he said. "She worked with K'os. Perhaps she knows some of the medicines K'os used."

He sent First Eagle and Night Man to help their wives with the dogs, then he waited, wondering if he wanted Aqamdax for the medicine she might have or for the comfort she would bring him.

"Chakliux wants you to come!" Yaa yelled at Aqamdax.

"Star is alive?" Awl asked.

"I think so. They need medicine. You're supposed to cross the river. I've crossed it twice. It's not deep, but the current is strong."

First Eagle and Night Man unhitched their dogs and carried each travois across. The dogs followed, all but Biter. He ran up and down the riverbank, then sat, whining. Aqamdax urged him to cross with them, but though the dog waded in a short distance, he turned back and sat on the bank, lifted his nose into the air and howled.

"Leave him. He will come," Night Man shouted to them. "He's crossed rivers before. Wider than this one."

His words nearly made Aqamdax turn back, but then First Eagle said, "Chakliux wants you to help Star."

She clasped Awl's arm, grabbed Yaa's shoulder, and together they crossed over, holding on to one another as the current swept up over their boots to their knees. Aqamdax's legs grew numb, but she kept her eyes on the river, as though somehow by merely looking she could tame its current.

The day was nearing its end, the sun just below the horizon, and Aqamdax pushed her hood back from her face, opened her eyes wide to let in as much light as she could, but still the river was dark, as though her feet were sinking into black stone. With each step Awl gasped, so that Aqamdax's heart sped in quick bursts like birds' wings fluttering in her chest.

Finally women were reaching for them, and also Chakliux, his hands firm on Aqamdax's arms. Aqamdax looked back, saw Biter still on the other side. She called to him, but Chakliux pulled her away, the people clearing a path.

Then she was beside Star, the woman breathing in slow, shallow breaths, her eyes closed, lips blue.

Twisted Stalk and several others were kneeling beside her. "We have done what we could," Twisted Stalk said. "You lived with K'os. Do you remember any medicine that clears the lungs?"

"Marsh marigold," Aqamdax said quietly. "But I do not have any."

Twisted Stalk stood, called out to Yaa. "Daughter, do you know the plant marsh marigold?" Yaa, her eyes fixed on Star, did not speak until Twisted Stalk asked the question again. "Daughter, you did not hear me?"

"I know marsh marigold," she said. "But I don't know where to find it except when we're at the winter village."

"In wet places. It always grows in wet places," Twisted Stalk said. "There hasn't been enough snow to kill it yet. You might be able to find some near the river."

"Get Sok to go with you," Chakliux told Yaa. "The sun has set. You shouldn't be away from the camp alone."

Aqamdax lay her hand against Star's belly, hoping to feel the baby move. Chakliux set his hand beside hers.

"The baby sleeps," Aqamdax told him. "Only that. He sleeps."

THIRTY-SEVEN

THE NEAR RIVER PEOPLE

Dii set her pack on the ground, shuddered as she heard Anaay bellow at her. "You think I want my tent there? It is wet. Find a better place! I did not bring you to make my life more difficult."

She carried a heavier load now that K'os was no longer with them, nearly twice as much as she had carried before, and that day Anaay had given her another of his own packs as well as a caribou hide. She had tied the hide on one of the dogs' travois, but the added weight pressed the travois down into the tundra, miring it in any wet spot that the snow and cold had not yet hardened.

By midday her back and shoulders were stiff with pain, but she had kept her thoughts away from the agony. She had been so tired by the time they stopped to make camp that she had unstrapped the heaviest of her packs and let it fall where she stood.

"Where do you want the tent?" she asked Anaay.

He lifted a hand toward her, and she crouched, prepared for his blow, but then he looked at the men and women who were watching. "Go with Blue Flower," he told her. "She has a little wisdom. Put my tent beside hers."

Blue Flower lifted her chin toward the east side of the camp, and Dii grabbed her pack, urged the dogs forward and followed the woman. Blue Flower bent to whisper to her nephew who walked beside her, and he ran back to help Dii drag the pack.

"Wife, you shame me," Anaay called to her, "allowing a boy to do your work."

But Blue Flower turned around, thrust back her parka hood and with all the camp listening said, "You should be the one ashamed, Anaay. It is a husband's work my nephew is doing. Are you so blind that you do not see your wife carries more than any of us and also watches three dogs?"

Blue Flower's words seemed to lend strength to Dii's arms, but she knew Anaay would not forget the humiliation, nor would he allow her to forget.

THE COUSIN RIVER PEOPLE

Yaa searched through the camp for Sok, but though she asked many, poked her head into the open sides of lean-tos, no one knew where he was.

Marsh marigold grew near rivers. She knew the plant well but had never seen it used for medicine. The round ruffled leaves grew on stems no more than a hand's length from the earth. They fanned out in a circle, and each spring the plant bloomed with bright yellow flowers. She knew she could find it herself, especially this close to a river, except for the snow.

She was glad Sok and not Twisted Stalk was the one who was supposed to go with her. Ever since K'os had been with them that one day, Yaa had been thinking of someone among the Cousin People who might have killed Cries-loud's mother Day Woman. She had considered each of the Cousin River men, but Yaa had heard the old women whispering about the tangle of furs and mats that had been Day Woman's bed. There had been too much of a struggle for the killer to be a man. A man would have easily overpowered Day Woman. So if not a man, then who?

Twisted Stalk was a woman of sharp words and strong temper. Yaa had seen her screaming in anger over small things that most women would allow to pass with only a scowl. Yaa could believe Twisted Stalk might take out her anger about the Cousin defeat on Day Woman. Day Woman was Near River.

She and Ghaden and Cries-loud had all been born in the Near River Village. What if Twisted Stalk were the killer? What if in her anger she decided to kill another Near River person? Once again Yaa wished for a long-bladed knife.

"What are you doing?"

Yaa jumped, then flicked her fingers in annoyance when she saw Ghaden.

"Chakliux told me to find some marsh marigold. Have you seen any growing here?"

"No. What's it look like?"

"Never mind. Why are you here?"

"Trying to get Biter to cross the river."

"Keep calling. He'll come. But leave me alone. I have to find . . ."

"I know."

Ghaden lifted his voice, called to the dog, and Yaa walked away from him. The snow was no deeper than a hand's length, but still it hid most plants. Too bad marigolds didn't grow taller, Yaa thought. Of course, their closeness to the earth gave the plants their power.

Yaa used her feet to push back the snow, bent low in the dying light to see the plants she uncovered. She came to a slope in the bank. It wasn't a true stream, but in spring it would funnel melt-off water into the river.

When she finally saw the clump of marigold, each leaf holding a cap of snow, she shouted her triumph. She wasn't sure if Aqamdax wanted leaves, stems or roots, so she gripped the plant with both hands and pulled. From the corner of her eye, she saw something move. She looked up and realized that Biter had kept pace with her on the other side of the river. He barked, and Yaa opened her mouth to call him, but at that moment the roots of the plant let loose, and Yaa fell, her heels slipping out from under her so she landed on her back.

She slid toward the river, cried out in a scream, heard

Ghaden's voice, then her eyes and mouth were filled with water, the cold so numbing that she could not move.

THE FOUR RIVERS VILLAGE

K'os curled herself into her sleeping robes, turned her back on Sand Fly, but the old woman still babbled. "There are better men than Cen in this village," she said. "Just because you knew him before, he should not be your first choice. What about Willow Stick and Jumps-too-far, or Gives-dogs? First Spear, our chief hunter, has four wives, but he might want another. . . ."

Her list went on, and she even included her own husband. Tree Climber better than Cen? Hoping that Sand Fly would shut her mouth, K'os raised up on her elbow and said, "Why do you think I want Cen? I would not choose the life of a trader's wife. What woman wants her husband away most of the summer and often in the winter? Besides, I am a healer. I do not need a husband. I can earn meat with the medicines I give."

"We are a healthy people. A healer in this village will not earn much," Sand Fly said. "I know the medicine you gave me has helped my joints, and for that I do not mind sharing my lodge. It is good to have the company of another woman. My daughter and her husband lived with us until this past summer, when he talked her into going to the Black Hills Village, where his brother lives. A fool, that daughter. She will not find anyone who takes better care of her children than I do. They will be back, at least by spring. But until then we have room for you."

"I will have my own lodge by the time your daughter returns," K'os said.

Sand Fly raised a finger. "One daughter, I have, and she is a fool. But you are wise. Anyone can see that. You will find a husband. There are many men in this village. Did I tell you about Fat Mink? Then there is Brown Eye. You have not seen him yet. He and his brother went caribou hunting, just the two of them. His brother has a wife, but he has none. He would be a good one."

K'os rolled herself again in her sleeping robes, tucked her head into the warm furs. The pelts blocked out Sand

Fly's voice, and K'os turned her thoughts to Cen and Red Leaf and how best to win her way into Cen's bed.

THE COUSIN RIVER PEOPLE

Chakliux, his hand on his wife's belly, called out, gladness in his voice. Then Aqamdax, who had been rubbing salve into cuts on Star's face, moved her hands to Star's stomach, felt the roll of the baby under her fingers.

She tried to bring Chakliux's joy into her own heart, but the feel of the baby suddenly reminded her of her dead son. She drew in a long breath, forced herself to smile, then asked Twisted Stalk if she had used marsh marigold before.

"I have not," Twisted Stalk answered. "It must be something K'os learned on her own and kept as secret."

"Then when Sok and Yaa come, if they have found the plant, bring it to me, I will make it into a tea. I am not sure it will bring her back to us, but—"

A man's voice interrupted her, Sok calling from outside the lean-to. "I went ahead to see what we might find tomorrow in our walking, if the river had changed its course or if caribou had come this way."

He came inside and was suddenly quiet. "What happened?" he asked.

"A limb from a tree. It hit the back of her head, knocked her into the river."

"Did you bring the marsh marigold, you and Yaa?" Twisted Stalk asked Sok.

"The what?"

"I sent Yaa to find you," Chakliux said. "We told her to bring us some marsh marigold, but I did not want her to leave the camp alone."

"Once my wife and sons were across the river safely, I left," Sok said. "Then, only a little ways downriver, I saw a moose. Tomorrow, when it is light, I will hunt."

Chakliux stood. "I will find Yaa. She cannot be far."

"Stay with your wife," Sok told him. "I will go."

Sok left, and Twisted Stalk raised her eyebrows at Aqamdax. "You should be at the moon blood tent. I will help here. If Yaa finds the marigold, I will come to the tikiyaasde so you can tell me what to do."

"I am sorry for what has happened," Aqamdax said, speaking to Twisted Stalk, but she hoped Chakliux knew the words were for him.

She left the lean-to and walked to the west side of the camp where she knew Awl would have set up their tikiyaasde. The space between the moon blood tent and the camp was dark, but Awl had built a fire, and its flames guided Aqamdax through that darkness. She squatted at the hearth, accepted the bowl of warm broth Awl handed her.

"Star?" Awl asked.

"She is alive, and I could feel the baby moving within her, but I do not think her spirit has returned."

"What if she dies? Is there some way to keep the baby alive?"

It was a foolish question. What baby not yet born could live with his mother dead? But then Aqamdax remembered Chakliux's face, the hope in his eyes when he felt his baby move. "There are stories told among my people of babies who were saved when their mothers died. The mother's belly was slit open and the baby taken out, but even if we did that, Star's child would be too small to live. She has . . ."

Aqamdax paused, looked up at the sky as she counted on her fingers.

"Six moons of pregnancy." She shook her head. "To save the child, we must save the mother. There is a medicine I saw K'os use made from marsh marigold. It will clear the lungs. Perhaps that will bring Star's spirit back. I do not want to see this child die. It would be like losing my own son again."

"I heard Hollow Cup say that your baby had died," Awl said in a quiet voice. "Did he come too soon? Or was his spirit called?"

"His father gave him to the Grandfather Lake," Aqamdax said, her voice harsh, her words cold.

Awl gasped. "The baby was . . . he was not strong?" she asked.

"He was perfect. Beautiful. My husband thought he belonged to another man. Someone who came to my bed before I was wife. But the baby was Night Man's child." Her voice broke.

"Even if he was not, what does it matter?"

"I hate Night Man, Awl. I do not want to be his wife."

Awl knelt beside Aqamdax, put an arm around her shoulders. "I could ask First Eagle if he would take you. It would be good to have you as sister. He is a gifted hunter. He would never kill your baby, even if it belonged to someone else."

Aqamdax wiped the tears from her face. "You are a good friend," she said. "But someone else has asked me."

"Chakliux?"

"How did you know?"

"You are foolish to ask, Aqamdax. Everyone knows. Your eyes say what is in your heart, and Chakliux is the same."

"I want to throw Night Man away, but Chakliux says to wait until we arrive at the winter village."

"That is best. Why add to whatever curse has taken us?"

"There is no curse," Aqamdax said. "Star will be all right. Her spirit will return."

"You say that because you know or only because you want her baby to live?"

It was a question Aqamdax could not answer.

Awl warmed a bit of snow in a wooden bowl and added a pinch of powered crampbark from a packet at her waist. She stirred in the powder with her little finger, then took a sip, grimaced at the sour taste and swallowed. She held the bowl toward Aqamdax. "You want some?"

"I do not need it."

"You are not bleeding, are you?" Awl asked.

"Why do you think that?"

"I never see you change the pad you keep between your legs when we sit in the tent. I do not see you bury anything morning or night."

"Sometimes a woman needs to be in the moon blood lodge for other reasons," Aqamdax answered carefully.

"Sometimes women who are sisters of the heart must keep one another's secrets," Awl answered.

Sok went to his wife Snow-in-her-hair, asked questions about marsh marigold. What did a hunter know about gathering plants?

Snow-in-her-hair had grown thin in this hunting camp, though they had more food to eat than at any time since they came to live with the Cousin People. He reminded himself that she was the one who had insisted on bringing their baby son. The child would have been better left at the winter village. Ligige' could have taken care of him, and surely there was an old woman who had kept her milk over the years by nursing grandchildren.

Snow-in-her-hair handed Sok a bowl of meat.

"I have some dried marigold leaves that my mother gave me before we left the Near River Village," she told him. "Why do you need it?"

"You know Star fell into the river?"

"Who does not?"

"I did not. As soon as you and our boys crossed, I went upriver. There was a moose . . ."

Snow-in-her-hair crawled to one of the packs set at the open side of the tent. She untied the flap, pulled out a flat pouch.

"Marsh marigold," she said, and tossed it to him. "They need it for Star?"

Sok shrugged. "Twisted Stalk wanted it."

"My mother claims it sometimes draws a spirit back to a body," Snow-in-her-hair said.

Sok grunted and noisily slurped up the rest of his meat. Snow-in-her-hair's mother, Blue Flower, had long considered herself a healer, but she knew little. He would not trust her claims.

He lowered his bowl and licked his fingers clean. "I need to know where it grows, because Yaa has gone looking for the plant and has not returned."

"The little girl, Yaa?" Snow-in-her-hair asked. "Aqamdax's sister?"

"Yes."

"Why do you sit here and eat? Go look for her."

Surprised at his wife's outburst, he picked up the packet of dried marigold, but Snow-in-her-hair snatched it out of his hand.

"I will take this to Aqamdax. You look for Yaa."

She took their son, who was asleep in his cradleboard, and left the tent. Sok set down his bowl, wiped his hands on his leggings. He chose a short lance and went out. He walked west along the river, away from the camp, until the brush was so heavy that he was forced to turn back.

"Foolish girl," he said, looking up as though he spoke to the stars. They were so thick that the center of the sky looked white. The frost of his breathing rose to meet their light, and Sok wished he could be warm in his bed. He would find the girl quickly. How far could she walk? Then he would return to the tent, roll himself warm into his sleeping furs and dream of the bull moose, his wide antlers still stained dark from the blood of their growing.

THIRTY-EIGHT

The dog, his dense fur soaked and glazed with ice, packs still strapped to his back, jumped so quickly against Sok's chest that Sok almost had his lance into him before he realized it was Biter.

Sok slapped the butt end of his spear along the dog's ribs in reprimand, but Biter jumped up again, then lifted his head and howled. The noise raised the hair on Sok's arms, and he shivered, held in the harsh words that had risen to his mouth.

Biter started to run, looked back at Sok, and barked until Sok followed him. The dog stopped near a shallow pool at the side of the river. A cold wind dipped down into the water, and he saw Snow-in-her-hair and Ghaden pulling on a sodden heap of fur. It was Yaa.

Sok slid down to the pool and hefted the girl to one shoulder, grabbed Snow-in-her-hair's arm and helped her up the bank. Snow-in-her-hair fell to her knees, began retching. Sok waited beside her, stroking the back of her parka.

Finally Snow raised her head. "Our son is with Twisted Stalk. I decided to look for you . . ." She gagged and waved Sok toward camp.

"I will be back for you," he said, and was surprised to

see Biter sit down beside Snow and Ghaden, as though to protect them.

Aqamdax was walking toward Chakliux's tent when the first mourning cries began. She broke into a run, her hand over the top of the bowl that held the medicine she had made from Snow-in-her-hair's dried marigold. But when she arrived at the lean-to, she saw that Chakliux was still sitting beside his wife, and though Star's eyes were closed, her breathing seemed more regular.

"Who?" Aqamdax asked.

"It comes from the river side of the camp," Chakliux said, then took the medicine from Aqamdax's hands. He lifted Star's head to his lap and forced open her lips, poured the liquid from the bowl into her mouth. She swallowed, once, twice, but the rest spilled down her chin and into the folds of her parka. "You have more?" he asked.

"A little. Snow-in-her-hair had some dried marigold her mother had given her. She said she would help look for Yaa. . . ." Aqamdax's heart quickened. "Has she returned?"

Chakliux shook his head, then lay Star back against the bedding furs and crawled outside. "Stay here," he told Aqamdax.

Aqamdax knelt beside Star, raised a quiet chant, though it was a First Men chant and probably would not help a River woman. What hope did they have without a healer? They needed to be back in the winter camp, with Ligige'. She knew more of plant medicines than Aqamdax or Twisted Stalk.

Aqamdax sang until she heard Chakliux's voice scolding the women for their mourning cries. She went out to meet them, saw Sok with Yaa in his arms. Then she hurried ahead of him to make space in the lean-to so he could lay the girl beside Star.

Aqamdax covered her, tried to rub warmth into her hands. Yaa was not breathing, but Aqamdax felt a weak pulse at her wrists.

"I cannot stay," Sok said. "My wife was the one who found her. I need to get her back to our lean-to. She's wet. . . ."

He left, and others crowded in. Then Aqamdax heard Night Man's voice.

"Why are you here? You should be at the moon blood lodge." He began a string of accusations, but Aqamdax ignored him. What was more important? Night Man's anger or Yaa's life?

Then her thoughts were only on Yaa, and she tried to sift through the suggestions of those around her. If the heart was beating, did that mean there was a chance for the girl to live? Surely her spirit had not yet left her body.

There was something Aqamdax had heard, a story Qung had told her about a young man caught in the cords of his harpoon when he was taking a whale. They had somehow brought his breath back to him. What had they done?

She flipped Yaa over to her side and pounded on her back. Once when Ghaden had choked on meat, the pounding had helped.

"She has swallowed water?" Night Man asked, as though he had only just noticed the girl. The question made Aqamdax angry. He thought so little of others, this man she had once loved as husband.

He squatted beside her. "My brother . . ." He glanced up at Chakliux, pressed his teeth into a grimace. "My oldest brother once fell into the river from a raft. My father . . ."

He grasped Yaa's jaw with his right hand, pressed until her mouth opened. He lifted his chin toward Aqamdax. "Put a finger down Yaa's throat," he told her.

Aqamdax hesitated.

"Do it."

She stuck her finger down Yaa's throat.

"Farther."

Suddenly Yaa bucked under her hand, gagged. Aqamdax pulled her hand out, and Yaa began to vomit water. Aqamdax picked her up, turned her facedown and held her as the water poured from her throat.

Ghaden heard what the women said, though he wanted to cover his ears to their foolishness, to the whispers that his sister was dead. He buried his face in Biter's fur and hid his tears. If the mourning cries would go away, if the women would stop their sad talk, then perhaps all things would be as they had been. Ghaden would wake in the morning to find Yaa beside him, scolding him for something he had done or not done, but all the while smiling at him with her eyes.

How could she be dead? She was young. Now all he had for a mother was Star. The women said Yaa had traded her spirit for Star's. He had heard them say that. But why would she do that? Yaa knew that Star was not a good mother. But maybe it was because of the baby. If Star died, the baby would die, too. That was what happened to babies still inside their mothers.

He cried until his eyes seemed to hold no more tears, and when Aqamdax came to him, he clung to her so fiercely that when she said "Yaa wants to see you," the words were nonsense in his head.

Did Aqamdax mean he was to go with Yaa to the spirit world? He was not sure he wanted to do that. The old knife wound in his back began to ache, as though to remind him that he had been close to death once before.

"She is dead?" he finally whispered.

"No, who told you that? She doesn't feel well enough to sleep with you and Biter tonight, but she is not dead."

Aqamdax brought him to Chakliux's lean-to. Yaa was lying there beside Star, still and quiet, her face full of shadows in the flickering light of the fire. He knelt beside her, stroked her face. She did not move, and for a moment Ghaden thought Yaa had died in that short time it had taken Aqamdax to come and get him, but then Biter pushed his way to her side, licked her face, and Yaa turned her head away as she always did.

Ghaden laughed. "Why did you fall in the river, Yaa? Why did you do that?" Ghaden asked.

Yaa opened her eyes, and her eyelids drooped like they did when she was tired. She opened her mouth, but closed it again without saying anything, then she surprised Ghaden by breaking into laughter. She laughed until she choked, then gagged, and Aqamdax had to help her sit up.

Ghaden was afraid he would be in trouble, but Yaa only said, "I had to get Star the plant." She panted after saying just those few words.

"Did you get it?" Ghaden asked, then wished he had not.

But Aqamdax smiled and said, "She had it in her hand when Sok brought her back to camp."

THE FOUR RIVERS VILLAGE

In the morning, K'os took a turn at the boiling bags. The women were more busy than usual, scraping the new caribou hides, cutting meat, and preparing for the feast they would have that night. But K'os did only what she wanted to do, nothing as difficult as scraping hides. There would be enough of that during the winter.

When Red Leaf left Cen's lodge, she carried a throwing stick, stringer and basket, so K'os was sure she would be checking her traps, perhaps gathering crampbark berries, always sweeter after the snow came.

K'os walked quickly through the village, as though she had something important to do, and she carried a cilt'ogho of dried blueberries, a fishskin basket of caribou meat. She stopped at the hearths, added berries to each of the three boiling bags that hung near the fires. As she worked, she watched the people, memorized the new faces, those of the hunters who had just returned and the wives, the older children who had been with them.

Several women spoke to her, asked when she had come to the village. She told them the same story she had given Sand Fly, that she had been a slave. That she had escaped. She smiled sweetly and offered the women some of the berries in her cilt'ogho. Finally, when their attention was distracted by a child who brought them a first kill—a boy with a large camp jay, its breast pierced by a sharpened wood spear—then K'os slipped away. Let them rejoice over such a foolish thing without her.

She walked with quick strides to Cen's lodge, slipped into the entrance tunnel, did not scratch or call to announce her presence. She pulled aside the inner doorflap, curled her lips in derision when she saw Cen sitting cross-legged, Red Leaf's daughter in his hands. He was making soft noises into her face, and the baby was laughing with that surprising deep laughter that denotes a strong child.

"Gheli trusts you with her daughter?" K'os said, and saw the surprise on Cen's face. He was wearing a shirt, and K'os recognized Red Leaf's needlework on the back, a design of dark and light points that reminded K'os of grass in wind.

"Why are you here?" Cen asked her.

He carried the baby to her cradleboard and laced her in.

K'os slipped off her parka. She wore nothing under it save leggings and short woven grass aprons front and back. Aqamdax had made her the aprons, had said they were like those Sea Hunter women wore in their lodges.

"Your wife made you the shirt," K'os said, and squatted on her haunches, her knees wide apart, an apron hanging down between her legs.

She heard the soft intake of Cen's breath, saw that his eyes were on her crotch. "You have lived too long with the River People, Trader," she said to him. "Have you forgotten how Sea Hunter women dress? I had a Sea Hunter slave once. She made me this apron." K'os lifted the front flap. "She wove it from grass. Perhaps you should get some of these to trade."

She dropped the apron flap into place and walked over to Cen, took his hands in hers and raised them to her breasts.

He jerked away. "Leave this lodge, K'os," he said, his voice hard. "I have a wife. I do not need you."

She raised a hand to his face, scraped a fingernail along his jaw. "I have spoken to your wife. She told me she would welcome a sister. Ask her yourself. She says it's lonely being wife to a trader, a man who also hunts. Consider the joy of having two wives. One who stays here in the lodge to keep your food cache safe and raise your children, another who travels with you to warm your bed when you sleep in a trader's tent."

"A wife who will also warm other men's beds when she thinks I do not notice," Cen said. "A wife who will plot against me. You think I need a wife like that? Leave, K'os. You are not welcome here."

He turned his back on her, and K'os made signs for curses against him and against Red Leaf's daughter. She waited to see if he would say anything else, but he did not. And finally, when, with his back still turned, he slid a knife from a sheath at his waist, held it up so she could see the sharp edge of the long chert blade, she slipped on her parka and went back to Sand Fly's lodge.

She squatted on her haunches just outside the entrance tunnel and thought of all the young men in the village. They would not be difficult to get into her bed, but they did not have a son in the Cousin River Village like Cen did. They would have no reason to visit the Cousin People, especially so soon after the Cousins's defeat. Why risk bringing the curse of that bad luck to the Four Rivers Village?

Finally, she got up, went again to Red Leaf's lodge, crawled into the tunnel and pulled aside the doorflap. Cen looked up, scowled when he saw her.

"You thought I was Gheli?" she asked, her voice curling around the words, twisting them from sweetness into spite. "You think she is the woman you need? She will give you sons? But what about that son you already have? Did you know that Chakliux has him now?"

"Why would Chakliux have the boy?"

"You know the elders gave Ghaden to Star," she said. "Chakliux took her as wife. You know Star well enough. Why do you think Chakliux wanted her? Perhaps he is a fool, or perhaps Chakliux, with his otter foot, wants the assurance of a son who will care for him in his old age."

K'os felt a sudden gust of cold air, turned and saw that Red Leaf was peering into the entrance tunnel. The woman's eyes were round with fear. She held up a handful of raspberry branches. "For tea," she said, her voice weak. "And I have hares from my traps."

"I was telling your husband something you should know," K'os said. "About his son, a boy named Ghaden."

"I have told Gheli about Ghaden," Cen said.

"Has he told you that someone in the Near River Village, that place where I was slave, killed the boy's mother and wounded Ghaden?"

"Yes," said Red Leaf. Her voice was even and controlled, but her hands trembled.

"But there is something I am sure neither of you know," K'os said. "Did you know, Gheli, that the elders in the village thought Cen was the one who killed Ghaden's mother?"

"I did not know," Red Leaf said slowly, but kept her head down, her eyes away from Cen.

"Leave us, K'os," Cen said. He turned as though K'os had already gone and said to Red Leaf, "I did not kill Ghaden's mother."

"I know," Red Leaf said.

She could not keep her eyes from the mutilated finger on Cen's left hand. She knew the story of that finger, given as sacrifice to save Ghaden's life when the boy lay dying of wounds from Red Leaf's knife. The guilt of what she had done pressed down over Red Leaf's head until she thought her neck would snap under its weight. The pattern of circles that danced from the walls of Cen's lodge no longer looked like clouds, but seemed to be eyes, watching, dark in accusation.

Red Leaf opened her mouth to confess what she had done, but before she could speak, K'os said, "If you are so concerned, Cen, you should have returned to the Cousin River Village to claim Ghaden after the fighting. Why did you leave him with a people who had been defeated?"

Cen turned on her, anger coloring his face. "Why do you care?"

"I do not," K'os said sweetly, "though it might bother your wife to think you have less concern for your son than you would for one of your dogs."

Her husband's pain pulled Red Leaf from her guilt. "Enough, K'os," she said. "You should leave."

K'os breathed out a laugh. "Ah, but Gheli, I have not told you what you both will be glad to know. The Near

Rivers found the one who killed the Sea Hunter woman. It was Sok's wife. Her name is Red Leaf.

"Do you remember Sok?" K'os asked Cen.

Cen frowned. "I remember him, but not his wife."

"A pity," K'os said.

"Why did she kill them? Does anyone know?" Cen asked, and K'os laughed inwardly at the change in the man. Had he forgotten how eager he was to have her leave?

"She killed the old man because he was chief hunter and she wanted Sok to be given that honor. She killed your son's mother and tried to kill your son only because they happened to see her."

"They were returning from . . ."

Cen's words drifted into silence, and K'os said, "From your trader's lodge."

"What did they do to the woman?" he asked, his voice suddenly hoarse.

K'os looked hard at Red Leaf. The woman seemed frail, as though she had suddenly grown old. "They killed her," K'os said. "With a knife. The same way she killed Ghaden's mother. They say Sok himself did it."

THIRTY-NINE

THE NEAR RIVER PEOPLE

The sound came so gradually that at first Dii did not know what it was, but when the smell of salt came to her on the wind, then she realized it was the sea.

They topped a rise, and the land fell beneath them into a wide, flat expanse of wet mud, marked at the tide line by ridges of ice.

They were not a people of the sea. They understood rivers, wild at times and dangerous, but still confined by the land. The sea was too immense. Who among them knew the spirits that controlled it or the chants needed for protection? What would be considered an insult? How should a people act to show respect?

The women crowded close behind their men, clung to their children.

Dii shuddered at the sight of water spreading to the far horizon. Some storytellers said it curled up the curve of the sky in quest of the sun, to capture the warmth of its fire. But others said no. Why would the sea want to leave its bed? How would the fish live, the seals and whales?

Dii did not notice when the people's awe first gave way to grumbling, but finally, as she took in the vast tide flats, she understood that her husband's dreams had again been wrong. They had come to the end of the land, and there were still no caribou.

All eyes rested on Anaay, men and women watching. Dii felt as if she could not breathe. She waited for accusations to fly against him, waited and was surprised when they did not come. At first, Anaay seemed to shrink down inside himself, but then he filled his chest with air, puffed out his stomach and cried, "Again the Cousin Rivers have cursed us."

But as he spoke, the men around him rudely turned their backs, motioned to their women, and in silence they left Anaay standing at the crest of the hill, Dii alone behind him.

THE FOUR RIVERS VILLAGE

It was night, three days after the hunters' return, when K'os heard the scratching outside their lodge. She waited to see if Sand Fly would hear, but when the old woman did not call out, K'os spoke a welcome.

The inner doorflap was thrust aside, and from the corners of her eyes, K'os saw Tree Climber move toward his weapons. She held up one hand. "This man, I know him," she said to Tree Climber, and gestured for the hunter to come into the lodge. "He is Near River, and his name is River Ice Dancer."

River Ice Dancer held out his hands in greeting, palms up. He nodded at Sand Fly and Tree Climber, but did not seem interested in knowing their names. Instead he looked at K'os and said, "When I did not find you at the Cousin River winter village, I thought you might have come here, where your brother once lived."

K'os smiled to herself. She had forgotten that during one of their times together she had told him about her brother.

"One of the women at the cooking fires told me you lived in this lodge."

"You see she was right," K'os said, trying to keep from laughing at his seriousness.

"I brought what I could," he said. "My dog and furs

and pelts, a tent. I cannot offer you a lodge, but I have enough caribou hides to make one."

K'os studied him from narrowed eyes. Was he telling her the truth? Did he have lodge skins? When the caribou had overrun the Near River hunting camp, few men had been quick enough even to rescue their weapons. Where had he gotten his hides?

"You took enough caribou to have hides for a lodge?" she asked, and waved away Sand Fly, who was trying to offer River Ice Dancer a bowl of meat.

Sand Fly sat down with the bowl in her lap. K'os sucked in her cheeks to hide her smile when she saw River Ice Dancer's eyes on the food. If he had come here to make a bride offer, let him make it. He could eat later.

"I took one caribou that day, and my father did also."

"Better than most," K'os said, and noticed that Sand Fly had begun picking meat from the bowl, licking the juices from her fingers. "But two hides are not enough for a lodge."

"I went to the Cousins's winter village looking for you," he answered. "They had a few good hides in one of the caches. I took what I needed and a travois. In the night, I slipped away. I thought they would come after me, but they did not. Of course, they are only a village of old women. What could they do?"

"So the hunters have not yet returned," K'os said, mumbling the words to herself. She straightened and looked into River Ice Dancer's face. "And you have come to me for something? All I can offer is medicine."

Sand Fly thrust out her hand to show a scar, neatly healed.

K'os hid her surprise. The scar was old, and she had given Sand Fly nothing for it. But it did not hurt to have an ally. Who could say when the words of an old woman might do some good?

"I have come to ask for you as wife," River Ice Dancer said.

K'os opened her eyes wide, as though to show surprise. "I do not want to return to the Near River People," she told him. "The women there will always see me as slave."

"We will stay here," River Ice Dancer answered foolishly, as though he had the power to make the Four Rivers People accept him as their own.

Tree Climber tottered to his feet, thrust a gnarled finger into River Ice Dancer's face. "You think you are worthy of such a woman? You're hardly a man. How do we know you can provide enough meat for her? Do you have a cache in this village, or some other, to keep her fed through the winter?"

"I have a pack of meat, a good dog and the caribou hides," River Icer Dancer said.

"And where will you live? You think I have enough to feed you? Leave your caribou hides here, then go and hunt. Bring back meat so we can see that you are worthy of this village."

River Ice Dancer stuck out his lower lip, pouting as though he were a child. K'os held her laughter in her throat. Did he think there was nothing to winning a wife? Of course, he had come a long way and was willing to leave his own village. But how foolish to give so much for the first woman who had welcomed him to her bed. She stood up and went to the boiling bag, filled a bowl with meat. Sand Fly offered River Ice Dancer the bowl in her hand, now half empty.

"He has come a long way, Aunt," K'os said gently. "He is hungry." She gave him the full bowl and also a bladder of water. "Eat," she said. "Then we will talk about this."

She sat and watched him, thought about his offer, considered sending him away to hunt as Tree Climber had suggested. When he returned, if she had decided she did not want him, she could put baneberries into his food. After he died, she could keep his caribou hides and the meat he managed to bring back. But perhaps it would be to her advantage to have a husband. She tilted her head, studied him. He was not a handsome boy; his lips were too large, his nose misshapen. He was strong, though, and she had enjoyed his fumbling attempts to please her.

River Ice Dancer looked up from his food, smiled at her. K'os lowered her eyes slowly, as though she were a girl being courted for the first time.

Perhaps River Ice Dancer would be a good husband, she thought. And if not, then there were many ways a husband could die.

THE NEAR RIVER PEOPLE

Dii reached into the food pack. Many Words had given Anaay the hindquarters of a fresh-killed hare, and Dii had wrapped it in a well-scraped piece of hide and tucked it at the top of her pack, but it had slipped down the side. She was tired enough to want to leave it there, but knew she should get it out before it became soft and seeped through its wrap to foul the dried meat she carried.

She had set her tent on high ground, layered spruce branches then grass mats over the frozen earth, but as she pushed her arm into the pack, her foot slid between two mats and slipped on the spruce branches. She fell against the pack and the sides split open.

She pulled the hare out, clenched her teeth against angry words. They were a long way from their winter village; no use in cursing a pack she still needed. She skewered the hare on a sharpened willow branch and propped it into place over the fire she had started just outside the lean-to.

She took meat from the carrying pack until the side was loose enough for her to relace the awl holes, then she dragged the pack to the side of the fire where it was bright enough for her to work.

Anaay came to her tent after she had finished repairing the pack. He spoke curtly to her, criticized the taste of the meat when he ate, but Dii ignored him. She was setting the last rawhide packet into the top of the carrying pack when she realized it was the medicine K'os had given her for Anaay. Dii had nearly forgotten it during all the problems of the hunting camp.

What had K'os said? It would help Anaay give Dii a son.

She had intended to wait until they were back at the winter village to use it, but she had thought they would return long before now. She lived with the hardships of being Anaay's wife. Why not have something to give her joy? Perhaps, if she bore Anaay a child, he would be a better husband. She opened the packet. It was filled with a powder, light green, nearly white. She mixed some into a cup of water, pushed the cup into the fire coals and waited until the water was hot. Then she poured the mixture into a clean cup and gave it to Anaay.

"A tea to strengthen you," she told him.

He took a sip. "Cranberry?" he asked.

"It is something we Cousin women know," she said, and wished K'os had told her what plant the powder was from. "Something for hunters."

Anaay narrowed his eyes and held the cup out to her. "You drink," he said.

She considered telling him that K'os had given it to her and that it would strengthen his seed, but why chance that Anaay would see her gesture as an insult? Better to drink some herself and assure him the medicine was harmless.

"It is usually only for men, hunters," Dii said, but she lifted the cup to her lips without hesitation.

Anaay grabbed it from her before she could drink and swallowed down the rest. "Why curse it, then?" he said with a smirk.

THE COUSIN RIVER PEOPLE

Sok sat beside Snow-in-her-hair, stroked her forehead with a strip of hide wrung out in cold water. She was hot to his touch, and in just three days her milk had dried up. Carries Much now ate at Willow Leaf's breast.

Snow opened her eyes and looked at him, mumbled that she must find Yaa. He told her again that Yaa was all right, that she was strong enough to leave her bed, had even come once to sit with them.

Snow gasped for breath as she did each time she spoke, and Sok's chest also ached, as though he, too, fought to breathe.

Aqamdax and Twisted Stalk had heated strips of caribou hide layered with spruce pitch and packed them over her chest. They had forced marsh marigold tea and lungwort down Snow's throat, had rubbed her back and neck with caribou leaves, but nothing seemed to help. Sok lowered his head to his arms, closed his eyes only for a moment. How long since he had slept?

Dreams hovered close, and though his eyes were closed, he saw Star walking toward them. She was better, Chakliux had told him, but Sok hadn't known she was able to leave her bed.

"You are well?" Sok called to her.

She looked at him and smiled, but did not answer.

"I am glad you could come," he said.

Still she did not speak. He watched her as she knelt beside Snow-in-her-hair, as she leaned close. Sok thought she had some secret to whisper, but then she opened her mouth wide, set it over Snow's mouth, sucked in as though to draw the breath from Snow's body.

Sok cried out and jumped to his feet, but Star was gone. A wind cut in from the open side of the lean-to, brought a cloud of smoke from the fire. It settled into his throat, made him cough. He went outside and drew the night's cold deep into his chest. The camp was dark except for hearth coals.

"A dream," he whispered, and went back to his wife.

"She is awake," Twisted Stalk told Chakliux.

Chakliux was so deep into his thoughts that the old woman had to repeat her words before he understood what she had said.

"Your wife is awake. You should go to her. She asks for you."

"She's awake?"

"She asks for you."

He followed Twisted Stalk from the center of the camp to his tent. Aqamdax was at the entrance, had stayed each night with Star, catching what sleep she could during the day.

"She is hungry," Aqamdax said.

Chakliux ducked into the tent. Star's eyes were open, her face pale but no longer fevered.

"Twisted Stalk said you are better."

"I'm well now," she told him. "Tired, though," she said. She clasped his hands, pulled them down to her belly. The baby moved.

FORTY

THE NEAR RIVER PEOPLE

Anaay finished the medicine, then narrowed his eyes. "A woman should always go first to her husband's tent," he said to Dii. "I should not have had to come here to eat."

But what could she say? She had lingered in her own tent because she did not want to hear his complaints, did not want to chance that he would take his anger out on her.

"I was coming," she finally told him, "but the food was not ready. You know the hare is from Many Words?" Perhaps the surprise that Many Words had brought a gift of meat would calm Anaay's anger.

Anaay grunted, grabbed his walking stick and began to push himself to his feet. Dii's heart quickened, and she stood also. Better to give herself some chance to run, though in the darkness, she would not go far. She preferred her husband's walking stick to whatever night spirits lurked this close to the cold and ice of the North Sea.

But when he was almost to his feet, he slumped suddenly, clasped his belly and groaned. Dii waited, wondering if he was using some ploy to get her close so she could not run from his anger, but he loosed his clasp on the stick, collapsed to the floor mats and tucked himself into a ball.

"What have you done to me, Wife?" he rasped out, his words thick, harsh.

"Nothing. I did nothing," Dii said, fear pulling her denial into a child's voice.

"The hare," he gasped.

"Many Words . . ."

"He—" Anaay cried out, twisted against the pain.

"I saw him kill it. He used a throwing stick," Dii said. She was crying now, her words broken. "I saw him skin it and . . . he gave the hindquarters to me. . . ."

Anaay, in his agony, did not seem to hear her. She had watched Many Words, had not taken her eyes away from him. She had even checked the hare's legs for splintered bones and had eaten a few bites herself. She sat back on her heels, waited to see if she would have any pain. There was nothing.

"I ate the hare, too," she told Anaay. "I'm not sick."

He seemed to consider her words, clenched his teeth as another pain took him.

"Perhaps Blue Flower will have something," Dii said. "A tea or—" She stopped. The remembrance of the tea she had given Anaay tore into her thoughts, squeezed her heart tight.

Then Anaay, too, gasped. "The tea. Who gave it to you?"

"No one," she answered, too afraid to tell him the truth.

"K'os," he said, whispering the name.

Dii did not answer.

"K'os!" he shouted, then doubled again in agony.

"K'os," she answered.

"She told you to kill me?"

"She said it would help you give me a son."

He ground his teeth, spat out, "You do not know that she wants me dead? She did not tell you . . . about the Grandfather Rock?"

"Only that you saved her, that you helped her kill—"

His sudden laughter turned into a scream of pain. His eyes rolled back in his head, and a stench suddenly permeated the tent. He groaned, and she saw the discoloration of his caribou hide leggings, the stain that was a mix of dung and blood. She ran from the lean-to, thinking only to get help. Blue Flower, where had she set her tent?

Dii made her way in the darkness, hearth fire to hearth fire. Most were now only coals, shedding little light, so that she stumbled often as she ran.

She recognized Blue Flower's tent by the string of raven skulls hung at the entrance, charms once owned by her shaman husband. She called out, tried to keep the tremor from her voice.

"I am asleep," Blue Flower answered.

"My husband, Anaay, needs medicine," Dii said, and held her breath until the woman drew aside the tent flap.

"What's wrong with him?" Blue Flower asked, her face a pale moon peering from the darkness.

"Stomach pains," Dii answered, afraid to say more.

"Diarrhea?"

"Yes."

"Wait."

Dii had not taken time to put on her boots. She stood in her lodge moccasins, and the cold of the ground seeped into her feet, made her bones ache. Finally Blue Flower poked her head out again. "Nagoonberry root," she said. "Let him chew it, or make a tea."

Dii had many questions, but Blue Flower closed the doorflap in her face. She went back to her tent, could smell her husband's sickness before she even stepped inside. He was lying with his knees drawn to his chest. She knelt beside him, broke off a piece of the root, pressed it against his lips.

"It will help you," she said. "Blue Flower sent it."

He opened his mouth.

"Chew it," she told him. "I will make a tea." She waited until he clamped the root between his teeth, then she put the rest into her own mouth, chewed until it was pulp, then spat it into a cup and poured in a little water. She pushed the cup into the coals and waited until the water was warm, then she took it to Anaay, tried not to see the mess he was lying in. She tipped his chin up, pulled what remained of the root from his mouth, then dipped her fingers into the cup and dripped the mash down his throat.

He seemed to relax, and Dii let herself hope that the nagoonberry was working. Suddenly his teeth clamped on the edge of the cup. His head snapped back, and his arms and legs flailed. She tried to hold him still, but he broke away from her, continued to twitch and jerk.

She lifted a chant, clasped the amulet her father had given her when she was still a child. Fear made her tremble. What hope could she have for protection when Anaay himself was so cursed? She began to cry, tears dropping from her cheeks to the front of her parka, but she did not stop singing until finally Anaay lay still. His eyes were open and had rolled up into his head so she could see only the whites. He jerked, and she jumped away, dropped the cup of mash. Then he was looking at her. Perhaps the tea and her prayers had worked.

"I'll get you clean clothes, Husband," she told him. "You can sleep here in my tent. . . ."

Then she noticed he had not blinked, and suddenly she knew that he was seeing nothing at all.

THE COUSIN RIVER CAMP

Sok shook himself awake. He thought he had heard a fox barking. Had it been true or only a part of his dreams? Either way, what else could it mean but death? He crawled to the open side of the lean-to, saw that Owl Catcher, sitting beside Snow-in-her-hair, had fallen asleep. One look at his wife froze his heart.

Her mouth and eyes were open. Sometime during the night, her spirit had found its way from her body. He tried to begin a mourning cry, but no sound came from his throat. Perhaps when Snow left, she had taken his voice with her. He leaned over his wife's body, gathered her into his arms, wept silently.

"I'm strong enough," Star said.

"You may be," Chakliux told her, "but what about Snow-in-her-hair? What about Yaa?"

"Let them stay here with Sok. He can care for them. I need to get back to my lodge. My baby is growing, and soon I will not walk so easily."

Chakliux sighed. He slipped on his parka and boots. When Star was in such a mood, there was no way to reason with her. But perhaps she was right. They were only four, five days from the winter village. Why not allow most of the people to go on to the village? Why should everyone stay for the few who were too weak to travel? The women needed time to repair their lodges for winter, and the men needed to divide out the caribou among the families.

As Chakliux started toward Sok's lean-to, Star crawled out after him, whining that he should fill the boiling bag and bring more wood for the fire.

"If you are well enough to walk to the winter village, you are well enough to feed yourself," he told her, and grabbed several strips of dried meat from a rack at the side of the tent, ate as he walked.

When he drew closer to Sok's lean-to, he heard Owl Catcher's voice, thin and broken, chanting a mourning song. Suddenly the meat Chakliux had eaten was like something rotten in his belly. He threw the rest of it to one of the dogs tied beside the tent, then he went inside. He wrapped his arms around Sok and let his tears join his brother's.

THE FOUR RIVERS VILLAGE

"I think you are wrong about K'os," Red Leaf said to Cen. She would have never spoken to Sok in such a way, but Cen was a man who would listen to a woman, even his wife.

"She's not a good woman," he told her. "You do not know K'os like I do."

"She makes beautiful parkas."

"You make beautiful parkas."

"Think how much you will get if both of us are making parkas for you to trade."

She saw Cen raise his eyebrows at the thought, and her heart beat hard in hope.

But then he said, "I lived with her once. In her lodge in the Cousin Village. I intended to take her as wife, but one day when I came home, she was in her bedding furs with another man."

"She was not your wife, you said."

"It would have been no different if she had been. The hunters laughed at my anger, told me she welcomed any man into her bed if he had enough beads or furs."

"So let her sleep with them," Red Leaf said. "When she's your wife, what she gets in beads and furs will belong to you. You will have more to trade."

She thought Cen would be angry with her for saying such a thing, but to her surprise, he laughed. Then he stood and pulled off her caribou hide shirt. He pushed her back into his bed. She opened her legs to him, and for a little while she did not think about K'os.

FORTY-ONE

THE NEAR RIVER PEOPLE

Dii's first thought was to go to Sun Caller. He was an
elder; he would know what to do. Perhaps she should also
get Blue Flower. But when she looked again at her husband, shrunken in death, lying in a pool of his own blood
and feces, she knew they would guess he had been poi-
soned.

And who would believe K'os had done it? She had left
them so long ago. Dii still bore the marks of Anaay's
beating. It would not be difficult to think she had taken
revenge.

She could steal one of the dogs. She had food and her
tent. . . . No. The Near Rivers would come after her. The
people had to avenge his death. Would Anaay's spirit be
any more forgiving than Anaay had been?

Dii went outside, looked up at the stars. She still had
most of the night left, and Anaay owned three strong
dogs, two travois. Dii was small, did not eat much. With
Anaay's share of the caribou, with fish she had caught
and dried and the supplies they had brought with them,
there was enough to get her back to the Cousin Village.
What was that from here? Four, five days' walk. Perhaps
a little more.

She packed the travois carefully, tied Anaay's weapons

and his walking stick to the largest. Then she used lengths of babiche to bind Anaay's joints so his spirit could not harm her, then to tie him and his mess into the grass mats she rolled around his body. She layered the travois with spruce branches from the tent floor and dragged Anaay to it. She tied him to the poles, took down her tent and draped it over him, bound it and the tent poles to the travois.

She crept through the village to Anaay's tent, took it down also. She had wanted to leave it, but who would believe a man as selfish as Anaay would leave without taking his lean-to, even battered as it was by the caribou's hooves?

It took Dii four trips to carry everything back to the travois. She harnessed the strongest dog, a golden-eyed male, to the travois that held Anaay's body, then tied the other male to the second travois. The third dog, a young female, she loaded with packs that held Anaay's bedding and his extra clothing.

Before the sun rose, she led the dogs in a wide circle around the camp, away from the sea and east toward the Cousin River Village. She would travel most of the day, find a place to leave Anaay's body, then return to her own people. Perhaps a woman with three dogs and two travois would find a man willing to take her as wife. If not, surely one of the old women would welcome her.

And who among the Near Rivers would doubt that Anaay had chosen to live somewhere else rather than admit he had claimed caribou where there were none?

THE COUSIN RIVER HUNTERS

"She is dead," Chakliux said.

Aqamdax glanced up at him, was suddenly frightened that he looked so tired, so small.

"Snow?"

"Snow. How is Yaa?"

"Stronger."

"Strong enough to travel to the winter village if we make a travois for her? Sky Watcher says he will pull it."

"You will leave before the mourning is ended?"

"I cannot," he said. "I'll stay with Sok, but why keep everyone four days in this place when we are so close to the village?"

"I'll stay. Yaa and Ghaden and I. It's better not to move Yaa."

"If she's strong enough, it would be best to have her at the village. Ligige' is there. Her medicine is good. She might have been able to save Snow. I should have sent a hunter for her. I should . . ."

Aqamdax stood and lifted a hand to Chakliux's face. "The river took her, Chakliux," she said softly. "Do not waste your days in regret. Your brother needs you. He has lost much."

"All things were going so well, Aqamdax, until that time we were at the river. Perhaps by what we did—"

Aqamdax placed her fingers over his mouth, stopped his words. How could she bear to hear what he said? What they did was a betrayal to Night Man and Star. Not to anyone else. Why should Snow be punished? Or Yaa?

"We have lost our luck, you and I," Chakliux said.

"No," said Aqamdax. "Nothing has changed for us. How many times in a hunt do people die? Hunters drown; women become sick. Children are lost in the traveling. Yet on this hunt, only one has died. Do not say our luck is gone. I'll go to the winter village, and when I get there, I'll throw away Night Man. When you and Sok return, then I will be your wife."

She leaned close to him, and he put his arms around her. When she went back to the tent to prepare Yaa for the journey, Aqamdax was crying.

Chakliux helped the people load their supplies, and though Star whined and pleaded to stay with him, he sent her back with the others. Sky Watcher pulled Yaa's travois and fended off Star, who thought she should ride with Yaa. Once, Aqamdax looked back at Chakliux, then she set her eyes on the trail and did not turn. Ghaden and Biter walked beside her. She carried her own packs and some of Star's.

With their loads, it would take them five days, Chakliux

thought—at least that with Star causing trouble and Yaa on the travois.

Chakliux watched until trees and hills hid them from his view, then he went back to his brother, to the bundle that was Snow-in-her-hair. The women had made a short mourning for her, had washed her and dressed her in the best clothing they could find in the camp—boots from one woman, leggings from another, a necklace given, a stone from an amulet. But now only he and Sok remained to mourn, and Chakliux wondered if, without the women, a proper mourning could be made. Perhaps Aqamdax was right. She should have stayed.

He had set several charred coals on the hearth stones. When they were cool, he used the handle of his sleeve knife to pound them into powder. He sifted the powder into a bowl of rendered caribou fat and used his fingers to knead the mixture until it was smooth. Then he blackened his face, watched as Sok did the same.

Sok pulled a knife from his belt scabbard, lay his left hand on a rock, held the blade, trembling, over his smallest finger.

Chakliux reached out, caught Sok's wrist. "No," he said. "You would honor the ways of the North Tundra People to mourn your wife?"

As Dzuuggi, Chakliux knew those stories of the men who crossed the North Sea to trade with the River People and the Walrus Hunters. He had heard how they mutilated themselves to show mourning. "Will she know it is from you, that finger?" Chakliux asked his brother. "She will think some Tundra hunter remembers his dead wife."

Chakliux took the knife, pushed up his parka sleeve and slashed his forearm, once, twice. He stood and allowed the blood to drip into the fire, to rise with the smoke in honor of Snow-in-her-hair. He gave the knife to Sok, watched as Sok slashed his arm four times. Then Chakliux began the mourning chants.

A storm found the Cousin People during their second day of walking. By midmorning, the wind whipped the snow until it blasted their faces like sand. The dogs fought their harnesses, and women fell under loads made heavier by the weight of ice.

At noon they found a strand of black spruce to shelter them. The men helped the women set up their lean-tos, but even in the lee of the trees, the wind and cold made tent poles splinter.

Aqamdax dug a cave in the snow, and the ice-hardened crust cut its way through her caribou hide mittens to score her hands. When she reached bare ground, she made a flooring of haired caribou hides, warming the hides with her breath and hands, then unfolding them slowly so they did not crack in the cold. She unharnessed Night Man's dogs, set the packs around the snow cave like a wall, then she and Star, Night Man, Ghaden and Yaa huddled together, sharing each other's warmth. Her thoughts carried her back to Sok and Chakliux, alone with Snow-in-her-hair, and she prayed for their safety.

Chakliux's dreams seemed to come to him from the snow, and they filled his mind with fear. He watched as though he were an eagle, seeing all things from the sky. He saw himself walking with Sok, and together they dragged a travois. It was filled with packs, and also a body wrapped in the way of the dead, knees drawn up to the chin, arms crossed and tucked close to the chest. The head was covered with a caribou hide, and as they walked, the wind lifted the hide. Then Chakliux saw that the dead one was not Snow-in-her-hair but Aqamdax.

He woke to his own cries and was afraid to return to sleep. How could he risk that his dreams would again find Aqamdax and steal away her spirit?

THE FOUR RIVERS VILLAGE

The men had cut her lodge poles, and K'os paid them well for their work. They showed her the sunken ground, dug out long ago by the first one to put a lodge there. Even stones and sand were still in place for the hearth. She had scraped the hides River Ice Dancer gave her, added them to her own, and sewed them into a lodge cover. It was a small lodge, but K'os's stitches were even and tight; the sinew she had borrowed from Sand Fly was well twisted and strong.

She moved into the lodge the day the storm began. She stayed there alone, fighting to keep the snow from finding its way down the smoke hole and in through the entrance tunnel. Usually she did not like storms. What could anyone do to stop them? But this storm, she decided, might be a good one. She doubted that River Ice Dancer would survive it. On the third day of the storm, she heard a scratching at her lodge wall. First she thought it was only the wind, but then someone called her name. She crawled into the entrance tunnel, pulled aside the flap. The one who stood there was so caked with snow and ice that she did not recognize him until she had brushed the snow from his parka.

River Ice Dancer. He smiled at her, and in spite of her disappointment, she returned that smile. Most likely he had not brought back the meat he had promised Tree Climber. How could he? He had been gone scarcely more than two handfuls of days.

"My dogs are outside," he said to her without any greeting of polite words, but in such a storm K'os did not expect politeness.

"They can stay in the tunnel," she told him. "But only until this storm has passed. I do not need their fleas in my lodge."

He went out, heaved several large packs in through the door, and she pulled them into the lodge. Finally, he brought the dogs into the tunnel. He cracked the balls of ice and snow from their feet, rubbed his hands over their eyes and noses, the tips of their ears.

K'os went into the lodge, brought out water, dried fish. She had not yet convinced one of the village hunters to make her a cache, so she kept her meat and fish with her in the lodge. Why chance leaving them in Sand Fly's cache? No doubt the old woman would use them up before she touched her own meat, and K'os did not have enough to get through the winter as it was.

She gave fish and water to the dogs, then motioned for River Ice Dancer to join her in the lodge. He waited as she hung his parka on a lodge pole, then helped him out of his leggings and inner parka. The inner parka was wet with sweat, rimed with ice, and so she knew he had walked too hard, too far, had taken a terrible chance in trying to get back to her.

She gave him a hare fur blanket, and he wrapped himself in it, groaned as he finally sat down beside the fire. "I thought I would not get here," he told her. "Even when I came to the village, I thought I might not have the strength to make it to your lodge."

"How did you know which lodge was mine?" K'os asked.

"I saw this lodge, new, sitting where there had been no lodge, and I hoped it was yours."

She gave him a bowl of food, watched as he curled his fingers around its warmth. His mouth was bloodied from splits in his lips, and his nose and cheeks were spotted with frostbite. She went to her medicine bag, took out powdered plantain leaves and mixed the powder into goose grease. She tilted back his head, and though he tried to turn away, she smoothed the grease on his face.

"Be still," she told him. "It will help pull the cold from your skin."

When she had finished, he held out his food bowl.

She filled it again and watched him eat.

"I have enough for a bride price," he said, his mouth full.

She raised her chin, looked at him through slitted eyes. Perhaps he was lying, but she did not think so. It was too easy for her to check his packs.

He was a boy, yes, but tall and big, perhaps more handsome than she had thought. She had first seen him when she and her husband Ground Beater traveled to the Near River Village. River Ice Dancer had been a leader then among the children. She smiled as she remembered. He had refused to tell her his name. Wise even then. Why give a stranger the power of knowing your name?

Perhaps he would be a good husband. "River Ice Dancer," she said, holding out her hand to him, "you are cold, and my bed is very warm."

FORTY-TWO

Dii walked for nearly two days before leaving Anaay's body. She found a clearing inside a stand of alders, the snow in sharp-ridged drifts where the trees had stolen it from the wind. What was more fitting than alders, with their weak branches and poisonous leaves? Dii asked herself.

She rolled his body from the travois, set his weapons beside him, then sang a mourning chant. She sang loudly, hoping to appease his spirit so he would not follow her and take revenge, but when the words came from her mouth, they seemed to fly into the grass mats that wrapped Anaay's body, and were sucked away so quickly that she did not hear them as song.

During her walking, she often spoke to his body on the travois. She explained that she had made him the tea only so she could bear him a child. K'os had tricked them both, giving poison rather than medicine. But Dii doubted that her explanations would be enough to turn away her husband's anger. When had Anaay ever given in to reason?

Dii used her woman's knife to cut the dried grass that stuck up through the snow, and she laid it on Anaay's body to hide him from anyone who might pass near the alders. Over the grass, she piled spruce branches she had brought from the Near River camp. The grass and the spruce were too light to hold down Anaay's spirit if he decided to follow her, but perhaps the bindings she had put at each of his joints would delay him until she was far enough away that he could not find her.

She repacked the travois, fed the dogs, all the while remembering her life with Anaay. She saw him in the fine parkas his first wife, Gull Beak, had made him, saw him as he stood in front of the hunters in the village, explaining his visions.

Then it seemed as if Dii's eyes cleared, and she remembered her husband in another way—as a man who did all things for himself and nothing for others. Perhaps he is not strong enough to take revenge, she thought.

She had not walked far after leaving Anaay when snow began to fall. She lifted her head to welcome it. What better way to bury her husband's body? But soon the snow was so heavy she could not see beyond the step she was taking. She stopped and made a shelter, setting the travois so they would block the wind. Why continue to walk when she could not see? She would probably only wander in circles.

She fed the dogs dried fish, hoped full bellies would help them sleep through the storm, then she curled under her tent covering, ate and tried to sleep. But the wind sang sharp, bitter songs, and scared away the comfort of dreams, so that Dii began to wonder if Anaay had sent the storm to kill her. How better to take her with him, still wife, still slave?

Chakliux guided Sok as though the man were a child, held on to his parka for fear of losing him in the storm. They had made a death platform and put it high in a spruce tree. He had promised Sok they would return the next summer and take Snow's bones to a sacred place, perhaps the Grandfather Lake, where Sok could visit them if he wished.

After four days of mourning, they had begun their journey to the Cousin River Village in spite of storm winds. The first night Chakliux had dug out a shelter where they planned to stay until the storm ended, but the next morning the winds were not as fierce, so they started out again. They fought the snow with each step, felt it weigh them down as it gathered on their parkas, stiffened their leggings, blinded their eyes.

Sok kept trying to sit down, mumbling explanations Chakliux could not hear above the wind. Finally Chakliux stopped and made a camp, allowed Sok to sit alone while he dug a shelter in the snow, lining it with spruce branches and caribou hides. He set his packs as a wind block at the opening and called for Sok to do the same. Sok did not answer, and with sudden fear, Chakliux realized that in the snow and darkening twilight he could not see his brother.

As he circled the shelter, the falling snow gave life to the closest trees, so that each seemed to jump out at him when he neared it. Then suddenly, within the curtain of snow, he saw Sok standing, one hand lifted to shade his eyes as if he were trying to see in bright sun.

"I heard Snow-in-her-hair," he told Chakliux.

Sok's words were like ice on Chakliux's spine, but he guided his brother to their shelter. A drift had already formed across the narrow opening Chakliux had left between the packs, but he broke it away with his foot and pulled Sok inside. He wrapped his brother in a hare fur blanket and gave him some of the dried salmon he carried in a pouch at his waist. Then Chakliux made chants, those few that were most powerful, and he hoped they were strong enough to keep Snow-in-her-hair from finding their small shelter.

Through five days of storm, Chakliux and Sok huddled together in their lean-to. They kept a warming fire alive until it had eaten all their wood. Then they borrowed warmth from one another, lying together under the howling voice of the wind.

It seemed to Chakliux as though they fought more than a storm. Could the wind truly be Snow-in-her-hair screaming for Sok to join her? Could a dead wife use a storm to pull away her husband's spirit?

A man could fight wind and snow, but what weapon

could stand against a spirit? Knives? Spears? Chakliux had used all his chants. . . . But perhaps whatever power he had held within his own spirit was gone. He had broken the taboos of The People, taken another man's wife without thought for anything but his own pleasure. Was there no punishment for such a thing?

Had his weakness cost Snow-in-her-hair her life? Did it threaten Sok's spirit? And what about the rest of the Cousin People? With the storm raging, had they managed to get to the winter village? Could a curse grow like the branches of a tree, reaching out to others who had done nothing to deserve hurt?

Once a taboo was broken, what did a man do to protect himself? More important, how did he protect those closest to him?

Chakliux's thoughts swirled as though driven by the same wind that had brought the storm. He steadied his mind with the stories and riddles he had been taught as a child. At first he did not realize he was telling those stories aloud, that his voice had risen above the storm noise, but then he saw Sok push back his hood and bend his head to listen. So Chakliux spoke into the darkness of their shelter, hearing the words that came from his own mouth as though for the first time, hoping to find some story that told how to earn forgiveness.

THE COUSIN WINTER VILLAGE

Ligige' pushed herself from her bed. Had someone scratched at her lodge door or had the sound been something from a dream? She stirred the hearth coals and looked over at Long Eyes. Chakliux would be surprised when he returned. Some days Long Eyes was almost normal—eating, working, even speaking.

She heard the scratching again, picked up her walking stick and thrust it into the entrance tunnel. Some animal perhaps, she thought. This time of year they were all seeking winter dens. Perhaps a fox or wolverine had decided on her lodge. She felt nothing with her stick, heard no growls or hisses, so she crawled into the entrance and called out a welcome.

"Twisted Stalk?"

"You are Twisted Stalk?" Ligige' cried, and in gladness thrust open the doorflap, but caught her breath when she saw the shadowed face of a young woman.

"You're not Twisted Stalk," the girl said. "Is this the Cousin People's winter village?"

"Yes," Ligige' told her. "You are alone?"

"I have dogs," she said, and stepped aside so Ligige' could see the three dogs behind her.

"I thought I knew all the people in the Cousin River Village," Dii said softly, more to herself than to the old woman who welcomed her.

Then suddenly she was afraid. Was the woman lying, claiming that this was the Cousin Village when it was not? Had Dii, in her desire to get away from Anaay, gone to a different village, one not her own? No, how could she? She had known this place since she was a child, had traveled to it many times from fish camps and hunting sites.

"I am Ligige', aunt to Chakliux. Do you know him?" the old woman asked, and gestured for Dii to follow her through the entrance tunnel.

Dii crawled into the lodge. The hearth coals made a faint red glow in the center of the floor, and Dii could see an old woman sitting up in her bedding furs, a woven hare fur blanket wrapped around her shoulders. Then she caught her breath in gladness.

"Long Eyes," she said, so pleased to see someone she knew that she forgot to answer Ligige' 's question.

"Who are you?" Long Eyes asked, and Dii was surprised to hear her speak.

"Her spirit has returned?" she asked Ligige'.

"Some think so. Who are you?"

The bluntness of the question matched rudeness for rudeness, and Dii began to apologize.

"She is Sun Girl," Long Eyes said, answering for her.

"Yes, Aunt, though now I am called Dii." Then she said to Ligige', "I know Chakliux."

"He and all the men in the village and their wives went on a caribou hunt," Ligige' told her. "We are just old women here. Were you one of those taken as slave to the Near River Village?"

"I was, I and my mother, though the Near River men killed her."

"Keep Fish?" Long Eyes asked. "She is dead?"

Dii shuddered to hear her mother's name called out in such a way. Keep Fish had been a good mother, but surely she would seek revenge for her death. Perhaps she was angry that Dii had become wife to one of the Near Rivers. But then her mother might consider Anaay's death a fitting revenge. Dii waited for some noise of wind, the voice of animal or bird to give sign that her mother had heard, but there was nothing. Perhaps with her husband and sons also dead, Dii's mother was content to be as she was—spirit among spirits.

"Be still, Long Eyes," Ligige' said. "Do not think about those who have died, be glad rather that this daughter has returned to her own village."

Long Eyes picked at the fur of her blanket, and Dii noticed that a wide patch of the woven pelts had been picked clean. "My husband once wanted Keep Fish," Long Eyes murmured. "For second wife. I would not let him." Her fingers picked more frantically. "Do you think she is mad at me?" She lifted her hands, held them curled like claws.

"No," Dii said. "She liked you. She told me that."

Long Eyes nodded and laid her hands on the blanket. Ligige' raised her eyebrows at Dii, showing her approval, then lifted her chin toward a stack of bowls that hung in a net tied to the lodge poles. "There is meat in the boiling bag, only hare, but it is fresh."

"Thank you, I will eat after I have seen to my dogs."

As Dii left the lodge, Ligige' settled Long Eyes back into her bed, gently scolded her for pulling the fur from her blanket. Then she squatted beside the hearth coals, held her hands out to gather heat into fingers bent and old.

"You ran away or were thrown away?" Ligige' asked. Dii lowered the bowl from her mouth. "I ran away," she said. "Though he was angry enough to throw me away. I was surprised each day that he did not.

"My husband dreamed of caribou and convinced the people to follow him to the North Sea. But when we came to the sea, there were no caribou, nothing but ice and water."

"You left then?" Ligige' asked.

"I had dreams of my own that came to me, songs the caribou sang into my bones. The rhythm of their walking was like the beating of my heart. I told my husband, and he was angry with me."

Ligige' 's eyes gleamed. "You dream caribou?" she asked softly.

Then Dii wished she had not told the woman. What good had ever come from her caribou dreams? "Perhaps my dreams are wrong," Dii said.

"Perhaps they are not," Ligige' whispered.

Dii shrugged. "It does not matter," she said. "The Cousin men always hunt the same river. They do not need dreamers, and the Near Rivers would not listen to me."

"When you told your husband, what did he say?"

"He beat me."

"And you left him."

"Not until we came to the sea. There he blamed me for his own false dreams. Then I left him. I took his dogs and came here."

"Your husband, who is he?"

Dii's skin prickled, and she felt a weight against her shoulders, as though Anaay were standing behind her. "I cannot say his name. He died before I left, and I do not want to call his spirit."

Ligige' wrinkled her brow. "Did you . . ." she began to ask, but then said, "This husband, did he have another wife?"

"Gull Beak."

Ligige' 's lips thinned into a smile. "How did he die?" she asked.

For a long time Dii did not answer. Her hands had begun to tremble, and when she spoke, her words were broken. "Someone, it was someone who did not know what she did . . . that one . . . killed him."

"This husband who died," Ligige' said, "maybe he needed to be dead. Perhaps we should not mourn but celebrate."

FORTY-THREE

They came out of the storm like ghosts. Ligige' clutched a hand to her breast, dropped the stick she was using to break the ice from the smoke hole of her lodge.

"If you take me, who will care for Long Eyes?" she said to them, but the wind whipped the sound from her mouth, swirled it into the storm as though she had said nothing at all.

She stood defeated, without protection of stick or words, but straightened her shoulders and waited for what would come. After all, she was old. She had known death was watching her. Many people died in storms, not only the old, but young, strong men, new mothers, children. Why should she expect to be favored?

They carried packs, these ghosts, so with sorrow Ligige' realized she would be traveling far. She had hoped the journey to the spirit world would be a quick one, easy on an old woman's bones.

"Aunt," one of them called, and lifted a hand in greeting.

She glanced down at herself, wondering if she was already spirit. Her arms and legs looked the same, but the ghosts were around her, laughing, lifting packs from one another's backs, and she recognized Sky Watcher and his wife Bird Caller, the old man Take More, and Aqamdax.

She opened her arms to Yaa and Ghaden. The boy's dog, Biter, packs still strapped to his back, knocked her down with his jumping and licked her face until Ghaden pulled him away.

"You dog turd, Biter!" the boy yelled out, his voice loud even in the wind.

Then Ligige' knew they were not ghosts, and she added her laughter to theirs.

"So they stayed with the dead one," Ligige' said, for once following respectful ways and not saying Snow-in-her-hair's name.

"They said four days, then they would come," Aqamdax told her, and Ligige' saw that her fingers trembled. Aqamdax picked up the empty bowl she had set on the floor mats, wrapped her hands around it.

"You would like more?" Ligige' asked, pursing her lips toward the bowl.

"No, I have had enough."

"It is good to see smoke coming again from all the smoke holes in this village," Ligige' told her, and waited for Aqamdax to say something.

Aqamdax was not one to sit and talk when there was work to do—food to put in caches, hides to stack in lodges, firewood to dig out of the snow, parkas to repair—so much work that the women would not finish it until winter was nearly over. So why was she here? And why, when Ligige' introduced Dii, had Aqamdax shown only politeness, no delight that Dii had returned to their village, no mention of the other women who had left their Near River husbands?

Ligige' felt the silence press in against her, as though the walls of the lodge were suddenly too close, but finally Aqamdax said, "Long Eyes is better." She turned her head and lifted her chin toward the old woman. Long Eyes sat beside Dii, legs crossed, a boot in her hand. She was sewing the sole to the upper, threading a length of sinew through awl holes.

"She is much better," Ligige' said. "Sometimes she speaks, and if I give her simple tasks, she almost always does them. But she has had to learn everything again, even her own name, and she still does not sleep well at night."

"Star will take Long Eyes into her own lodge tomorrow after the hearth fire has warmed and dried it," Aqamdax said. "She wanted me to tell you that." Then, as though she had said nothing about Long Eyes, Aqamdax leaned forward and whispered, "I have a problem, Aunt. I need your advice."

Ligige' raised her eyebrows to show her willingness to listen, tried to be still and patient while Aqamdax made several beginnings, struggling for words. Finally she sighed and said, "I want to throw Night Man away."

Ligige' 's only surprise was that Aqamdax had waited so long to do it. A husband who kills his own son is not a man any woman should keep. But Aqamdax had asked for advice, not agreement, so she asked, "Where would you stay? You have no lodge of your own."

"I have a share of caribou skins from the hunt, and before then I had two hides of my own, already scraped and sewn together."

"You know that winter is not a good time for a woman without a husband."

"I have lived through other winters without a husband," Aqamdax answered.

"You know there are not enough men in this village."

"First Eagle will take me as second wife."

Ligige' studied Aqamdax. "But you have another."

Aqamdax's cheeks reddened.

"Chakliux?" Ligige' asked.

"Yes."

"Will you leave your husband before Chakliux returns?"

"I do not want to stay with Night Man until then. I do not want another of his sons in my belly."

"So you have come here." Ligige' turned her back on Aqamdax and addressed Long Eyes. "What do you think, Sister? There is too much throwing away of husbands and wives among our children."

"Yes," Long Eyes said, her voice without inflection, her head still bent over her sewing.

"Throwing away is not a good thing."

"Yes."

"Husbands and wives are better to stay together. There are fewer problems that way."

"Yes."

"He killed our son," Aqamdax said, interrupting the strange conversation.

Ligige' looked at her. "If he was my husband, I would throw him away. Tomorrow, when Long Eyes goes to live with her daughter, I will have room enough in this lodge. Then come and stay here."

THE FOUR RIVERS VILLAGE

In the daylight, K'os counted the packs, recounted the dogs. Three handfuls of packs, eight dogs. There were six travois altogether, and she still did not know how River Ice Dancer could have controlled so many dogs. The storms had been in his favor. Otherwise, the Near River hunters would have surely caught him, though he raided their caches on a moonless night, and so had a start on them before they realized what had happened.

Much of what he brought was meat—smoked salmon; dried muskrat; goose meat packed in fat; caribou, some frozen, some dried; moose; small bales of blackfish; spruce grouse stored whole in oil and packed into large caribou bellies. But he had also managed to get bundles of hides: caribou, wolf, fox, lynx. There was a sack of beads, another of spearheads, several pairs of boots, two summer parkas and, best of all, a lodge cover, the hides fresh, newly sewn together and ready for lodge poles.

She and Sand Fly packed the meat and hides in K'os's entrance tunnel. When that was full, they took most of the remainder to Tree Climber's caches. River Ice Dancer did not do much to help them; he was too busy telling everyone the tale of his journey: how he and the dogs had waited out storms, that they made a false trail toward the Cousin River Village.

When all things were put away, K'os told Sand Fly her plan to have a giveaway. How better to share her bounty with others and to celebrate her marriage? Then K'os went from lodge to lodge bringing the news.

She saved Red Leaf's lodge for last. Cen himself beckoned K'os inside, but he stood while she spoke, though K'os settled herself comfortably beside the hearth fire, acting as though there were no enmity between them.

She told them that River Ice Dancer had won permission to live in the village as her husband. She had to bite her cheeks to hide her smile when she saw Red Leaf's relief. The woman would not be rid of her so easily.

When she said there would be a celebration, a giveaway, both Cen and Red Leaf had many questions. How had River Ice Dancer managed to bring so much wealth to the village? How had he controlled eight dogs? With ropes and harnesses, K'os told them, but more than that she did not know. It was River Ice Dancer's story, not hers. He would tell it the evening of the celebration.

When K'os left the lodge, Red Leaf, in politeness, went with her to the entrance tunnel. There K'os leaned close, whispered that it would be good if Cen would help River Ice Dancer set up their new larger lodge, if he would help find long, straight lodge poles. She leaned back, looked into Red Leaf's face, was pleased to see that the fear had returned to Red Leaf's eyes.

THE COUSIN RIVER VILLAGE

Night Man nodded toward the dwindling pile of wood, and Star hissed at him. "You are the one who sits doing nothing," she said. "Who brought all our supplies into this lodge? Who started the fire and hung the cooking bag? Who brushed the snow from your parka? You go get the wood."

They were alone in the lodge; Yaa and Ghaden had been sent to help others unload supplies and fill caches. Night Man leaned close to his sister, lifted her chin with forefinger and thumb, pinched. Star pulled away from him.

"You spend so much time thinking about yourself that you do not see what is happening around you," Night Man told her. "Why did Aqamdax leave this lodge as soon as her packs were in the entrance tunnel? She is planning something."

"A new lodge. That is what she plans, lazy one," Star said. "A wife should be ashamed to live with her husband's sister."

"You think those are her only plans?" Night Man asked. "Nothing more? You have not noticed that Chakliux's eyes are always on Aqamdax, and that she mentions him as often as she can when she speaks?"

"You lie," Star said, her voice low, shaking.

"Why would I lie? Do you think I want to see my sister hurt? Do you think I want to lose my own wife?" He brushed the fur of his inside parka. "Look," he said. "She made this. She made me sealskin boots. Is there another woman in this village who knows how to make waterproof clothing?"

"She said she would teach me," Star mumbled.

"But have you learned?"

"I have too much work to do. When do I have a day to learn Sea Hunter ways?" Star raised her fingers to her mouth, began to gnaw at the ragged edges of her nails. "You think Chakliux will take her as wife?" she asked.

"I think he wants her. I do not know if he will take her. But why worry? He will not throw you away." He pointed rudely at her belly, then uttered a coarse word for the child she carried.

She flicked her fingers in insult, and he shrugged. "You think I should feel sorry for you?" he asked. "You still have a husband to hunt for you. What will I do without a wife?"

"What about Sun Girl?" Star asked. "She has just returned from the Near Rivers and needs a husband. You can always get an old woman. An old woman would be better for you since you do not want babies."

"Why do you think that?"

"You killed your son."

He turned on her, his face suddenly dark, his lips pulled back from his teeth. "He was not mine. You think I would destroy my own son?"

"Why should it matter what I think?" Star said. "It will

not change what you did. But have you ever considered that you might have been wrong?"

"It is better. There is not so much wind," Chakliux called down to Sok.

Chakliux had burrowed an opening from their shelter out to the sky. The snow had nearly stopped, and though the wind was still strong enough to form drifts, it was no longer a storm wind.

Sok pulled his parka hood up over his ears, tightened the drawstring so the ruff covered all but his eyes, then joined his brother. They broke their packs from the snow, beat the ice from the tent hide they had used to cover themselves. It was frozen too stiff to fold, so when he had his pack in place on his back, Chakliux wrapped the hide like a sheath around his shoulders.

Sok moved as if he were asleep, his motions slow and clumsy, but finally they were ready, and Chakliux, using the few stars they could see during those times the wind died, set their course toward the Cousin Village.

They had seemed to walk forever in the storm, but perhaps they had not come as far as he thought. Were they foolish to be walking at night with the wind watching from the edges of the sky? Perhaps it had only been waiting for them to leave the security of their shelter, then would again become storm.

THE COUSIN RIVER VILLAGE

When Aqamdax heard Biter bark, she sat up in her bedding furs. A blow to the side of her face stunned her. She raised her arm, turned her head, then heard the whispers of the one who had hit her. Star. Aqamdax's fear turned to anger. She was not an infant; she could fight back. But then she heard Biter growl and knew that he would attack. Aqamdax dropped as he jumped, rolled away as the dog took Star to the floor.

Star cried out in short harsh screams, and Aqamdax gave Biter a stern command to stop. He loosed his hold, stood over Star, growling, his teeth bared and gleaming in the light of the hearth coals.

Aqamdax looked up, saw Night Man crouched at the lodge entrance. "You are leaving?" she asked him. "You are not man enough to help your sister?"

She grasped the braided collar at Biter's neck and dragged him past Night Man. Biter lunged toward Night Man's weak arm, but Aqamdax thrust her weight against the dog and pulled him from the lodge. She fastened him to a tether, then went back inside for her parka, leggings and boots.

Night Man was roaring insults at Star and Ghaden, the boy still groggy with sleep. When he saw Aqamdax he lashed out at her, but she pretended she did not hear. When she was dressed, she stood in front of her husband, said quietly, "I throw you away." Then she left. She cut Biter's tether at the snow line and led him to Ligige''s lodge.

Though it was night, the old woman met her at the entrance tunnel. She was wearing her outside parka, boots and mittens.

"Your husband has a loud voice," Ligige' told her.

"He is not my husband," Aqamdax said.

"We will make room for you here tonight," Ligige' told her. "What is one more person in a small lodge except a little more heat?"

They tied Biter and returned to Star's lodge. Aqamdax's blankets, her baskets, hides and sewing supplies were all lying in the snow. Beside them was everything that belonged to Chakliux—weapons, bedding, and the clothing he had not taken with him on the caribou hunt.

It took them several trips, though Dii left her bed to help. When finally only a few baskets were left sitting in the snow, Ghaden poked his head out of the entrance tunnel. His face was too shadowed for Aqamdax to see his eyes, but when he spoke, she could tell he had been crying.

"Night Man told me you do not want to live with us," he said.

Aqamdax went to her brother, squatted on her haunches in front of him. "I will stay with Ligige'," she said, "so we will not be far apart. "I am no longer wife to Night

Man, but I am still your sister. I will always be your sister."

"He says Biter hurt Star."

"Only because Star tried to hurt me."

"Star thinks Biter should be made into dog stew."

Aqamdax set her hand on his shoulder. "Do not worry about Biter. He is safe at Ligige' 's lodge."

"Can I sleep there, too, and Yaa?" Ghaden asked.

Aqamdax turned to look at Ligige'.

"Star is still your mother," said Ligige'. "You must do what she says. When Chakliux returns, we will see what he says." She picked up a basket, shook the snow from it.

Aqamdax hugged him, felt him hiccough. "I wish you could come, too," she said softly, then he was gone, scooting back into the entrance tunnel. Aqamdax picked up the last of her belongings and walked to Ligige' 's small lodge.

FORTY-FOUR

Sok and Chakliux walked three days, camped three nights. The winds were bitter, driving the cold through their parkas and deep into their bones. But the air was dry and it did not snow.

The fourth day they began walking in the darkness of early morning. By the time the sun peaked in its shallow arc across the southern sky, Chakliux saw the smoke from the village hearths, a layer of haze that hung flat and still just beyond the hills that stood between them and the village. The ache in his leg, the cramps in the side of his otter foot, made him glad that their journey was almost over, but as he neared the village, his fears returned. If a leader falls from respectful ways, does he also pull his people down with him? Had his people arrived safely at their village or had some curse, brought on by his own selfishness, blinded them to the way they should go?

Chakliux's thoughts drew his eyes from the trail ahead, so when Sok called out, he was startled. He looked up, saw someone walking toward them. Sky Watcher. Who else was so tall, so thin, with shoulders not quite filled out to a man's size? Sky Watcher lifted his hands in a sign of welcome, and though Sok was the elder and expected to speak first, Chakliux knew his brother's sorrow would hinder his words.

Chakliux lifted his voice in a traditional greeting, and before Sky Watcher could reply, asked, "Everyone has returned safely?"

"Everyone," Sky Watcher answered.

"And the old ones left behind?"

"All good."

"The dogs?"

"Fighting as always." Sky Watcher laughed, cleared his throat, and lifted his hand toward the hills that hid the village. "All the meat is in the caches, and our women work at scraping hides and finding firewood." He kicked at the snow. "Your sons, Cries-loud and Carries Much," he said to Sok, "they are staying with us in my wife's lodge. She is glad to have the children near." He looked into Sok's face. "You are welcome to stay with us."

"My wife?" Chakliux asked, stopping himself before he asked about Aqamdax.

Sky Watcher looked away, his eyes darting as though he were watching for hares or ground squirrels. "Star is angry," he finally said. "Aqamdax threw away Night Man. Now Star believes you plan to take Aqamdax as your wife. The old women say she threw you away, too, and that Aqamdax has stored your things in Ligige''s cache."

The man looked at Chakliux, and Chakliux met his gaze. "I will take Aqamdax as wife," he said, and saw that Sky Watcher was not surprised. "But I did not intend to throw away Star. Who would take her?"

"Perhaps she and Night Man will live together," Sok said, and Chakliux was surprised that his brother was listening.

"There are enough old women in the village. Night Man will not be long without a wife," said Sky Watcher.

"Where is Aqamdax staying?" Chakliux asked.

"With Ligige'."

"Then that is where I will go."

Someone scratched at the side of the lodge. Aqamdax set aside her sewing and glanced at Ligige'.

"Why are you afraid?" Ligige' asked her. "What can he do to you?"

Aqamdax pulled aside the inner doorflap, called a welcome into the entrance tunnel. When she saw the top of Chakliux's parka hood, she cried out her joy and met him in the tunnel. He pulled her into his arms.

"I was afraid . . ." she whispered. "I was afraid . . . you would not . . ."

"Hush, be still," he said, and slipped off his mittens to run his hands over her face, to touch her lips, her hair.

She led him into Ligige''s lodge, brushed the snow from his parka and hung it from a lodge pole, then sat beside him. Ligige' offered him a bowl of food, and he grunted his thanks, eating quickly, as though he had had nothing for many days, making much noise smacking his lips in his gratitude for broth and meat.

Ligige', pleased at such a compliment to the food she served, nodded her approval, then saw that Chakliux's eyes, even as he ate, were studying the piles of blankets, baskets and packs that crowded her lodge.

"Ghaden and Yaa are still with Star?" he asked.

Ligige' chuckled. "You are surprised to see so many supplies in an old woman's lodge? You think I might have decided to become a trader in my old age?"

He laughed.

"You remember the child called Sun Girl?" Ligige' asked him. "She was one of those K'os took to the Near River Village."

"I remember. Her mother was—"

"Her mother is dead, as is her father." Ligige' flicked her fingers as if to push such a remembrance from her lodge. "Sun Girl left her Near River husband and came here. She brought her husband's dogs and two of his travois with her."

"He did not come after her?"

"He, too, is dead. You knew him, I think. He was once second husband to your mother and called himself father to you and Sok."

Chakliux's eyes opened wide. "He is dead?" he asked, leaning forward as though afraid to believe Ligige''s words. "How?"

"That is something you should ask Sun Girl. She calls

herself Dii now. She came during a storm and found my lodge first, so for a few days she stayed with me; now she has moved into her aunt's lodge."

"Twisted Stalk?"

"Yes, but all this you see near the door of my lodge, these are Dii's things. Each day she comes and gets a few more. She says Twisted Stalk complains they do not have enough space, so she does not take much at any one time."

Ligige' lifted her chin at him, tilted her head. "You will mourn her husband?" she asked.

"No," Chakliux replied, his answer short, harsh.

A thin whine came from the back of the lodge, and Chakliux jumped. "You have a dog in here?"

"Biter," Ligige' said. "You know Aqamdax threw away Night Man?"

Aqamdax drew in her breath, worried that Chakliux would be angry she had done so before he returned.

"Sky Watcher told me," he said.

"You did not want me to?" she asked.

"I am glad you are not his wife," he answered, and smiled, but the smile was shallow, like a ripple of water made by the wind. He looked tired, sad.

"Some say Star has thrown you away," Ligige' told him, and Aqamdax wished the old woman would be quiet. Chakliux had enough to think about with Night Man.

"So Sky Watcher told us. I will go see her myself," Chakliux said, "and find out what is true. I want to be sure she will take care of Ghaden and Yaa. But why do you have Biter?"

"Night Man told Ghaden he would kill the dog."

"Why?"

"Biter attacked Star."

"He what?"

"He was protecting me," Aqamdax said. "It is nothing for you to think about." She wanted to ask about Sok. Did he plan to return to his dead wife's lodge? Did he need help with his children? Perhaps she and Chakliux could live with him in Snow-in-her-hair's lodge for the winter while Aqamdax finished sewing her lodge cover.

Ligige' pointed with her chin at Aqamdax. "This

woman here does not have a husband," she said. "That is something for you to think about."

Aqamdax wanted to leave the lodge, to hide her face from Chakliux's eyes. Would he think she had complained?

But Chakliux acted as though he had not heard Ligige''s words. He stood and said, "I will be back later." And as suddenly as he had come, he left.

Ligige' snorted, and Aqamdax spoke without thinking. "You were rude," she said. "He will take care of me."

"Too often, he considers those who do not deserve his concern before those who have earned his respect," Ligige' retorted.

"A man who leads his people must consider himself last," Aqamdax said. "His wife and children, his parents, are part of him, and must take their place after the others."

Ligige' clicked her tongue. "If he cannot take care of his own family, what right does he have to watch over others? It is good I came to this village. Where would you go if I was not here?"

"I would be cold and hungry, Aunt," said Aqamdax. "I will not forget what you have done for me."

Again Ligige' snorted, but this time she smiled.

Chakliux ran his hands over the knives he carried. One was strapped to his leg, another to his belt, a smaller knife hung under his parka like a necklace. "No fighting," he breathed, lifting the words like a prayer. "No fighting."

He entered Star's lodge without a greeting, as though he were still her husband. Star shrieked when she saw him, covered her mouth with both hands and stood behind her brother.

"You did not hear that Star has thrown you away?" Night Man asked.

"I heard. I have come to ask her to again be my wife."

Night Man looked up at his sister. "He misses your warm lodge," he said to her.

Chakliux saw the hurt in her eyes and held back the anger that made him want to insult Night Man. He almost told Star she had been a good wife, and for that reason he wanted her back. But how could he say something that was not true? He wanted her for the child she carried in her belly, for that son or daughter. Otherwise he would rather she belonged to some other hunter.

"I have a warm lodge where I can live," he said.

Again Night Man looked at his sister. She moved her hands from her mouth and stood like a child, twisting her fingers into her braided hair. "He does not want you for your cooking or sewing, and he does not need this lodge," Night Man said. "He has another woman to warm his bed." He reached up and patted her belly. "It must be this he is after." He looked at Chakliux. "You have not considered that it might be a daughter?"

"Why should that matter?" Chakliux asked.

Night Man laughed. "See, Sister. It is not you he wants. Get a good bride price for yourself. He will pay much for that baby."

"You have never looked at your sister before, Night Man?" Chakliux asked, his voice soft. "You have never seen her hair, dark as night? Her face shining like sun on water? You do not know that she is beautiful to look at? Where are your eyes?" He smiled at Star. "What do you want for a bride price?" he asked her.

Star looked at Chakliux, then down at her brother. "That you help me move my brother's things from this lodge," she said to Chakliux, and snapped her fingers in a gesture of insult. "He will not live here anymore."

FORTY-FIVE

Sok invited Chakliux and Aqamdax to live with him and his two sons, and asked Aqamdax to care for the children until he took another wife. It would be better for Star and Aqamdax to live in separate lodges, he had said, and how could Aqamdax disagree with him?

As she moved from Ligige' 's lodge, Aqamdax could not help but remember those days when she had been Sok's wife. He had pretended to be what he was not—a man who needed a wife. Aqamdax had believed him, had allowed his wide shoulders and strong arms to blind her to the truth, and then had hated him when he tried to trade her to the Walrus Hunters. He had thought the magic of her storytelling would entice the Walrus people to give much in trade for her, enough to pay the bride price for Snow-in-her-hair.

But now, seeing Sok in his sorrow, moving as though he were an old man, she had no more anger. Could she pretend she had never done anything selfish? Could she say she had never hurt anyone else to get something she wanted?

So when Chakliux came to Ligige' 's lodge, promising gifts of caribou hides, meat and necklaces, Aqamdax accepted not only a new husband but also his brother and his brother's children.

"By spring, he will find a wife," Chakliux had said to her. "By spring you will have the lodge cover sewn, and we will have our own lodge."

"And Star?" Aqamdax asked.

"She is still my wife," Chakliux told her.

Ligige' tottered to her feet, pulled on a parka. "I will go there, to stay with Star and Long Eyes, Ghaden and Yaa tonight," she said. "Star knows that you have claimed Aqamdax as wife?"

"She knows," Chakliux said, then offered to carry the boiling bag of food to Star's lodge. "I do not know if she has anything ready to eat."

Ligige' shook her head at him. "Yaa is there. She is woman enough to take care of all of us."

He held the doorflap open for Ligige', went outside with her, and Aqamdax knew he would accompany his aunt to Star's lodge, make sure Star accepted the old woman in politeness.

When he returned, his arms were full, his back bowed under the weight: a caribou hide, several long-furred wolf pelts, necklaces, boiling bags, a packet of beads—more than would be given for most first wives, let alone a woman who had been wife to two others, had once been a slave.

Aqamdax took the gifts from his arms one by one, hid tears by pressing her face into a wolf pelt. "There are more caribou hides, enough in my cache to finish a lodge cover, but I thought you would not mind if I left them there."

Aqamdax began to laugh, then her voice broke with her tears, and she busied herself arranging the gifts in a pile at the women's side of the lodge. She set out food for her husband, a bowl of caribou meat flavored with iitikaalux and boiled in broth, several dried fish, warmed near the hearth fire, and a bowl of fish oil to dip them in.

"One more gift," he said when he had finished eating.

"The lodge is full," said Aqamdax, laughing. "What more can you give?"

"It is not a gift for the eyes but for the ears," Chakliux said quietly. Then he motioned for her to sit beside him, pulled her close and began to tell stories. They were ancient stories, each sacred to the River People, and Aqamdax had not heard them before. She listened in joy, felt his heart like a drumbeat set the rhythm for the words, so that each story was like a dance made with voice rather than feet and hands. And her love for him grew in the gratitude that he would trust her with something so sacred when she was only a woman, second wife, not even born to the River People.

Yaa helped Ghaden with the snowshoe he was webbing, then took a water bladder to Long Eyes and watched to be sure the old woman drank. When Star began an argument with Ligige', Yaa was the one to distract her with a request for help with the boiling bag, and to remind Ligige' with raised eyebrows and a quick frown that Star was only a child, though she wore a woman's body.

Ligige' pinched her face into stubbornness, and Yaa found her thoughts again on Day Woman, that dead one. Could Ligige' have killed her rather than Twisted Stalk? If so, why would Ligige' have worked so hard to save Day Woman's life? Perhaps Star was the killer, but why would Star hurt Chakliux's mother? For that matter why would Ligige'?

Yaa sighed. Perhaps no one would ever know who the killer was, and since there had been no more trouble in the village, why worry about it?

But then she thought of Cries-loud, his eyes shadowed with sorrow. It would be good if they could somehow prove Red Leaf was innocent, good for Cries-loud and even for Sok.

Someday, if she was Cries-loud's wife . . .

Yaa squeezed her eyes shut in embarrassment at the boldness of that thought and felt her cheeks grow hot.

Long Eyes let out a sudden squeal of anger. Yaa left Star and went to untangle the length of sinew thread that hung from the old woman's needle. Long Eyes smiled at her and patted her hand, then resumed her sewing.

"Someday you will be a good wife," Ligige' said and nodded her approval at Yaa.

Yaa lowered her head so Ligige' would not think she was too proud, but she hugged the compliment to herself. A good wife, she thought. She would have to be a very good wife to help Cries-loud forget his sorrow and learn to smile again.

When he finished the stories, Chakliux stood and reached up to the rafters, took a bladder of rendered oil and pulled out the stopper with his teeth. He stripped away Aqamdax's clothing and stroked the oil into her skin, standing to comb it through her long hair, kneeling to rub it into her legs. He warmed her with his hands, cupped her breasts, then her belly, her buttocks. Then he took her to her bed, removed his own clothing and lay down beside her. His hands continued their dance over her skin, and she found herself moving beneath his touch. She reached out for him, to bring him also into the celebration of their joining.

When he finally raised himself over her, entered her, she heard the storm winds outside, beginning anew, howling through the walls of the lodge. Later, as they lay still and quiet, Aqamdax felt the lodge begin to shake.

Fingers of cold crept in through the seams and awl holes of the caribou hide lodge cover, and though Chakliux wrapped her into his arms, the wind's voice would not let Aqamdax sleep. Through the night, she heard her husband murmur quiet prayers, but the words seemed too small, too quiet, a child's chant against the wind.

THE FOUR RIVERS VILLAGE

The storm began just as the feasting had started. K'os moved the tripods and cooking bags into Sand Fly's lodge and continued to feed the people until there was nothing left. When the food was gone, she opened the packs she had chosen from those River Ice Dancer had brought and gave each person a gift.

When she had first told River Ice Dancer her plan for a giveaway, he had protested.

"I have enough here to become a trader," he told her.

"I will have the finest dogs, the best parkas, and you and our children will never be hungry."

She did not bother to tell him that she could not give him children. If he began to worry about having a son, she could claim a pregnancy, steal a child. There were ways to do such things.

"Wait and see what happens," she had told him. "With each gift given your worth will grow in the eyes of the people. You will be seen as wise and generous, a leader."

He had turned his back on her, pouted like a child, but she slipped her fingers under his breechcloth, and soon he was stiff and ready in her hands. When he was sated with their lovemaking, he had no more protests about her give-away.

When the sky grew dark, the people left, walking out into the hard stinging snow, clasping one another as they moved from lodge to lodge. River Ice Dancer went with the old ones, guiding them to their own lodges, and when he returned, K'os took off his ice-crusted parka, brushed the snow from the fur, then rolled out his bed next to hers.

K'os lay awake long after she had satisfied River Ice Dancer into sleep. She had given much away—even a fine fishskin basket to Red Leaf, a beaver fur hood to Cen. In the quiet of the lodge, she listened to the wind. As always, it spoke with many voices: in anger, in bitterness. But this time, it also carried the whispered words of the men and women who lived in the Four Rivers Village—praises for River Ice Dancer and for his wife, that generous one, K'os.

THE COUSIN RIVER VILLAGE
Four, five times in the night, Chakliux used a walking stick to knock the snow from the smoke hole, and in the morning, when he and Aqamdax opened the inner door-flap, they found that the entrance tunnel was nearly full of snow.

Aqamdax went through Ligige''s storage baskets until she found several old caribou skin boiling bags. Chakliux filled them with snow and hung them over the fire so the snow would melt into water, then he pushed his way from the lodge and went outside. The wind still blew, sent ice fingers through the fur of his parka ruff, scratched his face and eyelids. He had pulled the drawstring of his hood tight so he breathed through the fur, but still his lungs ached with the cold.

He could not remember such fierce weather so early in the winter, with the sun yet so high in the sky. He wondered if Sok would claim that this storm, too, was Snow-in-her-hair calling from the spirit world. As Dzuuggi he knew stories of such things happening, but that had been in times long ago. Snow-in-her-hair was not some shaman, not even a woman of great power or age. How could she know enough to make such storms?

When he reached Star's lodge, Chakliux found he had to dig out the entrance tunnel. He heard no voices coming from within, and dug more quickly. Sometimes when the wind found a lodge sealed with snow, it would react in anger at being shut out and steal the breath of those inside.

He was halfway through when Biter bounded out, knocking him back, tangling him into a welcome of tongue and paws. Ghaden followed, whooping at the depth of the snow, calling for Yaa to join him. Chakliux warned Ghaden to stay close to the lodge. The wind was still strong, whipping the snow into a blanket that hung thick around the lodges, blocked vision of anything more than two or three steps away.

Inside, the women sat close to the fire. "Another storm," Ligige' said.

"Not as bad as the first," Chakliux replied.

"Not as bad as the first," Long Eyes repeated without looking up.

Star sat with her back to the entrance tunnel. For once she had work in her hands, but, of course, Ligige' would not allow her to sit idle while others sewed.

"You have enough food?" Chakliux asked.

The lodge belonged to Star. She should be the one to answer, but she acted as though he were not there. Chakliux asked her again, then offered to break a trail to the cache.

Finally she looked at him, and he saw the anger in her

eyes. "Your new wife," she said, "is her bed warmer than mine?" She dropped the caribou hide she was sewing. "I am the better wife." She patted her round belly. "Look. Here is your son. Have you forgotten him?"

"I would never forget him or you," Chakliux said patiently. Then, as though she had said nothing, he continued. "I will break a path to the cache. It will not be open long. You will have to go soon if you need meat."

He left, but not without inviting Ligige' back to her own lodge, telling her that Aqamdax would move to Sok's lodge that day.

"Take your dogs, Husband. I will not feed them," Star called, and he heard something hit the lodge wall just as the inner doorflap fell into place behind him.

He calmed himself with thoughts of Aqamdax, then called Ghaden and Yaa to help walk a path through the snow to the caches. He loaded them with food to take back to Star's lodge and went on to his own cache, brought back several frozen chunks of caribou meat for himself and Aqamdax and a caribou skin of dried fish for his dogs.

He took most of the food to Sok's lodge. The lodge was empty and cold, but there was a stack of wood beside the circle of stones and sand that marked the hearth. Chakliux used a fire bow and scraps of birchbark to start a fire, fed it patiently until it had burned several of the larger chunks of wood into glowing coals, then he took some of the meat and enough fish for Ligige' 's dog to her lodge.

She had not returned yet, but Aqamdax was there waiting for him. He wanted to tell her to unroll their bedding furs again, wanted to enjoy a last time in this lodge together, but how could he risk leaving the fire in Sok's lodge burning with no one to watch? Storm winds did strange things in empty lodges.

"I have started a fire in Sok's lodge," he told her. "We should move our things there."

"Now? In the storm?" she asked, looking up at him with worried eyes.

"Star wants me to move my dogs from around her lodge. She says she will not feed them, and in this cold they need food. You can stay if you want. Ligige' should soon be back, but Sok also needs to return to the lodge, to have a place for himself and his children."

He saw that she sucked her bottom lip into her mouth, worried it with her teeth. "You do not want to live again in the same lodge as Sok?" he asked.

She looked at him with surprise in her eyes, frowned for a moment, then said, "No, I was not thinking of that." She smiled at him, her eyes crinkling into curves like slices of the moon. "He needs me to help him with his children. I was wondering if my milk might start again if I nursed the baby."

"Sky Watcher's wife nurses him," Chakliux said.

"You did not know she again carries a child?" Aqamdax asked, and laughed at his surprise. "So her milk will not be as plentiful." She patted her own belly. "I will have a few moons before the babe we have made does the same to me."

He opened his mouth in surprise. No woman could know so soon.

She laughed, and he joined her laughter. He was not used to a wife who made jokes.

He squatted beside her, placed his hand on her belly, and soon they were lying together on the floor mats, his parka, still wet with snow, flung aside. And for a few moments, Chakliux no longer heard the storm or thought about dogs. What man should allow such worries to steal his pleasure with a wife he loves?

Sok kept his eyes from the pity on Sky Watcher's face. He tried to eat the food Bird Caller had given him, but finally set his bowl, still half full, on the floor. Bird Caller held Carries Much, and Sok lifted the child from her arms. The baby gurgled his delight, and Sok could not help but notice that the boy had Snow's eyes, her nose. He gave the child back to Bird Caller, let himself imagine how he would feel if he were handing the boy to Snow.

But no, he would not have noticed such a small blessing as that. Perhaps the spirits punished him for his lack of gratitude. Perhaps that was why Snow had died.

He thought about other men, some much worse than he was. Take More was always grumbling about his wives. Even during the feast after their first successful river hunt, he had complained about the piece of meat one of his wives had given him. Yet in his old age, he had three wives: two old women good with sewing, and one of the young girls who had chosen to return from the Near River People. Surely Sok was a better man than Take More, but both Sok's wives were dead and one of his sons. Was he truly that cursed?

Perhaps he should give what he had left—his two sons, his dogs—to Chakliux. In that way he might protect them from whatever bad luck he was carrying. But then, Chakliux had Star and Aqamdax as wives. What man would want Star to raise his sons? Aqamdax was not terrible, but she was Sea Hunter. Carries Much and Cries-loud deserved better.

Star, not Snow-in-her-hair, should have been the one to die at the river. Who would have missed her? Her old mother, Long Eyes, seldom knew what was happening around her. Her brother, Night Man, was too selfish to care whether Star was dead or alive.

Truly it had seemed that as Star grew stronger, Snow-in-her-hair grew weaker, as though Star's spirit used Snow's strength to pull itself back into the world. He turned suddenly to Sky Watcher and asked, "You need food from your cache?"

"For the dogs," he answered.

"I will get it."

"Bring a little caribou meat," Bird Caller told him.

Sok pulled on his outside clothes and left the lodge. The snow cut hard into his face, but he welcomed its pain, pushed his parka hood back from his face so he could feel the bitter cold bite into his skin. A drift behind Bird Caller's lodge was nearly to his hips, the snow hard and crusted with ice, but he forced his way through. The wind sang, and now that he was outside the lodge walls, he recognized its voice.

Snow-in-her-hair was calling him, singing, singing, her cold fingers caressing his skin.

FORTY-SIX

The storm lasted three days. During that time Sok was quiet, seldom spoke, even to his sons, but he cared for his dogs, went hunting once with Chakliux, though they returned only with ptarmigan.

The wind finally blew the storm north, and the sun cut through the layer of clouds to reveal the pale blue of a winter sky. Neither sun nor wind was strong enough to keep the clouds away, and two days later they circled back, at first in a thin layer, so Aqamdax thought they were only the smoke from village hearths. But soon the wind caught bitterness again in its mouth and flung it in ice and cold over the village. Once again the dogs curled tight in the lee of drifts, and old women covered themselves with caribou hides so the cold, on its way to their bones, would be trapped in the hides' thick hair.

The first night of that new storm, Sok woke Aqamdax with his mourning songs, and as his wailing turned to words, she realized that he was speaking to the wind as though it were his dead wife.

In the darkness of the lodge Cries-loud crept to Aqamdax's bed, and though he had eight summers, he huddled close like a small child awakening from bad dreams.

Chakliux stirred beside her, and Aqamdax whispered, "You need to get Sok away from here."

"In this storm?"

She could hear the anger in Chakliux's voice, knew that it was not at her but at the sorrow that seemed to tear Sok away from who he was. She took his hand, guided it to Cries-loud so he could feel the boy trembling beside her.

"Where?" Chakliux asked, his voice again gentle.

"The hunters' lodge?" she said, giving her suggestion as question.

Chakliux pulled on boots and parka, got Sok into his outside clothing. After they left, Aqamdax put Cries-loud back into his own bed, then she took Carries Much from his cradleboard and held him, singing the lullabies she had learned as a child living with the First Men.

Chakliux did not return until the next morning, and then he came by himself.

"Sok stayed at the hunters' lodge?" Aqamdax said.

"The men asked him to tell hunting stories. I came to feed the dogs and see if you need anything, but I should go back."

Aqamdax kept her disappointment hidden. Only a moon before he had not been her husband. Then, a quick smile when others were not looking was all they dared. How could she complain now that they belonged to one another?

"How bad is the storm?" she asked.

"Like the others," he replied, and shrugged his shoulders as though it did not matter, but she could tell it bothered him. How could a man hunt? How could a woman keep her traplines open?

She gave Chakliux food, filled his bowl again so he would stay longer. When he left, she sang songs to fill the lodge, and told stories, Cries-loud begging for more even when her voice grew hoarse from speaking. Later in the day, Yaa and Ghaden came to the lodge, and Aqamdax taught them all a First Men song.

She fed the children, took Carries Much to Bird Caller so the woman could see him. Aqamdax herself was nursing the baby now, and each day she had more milk. She fought the storm back to Snow's lodge, told Ghaden and

Yaa she wanted them to spend the night, but in the early darkness of that evening, Star came, scolded both children for worrying her. Then when the children begged, she agreed that Cries-loud could come and stay in her lodge with Ghaden and Yaa.

Aqamdax met Star's eyes boldly. "You know I cannot let him go with you," she said.

"You trust your brother and sister with me and yet not Cries-loud?"

"I have no choice with my brother and sister," she said, "but Cries-loud belongs to Sok. You must ask him."

"Where is he? I thought he would be here."

"He and Chakliux are at the hunters' lodge."

"A new husband does not live with his new wife?" Star asked, mocking her with raised eyebrows.

Aqamdax did not answer. She knew the truth. What else mattered?

"I will go to the hunters' lodge and ask," Star told her, but Aqamdax put on her outside clothes, bound the baby under her parka and went with her. Together they stood outside huddled with Yaa as Ghaden and Cries-loud went in. Finally Chakliux came out, said Sok wanted the boy to stay in Snow's lodge until the storm ended.

Star thrust her lip into a pout, and grabbing fistfuls of Yaa's and Ghaden's parkas, dragged them with her to her lodge.

"Wait for me," Chakliux told Aqamdax, and he followed Star to her lodge.

Aqamdax and Cries-loud waited, crouched beside the hunters' lodge, heads turned away from the wind. When Chakliux came back, his face was grim, but Aqamdax asked no questions, said nothing about Star. Chakliux walked Aqamdax and Cries-loud to Snow's lodge, stayed with them there through the evening before returning to his brother.

That night Chakliux dreamed he was with Aqamdax. He turned in his sleep, flung an arm over her to pull her close, then sat up, suddenly awake. He heard the sleep noises of the men, smelled the thick odor of their breaths, rich with the meat they had eaten the day before.

Sok was not in his bedding furs. His parka no longer hung on the clothing pegs. Take More sat beside the hearth fire, was feeding thin sticks into the coals.

"He left," he said to Chakliux.

"You did not stop him?" Chakliux asked.

"Is he a child that I must stop him?"

"Did he say anything to you?"

"That someone was calling him."

Chakliux dressed and went outside, studied the footprints the snow had not yet covered. The largest went toward Sok's lodge, and Chakliux began to hope his brother had stopped for food and supplies.

Then, through the darkness, Chakliux saw Sok leaving the lodge, a pack on his back. He did not take any of the dogs, but instead started toward the caches. The new snow, not yet hardened by the wind, reached Chakliux's knees, and his otter foot slipped. He toppled into the snow, but he pushed himself up and caught Sok before he reached the caches.

When Sok saw Chakliux, he said, "My wife is calling me. I cannot pretend anymore that I do not hear."

"Where are you going?"

"To find her."

Chakliux grasped his brother's arm, lifted his voice above the screaming wind. "What if she is calling you to her world? Who will raise your sons? Your wife would trust them to another?"

"They are yours if I do not return," Sok said, then continued toward their food cache.

Again Chakliux caught his brother's arm. "I am going with you."

Sok shook his head. "Who will take care of my children if both of us are called into that spirit world?"

"She does not call me."

Sok stomped his feet against the ground, brushed snow from the ruff of his hood. "Come if you must," he finally said.

"I cannot go without telling Aqamdax."

"I will get meat while you speak to her."

Chakliux clamped a hand on his brother's shoulder. "You will wait for me?"

"Yes."

Chakliux turned and ran to the lodge.

Aqamdax was feeding Carries Much when her husband burst into the lodge. She was relieved to see him, began speaking before he could say anything.

"Sok was here. There is something wrong. You need to talk to him. He would tell me nothing. He took Carries Much from his cradleboard and whispered into his ears. Then he gave Cries-loud one of his best spears. The long one he uses for caribou."

Chakliux crouched in front of his wife and looked into her face. "I saw him. He thinks his dead wife calls him from the storm. He says he must go to her."

"Do you think she is calling? Why would she want him to leave her new son? What if the wife calling him is not Snow but Red Leaf?"

"I am going with him."

"No! Chakliux, look at me. I have a baby to care for, and Cries-loud, and my brother and Yaa. . . ." She saw the sorrow in his face, the worry, and she choked down her protests. "I have taken care of children before," she said softly. "But I cannot lose you. Please, Chakliux . . ."

He enclosed her in his arms, whispered into her hair, "If I let him go alone, he will not come back. If we go together, I have a chance to bring him home. But whatever his decision, I will be back. I will never leave you. You are always at the center of my heart."

Then he had weapons in his hands, a pack, and before Aqamdax could think of other arguments, he was gone. She cradled the baby in one arm and crawled into the entrance tunnel, lifted the doorflap to watch Chakliux leave, but the snow swallowed him, and she could see nothing but the storm.

She went into the lodge. Cries-loud had squeezed himself into a ball, knees drawn nearly to his chin. The spear Sok had given him was in his hands, the butt end resting against the floor, the spearhead pointing up as though to threaten the wind.

Aqamdax sat beside him, adjusted the baby at her breast, began to rock and hum. Then a story came into her mind, a silly tale of gulls and kittiwakes, and she began to speak. Soon Cries-loud was leaning against her, the spear between them, and Aqamdax told stories long into the night.

FORTY-SEVEN

The day dawned bright and clear, as though the storm had never been. Ligige' stomped out a path through the snow to her dog, was welcomed by his yips. When he had first belonged to the Near River shaman, Wolf-and-Raven, the animal was nearly wild, snapping at anyone who came close, but as the years passed he had gentled, and after Wolf-and-Raven's death, when his widow gave the dog to Ligige', he was nearly as much a pet as Ghaden's dog, Biter.

Ligige' fed him a large fish, then tossed out several chunks of fat. If people saw her giving him the fat, they would think she was foolish, but she told herself that if starving times came, she could always eat the dog, so any fat given was not really wasted. The winter promised to be a bad one. During the next storm, she would let the dog sleep in the entrance tunnel. After all, what could anyone say to her? She was not a child to be scolded. Old women had earned the right to do things differently if they wanted.

When the dog finished eating, Ligige' ran her hands over him, broke away ice from his tail and feet, endured the slimy warmth of his tongue against her face.

When she was satisfied he had survived the storm well, she stood up, looked at the Cousin People Village. The domed caribou hide lodges sent thin spirals of gray smoke into the blue sky, and the snow glittered under the sun, so bright it hurt her eyes. She sighed. It was too beautiful a day to go to Star's lodge, but now that Aqamdax was no longer wife to Night Man, who would watch over Yaa and Ghaden if she did not? She sighed again and, leaning on her walking stick, tottered through the snow on her old-woman feet.

She could hear Star yelling even before she came to the lodge. When her scratching brought no response, she pulled aside the doorflap in disgust and went inside. Yaa and Ghaden were huddled together between two stacks of baskets. The dog Biter, allowed once more in Star's lodge, lay in front of them as though to offer protection from her words. Night Man had returned also, and he was laughing. His laughter seemed to add to Star's rage, and until Ligige' raised her voice to scream out a greeting neither noticed that she was in the lodge.

Star was suddenly quiet, but her mouth stayed open as though an abundance of unspoken words still forced her teeth apart. Ghaden took advantage of the silence by jumping to his feet and running to Ligige', crying out, "Thank you for asking us to stay with you tonight."

The boy grabbed his pack and parka, called Biter and was into the entrance tunnel before anyone could react.

Star lifted her voice into a howl, but Ligige' asked Night Man, "You do not care if I take them?"

"It would be best," he said.

Yaa scrambled to her feet, got her things and joined her brother. Ligige' nodded toward Long Eyes, who sat at the back of the lodge. "You need me to take her also?" Ligige' asked.

"Some other day perhaps," Night Man said. Ligige' thought he tried to smile, but with Night Man it was difficult to tell. His smiles were usually of derision, not gratitude. She followed Yaa and Ghaden into the brightness of the snow, called them back to her when they began to run toward her lodge. They whooped when she lifted her chin toward Aqamdax's lodge, and without greetings or the politeness of scratching, tumbled into the entrance tunnel, Biter following them.

Ligige' shook her head and chuckled. How could she scold them? They only acted out their joy. She had let them stay too long with Star.

Aqamdax heard the voices before anyone scratched, felt her spirits lift. Cries-loud jumped up from where he was poking at a bowl of food, and Aqamdax was happy to see a smile light his face. The boy had lost too much in the last few moons—a brother, two mothers and perhaps now a father.

He pushed opened the doorflap, and a rush of cold air came from the entrance tunnel. Biter bounded in and began to bark. Aqamdax hushed him and checked the baby, sure the chill and noise would wake him up, but he slept on. Then Ghaden and Yaa were in the lodge, filling it with their happy voices, and Ligige' followed close behind them.

Aqamdax offered them food and tried not to act concerned when Ghaden and Yaa gobbled their meat and Biter whined more piteously than usual for a share.

She leaned close to Ligige', whispered, "You think Star has been feeding them?"

Ligige' pursed her lips. "Not as much as she should. I will try to watch them better. Perhaps Sok can help us, at least until Star will again welcome Chakliux into her lodge."

"You had not heard that Sok left the village?" Aqamdax asked, then saw the surprise on Ligige''s face, a quickly hidden look of concern.

"Hunting?" she asked.

Aqamdax looked past Ligige' to Cries-loud, then said, "Yes, hunting," and saw that Ligige' understood. "Chakliux went with him."

Ligige' began to ask questions, but Aqamdax shook her head, then said to the children, "When you have finished eating, I have something for you to do. There is much work. You cannot always play."

Ghaden groaned, and Yaa scolded him, but when Aqamdax brought out the caribou hide, the flesh side well scraped, all three shouted out their gladness and set their food bowls down to lace boots and find mittens.

"Take it to the hill at the east side of the village. The snow should be packed hardest there, and be sure you keep the hide hair side down."

Their sliding would rub much of the hair from the hide, and she would have less to scrape. When the children were gone, Aqamdax told Ligige' what she knew, then the two sat together, Ligige' speaking of everyday things, telling funny stories that made Aqamdax laugh and lifted her heart, if only for a little while.

THE FOUR RIVERS VILLAGE

K'os kicked away the snow at the entrance of Red Leaf's lodge and called out.

Red Leaf pushed aside the outer doorflap. "I would invite you inside, but my husband forbids me."

K'os had seen that no one had left the lodge that morning; her own footprints were the first in the new, untrampled snow, but she said, "You think I believe you? Perhaps you do not want to share your food. Perhaps you are that selfish, even after the gifts my husband gave you."

"You know Cen is here," Red Leaf said, and looked past K'os at the path she had made with her snowshoes. "No one has left this lodge yet today."

"You know I have a husband now," K'os said. "I came only to warn you that he has promised vengeance for me on my son Chakliux. He will soon go to the Cousin River Village, and of course he knows who you are." K'os shrugged her shoulders. "He has decided to tell Sok that you are here. I tried to reason with him. After all, what harm can come from having you in this village? But he is a man much concerned with curses."

"I have meat in my husband's cache," Red Leaf said, her voice quiet. "Beautiful fox pelts, better than any I have ever seen before, wolf pelts, and a fur seal pelt my husband took in trade. . . ."

K'os tilted her head, looked into Red Leaf's eyes. "You have nothing I want," she said. "Now that I have a husband, I do not even want Cen. How sad for you. You had the chance, but now . . ." She lifted her hands, her mittens spread wide over her splayed fingers.

"Of course, you could hide again, but what chance would your daughter have? It is difficult enough for a child to survive winter in a strong village, let alone with only a mother to provide for her. You could leave the child, but then Cen would wonder why you went. I think he would follow you. I do have a plan that might work for you so at least your daughter could be saved. But go now and be with your husband." K'os reached out and patted Red Leaf's shoulder. "Enjoy him and the warmth of his lodge while you can. I will be back later when you and I can be alone."

She saw the despair on Red Leaf's face, the fear, and left with a smile hidden inside her cheek. How good that she had come to this village where Cen lived. How wonderful that Red Leaf, too, had found her way here.

K'os allowed her thoughts to drift back through the years to Chakliux's poor ugly wife, Gguzaakk. That woman, like Red Leaf, had stolen something that in truth belonged to K'os. K'os remembered Gguzaakk's slow dying, the sickness brought on by poison. She sucked in her cheeks and savored the thought of Red Leaf dying in the same way. Of course, Red Leaf was not as strong as Gguzaakk had been. She would not die so bravely. And who would Cen have to blame for that death except himself, fool that he was to claim a murderer as wife?

THE COUSIN RIVER VILLAGE

Ligige' stayed with Aqamdax most of the day, and the children, in their sliding, wore the hair from two caribou hides. Aqamdax and Ligige' staked the first hide hair side up over a portion of the lodge floor, then scraped and smoothed the hide with bone drawknives and sandstone.

When the shadows grew long, Aqamdax called the children inside. Wolves would be out on a warm day after a storm, and what was easier to catch than a girl or boy in deep snow?

When Cries-loud begged to go with Yaa and Ghaden

to Ligige' 's lodge, how could Aqamdax refuse him? His face was pink and glowing, and his eyes danced. Could she ask him to return to the fear and emptiness he had endured the night before? Ligige' reached out to touch Aqamdax's cheek before they left, and Aqamdax felt the trail of her fingers like a smooth path through her pain.

"You will be all right here alone?" Ligige' asked.

Aqamdax forced a smile. "I am not alone," she said, and nodded toward the cradleboard. Carries Much was awake, his dark eyes a brightness in the shadows of the lodge.

"Aaa, babies are good company," Ligige' said, "but much work."

"Today I am glad for busy hands," Aqamdax told her.

Then they were gone, and Aqamdax was left alone with Carries Much in Sok's lodge. How strange, she thought, remembering back to the first few moons she had lived with the River People. She had been Sok's wife then, had hated him, and did not yet understand that she was growing to love Chakliux. Then, she would have welcomed time alone.

She went back to the caribou hide she and Ligige' had been scraping, and as she worked she sang to Carries Much. Her song took her back to the warm earthen lodges of her childhood, and her voice filled the emptiness so it seemed that many were listening.

She closed her eyes, thought of those days when she was a storyteller for her people. Then her lodge was crowded, and everyone was eager to hear her words. Now, only the wind listened, waiting at the smoke hole. Aqamdax raised her voice until her song was loud enough to reach the top of the lodge so the wind could hear and would not be tempted to come closer, squeezing in through awl holes and lodge seams to sit with her near the hearth fire.

FORTY-EIGHT

At the first hint of dawn, Ligige' left her bed and slipped into her outside clothing. She sighed at the sound of the wind. What a difficult winter it would be if the storms continued to come one after another. At least their caches were full.

She woke Yaa, asked her to make sure the boys did not go far from her lodge, then told her that she would check her snares, reset them, though that was probably a useless thing to do with a storm so near.

"I will not be gone long." She lifted her head toward the top of the lodge. "You hear the wind?" she asked.

"With wind like that you should not go," Yaa said.

"I set my snares close to the village," Ligige' told her. She finished strapping on her snowshoes and went outside. Yaa followed her.

"You are taking a dog?" Yaa asked.

Ligige' pointed with her chin at her dog, standing now, stretching his tether to its full length.

"If you do not come back soon, I will go out after you."

"No, you will not," Ligige' said. "You will stay here with your brother and Cries-loud. Better to keep two young hunters safe than worry about an old woman."

Ligige' gave the dog a chunk of dried fish, then untied him. He gulped the fish down whole and followed her from the village. The wind was already strong and coming from the east, though the snow was light.

Ligige' walked toward the spruce woods. When she reached the trees, their branches and shadows darkened the dim morning light, but she was glad for their shelter from the wind. She walked to the sunken area that in spring held a marshy rivulet. She had set her snares there in the narrow trails that wove patterns through the brush. She trapped one half of the rivulet, Twisted Stalk the other. The two oldest women in the village should not have to walk far to set their traplines, Chakliux had decided when dispute for the area arose among Twisted Stalk, Ligige' and Star.

Ligige' 's first trap held a fat hare, limp and dead, strangled by the sinew noose that had caught it.

Ligige' removed the hare, reset the noose, then went on down her line. The snares were empty until she came to the last. When she saw what she had trapped there, she dropped her walking stick, held both hands over her mouth.

She backed away, took a long breath and picked up her stick. She slapped it into the snow and cried out, "You, caught there in my trap. You parka hood ruff, why do you visit an old woman? You know I cannot kill you. You know I cannot end your suffering. Do you think I am so foolish as to bring such a curse on myself?"

She slapped her stick again, and then noticed that the animal did not move. Could it be dead? But how could a snare set for hares catch something as powerful as a wolverine? What animal had a stronger spirit? Not even the black bear demanded more care and respect. She did not want to get too close. Perhaps it only slept. Perhaps it pretended to be caught, using itself as bait in a trap to catch her. Then what chance would she have, old and brittle as she was? A wolverine could snap her legs in two quick bites. She took a step closer, extended her walking stick, poked the animal and quickly jerked the stick away. The wolverine still did not move.

She went closer, poked again. Her dog whined, tucked his tail and tried to slink away.

"Stay!" Ligige' demanded. "It is only a parka ruff. Only a few teeth for a necklace. A tail for Ghaden to sew to his belt, something to help him run fast. You are afraid of that?" But she trembled once she had spoken. What was the matter with her? She was old and still could not control her tongue. What if she had offended the animal? She muttered a chant, thought of a praise song she had once heard about a wolverine, but when she started to sing it, she could not remember all the words.

Perhaps she should leave the animal, go get some man to bring it to the village. But who? Sok and Chakliux were gone, and who could trust Night Man, Man Laughing or even Take More to carry the proper respect? She might ask Sky Watcher or First Eagle, but they were young and her choice of them over the others would be seen as an insult. Besides, Ghaden or Cries-loud, one of the two, had said Sky Watcher and First Eagle were away from the village, hunting.

Finally she cut the line, took the wolverine, noose and all, and tied it to her belt. She sat on her haunches then, spliced another line of sinew, tied it into a noose and fastened it to small sticks set on either side to keep the sinew loop open.

She stood up, but the cold kept her knees bent, and she had to take several steps until she was steady on her feet. "There, home now," she said to the dog.

He whined at her but lifted his ears, hurried away from the snare line, angling into the woods. She almost called him back, then thought better of it. Let him go. He shouldn't walk the snare line more than necessary, leaving his dog smell. Besides, the wind did not seem any worse, nor the snow. She would have left him at home had she not feared a storm.

She started back toward the village, the hare hanging on one side of her belt, the wolverine, weighing her down, on the other, their bodies bouncing against her sides as she walked.

She stopped twice on her way out of the forest, once to urinate, the second time at the edge of the woods to call her dog. She did not need him to precede her into the village, start fights with dogs tied to lodges. He came bounding back to her from the trees, and she was surprised at the amount of snow on his coat.

But when she stepped out into the open, she felt the full force of the wind, saw the snow driven hard before it, and she understood. She waited until a brief lull in the wind allowed her to see the dark shapes of the village lodges, small and dim in the distance, then set herself toward them, wrapped her hand into the fur at the dog's neck and pulled her hood far forward, making a shield for her face. With each step, she plunged her walking stick ahead of her and coaxed the dog forward into the wind.

Yaa waited at the entrance tunnel. She had known worse storms, winds and snow so heavy that you could not see the lodge closest to yours. She could still see Twisted Stalk's lodge, and Star's, could almost make out Aqamdax's.

She had dressed in her parka, leggings, boots and snowshoes, was debating with herself as to whether she should go out into the storm and look for Ligige'. Yaa knew where the old woman's trapline was, but what if Ligige' had already returned to the village, had decided to stop at another lodge—perhaps even Star's, to ask if Yaa and Ghaden could stay another night?

No, she wouldn't be at Star's lodge. Yaa had been watching from the entrance tunnel a long time. She would have seen Ligige' pass this way. Perhaps she was with Aqamdax. But maybe the wind had pushed Ligige' down into the snow. She was an old woman. She could not survive a day caught in a storm. The thought made Yaa's heart pound too hard, made her feet anxious to be doing something. She crawled to the inner doorflap, looked in on the two boys.

"I'm going to see if I can find Ligige'," she told them.

"You have to stay with us," said Ghaden.

"You shouldn't go out there in the wind," Cries-loud said.

"Stay," Ghaden begged.

Biter whined, then snapped out a quick, sharp bark.

"I'm going," Yaa said, and let the doorflap fall back into place.

Then Biter was in the entrance tunnel. "Take him, Yaa," Ghaden said, peeking in at her.

She looked at her brother, sighed. "He'll be a problem."

"He'll bring you back if you get lost in the storm."

"I won't get lost."

"Take him."

"Biter, come," Yaa said, and ignored the grin on her brother's face.

Ligige' crouched beside her dog and tried to see through the snow, but it came at her with such force that she could make out nothing except white. Once she thought she saw a dark shape, moving. She called, but no one answered, and she wondered if her eyes felt they must show her something for all her looking, even when there was only snow.

She had taken her heading toward the village when she left the woods, and she assured herself that she still traveled in the same direction. She stood, her knees protesting, took several wobbly steps, then had to stop.

She wondered if she should leave the wolverine. It was heavy, and perhaps its spirit was making the wind stronger so she would leave the body near the woods. She tried to untie the babiche that held it, but the snow had made the knot swell. See then, she told herself, it wants to stay with you.

Suddenly the wind blew with new force, driving the snow so it felt like needles against her skin. The dog stopped, curled itself at her feet, and Ligige' tripped over him. She pushed him up, forced him on, both hands on his back, her walking stick lost somewhere in the snow behind her. Again the dog stopped, curled; again she forced him to his feet.

"It can't be far. We have come a long way," she said, but the words were lost in the storm.

She fell before she saw the thicket, recognized where she was as she pushed herself away from the stiff, snow-coated branches.

She had somehow skirted the village and made her way to the women's place. On which side did the thicket grow? Her mind seemed as hindered by the cold as her body. The north side. She crawled on hands and knees, heading again toward the village, but her snowshoes caught and her legs would no longer hold her up.

The dog growled a warning. Some animal was near. Bear? No, not in this storm. Fox? Wolf? Not likely. Animals were wise when it came to storms. It must be a dog. Tainted by living with people, they sometimes did foolish things.

"Naax!" she called out, a command familiar to village dogs. "Naax!"

Ligige' 's dog whined and barked. There was an answering bark, and Ligige' called out again.

The dog came to her. It was Snow Hawk, one of Sok's animals. A tether line dangled from a braided collar, and Ligige' saw that the tether had been chewed. The animal was most likely pregnant, Ligige' thought. It was not unusual for a bitch with a litter in her belly to chew away her tie line and escape to the women's place, drawn there by the feces ripe with the smell of caribou meat. Ligige' crawled toward the dog, held out her hand, let Snow Hawk sniff. Though village dogs often fought, with Snow Hawk female and her own dog male there was less likely to be a problem, and with two dogs to warm her, she might live through the storm. She pushed her way into the thickest part of the alder brush, mounded snow at her back, then called the dogs. Her dog came, curled beside her, but the bitch stood away, the snow almost blocking her from Ligige' 's sight.

"Snow Hawk, come! We will be warm here together," Ligige' said.

She took off one of her heavy mittens and slipped her fingers up into her parka sleeve. As always when she left the village, she had tucked several thin strips of smoked caribou meat into her parka. It was good meat, cut from the rump and greasy with fat. She hated to give it to a dog, but better to lose a little meat than to freeze to death. She pulled a strip from her sleeve, held it out.

Snow Hawk growled. Ligige' was cold and tired, angry with herself for going to her trapline, angry with the dog. Why would she refuse food?

"Stupid dog," she muttered. "You stupid, stupid . . ." She held the meat out, coaxed, moving forward as she spoke, but her snowshoes caught again on something buried in the snow and she pitched headfirst into the drifts.

She came up shouting curses, but then she saw that she clutched a fistful of bloodied snow. Snow Hawk whined, came to her, began to dig. Ligige' pushed away the snow, and screamed when she saw Star's face, white and frozen beneath her hands.

FORTY-NINE

Yaa walked from lodge to lodge looking for Ligige', but no one had seen her. She finally went to Ligige''s trapline and found the old woman's trail, snowshoe prints threading among the trees, each print nearly drifted over, but once the trail led beyond the spruce forest, the wind-driven snow covered it.

Biter huddled at Yaa's feet, tucking himself so close that sometimes Yaa tripped over him. They fought their way through the storm back to the village, fear growing with each step that she would somehow miss the lodges and walk out into the tundra. But suddenly Twisted Stalk's lodge loomed before her, dark and shapeless through the snow. Yaa went inside and was welcomed by Twisted Stalk's niece Dii. They made her drink a bowl of hot broth, then against Twisted Stalk's advice, Yaa again went out into the storm, again inquired at each lodge.

When she came to Aqamdax's lodge, she could no longer hold in her tears.

"Ligige' is lost," Yaa sobbed as Aqamdax pulled her inside and brushed off her parka. "I should have made her stay with us."

"You think she would have listened to you?" Aqamdax

asked her. "You did what you could. Perhaps she stayed at her trapline."

"I was there," Yaa said, and saw the amazement in Aqamdax's eyes.

"By yourself, you went there?"

"I have been in worse places," Yaa said. She saw Aqamdax nod, and knew she was remembering that Yaa had once walked from the Near River winter village to this village, searching for Ghaden.

"Perhaps even now Ligige' has returned to her own lodge," Aqamdax said. "I will go back with you. I think we will find her there."

Aqamdax bundled Carries Much into his cradleboard and put on her parka and snowshoes. They swaddled a woven hare blanket around the baby, and Aqamdax carried him in her arms, bending over the cradleboard to protect him from the worst of the storm.

At Ligige' 's lodge, Ghaden and Cries-loud were playing a game with small marked throwing sticks. The dog burst into the lodge, shaking snow and ice from his fur and scattering the boys' game.

Aqamdax interrupted Ghaden's protests.

"Ligige' is not back yet?" she asked.

"Not yet," Cries-loud said.

Ghaden came to Yaa and wrapped his arms around her, then went to Aqamdax and did the same. Aqamdax hugged him and hung the cradleboard from the lodge poles. The baby began to cry.

"I will feed him," Aqamdax said to Yaa. "Then I will go out and see if I can find her. Ligige' is not foolish. She has probably dug herself a cave in the snow and is as warm as we are."

"She took her dog with her," Ghaden said, then draped an arm over Biter's neck, pulled the dog down to sit beside him.

"Then she is all right," Aqamdax said.

But Yaa saw the pinched look on Aqamdax's face and was afraid.

*   *   *

Again Dii heard someone in the entrance tunnel. In a storm most people stayed put in their lodges. It was foolish to be outside. Even to walk from a lodge to a food cache might cost a woman her life. Who had not heard the stories of Cold Girl and Fast Bird Woman? Both had died in storms. Even now you could see Cold Girl, frozen into rock by the storm winds, crouching beside the trail that led to the Grandfather Lake.

"Perhaps it is Ligige'," Twisted Stalk said, and Dii hoped her aunt was right. How much chance did an old woman have in such a storm, especially if it lasted two or three days?

But then Night Man came into the lodge. In politeness, Dii brought him a bowl of broth. They did not have much, she and Twisted Stalk, but they would not starve. The people were generous and would share their meat, but she knew her aunt was a proud woman. Dii would be the one who asked for food if they ran out. Between storms they had been fortunate in their trapping, had brought in at least one hare almost every day, and Awl had promised to take Dii to a place she had just found full of highbush cranberries. Where better to look for ptarmigan, those fat winter-white birds? They would burst so suddenly from their snow burrows, sometimes in groups too large to count, that a woman with a bird net, throwing stick or bola could get enough to feed her whole family. Dii could already taste those birds simmering in Twisted Stalk's boiling bag or skewered over their fire, dripping fat into the hearth.

"You are looking for Ligige'?" Twisted Stalk asked, breaking the rules of politeness and not waiting for Night Man, a hunter, to speak first.

He finished his broth, smacking his lips before he answered her. "For my sister," he told them. He set down his bowl. "For Ligige', too, if I see her. But my sister left our lodge before I awoke this morning and has not been back. She is one to visit others and sometimes does not have much sense, even about storms. I thought she might be here with Dii."

Twisted Stalk lifted her hands, spread her fingers wide.

"She has not been here for two or three days." She looked at Dii, raised her eyebrows for confirmation.

"Three days," Dii said.

Night Man had not taken off his parka, so Dii began to brush the snow from it.

"If she comes to you, make her stay here. Do not let her back out into the storm."

Twisted Stalk agreed, went with Night Man as he crawled into the entrance tunnel to strap on his snowshoes. Dii stayed inside, wiped out his bowl with her fingers and licked them clean. It was fine for Twisted Stalk to say they would keep Star in the lodge, but Star would rave and whine to have her own way. It would be difficult to make her stay if she did not want to. Ah well, perhaps she would not come. Perhaps in this storm, she had already found her way to some other lodge in the village.

Aqamdax had just finished feeding Carries Much when Night Man came into Ligige' 's lodge. He came rudely, without scratching, without clearing his throat or calling out, so for a time Aqamdax did not look at him, but instead fussed over the baby in her lap.

When he finally spoke, she heard the worry in his voice and regretted that she had ignored him.

"Star has been here?" he asked.

"Was she here before Yaa and I came?" Aqamdax asked Ghaden and Cries-loud.

"Not today, not last night," Ghaden said.

"Ligige' went out to check her traplines," Yaa told Night Man. "She should be back by now. Have you seen her?"

"No, but an old woman should know better than to do such a thing."

His answer was harsh, and Aqamdax knew he spoke out of his worry over his sister, but still she could not hold back her words. "Yaa did not tell her to go. Why yell at her? If Star comes to this lodge, I will be sure to bring her home."

"Just keep her here," he said. He looked at Yaa. "If I find Ligige', I will bring her back to you."

"She has a dog with her," Ghaden called as Night Man left the lodge.

Aqamdax put on her parka, laced her boots and went into the entrance tunnel. "I will check the lodges again and then go to the women's place," she told Yaa. "Do not go out except to clear the smoke hole or bring in wood, and even then, take Biter with you."

At each lodge Aqamdax received the same answer. No one had seen Ligige' or Star. She saved Bird Caller's lodge for last, reassured her that Carries Much was safe and healthy, that she had enough milk for him.

"These storms that have come on us this winter are different," Bird Caller said. "Perhaps Sok was right about his dead wife calling him. That is why I worry about Carries Much. What if she tries to take him? I wish my husband had stayed in the village. Why risk a hunting trip when the storms follow each other so closely? We have enough meat. What if Sok's wife tries to call my husband, too?"

"Sok speaks out of grief," Aqamdax told her, but the wind that battered against the caribou hide walls of Bird Caller's lodge seemed to find its way into Aqamdax's chest and slow her heart with its chill.

First Sok and Chakliux had left them, then Sky Watcher and First Eagle. Now Star and Ligige'. Did Snow-in-her-hair hope to bring the whole village to live with her in the spirit world?

THE FOUR RIVERS VILLAGE

K'os opened the doorflap and was surprised to see Red Leaf standing outside. "I have come to talk to you," Red Leaf said.

K'os stretched her lips into a slow smile. "How did you know my husband was gone?" she asked.

"I have been watching your lodge."

K'os motioned for Red Leaf to follow her inside. "River Ice Dancer cannot bear to stay too long in one place. And Fat Mink likes to play at the throwing bones."

"You are not afraid he will gamble away all your meat?"

K'os laughed. "I have ways to get it back."

She watched as Red Leaf took off her parka, hung it on a pegged lodge pole. "Where is your daughter, Daes?" she asked, and smirked when she saw Red Leaf cringe at the name.

"Cen is watching her. I told him I was going to get wood."

"I am surprised he let you go out in a storm like this."

Red Leaf raised her head as though listening to the wind. "It is better than it was," she said. "The snow has stopped. Now it is only wind."

K'os nodded but said nothing. She did not intend to offer the woman food. Why feign politeness? She knew the reason Red Leaf had come.

"When will your husband go to the Cousin River Village?" Red Leaf asked.

K'os shrugged. "Not in this storm," she said.

"There is nothing I could offer to keep him from telling Sok where I am?"

K'os smiled. It was the first time Red Leaf had admitted who she was. "There is nothing," K'os said. "He is afraid of a curse. I told you that."

"I have thought about what you said. You are right. If I leave with my daughter, we will both die. If I go alone, Cen will come after me." She raised a hand to brush a strand of hair from her face, and K'os saw the woman's fingers tremble. "Do you . . . do you have something . . ." Red Leaf's voice broke. "Is there something you can give me that if I eat it, I will die?"

K'os widened her eyes as though surprised, but she had expected Red Leaf's request. "You would kill yourself?" she asked, whispering the words.

"If you have something that will make death seem to come because of illness."

K'os looked long into the hearth fire, watched the flames eat the wood. "I might have something. You could not nurse your daughter or she might take the poison through your milk."

K'os got up, brought out her river otter medicine bag and took a packet tied with red-dyed sinew, bound with four knots. "It takes only a little," she said. "It will make your stomach cramp and you will vomit, but there is little pain. If you took only a pinch the first day, then a little more the next . . ." She pretended to consider, then nodded. "Yes, that would do it, and Cen would believe that you were sick." She offered the packet to Red Leaf. "Do you want it?"

Red Leaf reached out, but, like a child playing a game, K'os pulled the poison away. "You think I will give it to you for nothing?" She saw the sudden weariness in Red Leaf's eyes.

"You said I have nothing that you want," Red Leaf answered.

"Perhaps I was wrong," K'os told her. "You said you have wolf pelts."

"I do. If you want them, they are yours."

"For something like this," K'os said slowly, "it might seem that a few wolf pelts are not enough. Would you give me your daughter?"

Red Leaf met K'os's eyes. "I would feed her the poison myself rather than give her to you," she said. She stood and pulled on her parka. She stopped before she went into the entrance tunnel, said to K'os, "Do not forget she is Cen's daughter as well as mine."

K'os tilted her head as though conceding defeat. "Wolf pelts, then," she said, "but I will keep the poison here. Tell me when you are ready for it."

"Tomorrow, I will bring you the pelts," Red Leaf said.

K'os held in her retort until Red Leaf was gone. But then, as though the woman were still in the lodge, K'os said, "You think Cen will stop me from taking your daughter? You think he will turn down that good woman, Sand Fly, when she offers to care for the child? You know that though she is a grandmother she has kept her milk by nursing the babies of this village through the years. How sad that while Cen is away on one of his trading trips, Sand Fly will become sick and die. Then who better to take the child as her own than a wife who has none?

"Ah, Gheli, there are so many ways a woman can get herself a daughter."

FIFTY

Ligige' sat in the wind, held the frozen baby in her arms and waited for death. The dogs huddled close to her, but their warmth was not enough to pull away the cold that numbed her. Ravens had taken Star's eyes, left pink hollow sockets. Foxes had shredded her tongue, reaching into a mouth left open by death. They had not touched the baby. It was beautiful, hair and eyelashes dark against its white and frozen flesh. It was a daughter, and Ligige' grieved for it and for the child's father. Chakliux had lost too many children: his first son; then Aqamdax's son—though not of Chakliux's flesh, the boy would have surely been his own—and now this one, a small and perfect daughter.

Whoever had killed Star had killed her with a knife thrust into her throat. Star's hands were bloody. She must have staggered away, clutching her neck. When she fell, the killer had slit open her belly and ripped the child from her. There were legends of giants—nuhu'anh—who ate people in winter. Perhaps a nuhu'anh had done this thing. Surely there was no one in the village who would kill like this. But then a quiet voice of reason came to Ligige', spoke in whispers she did not want to hear. A nuhu'anh would have eaten Star and the baby. What nuhu'anh did not kill to eat?

Ligige' looked up and saw a dark form moving toward them through the snow. She was afraid, but she did not call out. Her dog, growing deaf in his old age, was curled into a tight circle, nose protected by the thick fur of his tail, but Snow Hawk growled.

"Go now," Ligige' said to her. "There is no need for you to fight. You have pups coming soon. We are old, my dog and I. Leave us."

Snow Hawk stood as though she understood Ligige' 's words, but then she moved to straddle Ligige' 's legs, as if to protect the old woman and the dead baby. The dog's courage pulled away some of Ligige' 's fear. She took a sleeve knife from her parka and held its fragile blade up into the wind.

"The baby is yours," she called out, "and the woman here beside us, but I will not yet go with you, nor will these dogs."

"Ligige'?" It was a man's voice, no surprise, surely most nuhu'anh were men, but the voice was not as harsh as she would expect.

"Ligige'!" he called. "Ligige'!"

Then Ligige' saw his face. It was Night Man, and in her relief, Ligige' felt suddenly very old, very tired.

"I have been looking for you, and for my sister."

Ligige' tucked the baby into her arms. "You have found us," she said softly.

Night Man crouched beside her. "You are hurt?" he asked, but then he looked down at the baby in Ligige' 's arms. She followed his eyes to the blood. The sound in his throat was first like something strangled, then rose into a scream that cut through the snow like a blade.

They gathered in Star's lodge, around the dead woman. The baby was beside her, naked, still marked with blood. Star's parka was pulled down over her gaping belly, but otherwise she lay as death had left her, without eyes, without tongue. Each old woman who came in begged to clean the body, to sew shut the eyelids, to tie the jaw, brush the parka, at least find her death boots, decorated with carved beads and porcupine quills. Surely she had death boots waiting for her. Did not every woman? Did not every man?

But Night Man kept them away, bared his teeth at them, pointed with rude fingers, and shouted to tell them where to sit.

Aqamdax ignored Night Man as he directed her to the far side of the lodge. Instead she sat next to the body, a sister-wife giving some shield of privacy, as though Star were merely relieving herself on a hunting trip and needed shelter from men's eyes.

When everyone was in Star's lodge, Aqamdax saw what a small group they were—without Chakliux, Sok and Snow-in-her-hair, without Sky Watcher and First Eagle, and now without Star. Long Eyes sat alone near the entrance, wrapped in a hare fur blanket, her hands busy twisting sinew, her eyes on her work.

Aqamdax felt Star's presence. Perhaps her spirit still clung somehow to that poor body, lingering to be sure her child would follow her to the place of spirits. Aqamdax's people, the First Men, knew that place to be what the River People named Yaykaas, those dancing lights that colored the northern sky. But the River People seemed to have only vague ideas of where their dead went. Some believed one thing, others another. None of them honored that maker spirit the First Men knew to be above all things. Not a good way to live, she thought. How would their spirits know where to go when they died?

Perhaps that was why Star seemed to be with them. Or perhaps she only wanted to be alive and did not think beyond that to the new life she should be living.

Aqamdax had slung Carries Much in a strap under her parka. She unfastened the strap and pulled him onto her lap. She should have brought his cradleboard, but when Dii had found her in the storm, brought news of Star's death and assurances that Ligige' was alive, Aqamdax thought of little else but joining the women in Star's lodge to prepare the body.

In her hurry she had forgotten the cradleboard; she had forgotten to bring food and a dry parka for Ligige'. But Twisted Stalk had brought an extra parka, and other women had food. Perhaps it was enough that she was here, watching over her sister-wife's body.

Ghaden sat with the men, Biter beside him. He would have rather been with Aqamdax, but she sat close to Star, so perhaps it was best that Night Man had made him stay here. When his first mother, Daes, had died, Ghaden had wanted to die, too, so he could go with her to the spirit world. But he did not want to go with Star—mother yet not mother—and he tried to hold his thoughts on other things so she would not be reminded that he was here, a son nearly a hunter who could go with her.

At first everyone was quiet, as though they were waiting. But finally one of the old women began a mourning song, then others joined. Those songs always made Ghaden shudder. He clamped his teeth tight together and told himself that a man did not shake at the sound of mourning.

At least the songs were familiar, a sign of things being done in respectful ways. Not like this death. What animal would have ripped the baby from Star's belly and not eaten it? He heard Cries-loud and Squirrel whispering about nuhu'anh, but nuhu'anh were too terrible to think about. Anyone from your own village could be nuhu'anh and you wouldn't know. They would look ordinary and live ordinary lives, but in the cold days of winter would become nuhu'anh, then kill and eat people.

Ghaden was sitting on the side of the hearth opposite the women. Though Aqamdax hid most of Star's body, Ghaden could still see her hair spilling out over her hood. He moved so he was sitting on his haunches, his knees raised. He remembered his first mother sitting this way, and Aqamdax did also. He crossed his arms over his knees, lowered his head to his arms, and hid his eyes.

When he had come into the lodge, he had looked at Star, had seen that her eyes were gone. Did that mean that she was blind now as spirit? Would she try to take someone else's eyes before she left the village? His eyes began to ache. He thought of himself as Star was now, with pink hollows where his eyes should be, small, toothless mouths, open as though Star were trying to swallow up as much as she could before she was wrapped for burial.

"I am a hunter," Ghaden told her in that voice that lived in his head. "Hunters need their eyes. Find someone else. Some animal. The old men say foxes see better than we do. Go get yourself fox eyes."

Almost, he could hear Star's voice arguing back at him, but his conversation with her was interrupted by Night Man's shouts. The women stopped their mourning song, and Cries-loud moved closer to Ghaden. Biter growled, and Ghaden reached out to clamp a hand over the dog's mouth. Why draw Star's attention? She might decide she wanted Biter's eyes. Then how could he hunt?

"You see this woman, my sister!" Night Man was shouting, and he repeated the words again and again. "You see this woman, my sister! You see this woman, my sister!"

Faster and faster he spoke, until the words no longer made sense but were like a healer's chants.

Then his voice slowed and changed, and Ghaden realized that Night Man was saying, "You see this child, my sister's daughter." Then those words, too, were spinning away from Night Man's mouth, whirling into the hearth fire, scraping against the inner wall of the lodge like a knife taking flesh from a hide.

Finally Night Man spoke normally, sometimes shouting, but at least in words that Ghaden could understand.

"You see them. They are dead. Not killed by a storm or by an animal. I hear some of you whisper of nuhu'anh. What nuhu'anh kills but does not eat? What nuhu'anh would be frightened away by an old woman and her dog? I have left these two, my sister, her child, as Ligige' found them. Look at my sister. See her throat. We all know the mark of a knife. Look. See the cut."

Cries-loud was brave enough to rise to his feet so he could see Star's throat. The hunters around him did the same, but Ghaden stayed as he was, his arms around his knees, and when Biter also stood, Ghaden grabbed the babiche braid that circled the dog's neck and jerked him down again.

The men began to mutter, and Ghaden could hear the fear under their words, the anger. He wanted to block his ears, but he sat very still. Star was here with them. Couldn't the others tell that? Why draw her attention?

"Do you remember the woman who was Chakliux's mother?" Take More asked. "She died in that same way— by a knife."

"Sok's wife, now dead, did that in trying to escape," Man Laughing said. "You think she came back to kill Star?"

"Who can say? There are stories about such things," said Take More.

He looked at Aqamdax, and Ghaden knew Take More wanted her to tell them of such a story, but Ghaden squeezed his eyes shut tight, shouted at Aqamdax in his mind to say nothing, sit still, don't move.

But even had she wanted to talk, Night Man's voice rose loud over everyone's. "Sok's wife is dead. She did not do this. The dogs would have seen her. We would have heard them. Did anyone hear dogs barking this morning, early, when it was still dark?"

"How would they see her through this storm?" Take More asked.

Night Man ignored him. "You think some spirit did this? No. Someone here in this village killed her."

"What reason would any of us have to kill her?" Twisted Stalk asked. "She had done nothing to us. We needed her child." She lifted her chin at Ghaden and Cries-loud, then turned her head toward Yaa and Carries Much, at Squirrel and Black Stick, sitting beside their mother. "Look how few children we have. Can a village survive without children?"

"Perhaps it was one of the Near Rivers," Take More said. "They hate us."

"There is that chance," said Night Man, "but if they wanted to kill our women, why not attack us on our return from the hunting camp? We would have been easy to kill, laden with packs as we were. Or why not attack the village while we were still hunting? Our old women could not have defended themselves. If the Near Rivers wanted to kill or raid our caches, why not come to the village when those caches were full of summer salmon and the old women were here alone?"

He looked at Ligige'. "You were out checking your traplines this morning," he said. "Did you see anyone?"

Ligige' roused herself as though she had been asleep through all Night Man's yelling. Her voice was thick and her words difficult to understand. "After I left my traplines, I saw nothing but my own dog," she said slowly, "then the dog Snow Hawk and these dead ones."

Night Man squinted at her. "You saw nothing but two dogs, your own and Snow Hawk. Snow Hawk is Sok's dog, nae?"

"Sok's or Chakliux's," Ligige' answered. "I am not sure whose."

"Sok's," Aqamdax said quietly, and Ghaden sucked in his breath, shook his head at her, but she did not notice him.

"Sok is away, but you live in his lodge," Night Man said to Aqamdax.

"Be quiet, be quiet," Ghaden moaned under his breath. "Be quiet, Aqamdax. Star will hear you. She will steal your eyes."

But Aqamdax answered, her voice clear, her words loud. "Yes, I live there with my husband and Sok's sons. I take care of their dogs."

"You let Snow Hawk go this morning? You let her out into the storm?"

"No. She chewed through her tie. I did not even know she was gone until you and Ligige' brought her back."

Night Man nodded, then turned to Ligige'. "You went out into the storm, Aunt," he said. "Why?"

"To check my traps. An old woman will not live through the winter if she does not help feed herself."

"But you took a dog with you. Do you usually take a dog when you check your traps?"

"No. But I needed his eyes in this storm. And if I got lost, I knew he would keep me warm until the storm cleared."

"Do you think most people would take a dog with them

if they had to go out into a storm?" Night Man asked.

Ligige' narrowed her eyes. "I know only what I would do," she said. "How can I tell you what others might do?" She flipped one hand toward the circle of people in the lodge. "You should ask them, not me."

Ghaden watched Night Man, saw he was angry at Ligige'. Why? She had found Star, but why be angry about that? Someone had to find her.

"Twisted Stalk," Night Man said, "would you take a dog?"

"I would not go out," said Twisted Stalk. "Not in a storm."

"If you had to. If you had no choice," Night Man persisted.

Twisted Stalk shrugged. "I might. How do I know what I would do?"

"I would take a dog," Take More said. "And I think most people would."

Night Man smiled, but it was not a smile of happiness. Ghaden felt his legs begin to tremble, and he had to hold his arms tight around himself to stay still.

"Perhaps Snow Hawk did not go by herself to the women's place," Night Man said. "Why would a dog go out into the storm?" He lifted his head toward Cries-loud. "Where is the dog?" he asked.

"I tied her again at our lodge," Cries-loud said, and Ghaden, sitting beside him, felt Cries-loud begin to shake.

"Go get her."

"It is enough that you ask us all to come to your lodge in this storm," Ligige' said. "Now you want this boy to risk the storm alone? Do you ask him to do such a thing because his father is not here to defend him or because he is Near River? If you want the dog, go get her yourself."

"Who are you, old woman, to tell me what to do?" Night Man asked. "Who are you, a woman of the Near River Village, to speak to a hunter of the Cousin People in such a way?"

"Who are you, a man who sits all day feeling sorry for himself, to show such disrespect for an elder?" Ligige' retorted. She lifted the hare still hung at her waist, then the wolverine. "At least I bring in meat."

Several of the hunters hissed at her, and the women covered their mouths.

"You speak boldly for an old woman who has no one here in this village who belongs to you. Have you forgotten that your nephews have left us?" He lifted his hand toward the top of the lodge. "You hear the wind. Who knows whether they will return?"

"Pray your words stay in this lodge," Aqamdax said. "What will we do in this village without them?"

Then, to Ghaden's amazement, Night Man tilted back his head and began to laugh. It was not a good laugh. Biter began to whine, and again Ghaden clamped his hand over the dog's muzzle.

Suddenly Aqamdax stood. "Since you yourself are afraid of the storm," she said to Night Man, "I will get Snow Hawk for you."

Ghaden waited, thinking Night Man would go, but he did not move. Aqamdax handed the baby to Ligige' and pulled up her parka hood.

"Biter and I will go with you," Ghaden said, and did not care if his sudden words brought Star's attention. She was a lazy one and even as spirit would not want to follow them into the storm.

"You will stay here," said Night Man.

Ghaden looked at him in surprise. Why would he care what Ghaden did?

As though Night Man knew Ghaden's thoughts, he said, "My dead sister took you in as son. Now you are mine."

Then Yaa was on her feet. "We do not belong to you. Now your sister is dead, we belong to our sister, Aqamdax. We do what she says."

Aqamdax raised her eyes to Night Man's face. "Ghaden, you stay here," she said. "But I would be glad to have Biter go with me."

Ghaden took his dog to Aqamdax and watched as they left the lodge. Then he sat down beside Cries-loud and listened as Night Man spoke. Night Man's words were filled with tears as he talked about his sister, but gradually the crying left his voice, and Ghaden realized he was not talking about Star or the one who killed her but about the Near River People, and about those who had died in the fighting. He spoke about the Cousin men who had given their lives, the Cousin women who still lived in the Near River Village, lost to their families. He spoke of burned lodges and empty caches. He spoke about revenge.

FIFTY-ONE

Aqamdax and Biter returned with Snow Hawk, both dogs whining as they walked back to Night Man's lodge. The wind had shifted again and now blew from the south. A good sign. The worst storms often began with a wind coming from the east, changing gradually to north and then west.

Biter nosed his way past the outer doorflap of Star's lodge, and Aqamdax pushed Snow Hawk into the entrance tunnel. Snow Hawk snapped at her, but Aqamdax spoke in a soft voice. From the time Snow Hawk was a pup, she had been trained to stay outside. Aqamdax, her hand on Snow Hawk's back, could feel the low rumble of the dog's growling and knew she was frightened, forced into the dark, low entrance tunnel of someone's lodge.

As Aqamdax removed her snowshoes, she heard Night Man's voice coming from inside. His words were harsh and loud, filled with hatred. A fool that one, she thought, but still she understood his anger. Someone had killed his sister. In considering all the people living in the village, Aqamdax could not imagine any of them doing such a thing.

But then, it had been difficult to believe Red Leaf had killed people, had continued that killing, even taking Day Woman's life. So perhaps Red Leaf had not died. Perhaps she had been able to stay alive, and she had killed Star. But why?

Aqamdax could imagine K'os doing such a thing, but K'os would kill more subtly. A woman who knew plants like K'os did would use some poison like baneberry. Perhaps Awl was right. Aqamdax had heard her whispering of nuhu'anh. The First Men had no stories of nuhu'anh, but Aqamdax had heard Chakliux's tales of those wild ones, giants who lived by eating other men.

Biter pawed at the weighted doorflap, and Aqamdax pulled it aside. He trotted in, stepped over several people until he found Ghaden, shook his wet fur, then lay down beside the boy. Snow Hawk set her feet, and Aqamdax had to pull her into the lodge.

"She has not been inside much," Aqamdax said, though the explanation was unnecessary. Aqamdax tucked her legs under herself and knelt beside Snow Hawk, one hand on the dog's back.

"You say she chewed off her tie strap?" Night Man asked.

Aqamdax nodded.

Night Man lifted his chin toward the strap dangling from Snow Hawk's neck. "It does not look chewed," he said.

"I put a new one on her." Aqamdax lifted the strap. She had found it in Sok's supplies. It was dark with age, but wide and strong, a braid of spruce root.

"It looks old," said Night Man, then came around the hearth fire to squat in front of Aqamdax and the dog. He lifted the strap. Snow Hawk growled.

"Yes," Aqamdax said. "I found it in one of Sok's packs."

"It has not been chewed," Night Man said, holding the end of the strap so others could see.

"No. It has not."

He leaned in quickly, then, ran his hands over Snow Hawk's belly. She jumped back, bared her teeth, barked. Aqamdax grabbed her collar.

"I am not strong enough to hold her if she decides to attack you," she told Night Man.

"If she attacks me, I will kill her. She should have been killed long ago." Night Man slipped a knife from its scabbard.

"Then be prepared to give Sok one of yours, and pups to replace those she carries in her belly."

"You are so loyal to a man who once threw you away?" Night Man asked.

"I believe in doing what is right. A dog for a dog."

"You believe such a thing," he said. "That is something your people teach? A dog given for one taken?" His smile chilled her. "Perhaps you also believe a child for a child," he said, and suddenly she understood what he was trying to do.

"I did not kill Star," she said, then regretted her words. Why put that idea into the minds of those who listened? Who did she have among them to defend her? Only Ghaden, only Yaa and Cries-loud, and they were children. Perhaps Ligige', but who could say?

Night Man pointed his knife at Snow Hawk. Again she growled. "Life for life," he said, and raised his knife as though to throw it.

Aqamdax slipped the tie strap from Snow Hawk's neck, lifted the doorflap and pushed the dog out. "Go!" she cried, and blocked the entrance tunnel until Snow Hawk had run out into the storm.

"Life for life, Aqamdax," Night Man said. "You killed Star's child because of your son."

THE FOUR RIVERS VILLAGE

K'os was startled when Red Leaf came into her lodge. In the supplies River Ice Dancer had brought back from the Near River Village, K'os had found several small drawstring bags filled with beads; some were common, made of birdbone, but others had been cut from shell and wood and polished. She had dumped them out on a caribou hide floor mat in front of herself, was playing with designs.

She glanced at Red Leaf, then jerked her chin toward the beads. "From my husband," she said. "I am making a pattern for one of my parkas."

"Better you should make it for him," Red Leaf said.

She lifted the bundle of furs she had in her arms. "I brought the furs. I decided it was best to take the poison now before I lose my courage."

K'os went to her medicine bag and took out the bound packet. "I will make you a tea," she said to Red Leaf, but Red Leaf shook her head.

"Do not worry," K'os told her, "you will not die here. I will make it weak so it takes a little time before the sickness comes."

Red Leaf held out a trembling hand. "Let me take it to my own lodge. I left my daughter there and I must get back to her."

"You think I am fool enough to let you have the poison?" K'os asked her. "How do I know what you will do with it? You might try to poison Cen or my own husband."

"Come with me, then," Red Leaf said. "I cannot be gone any longer from my daughter."

K'os laughed. "Your husband is away?"

"Hunting," Red Leaf said. "He will be back by night, he told me."

"That is good," K'os said. "You should not have to suffer without your husband near." K'os smiled in derision and handed Red Leaf the small packet, tied in four knots with red-dyed sinew. She got her parka, pulled on boots, outside leggings. "Well, you and I, we will have a nice visit," she said, then she picked up her knife from where it lay beside the hearth, slipped it from its scabbard and held the blade in the smoke rising from the fire.

"A reminder for the spirits to protect me," she said to Red Leaf, then strapped the scabbard to her leg as though she were a man and followed Red Leaf outside.

THE COUSIN RIVER VILLAGE

"That dog," Night Man said, and lifted his head toward the doorflap, "she was fat." He still had the knife in his hand, and he slapped the flat of the blade against his palm with each word. "She did not chew her tie loose because she needed food. You took her with you into the storm. You went to the women's place, saw Star there and decided it would be a good time for revenge. You killed her and cut the baby from her belly."

"I did not go out into the storm this morning," Aqamdax said.

"And you have someone who will say you did not?" Night Man asked.

"I will say," Ghaden said, standing.

Aqamdax closed her eyes, her heart full of love for what the boy was trying to do and filled with regret for what would happen next.

"You were with her this morning and all night?" Night Man asked.

"I was with her. Me and Biter."

Night Man raised his eyebrows, rubbed the side of his knife against his caribou hide shirt. "Ligige'," he said, "where did this boy sleep last night?"

Ligige' pressed her lips into a thin line. "In my lodge," she said softly.

"Did he leave this morning?"

"I would not let him."

"Because of the storm," Night Man said.

"Yes."

"Just you and this boy?"

"Cries-loud and Yaa were there also," she said.

Night Man looked at Yaa. "You spent the night with Ligige'?"

"You said we could," she answered.

"Yes, I said you could. Did your brother slip away in the night? Perhaps sometime when Ligige' was sleeping?"

"I do not know."

"You do not know? How can you not know?"

"I was asleep. He might have. Sometimes he doesn't do what he's told to do."

"You think he and Biter might have gone to Sok's lodge?"

"I think so," she said.

"Cries-loud, what do you think?"

The boy jumped when Night Man said his name. "I was asleep," he said.

"So you do not know if Ghaden left Ligige' 's lodge in

the night and went with Aqamdax to help her kill my sister?"

Cries-loud's eyes grew wide and round. "He did not. He stayed with me. We slept under the same blanket."

"So you are telling me Ghaden stayed all night and all morning in Ligige' 's lodge."

Cries-loud lowered his head. "Yes," he said softly. "He didn't kill anyone."

Ghaden raised a hand to punch him, but Take More reached over and caught the boy's fist. "So this Sea Hunter woman taught you to lie and to hit those who tell the truth?" Night Man said.

"She didn't teach me that," Ghaden muttered, and wrested his fist from the old man's grasp.

"Leave the boy alone," Aqamdax said to Night Man. "He has done nothing. You know that."

Aqamdax looked at the faces of those in the lodge. Hollow Cup and Yellow Bird, those two old women, were watching, lips pressed tight, leaning forward to catch each word. They did not care whether Night Man's accusations were true, only that something had happened to break the boredom of their days. Take More was studying her as though he were seeing her face for the first time.

"I have heard that the Sea Hunters are a people not quite human," Night Man said.

Aqamdax spoke in anger, in fear. "We heard the same of you," she answered.

"What right do you have to accuse her?" one of the old women asked, and Aqamdax saw it was Twisted Stalk.

The woman's words gave Aqamdax hope, especially when Ligige' added in a sullen voice, "You are a fool, Night Man. You know she did not kill your sister."

But then Twisted Stalk said, "You killed her son. You and your sister. We know how you came and took the child when Aqamdax was still in the birth hut. What do you expect when you killed her son?"

"The boy was given as gift to the Grandfather Lake," Night Man told her. "You think our food caches are full because we are good hunters? You think the only reason we were blessed was because the caribou were pleased with our respect? I gave the child to assure we would have food for the winter."

"You lie!" Aqamdax screamed. She jumped at Night Man, scratched his face, clawed for his eyes. "You killed our son because you thought he did not belong to you. You told me that. You told Chakliux. Even Star!"

By the time Take More and Twisted Stalk had dragged her away from Night Man, his face was streaming blood.

When he was able to speak, he said, "You think she would not kill my sister?"

In the lodge, the people were quiet, and Aqamdax saw the fear in their eyes.

PART THREE

The old woman added wood to her hearth fire. It was good to be back in her winter lodge, her cache full of the summer's dried salmon. But soon most of the lodges in the winter village would be empty again. Already families had left to follow the caribou. Tomorrow, the boy would go also, but she would stay, she and the other old women. Like ghosts, they were, gray and brittle with years, not much good on caribou hunts. She shut away her thoughts of loneliness and smiled at the boy who was sitting beside her hearth.

"In the morning you will leave?" she asked him.

He nodded. "I will miss our stories."

"As will I," said the old woman, "but remember, each caribou hunt tells its own tale, so listen well and bring that story back with you."

The boy looked down at his hands. He was plaiting strips of tanned caribou hide into a four-ply braid. "My father gave me a dog," he said. "I am making a harness."

"Look! What do I see?" said the old woman, offering him a riddle. "With twists and turns it is made stronger."

"The braid," said the boy, but then his eyes widened, and she saw him smile. "A story," he said.

"Two answers for the same riddle, and both are right," the old woman told him. "But no more riddles. Today our story is riddle enough."

"The Cousin River Village," she said, and began to weave her words through the smoke of the hearthfire, around the boy's fingers and into the taut square braid. "Listen:"

LIGIGE', OF THE COUSIN RIVER VILLAGE

I spoke for Aqamdax, but my voice was small. My words were lost. We defended her, Yaa and Ghaden, Cries-loud and I, sure that because we were right they would listen. But who heeds the words of an old woman? Who listens to children? Unless Sok and Chakliux return, Cries-loud and I have no hunter to feed us, and now, because they stood against Night Man, neither do Yaa or Ghaden. We are nothing in this village.

But why would the others believe Night Man? Where are their eyes? Do they not see that, like his dead sister, he carries the seeds of madness? Perhaps when Chakliux is away from the village, we do not have enough strength to balance our weakness. Or perhaps the horror of what happened has stolen our wisdom.

I understand Night Man's reasoning, that Aqamdax would seek revenge for her son's death. But fear grows large within me that she would have been accused anyway, even if her baby was still alive. She is Sea Hunter. Who cannot see that difference in all her ways? Her voice carries the heavy sounds of their speech; her face is round and small-nosed like Sea Hunter faces. Even her stories and songs are different.

On the day Star's body was found, I could not miss the whispers of the old women. Sea Hunters are not like us, they said. Who can trust them?

Aaa! At one time I believed the same myself. And how much easier to think that what happened to Star was done by someone not raised in River ways. But now that I truly know Aqamdax, I have begun to understand that the differences between Sea Hunter and River are small things and have nothing to do with the soul.

How long until the old women's whispers close around another difference—that between Cousin and Near River, or those between families? How far will we go? Until there is only one person left?

And how would that one live, alone, without the strength of others?

FIFTY-TWO

Aqamdax stood in front of the people gathered in Star's
lodge. She reminded them that she had once been slave
to K'os. "If I had been a woman inclined to violence,"
she told them, "I would have killed K'os during those days
of my slavery. So how can you think I would kill my own
husband's child? How could I make him grieve in such a
way?" She looked at Night Man, met his eyes boldly,
hoping he would see her scorn. "I hold life sacred," she
said, and to her surprise, she saw he was afraid.

For a moment her own fear was replaced with a flow
of strength, but then the old women's whispers broke the
silence, and she heard their hissed insults.

Ligige', then Ghaden and Yaa, even Cries-loud, stood
and spoke for her, but for each word they said, Night Man
spat out lies, until Twisted Stalk, her feet on the treach-
erous path between the two sides, suggested they send
Aqamdax from the village.

"At least until her husband returns—if he returns,"
Twisted Stalk said. "Then let him speak to us about what
should be done."

Aqamdax watched in horror as the people in the lodge
nodded agreement, as they shouted down Ligige' 's attempts to speak again in her defense.

"Pack your things," Night Man told Aqamdax, and

turned cold eyes on her when she cried, "Who will nurse Sok's son?"

Twisted Stalk stood. "He will be a grandmother's baby, cared for by the old women," she said. "We have nursed enough grandchildren to keep some of our milk. Together we will keep him alive." She turned her face from Aqamdax's tears, but held up one hand to silence Night Man when he objected as Aqamdax asked Ligige' to watch over Ghaden and Yaa and Sok's older son, Cries-loud.

"They are not your children," she said, and Night Man had no argument.

When Twisted Stalk won a promise from Man Laughing that he would feed Sok's and Chakliux's dogs, Aqamdax left Star's lodge, walked out into the storm, let the wind scour the tears from her face.

She took as much meat and fat from Chakliux's cache as she thought she could carry, then rearranged his remaining packs, setting the dog salmon at the front for Man Laughing. She worried that he would take caribou meat for himself from Chakliux's share. But if all the dogs' fish was at the front, he would be less tempted to take what was not his.

She was unsure of the tradition of the River People. Would the whole village come to Sok's lodge, force her out with anger and shouting? Would they send a hunter, perhaps even Night Man himself? Or did they trust her to go alone?

Her tears touched everything she packed, and for a moment her hands hesitated over a small furred hood she had made for her son. She slipped it into her inner parka as something soft against her skin, a comfort to remind her of that little one who waited for her at the Dancing Lights.

She loaded a backpack, then a travois, one she considered her own. For how could she carry the weight of food and tent hides? When she finished, she waited in the entrance tunnel of Sok's lodge, wondering what she should do. Why go out into the storm any sooner than she must?

Finally, over the wailing of the wind, in the darkness of late afternoon, she heard voices. Her pulse pounded hard in her wrists and temples, and the thoughts she had held at bay—walking under the weight of her pack, trying to pull the travois, staying alone during the dark days of winter—twisted into her heart like knives.

Her eyes burned with tears, but she crept out of the lodge tunnel to meet the ones who came. Then, through the snow, she heard Ghaden's voice, and Biter bounded out to jump against her, knocking her back so she had to catch herself before she fell.

Ghaden and Yaa threw their arms around her, and Cries-loud pressed close to her side.

"They would not let me bring the baby to you, even to feed one last time," Ligige' said, her voice raised against the wind. "But even Twisted Stalk has a little milk. Do not worry about him. He will have enough to eat."

She reached across Yaa to grip Aqamdax's shoulder. "Chakliux will soon be back. Stay close, less than a day's walk. He will find you."

"I know he will, Aunt," said Aqamdax.

"You are ready, then?"

"Yes. Do I go, or is there some River custom that must be followed . . . something I must do?"

"I do not know Cousin ways," Ligige' said, "but in the Near River Village, there is no custom, nothing you must do. If you are ready, go. That is best."

Aqamdax bent down over the children, pulled each close. Cries-loud gave her a bola, something Aqamdax knew his father had made for him. She began to thank him, but tears broke into her words, shattering them as she spoke. Yaa gave her mittens, caribou hair on the outside with hare fur liners.

Then Ghaden leaned close to say, "I brought you Biter. He is the best thing I could think of."

Then even through her tears, Aqamdax forced herself to speak. "Biter is a wonderful gift, Brother," she said softly. "But you will have to keep him for me until I return. I cannot carry enough food to feed a dog as well as myself."

"You know he hunts. You know he brings hares and ptarmigans to us almost every day."

Tears closed Aqamdax's throat, and Ligige' said, "Your

gift is a good one, Ghaden. Now that Biter belongs to your sister, she has decided that she wants him to stay here in the village to watch over all of us. You do not expect my old dog to take care of four of us, do you?"

Then Ligige' pulled the children away from Aqamdax and said to her, "Go now, before Night Man makes it worse for you."

They slipped away in the darkness of snow and wind, and Aqamdax strapped the pack on her back, adjusted the pulling strap of the travois across her chest and started out alone into the storm.

THE FOUR RIVERS VILLAGE

Red Leaf held the open pouch in one hand, a cup of water in the other. "How much?" she asked K'os.

K'os pressed her forefinger and thumb together. "Only this," she said.

Red Leaf pinched her fingers into the gray-green powder, sifted it into the cup.

"Tomorrow, you will take more," said K'os. "Two, three pinches." She narrowed her eyes, looked at the baby hanging in her cradleboard, asleep. "Do not nurse the baby," she said.

"You think I want my daughter dead?" Red Leaf answered. "You think I would drink this cup if it were not for her?"

K'os merely smiled, waited as Red Leaf drank, then said, "Fill it again, drink again, then wipe it out."

Red Leaf did as K'os told her, and handed K'os the pouch. She tied the pouch shut again, carefully knotting the red sinew four times. "I will be back tomorrow, Gheli," she said. "And if you refuse my medicine, I will tell your husband who you are."

FIFTY-THREE

THE COUSIN RIVER VILLAGE

Take More joined Aqamdax just as she left the village.
He was leading Snow Hawk on a tether, the dog fighting
him at every step, and he carried an old hunting spear.

"You have your belongings?" he asked, shouting over
the noise of the storm.

"What I could carry," she told him. She turned her head
toward the spear. "Night Man told you to kill the dog or
me?" she asked.

For a time Take More did not answer, though the wind
played tricks with Aqamdax's ears, made her think he was
speaking when he was not.

"Both," he finally said.

"And what will you tell Sok when he returns? The dog
belongs to him."

"The truth," he told her. "That I did what had to be
done. How can we allow a dog to live once it has tasted
human blood?"

"There were no marks of Snow Hawk's eating on Star's
body," Aqamdax said.

"Be quiet. Do not speak about her."

"Why should I be afraid? I will soon be dead. You
should fear me more than her. If I did not kill Star, that
means you will take an innocent life. And if I did kill her,

389

then I am wicked enough to avenge my own death even if it is deserved. The people decided I should leave the village, not that I should be killed. It is no surprise to me that Night Man sent you rather than come himself. He has never been known for his courage."

Take More answered her, but his words were lost in the wind, and Aqamdax found she had no more breath to continue her arguments.

They walked until Aqamdax had to stop. She took the pack from her shoulders and crouched to huddle against it, a small protection from the wind. She did not look at Take More as he stood beside her, did not offer him food when she pulled a stick of dried meat from her parka sleeve, but when she got up to continue their journey, he slung the pack to his shoulders, strapped it to his own back. Then each time they stopped, Take More squatted on his haunches beside her, huddling in silence in the lee of pack and travois.

Finally in their walking, Take More pointed to a clump of trees, dark in the night against the snow.

"There is a spring in those trees," he told her, "open even in winter. Sometimes when I hunt, I come here to fill my water bladders."

"My death will curse your spring," Aqamdax said.

Take More did not answer her, the man striding toward the place with long steps so that Aqamdax, pulling the travois, could not keep up with him. The trees were willow and alder, their branches bending toward a small opening where water spoke in a voice much different from the wind.

Take More dipped his hand into the pool and drank, then said, "It flows back into the ground there." He pointed toward a gap in a pile of rocks. "It is called the Hunters' Spring. The River People say that many old men have come here to die."

Aqamdax unstrapped the travois, then squatted on her heels. She wondered why Take More continued to speak. Why waste his explanations on a woman cursed to die? Perhaps he was afraid she would fight him. Why not use words to distract her so she would not suspect the moment he planned to throw his spear?

"Animals come here to drink in winter," he said. "Someone who was good with traps or weapons could get a moose in this place."

The dog sat beside her, leaned against her legs, and Aqamdax was surprised. Snow Hawk was loyal only to Chakliux, bared her teeth at everyone else, even Sok.

Aqamdax wrapped an arm around Snow Hawk's neck, lay her hand on the dog's chest. "We were cursed by the same one, you and I," she said. She looked up and saw the shine of Take More's eyes in the darkness. "You do not worry that a woman's death will curse this place?" she asked again.

"Did you hate that one who was your sister-wife?" he said to her. "Did you want her dead?"

"She helped Night Man kill my son. I hated her for that. But I would not kill her. She carried Chakliux's child, a child he wanted very much."

"The old women told me that the baby was a girl," said Take More.

"That would not matter to Chakliux," Aqamdax said.

She looked at the trees around her, the fine darkness of their branches bending under snow and wind. She felt the cold against her face, heard again the voice of the water. She took a deep breath, held it until the rapid beating of her heart slowed, then she thought of her dead son and of Chakliux.

Take More lifted his spear, cradled it in his arms. He hefted it lightly in his throwing hand. Aqamdax felt the rumble of Snow Hawk's growling, and she tightened her hold. Chakliux had told her that the dog had killed one of Night Man's brothers. She felt Snow Hawk tense to spring, but just before Aqamdax released her, Take More slammed the butt end of his spear into the snow. The dog stood, the hair on her neck raised, her teeth bared.

"It is an old spear," Take More said. "I do not need it. The spearhead is socketed to the foreshaft and together they can be used as a knife. If you need a throwing board, you will have to make it yourself." He set a thin, flat piece of wood beside the spear. "I will tell Night Man that you and the dog are dead."

He walked away from her, head bent into the wind. At the edge of the trees, he stopped and called back, "If you are strong you will live."

Aqamdax stood, her hand clasped tightly in Snow Hawk's fur. "I am strong," she called to Take More.

THE FOUR RIVERS VILLAGE

Red Leaf scratched at another lodge. It was her third since K'os left her and would be the most difficult. Sand Fly and Tree Climber were like aunt and uncle to K'os. Red Leaf would have to be very careful with her words, perhaps say less than she had at the other lodges. There was even the chance that K'os was inside, or that she would come during Red Leaf's visit.

When Sand Fly called out Red Leaf crawled into the entrance tunnel, answered the old woman: "It is I, Gheli, and my daughter. We have brought dried blueberries for you."

Sand Fly pulled aside the inner doorflap and chortled a welcome. She took the berries, then brushed at Red Leaf's parka and unlaced the baby from her cradleboard.

Sand Fly squatted cross-legged on the women's side of the hearth fire. "She will soon be walking, this one," she said, settling the baby into her lap. "See how fat her legs are. You make strong children, Gheli. Cen is lucky to have you."

The old woman's words were a fine beginning for what Red Leaf wanted to say, and as Sand Fly played with the baby, Red Leaf scooted closer to the hearth fire, leaned near the smoke until her eyes teared. She drew in her breath with a gasp loud enough for Sand Fly to hear. When the old woman looked at her, Red Leaf raised her hands to cover her face and pretended to sob. From the cracks between her fingers, she watched, saw that even Sand Fly's husband, feigning sleep on a bedding mat at the back of the lodge, had raised up to look at her.

"Daughter?" Sand Fly said, her old woman's voice trembling. "What is the matter? Is it Cen? He is not hurt?"

Red Leaf took her hands from her face, sat with head lowered and allowed tears to drip to her lap. "No," she said. "He is not hurt. He . . . he is a good husband to me. It is . . ." She paused and took a shuddering breath. "I do not know what to tell you." She wiped her face with the edges of her hands, sniffed up the tears that had made her nose run, then she raised her head and looked at Sand Fly. "It is K'os. Has she said anything to you about my husband?"

Sand Fly looked puzzled.

"Ha! That one!" said Tree Climber. He pushed himself from his mats and tottered over to sit near the hearth fire. "She is always after the men, all of us."

"You think she wants you, old man?" Sand Fly asked, scowling at her husband.

"I say only what I know," he told her, speaking so loudly that flecks of saliva bubbled at one corner of his mouth. "You think you know everything about me, old woman?" He snorted, picked up a stick and poked at the fire.

"I know foolishness when I hear it!" Sand Fly said.

Red Leaf cleared her throat, hoping to interrupt the bickering, but Sand Fly threw out another insult, and Tree Climber answered, until Red Leaf, raising her voice to be heard, said, "K'os did not tell you that she will try to make Cen throw me away?"

Then husband and wife both looked at her, Sand Fly's eyes stretched wide, Tree Climber's mouth hanging open.

"She told Cen to throw you away?" Tree Climber asked. "She has a husband. Why would she want Cen?"

Before Red Leaf could find a good answer, Sand Fly said, "She told me once, before she married River Ice Dancer, that she would like to be a trader's wife. She said that, but I thought she was happy with her new husband."

"That makes me feel better, Aunt," Red Leaf said. "Perhaps the young women only try to make trouble with their whispering."

"They are fools, those young women," said Tree Climber. "They need more work to keep them busy." He prodded his wife with the stick he was holding. "Get this good daughter something to eat," he said. "What man would be fool enough to give up a strong, fat wife? If Cen throws you away, come here to this lodge. *I* will take you as wife."

Sand Fly rolled her eyes, but Red Leaf smiled at the old man's kindness and pretended his words had driven away her fears.

CHAKLIUX'S CAMP

Chakliux and Sok had set a hunting tent only two days' walk from the Cousin River Village. Chakliux had hoped to hunt, and so remind Sok of the good things left in life, but Sok had decided to fast, and how could Chakliux disagree with his brother's choice? Fasting brought spiritual strength. If Sok were to resist Snow-in-her-hair, he needed to build his own powers against her.

Chakliux knew it would double their strength if both he and Sok could fast, but fasting, though it strengthens the soul, weakens the body. Someone had to watch, to keep the fire, to hold Sok back if he tried once more to follow his dead wife into the spirit world.

As Sok fasted, Chakliux kept busy with small tasks, retouching the edges of spearheads and knives, straightening arrow shafts, calming himself with the knowledge of things solid and familiar, so that the rhythm of his hands made a framework for his prayers.

FIFTY-FOUR

THE FOUR RIVERS VILLAGE

Red Leaf moaned, her hands clutching her belly, her knees drawn up to her chest.

"Wife, you are sick?" Cen asked.

"My belly," Red Leaf gasped out. "It burns."

Cen used a stick to knock the ashes from the banked hearth coals, then fed the fire until it blazed. He brought her a water bladder, and she sat up, made a show of swallowing.

"Yes, that is good," she told him. She took a long breath, then suddenly doubled over, retching. "Go get K'os, Husband," she gasped out. "She has medicine . . ."

"You think I want that woman in this lodge?" he asked. "There are others in the village who know something about healing."

"Bring K'os," Red Leaf said, forcing tears from her eyes, pleading until finally he went, muttering his disagreement.

Red Leaf lay still, listened until she was sure he had left the entrance tunnel, then she crept close to the fire, kept her face near the flames until her skin felt tight and swollen from the heat. When she finally heard voices at the lodge entrance, she went back to her bed, lay on her side and moaned.

Cen came into the lodge, and Red Leaf made herself shake as though she were cold. K'os was with him, as well as Sand Fly and a second old woman—Near Mouse.

"Near Mouse has medicine, Gheli," Cen said, and Red Leaf stopped shaking enough to glance at K'os, to see the woman's almost imperceptible nod.

Near Mouse squatted in front of the hearth, demanded a cup of water.

"Hot?" Cen asked.

The old woman, rude in her sudden importance, answered Cen with a quick slash of one hand. He gave her a water bladder. From a pouch hung at her neck, she withdrew a gnarled and blackened root, bit off a piece and chewed it. When it was pulp, she spat it into the cup and squeezed water over it; she stirred the mixture with one finger and handed the cup to Cen.

"Make her drink it," she said.

Again Red Leaf stopped her shaking long enough to glance at K'os, but this time the woman gave her no sign. What was best? Did Near Mouse know what she was doing? Or was the root some other kind of poison, perhaps even stronger than baneberry? But no, whatever was in the cup could not be poison. Near Mouse would not risk chewing it herself if it was. Of course, K'os might have tricked the woman, slipped in some kind of poison, and with K'os, who could doubt that she would do such a thing?

Cen helped Red Leaf sit up. He raised the cup to her lips, but Red Leaf took it from his hands, lifted it with trembling fingers. She pressed the cup to her lips, tipped it, then pretended a quick and violent tremor. She dropped the cup, and Near Mouse howled out her disgust, but there was no change in K'os's face, no dismay, only amusement.

"I have something that will be easier for her," K'os said, and took the familiar packet from her medicine bag, untied the four red knots. She picked up the cup, dumped out what remained of Near Mouse's medicine, ignored the old woman's tantrums and shook powder into the cup. She filled it with water and handed it to Cen.

Red Leaf glanced at her, and K'os shifted her eyes to the baby sleeping in her cradleboard. When Cen offered her the cup, Red Leaf drank without protest.

THE HUNTERS' SPRING

"I should have seal oil," Aqamdax said to Snow Hawk.

After Take More left her, she set up a lean-to, but the sticks she used for tent poles were those she found in the woods nearest the spring, and the branches were weak and crooked. She thought with longing of the fine, straight poles she had left behind in the Cousin River Village, but then remembered what else was in that village.

She was afraid to make a fire, afraid the smoke would be seen, but she coaxed Snow Hawk into the lean-to, and they slept together, each giving heat to the other. Oil— burned in a stone lamp in the manner of her own people— would have given more than enough heat to warm her tent, and made little smoke, but where would she get seal oil except by trade, and what did she have to give in exchange?

At sunrise, she tethered Snow Hawk to a tree near her tent, told the dog to be quiet, then strapped on her snowshoes and went to set loop snares in the animal trails that led to the spring. It was nearly dusk by the time she finished. She squatted beside the last trap and looked up at the branches that patterned the sky.

She was tired and cold. She asked herself why she should even worry about traps. Would it matter if she caught enough to live for a few more days? If Chakliux was alive, he would come for her soon. She had food to last until then, but if he was dead, why should she live? Better to be with him and her son in death than here alone, far from her own people.

She laid her head on her arms and sat until the long shadows faded into winter twilight. The cold had nearly lulled her into sleep when something hit solidly against her side. She screamed and jumped to her feet. It was Snow Hawk, trailing a chewed line, the dog wiggling like a puppy, curling herself around Aqamdax's legs.

Like all village dogs, Snow Hawk was as wild as she

was tame, kept in her place with threats and blows, a tether and the promise of food. What had made her come to find Aqamdax when she had won her freedom?

Aqamdax stood and with stiff fingers took a knife from its scabbard at her waist. She cut the tether tied around Snow Hawk's neck. "You belong to yourself now," she told the dog. "If you hope to live, you will have to hunt. Keep away from the village. There is no place for you there, at least until Chakliux returns. Stay with me if you want."

Aqamdax did not allow herself regret when Snow Hawk ran away through the trees, nor did she shed the tears that pressed into the corners of her eyes when she found Snow Hawk at her tent waiting for her.

CHAKLIUX'S CAMP

Sok lived in the confusion brought by his grief, so that during his fast he forgot he was in a small shelter with his brother, his vision bound by the darkness of its walls.

In his thoughts, he was again in Snow-in-her-hair's bed, then with Aqamdax in those long-ago days when he had won her as wife by trickery. Someone offered him broth, hot and full of the sweet smell of caribou. Red Leaf? Did her hands cup that bowl? He slapped her away. Then the bowl was gone, and the smell of meat.

His dreams moved him to a lodge where he was knapping a spearhead. He made his chips straight and narrow across the breadth of the blade. But why was the blade shaped with blunt base and straight sides? Would the caribou honor a spearhead like that? He threw the stone away in disgust, and someone laid it back on his lap.

"It is wrong!" Sok said, his voice angling into the high scream of a child. "What man would use it? What caribou would honor it?" Then he saw again the close walls of his brother's hunting tent, the coals white with ash, hiding heat like a heartbeat at the center of the hearth.

He looked up and saw that Chakliux stood beside him. "What do we hunt?" Sok asked.

"Caribou," he heard Chakliux say.

"We hunt caribou?"

This time Sok heard no answer. He reached out for his brother, and his hand closed over nothing. He began to wail, and the sound of his own voice woke him.

He sat up in his bedding furs, reached for the bowl of broth thrust at him, reached not for the food but toward the one who offered it, closed his hand around his brother's arm.

THE HUNTERS' SPRING

The next day Aqamdax's traps took their first hare. She cut the flesh into thin strips, and she and Snow Hawk ate some raw, then she hung the rest to freeze and dry at the top of her lean-to. By then, she and the dog had begun to learn the woods that surrounded the spring.

The trees were spread in the shape of a tear, the rounded end south, the pointed end north, as though to show the way to the Cousin River Village. The spring was set at the center of the point, protected on the east by a ridge that boasted a few spruce and a gathering of cottonwoods.

Even after the coldest night, the springwater still bubbled, and the steam of its breath formed a cloud in the air. Ice webbed the edges of the pool only where the water flowed back into the earth. Berry thickets crowded close to the west side, black currant and highbush cranberry. Aqamdax filled a caribou bladder with berries, withered and sweetened by the cold.

She found eight more animal trails and set traps in each, and once dared to leave the protection of the woods for the tundra, where she scared up ptarmigan from their tiny snow caves and took them with her bola as they began their flight, wings slowed by the remains of their sleep.

She promised herself she would return to hunt again, and in the summer would find the hollow-sounding places that told of mouse food caches. Like the River children, she would dig out the small tubers the mice had stored for winter. Then, with a sudden catch of her breath, she reminded herself that she would not be in this place that long. By then Chakliux would have found her.

Even yet today, he might be back at the village. Then Take More would tell him that she was alive, here, waiting for him at the Hunters' Spring.

FIFTY-FIVE

THE COUSIN RIVER VILLAGE

"I have enough food for both of us," Dii said to her aunt, her voice soft as she strove to keep the fear from her words.

"Near River food," Twisted Stalk spat out. "You think I would take meat from them? Why not ask me to eat my own children, boil the bones of my grandsons!"

"First Eagle will take me as wife," Dii said softly, but she already knew her aunt's reply.

"He is Near River! What if he was the one who killed your brothers? How could you give a son to a man like that? What if your father's spirit came to that son and demanded that he take First Eagle's life? Could you deny your father his vengeance?"

"Let me go to Take More or Sky Watcher," Dii said.

"Take More is old and already has three wives," Twisted Stalk told her. "Sky Watcher hunts for too many of the elders. Who, except me, does not claim him as nephew?"

"Aunt . . ."

"I do not hear you," Twisted Stalk said, and raised her hands to cover her ears. "I promised, and you will go. He expects you now in the lodge where he lives. You are wife. Show your gratitude."

THE HUNTERS' SPRING

Aqamdax walked to the south end of the woods. There, a flat, marshy area was enclosed by the trees. Even now, in winter, the grass stood golden above the snow, still and stiff on this day without wind. She clutched Take More's spear in her right hand, a cluster of sticks, each sharpened to a point, in her left. The weapon Take More had given her felt awkward, the stone point heavy and out of balance with the slender shaft. She had seen many spears but, being a woman, had held only those made as a child's practice toy: sticks with fire-hardened points. Take More's spear was made in the manner of the River People, the spearhead knapped from quartz, one of the stones the River People considered sacred. She knew he had given it to her only because a large chip of stone was broken from one side of the head.

She thrust the butt end of the spear into the snow, so the weapon could watch her as she practiced. She called Snow Hawk to her side so the dog would not stray into the paths of her sharpened sticks, and then she began to throw, marking as her target a twist of grass the wind had bent in upon itself. Her first throw was poor, without enough strength for the stick to reach the grass, but her second and third were closer, and finally she was throwing with enough force, though each of her tries fell to the left of her target.

Snow Hawk had curled herself into a ball, face covered by her tail, but as Aqamdax prepared to throw her last stick, the dog raised her head and whined.

"You think I cannot learn to do this?" Aqamdax asked her. "What is so difficult about throwing a spear? Remember the men who have learned to do it—Fox Barking, Night Man, even boys no older than Ghaden."

Speaking her brother's name aloud brought a sudden catch to Aqamdax's throat, and she gritted her teeth, picked up the last of the sticks. She could not waste time on tears if she was to survive until Chakliux came for her. There had been moose tracks twice now at the spring. For a moment she allowed herself to imagine a bull moose, still fat during this early winter. What made stronger boots than moose hide? What tasted better than a stew of moose meat? She hefted the stick, found the place on the shaft where it lay balanced in her hand, raised her arm and threw. It hit her target, stood quivering in the twisted grass.

THE FOUR RIVERS VILLAGE

Throughout the day Red Leaf lay on her bed, clutching her belly. K'os came again just before dark, gave Red Leaf more of the powder, this time mixed into a tea flavored by a few dried berries.

"You did not feed the baby?" K'os asked.

"I have not," Red Leaf told her.

"I asked old Brown Foot's wife to come and feed her for you," K'os said.

Red Leaf grimaced. "You think that old woman would risk coming into this lodge when I am sick? She is afraid when she hears a dilk'ahoo cry. Everything to her is a curse."

"Who, then?" K'os snapped. "Sand Fly?"

"I have heard she still nurses children."

"That old one, she will expect payment. She does nothing without wanting something in return."

Red Leaf wrapped her arms around her belly and moaned, but did not take her eyes from K'os. "Get her. My daughter needs to be fed."

K'os, grumbling her complaints, left the lodge, and when she was gone, Red Leaf sat up. "Do not ask for my sympathy, K'os," Red Leaf whispered. "Like me, you have made your own troubles."

In the evening, when the sun had set, K'os brought several old women to Red Leaf's lodge. Sand Fly was among them, and she nursed the baby during her visit, making a show of the thin blue milk she still carried in her shriveled breasts. Red Leaf stayed on her bed, moaning out her gratitude in broken words and tears, sure in her thanks to mention K'os and her medicines, especially her kindness to Cen, and when Sand Fly finally made excuses for the women to leave, Red Leaf saw that they watched K'os

from the corners of their eyes, were careful not to touch
her or look into her face.

When Cen came to the lodge that night, his mouth was
pinched with worry. From her bed, Red Leaf held out her
hand. He knelt beside her, and she whispered, "Please,
Husband, I need K'os to stay with me tonight."

Cen shook his head. "What can she do that I cannot?"
he asked.

"She has medicine," Red Leaf said. Suddenly she stiffened, jerked, began to cry. "Please," she said, and begged
until Cen agreed.

He went to K'os, and Red Leaf stretched herself out on
her bed, easing the muscles that had cramped in her legs.
She smiled, closed her eyes and waited.

CHAKLIUX'S CAMP

Chakliux added more sticks to their fire. For two days
Sok had slept, waking once to go outside and relieve himself, but even then he had moved as if he were asleep,
and he had not responded to Chakliux's questions.

Chakliux wondered if Snow-in-her-hair, unable to take
her husband with a storm, had come into Sok's sleep,
called him instead through his dreams. But then Chakliux
told himself that his brother only needed to rest. If Snow-
in-her-hair had sent the storms, the violence of their wind
and ice, her dreams would also carry her anger. Would
Sok be lying quietly if Snow had lured him into sleep?

Chakliux calmed his mind by telling stories. His words
circled the small shelter, warmed the walls and spread
themselves over Sok like a blanket. Perhaps those stories
would be strong enough to push Snow-in-her-hair back
into the spirit world, he thought. Perhaps the words would
remind Sok that he was a hunter, that he had two sons
still here in this world of the living.

THE FOUR RIVERS VILLAGE

Red Leaf opened her eyes in the darkness and sat up. Cen
and K'os were asleep on opposite sides of the lodge, and
Sand Fly had taken the baby for the night. Red Leaf
packed blankets and mats under a sleeping robe to make

it look as if she were still in her bed, then she crept to the peg where she kept her parka and leggings. She took her clothing into the entrance tunnel, dressed and slipped out into the night.

The wind cut through the village, lifting loose snow into drifts. Another storm? she wondered. She moved from lodge to lodge, taking slow steps, staying away from the places dogs were tied. She tucked herself into the darkness at the side of K'os's entrance tunnel, waited, listening. It had not been so long ago that she had done the same thing in the Near River Village, but then she had planned to kill an old man. She had known she could overpower him if he fought her.

This would be more difficult. River Ice Dancer was strong. She would have to act quickly.

She slipped into the entrance tunnel. Waited until her heart slowed. If they found her now, she would act confused, would say she had come for more medicine. The thought gave her courage.

She pulled off boots, leggings and parka, untied her hair so it hung loose behind her ears, then she listened at the inner doorflap. There was no sound other than a man's snores. Red Leaf patted the knife that hung in its scabbard at her waist and crawled into the lodge. She waited again to see if the cold that had come with her from the entrance tunnel would wake River Ice Dancer. It would be more difficult to explain why she was here now, nearly naked, though perhaps she could pretend madness.

River Ice Dancer moaned, and Red Leaf's heart seemed to move into her throat, blocking her breath, but then he was quiet. She stood to pull one of K'os's parkas from its peg, draped it over her arm, then moved to the hearth fire. She sighed her relief when she saw Ko's's knife on one of the hearth stones. It was a sleeve knife, made like a man's, and K'os usually left it there, but Red Leaf had been afraid she would take it with her to Cen's lodge. How much better to use that knife than her own.

Red Leaf picked up the knife and went to River Ice Dancer's bed. She slipped her left hand in under his hare fur blankets, ran her fingers up his legs until she found his penis, flaccid in his sleep.

He startled, then gave a short laugh. Red Leaf lowered her head to his, pressed close, brushing her hair forward so he would think she was K'os.

"Sh-h," she whispered, and began to stroke him.

She got into his bed, climbed up to straddle him. Then she took the parka and, trying to imitate K'os's laugh, shoved it down over his face. He began to protest, and, with her left hand, Red Leaf pushed a corner of the parka into his open mouth. He bit down, but it was a gentle biting, and she knew he thought K'os was teasing him. He heaved against her, but she pulled her hand from his mouth, raised it to clasp his hair, then slid the knife into his throat.

FIFTY-SIX

THE COUSIN RIVER VILLAGE

Night Man pulled off his parka and thrust his bad shoulder toward her, but Dii's eyes went first to his right shoulder, well-muscled and large. She had heard the stories, how Chakliux had been attacked by Night Man and his three brothers. How he and the dog Snow Hawk had killed two of those brothers and wounded Night Man.

She had been a girl then, living here in the Cousin River Village. She remembered the whispers of the old women, predicting death when Night Man's shoulder festered. Sometimes a person passing close to Long Eyes's lodge would hear him cry out, demanding revenge even in the dreams of his sickness.

But during the time Dii had lived in the Near River Village, Night Man had recovered, though his arm never regained its strength. People said K'os had saved him, and perhaps that was so. Her medicines were strong. Who could deny that she saved as well as killed? But if she had, why did Night Man's illness linger until Aqamdax became his wife?

Perhaps it was the strength of that good shoulder that made the wounded shoulder look worse now than it was. Taken alone, it was not so terrible. New tissue, pink and shiny, wet with a trickle of pus, seemed to bubble from the hole left by Chakliux's spear. The shoulder and arm were withered, and a scattering of pimples ringed the scar, then spread out over his chest.

"Can a wife live with a husband like this?" Night Man demanded, his voice belligerent. "But perhaps a woman who has spread her legs for a Near River man would not even notice my wound."

"A good wife looks first to the strength that lives inside her husband," said Dii, meaning the words to be a compliment.

Night Man's face darkened, and he roared out an insult. "You think you have much value, woman?" he asked. "If you are so desirable, why would you take a husband like me?"

When Dii had been wife to Anaay, she accepted his insults, said nothing, only worked harder to please him. But his death had made her realize her own power. If she was as weak and worthless as Night Man wanted her to believe, how could she have hidden Anaay's body, then found her way home to the Cousin River Village? If she was not worthy, even to be Night Man's wife, why had the caribou chosen to sing their songs into her dreams?

"I am here to honor the wishes of my aunt," she said to Night Man, her words calm and firm. "If my days as your wife are to be filled with insults, I will leave. I have dogs and food from the Near River People, enough to survive on my own, with or without a husband." She stood up, started toward the entrance tunnel.

"And the hunter who takes you not only receives that food and those dogs, but also an old aunt with a complaining mouth," Night Man said.

Dii lifted her chin toward the side of the lodge where Long Eyes sat mumbling a rhythm of words as she sewed a boot sole to an upper. "And you offer the gift of a mother who can barely feed herself."

"She is stronger," Night Man said, his words too quick.

Dii studied the woman for a moment, shrugged her shoulders, but said nothing. Again she started for the entrance tunnel.

"I need a wife," said Night Man. "I have gifts."

"Keep your gifts," Dii told him. "As wife I ask but one thing. Respect."

"And this?" Night Man said, gesturing toward his shoulder.

"I have no problem with your shoulder," she said. "You are the one who has allowed it to be something too important. You are the one who has used that wound as an excuse to hate and to pity yourself, rather than grow strong within."

He clenched his teeth, and Dii thought he would order her from the lodge, but he said, "Please stay."

"I did not say I was leaving," Dii told him. She went to the entrance tunnel, brought in her blankets and mats, began to arrange her bedding on the women's side of the lodge.

THE FOUR RIVERS VILLAGE

There was blood—more than Red Leaf remembered from Tsaani's death. And River Ice Dancer had fought, but his efforts were undermined by his bewilderment that K'os would try to kill him. His fists had left bruises on Red Leaf's belly and arms, but he had been unable to wrest the knife from her hands. The first cut she had made, before he began to fight, was a death wound, and eventually the loss of blood slowed his hands and mind. Only when he finally lay still, in the last moments before his death, did he realize she was not K'os. Then, in his relief, he let his spirit go, and though Red Leaf crouched waiting in fear for some retribution, there was none.

She rolled him back into his bed, tucked his robes around him, and pushed the knife under nearby floor mats. Someone would find it there. Not K'os, she hoped.

She took a water bladder from the rafters, rinsed her hands and face. She suddenly saw herself caught by K'os or Cen, naked and bloody, River Ice Dancer dead on his sleeping mats, and she shivered. But no one came, and when Red Leaf had managed to wash away all the blood, she dressed again and went out into the night.

She walked back to Cen's lodge, listened long in the entrance tunnel, a lie resting on her lips: she had been to the women's place to vomit. Why curse others in this lodge with her illness?

She listened and heard nothing, so she finally crept inside. K'os and Cen were still asleep, both lying where they had been when she left the lodge. Red Leaf's bed was still warm. Had she been gone only that short a time? So quickly, a young, strong hunter was dead.

He was cruel, Red Leaf reminded herself. He was selfish. But she remembered his mother's joy when he had been born, only son of the Near River hunter Wolf Head. She remembered his first kill, the celebration over a hare taken with a boy's hunting stick. Red Leaf began to shake. She sat up and clutched the wooden bowl K'os had left next to her bed. Her retching woke Cen, and he squatted beside her, stroked her hair, murmured soft prayers until Red Leaf was able to lie down again. He stayed with her until she fell asleep.

In the morning Red Leaf felt someone bend over her. She opened her eyes to see K'os.

"You are alive," K'os said, her voice betraying her surprise. She prepared another cup of water laced with powder from the red-stringed pouch. Red Leaf drank it.

CHAKLIUX'S CAMP

In his dream, Sok again heard the wind. It was Snow-in-her-hair, though her voice was weak, as if she called from a great distance. He opened his mouth, cried out for her to wait. He went outside, saw the faint light of the new morning, the sun still hidden by the curve of the earth.

Then, as though Snow-in-her-hair were standing beside him, he heard her voice, clear and hard as ice. "I have waited long enough," she said. "I am going now. Come if you wish."

"Let me tell my brother that I go," Sok begged. "He has come all this way with me. He needs to know so he will not worry."

Snow-in-her-hair laughed, a laughter touched with anger. "You ask me to wait just so you can tell your brother? What kind of brother is he, trying to keep you here when you do not want to stay? Go, see if he is worth your concern. Then if you hurry, you will find me."

Her voice faded, and he ducked back into the tent, felt the heat of the banked coals pushing hard to keep the cold outside the caribou skin walls. He crouched beside Chakliux, saw that his brother had fallen asleep sitting up, leaning back against one of their storage packs, his fur blankets drawn over his head. Sok called his name, but Chakliux did not answer. Sok pulled away the blankets, saw the gleam of his brother's eyes, open as if in death. Sok called again, but Chakliux did not move. In growing fear Sok lay a hand against Chakliux's chest. There was no heartbeat. Snow-in-her-hair. In her fear that Sok would not come with her, she had taken Chakliux. Sok cursed his dead wife, and the curses rose with his mourning wails.

When Sok finally came to himself, he was outside, a pack strapped on his back, snowshoes on his feet. He felt like a child first coming to know the world. His chest ached as though from an old wound, but he found that his body moved in spite of his pain, and that his mind worked, his thoughts no longer the muddle they had been since Snow had died. But now he also mourned his brother, took each step in sorrow, drew each breath in fear. What if Snow, in her need for him to join her, had taken not only Chakliux but also the others who held him to the earth: his sons?

THE HUNTERS' SPRING

Aqamdax woke to nausea. She pulled back her bedding furs and crawled over Snow Hawk toward the doorflap. Outside, she began to retch, but her belly was empty, so she brought up only bile. When her stomach stopped heaving, she scooped up a handful of snow, let it melt in her mouth and trickle down her throat. She went back into the lean-to and rubbed her hands dry in Snow Hawk's thick fur.

The day before, she had decided to chance a hearth fire. The nights had grown too cold for her to survive without one. So now she coaxed the coals back to life.

"It is morning," she said to Snow Hawk, "though the

sun is not yet up in the sky. How is your stomach? Are you sick?"

They had eaten much the same things, the two of them, though Aqamdax knew Snow Hawk also hunted on her own. But the dog seemed well, and once Aqamdax had eaten a little, she felt better, as strong as though she had not been sick.

Snow Hawk spent more time away from Aqamdax each day. Aqamdax worried at first, thinking Night Man, on some hunting trip, would see the dog and know Take More had allowed them to live. She worried about wolves. What chance would Snow Hawk have against a pack, except the same chance any female had—that one of the males would want her? But each day at dusk Snow Hawk returned to take her share of food, to sleep outside the tent, untethered, to creep inside if the night grew too cold.

Each morning Aqamdax checked and reset her traps, gutting and skinning any hares she caught, then she rolled the pelts flesh side in to store with the carcasses under the caribou hide cover of her platform cache.

This day, her traps held three fat hares, and when she had finished skinning them, she took her spear sticks and walked to the south side of the woods. The wind had died, though it kicked up a skiff of snow now and again over the tundra beyond the trees.

Aqamdax had become more accurate with the spear sticks, and her muscles did not burn as they once had after time spent throwing. Now she was trying to learn to throw while making a short run. She had seen the men take game in such a way, but though her spear went farther, she found it more difficult to keep her eyes on her target, and so lost her accuracy.

She retrieved her spear sticks, had them in her hand, when a voice suddenly called out, "You need a throwing board."

Aqamdax whirled, a spear ready, but as quickly as she turned, she lowered her weapon. Take More stood at the far side of the marsh clearing, a dog beside him, a haunch of frozen caribou meat on the travois the dog was pulling.

"You would greet an old man in such a way, one who has brought you meat?"

Tears gathered in Aqamdax's eyes, but she called out as though she were a wife offering the hospitality of her lodge to one of her husband's friends. "You are hungry?"

"Perhaps I could eat. I started out this morning in darkness so my wives would not see what I brought you."

"You can stay for the night?" Aqamdax asked.

Take More laughed. "You are not afraid I will ask for more than food?"

"I think you respect my husband and will not ask his wife to share her bed."

Take More's face reddened, but Aqamdax pretended not to see. Perhaps, for bringing meat, the old man deserved more than a bowl of stew, but what wife could offer such hospitality without the approval of her husband?

He helped her put the haunch in her cache and answered her questions about the people in the village. He said that Ghaden, Yaa and Sok's sons were well, that Ligige' spent much time telling others how to live their lives, and that Sok and Chakliux had not yet returned. Aqamdax closed her eyes in quick sadness when he said that Twisted Stalk had given her niece Dii to Night Man.

When he had nothing more to tell her, Take More spoke of being young, hunting and marrying wives. Finally, he ran out of words. Then he left, and her tent seemed too quiet, too empty. But that night, as Aqamdax went to sleep, she repeated his hunting stories to herself, whispered them into her dreams, and she did not feel so alone.

FIFTY-SEVEN

CHAKLIUX'S CAMP
In the dream, Aqamdax was beside him, her hands gentle
on his face. She leaned close, and he raised up to gather
her into his arms. Suddenly she was not Aqamdax but
Star, her face white and drained of blood, ice glazed over
her cheeks, her eyes dark and sightless.

Chakliux cried out, and the sound of his voice woke
him. His heart slowed as he realized he had been dreaming, then he scolded himself. He had fallen asleep. In the
darkness of the tent, he looked over at Sok's bed, saw the
raised outline of a light-colored fur robe and sighed his
relief. Sok was asleep, but what if he had awakened while
Chakliux slept? He could have wandered outside. . . .

Chakliux crept forward on hands and knees, reached to
pat his brother's shoulder. The empty hare fur blanket
collapsed under his hand. He jerked the blanket away.
Even Sok's sleeping mats were gone. Chakliux quickly
pulled on his boots and strapped snowshoes to his feet.

Outside, he was surprised to see that the sun had risen,
a pale yellow disk barely above the horizon, the sky dark
toward north and west. New snow had come during the
night. Less than a hand's breadth had fallen, but it had
drifted over Sok's trail so that Chakliux found nothing but
the first few steps Sok had taken, heading west.

Why would Sok go in that direction? Their village was south and east. Then Chakliux knew Sok was following his dead wife, walking west toward the land of the spirits.

Aaa, Sok, Chakliux thought, after all this have I lost you?

Everything seemed the same, each ridge, each frozen stream like the one he had just crossed. Once a white fox trotted past him, once ravens circled, but otherwise, the earth and sky were empty. Sok sang his sons' names under his breath, a rhythm for his feet, a reminder of the direction he should travel and why. He pitched his parka hood back, allowed the air to cool his head so he would not sweat, and when his ears began to ache from the cold, he drew the hood forward again. As the sun moved in its shallow arc, he fought against sleep, walking with his head down, his eyes closed.

Sleep was escape, a place without decisions, without pain. There he would not have to tell Aqamdax that her husband was dead, killed by Snow-in-her-hair. He would not have to face each empty day without the wife he needed, without the brother he had learned to love. But he made himself walk, and he breathed his sons' names, with each step spoke them into his thoughts until their faces danced before him, until their voices were louder than Snow's as she called to him from the wind.

THE FOUR RIVERS VILLAGE

Brown Foot scratched at the side of K'os's lodge. He was mumbling small curses against an old wife too lazy to get up in the morning to feed her husband, and against River Ice Dancer's dogs, the animals barking as he waited.

"What?" he finally shouted out. "Are all women lazy this morning? Is everyone still asleep? Look!" He raised his walking stick toward the southeast. "There is the sun." He blew through his lips, a sound of rudeness, and pulled aside the outer doorflap. He went into the entrance tunnel and did not pause to call again before stepping inside the lodge.

When he saw K'os was not there, he stopped his flow

of curses. Then, glimpsing the thatch of River Ice Dancer's dark hair above his sleeping robes, Brown Foot slapped his walking stick against the floor and shouted, "What hunter sleeps away a good day?"

When the man did not answer, Brown Foot stepped closer and prodded him with his stick. "Where is your wife?" he asked. "Your hearth is cold." He squatted on his haunches and muttered, "She's a foolish woman, going out to the food cache before starting your morning fire. You might decide to get another. I have a granddaughter, you know. . . ."

He pushed a hand under River Ice Dancer's blankets, then his mouth fell open. He stared at his fingers. They were sticky with clotted blood.

"How is your wife?" Near Mouse whispered, standing on tiptoe to peer over Cen's shoulder into the lodge. Sand Fly scuttled past him, set the baby's cradleboard on the floor. She unlaced the bindings and stripped out the moss padding, full of the baby's wastes, then threw the moss into the hearth fire.

The two old women had entered as if the lodge belonged to them, and Cen clenched his fists to keep his impatience from becoming anger. He was tired, awakened in the night by Gheli's vomiting. She had quieted and then he had slept, but that sleep had been cursed with strange dreams and half-formed thoughts.

At dawn, K'os had given Gheli more medicine, tea made with a pale green powder.

"It is the strongest medicine I have," she had told Cen. "It should drive away her pain, loosen her bowels and force the evil from her body. But if those pain spirits are too great . . ." She shook her head. "It is the best I can do for her," she had said softly. "Perhaps you should ask one of the elders to come and make prayers."

Now, as Cen answered Near Mouse's question, he found his eyes tearing and had to look away. "Gheli is still sick," he said. "Is there anyone in the village who might know prayers?"

"Our shaman died two . . . no . . . three summers ago. He was old, and my husband told us—"

"I know," Cen said, interrupting her. Near Mouse was a woman of too many words, and he did not have time for her foolishness. "Is there anyone else?"

"Perhaps old Brown Foot."

Cen shook his head.

Near Mouse pursed her lips into a frown. "He is always after more than his share of food, that is true," she replied, "but he knows many prayers. He was brother to our shaman."

Cen glanced at Sand Fly; the woman was nursing his daughter. "He knows prayers," she said without looking up from the baby.

"I will ask him to come," Cen said, and pulled aside the doorflap, then stepped back in surprise as Brown Foot burst into the lodge.

He was babbling, his eyes wide, his words so scrambled that Cen could make out only K'os's name.

"What? What has happened?" K'os cried out. She grasped his shoulders, shook him until he said, "Your husband, that young man from the Near Rivers, someone has killed him. He is dead. There is blood all over. Blood on his bed . . . on the floor . . ."

He continued to babble, even as he followed Cen and K'os when they ran from the lodge.

Near Mouse crept close to Sand Fly. "He said K'os's husband is dead?" she whispered. She glanced up as Red Leaf moaned, leaned from her bed to retch, dry heaves that brought up nothing.

"And this one . . ." Sand Fly nodded toward Red Leaf. "You think she will live?"

Near Mouse shrugged her shoulders.

"It is strange," Sand Fly finally said, using a finger to break the baby's suction on her breast. She ignored the child's quick squeak of protest, lifted her to a shoulder and patted her back until she burped, then nestled her at the other breast. "Before Red Leaf was sick, she came to our lodge and spoke to my husband and me. She seemed afraid of K'os, but we did not think much of it. After all, she is a trader's wife, and claims her father was a trader, too. How can you know if a woman raised like that tells the truth? She said that K'os wanted Cen to be her husband."

"Why would K'os want Cen with a fine young hunter like—" Near Mouse stopped before saying the dead man's name.

For a time neither woman spoke, the silence between them broken only by the soft throat sounds of the baby's nursing, then Sand Fly said, "Before that Near River hunter came to our village, when K'os lived in my lodge, she had eyes for any man, even my husband." She raised a hand to cover her smile.

"Did she ever say anything about Cen?" Near Mouse asked.

"Yes, sometimes, and she watched him. I remember that she did. . . ."

"But she would not kill . . . why would any woman—"

Near Mouse's words were interrupted by a cry from Red Leaf. Even the baby jerked away from Sand Fly's breast.

"Who is dead?" Red Leaf cried. "Who has died? Tell me!"

Near Mouse glanced at Sand Fly, then hobbled to Red Leaf's bed. "Gheli, you are sick," she whispered. "You are sick. You cannot worry about what has happened. There will be time to think about that when you are well."

"River Ice Dancer?" Red Leaf whispered, her eyes stretched wide.

"Hush, child," Near Mouse said, and pressed a hand to Red Leaf's mouth. "Hush, now, do not say his name."

Red Leaf twisted away from Near Mouse's hand. "No!" she screamed. "No! She told me she would do it. She told me that if I did not give her Cen . . . if I did not give her my baby . . ."

"Be still, Daughter," said Near Mouse, and pushed Red Leaf back into her bed. "Be still, be still."

Red Leaf took a long shuddering breath, closed her eyes. "K'os has killed us both," she said. "Now she has killed us both."

FIFTY-EIGHT

THE COUSIN RIVER VILLAGE

"Your Near River husband, you left him?" Night Man asked.

Dii pulled the hare fur blanket more tightly around her shoulders. He had come to her during the night. In silence he had mounted her and taken her as wife. Now, this morning, even before she had left her bed, he was full of questions.

Be fair, she told herself. What husband would not ask a new wife the same thing? You have been away from this village too long. Have you forgotten that his mother, Long Eyes, cried each time her husband left to hunt? The people in Night Man's family care much for those who belong to them. His questions mean nothing more than that. Would you rather have another husband like Anaay?

But how much should she tell Night Man? Why take the blame for Anaay's death when K'os had been the one to make the poison? And why admit to hiding his body?

"Yes, I left him," she said. Not a lie. She had left him— at least his body—and she hoped she had not led his spirit to this village.

"Why?"

"He did not need me," she said softly. "He had another wife."

419

"What?" Night Man asked. "Why do women always mumble? How can I hear you when you whisper your words?"

Dii lifted her chin, turned her face toward him. "I left him," she said again. "He was not a good husband to me."

Night Man shrugged.

A foolish reason, no doubt, Dii thought. Remember what Twisted Stalk told you about Night Man and Aqamdax. You think he will have sympathy for your problems with Anaay?

"You blame *him* for your decision to leave?" Night Man asked, his question edged with bitterness.

Be wise, she told herself. Consider your words before you say them.

"You, Husband," she said, "could you stay with a wife who had killed your brothers or your father?"

"Your Near River husband was the one who killed your father and your brothers?"

"I do not know, but someone in his village did. I could no longer live among them."

"Ah," he said. His cold eyes skipped over her face and down to where her hands were crossed over her breasts. "Perhaps then this time I have chosen a good wife."

She opened her blanket to him, but though he raised his eyebrows in approval, he flicked his fingers at her and lifted his chin toward the hearth. Dii dressed and rekindled the fire, then went out to the cache. The first night was past—surely the worst of any she would face as Night Man's wife. She sighed her relief and watched the cloud of her breath rise into the shadowed blue light of the morning.

THE FOUR RIVERS VILLAGE

"You have forgotten that I did not want K'os to stay," Sand Fly said, standing up from her place among the women to point one bent finger at her husband, Tree Climber. "You were the fool who thought she would come into your bed."

A rift of laughter passed through the people who had gathered in the chief hunter's lodge, and two dark spots of red burned in Tree Climber's pale cheeks. "I heard no complaints when she gave you medicine for your joints," he said to her.

"It does not matter why she is here or who helped her when she came," Cen told them. "I knew her from another village, and still did not think she would kill her own husband. But now we must decide what to do with her. We cannot keep a woman like K'os in this village."

"She claims she did not kill her husband," Brown Foot said.

"Jumps-too-far found her knife under her dead husband's body," said Sand Fly. "I know it is K'os's knife. She had it when she came to us."

"Send her away," said Brown Foot. "It is winter. She will not live long without dogs or food."

"No," Cen replied. "If K'os killed her husband, she has no right to live. Is there some man here who will kill her? I will make it worthwhile for him. I have trade goods and meat."

"Always in this village," Tree Climber said, "when someone has killed or broken our strongest taboos, we send them away. It is best, especially with a woman. You do not know our ways, Trader." Tree Climber nodded at the chief hunter, a middle-aged man, short and broad, his eyes squinted as though he always looked toward far places. "First Spear, what is your choice?"

"Long ago, when I was a child, this woman's brother lived in our village," First Spear said. "He was a good man, married to my sister. He gave me my first knife."

K'os's knife lay at the edge of the hearth, bloodstains on the caribou hide that wrapped the handle. First Spear pointed with his chin at the weapon. "The knife found under the body looks like one K'os's brother made me," he said. "You know this brother of hers died long ago. Perhaps this is some vengeance K'os's dead brother planned. Perhaps he directed her to our village."

"This brother of hers," one of the oldest men said, "I remember him. He made that blade. See how it is knapped. Do any of you know a man in this village who makes blades in such a way?"

First Spear nodded at Cen. "Do you have any idea where the knife came from?" he asked.

"As I told you before, I knew K'os when she lived in the Cousin River Village. She had the knife then. It is almost like an amulet to her."

"Did she ever tell you where she got it?"

Cen pressed his lips into a tight line. "One of her brothers gave it to her," he said.

A soft hiss of breath went out from the people.

"So then," First Spear said. "There are things here not easily understood." He looked over the heads of the men to the women, who sat near the lodge walls. "Sand Fly, you said K'os gave you medicine. Did it help?"

"A little."

"And she gave medicine to Cen's wife?"

"Yes."

"The medicine helped?"

Sand Fly shrugged. "Gheli is no worse."

"What does that have to do with the killing?" Cen asked.

"How could a woman who heals also kill?"

"But what if she did?" said Cen. "You would let her stay here in this village, take the chance that she would kill again?"

One of the hunters stood up. "If she stays, my wife and I, my father and his wife, we will leave," he said.

Several others nodded their agreement.

"Send her away," said Brown Foot. "If she did the killing, her husband's spirit will take revenge. If she did not, then he will protect her, and she will find another village where she can live."

First Spear nodded, and the men, old and young, called out their agreement. Cen heard the women, their voices like a soft wind at the edges of the lodge as they talked among themselves. Finally Sand Fly stood and said, "Brown Foot is right. Why chance doing harm to someone innocent?"

When the elders left the lodge, Cen spoke politely for a few moments to those around him. Perhaps their decision was best. Who was he to question them? He had

never stayed long enough in any one village to understand
the loyalties and hatreds that bound the people to one
another and gave foundation for arguments, reasons for
choices. He was weary, anxious to return to his wife and
daughter.

The men of the village had left three young hunters
with K'os, and only at Cen's insistence had bound her
wrists and ankles, tied a gag over her mouth. He had
known her long enough to realize that she could charm
any young man if given the chance.

Near Mouse had stayed with Gheli, and now, as Cen
hurried back to his lodge, he was suddenly afraid that K'os
had escaped and found some way to kill his wife. But
when he went inside, he found Gheli and Near Mouse
sitting beside the hearth, playing with the baby. Daes was
lying on a hare fur blanket, her legs kicking as she reached
toward some trinket Gheli held just beyond her fingers.

"You are feeling better, Wife?" he asked, though the
question was foolish. Who could not see that she was
better?

Near Mouse looked up at him and chuckled. "I think
your wife is well."

Cen squatted beside them, lay his hand on his wife's
shoulder. Perhaps, then, the decision to allow K'os to
leave the village was the right one. He had a little daughter, a good wife. In spring he would return to the Cousin
River Village and bring his son, Ghaden, here to live in
this fine lodge with his sister Daes and his new mother,
Gheli.

FIFTY-NINE

THE FOUR RIVERS VILLAGE

K'os bent over River Ice Dancer's body, cut the thong
that held the amulet he wore at his neck. First Spear had
told her she could take it, but had said she was a fool for
wanting it. Did he think she was afraid of whatever power
that amulet carried? If it could not protect River Ice Dancer against the killer's knife, then it was good for only
one reason: to prove to the Near River People that he was
dead, and then to convince them to avenge his death.

She heard the murmurs around her—those who thought
she had killed her husband and those who did not, arguing
still over her guilt. The old women of the village had
dressed River Ice Dancer in his finest parka, and she noticed as she removed the amulet that they had bound a
scabbard at his waist. She was surprised to see the blood-
stained handle of her own knife protruding above the
leather that covered the blade, and she drew in her breath
as she suddenly realized that her knife had been used to
kill him. It was thirsty for blood, that knife, and had
served her well. She had used it to kill Chakliux's father,
Gull Wing, after he, Fox Barking and Sleeps Long had
raped her and left her for dead. How could she allow it
to rot with River Ice Dancer?

She lifted her voice in a mourning cry, then through

her tears said to the women nearest her, "I was making him a parka." She gazed around the lodge as though confused, then her eyes came to rest on a fishskin basket. She pointed, and the women passed it from hand to hand until it reached K'os. She pulled out the partially completed parka, held it up so they could see its intricate pattern of light and dark fur.

"Like water on ice," one of the women whispered. Then another murmured, "If K'os planned to kill her husband, why would she make him something so beautiful?"

K'os raised the parka, held it above her head, moved her feet in a slow dance of mourning, her shoulders heaving as she sobbed. Finally she threw herself over River Ice Dancer's body, covering him from chin to groin with the parka. She buried her head in the fur and cried out her anguish, but as she lay over his body, her hands worked under the parka to remove her knife from the scabbard. She slipped it up her sleeve even as three old women pulled her away, one cursing, two crooning their sympathy. They walked her to the entrance tunnel. There K'os hefted the pack they had allowed her, went outside and called the two dogs they said she could take. They were River Ice Dancer's dogs, and one pulled a travois laden with tent and tent poles, food and some of her belongings.

As she left the village, she sang mourning songs until she knew they could no longer hear her voice.

When the sun had nearly tucked itself again into the earth, K'os made a camp in a group of spruce trees. She set up the tent, tying the dogs near the entrance, and she built a fire, lighting it with the smoldering knot of spruce she carried in a birchbark container hung from her waist.

She huddled close to one of the dogs. He snapped at her. K'os snarled, and the dog tucked his tail between his legs, cowered and finally accepted a small piece of dried meat from her hands. The night would be long, and she was cold, but she would not die.

Her hatred alone would carry her to the Near River Village, but someday she would return to the Four Rivers.

Perhaps she would come in stealth, or perhaps with warriors, but she would return. Then Cen would suffer, for who but Cen could have killed River Ice Dancer? He alone had the strength and a reason.

Of course, for him to do such a thing meant that Red Leaf had told him of K'os's threats. Not the whole truth, K'os was sure, but some part of it.

K'os smiled, searched through her pack until she found her medicine bag. She drew out the small pouch tied with red sinew. At least she could comfort herself with the thought of Red Leaf's retching out her life, bleeding from nose and mouth until finally even her vomitus and feces were only clotted blood.

K'os tipped back her head and laughed. That night, in spite of the cold, she slept well.

THE FOUR RIVERS VILLAGE
Cen knelt beside Red Leaf, gently shook her awake. "Gheli?"

She heard his voice from her dreams, opened her eyes slowly and smiled at him.

"It is morning. Are you well enough for me to go and get wood? I will return as quickly as I can."

"Go," she said, her words broken by the dryness of her throat. "First, could you bring me some water?"

He untied a bladder, held it to her mouth, and when she had finished drinking, he tucked the sleeping robes around her shoulders. She watched him leave, waited for a short time, then rolled out of her bed. She went to her stack of baskets, chose one made of salmon skins, dark and translucent, sewn side by side, tail ends down to form the base. She pulled out a pouch of caribou hide, no larger than her hand. It was bound with red sinew, tied with four knots. She took it to the hearth fire and used a stick to tuck it into the coals.

She flexed her fingers. She was a large woman, a little clumsy, but her hands were as nimble as a child's, gifted with needle and awl, cunning enough to substitute a packet of ground willow root for one of baneberry and to do it so quickly that the trade was not even noticed by someone standing near.

As the poison burned, Red Leaf thought of that harmless pouch K'os now carried in her medicine bag. And she wondered what other lives she had saved. Perhaps they would count as a payment for those she had taken.

THE HUNTERS' SPRING

Aqamdax wiped her hand across her mouth, lay back on her bed. Snow Hawk tried to lick her face, but she pushed the dog away. She patted the floor mats, and Snow Hawk lay down.

Was this the third or fourth morning that she had awakened to light-headedness and nausea?

"I do not need to be sick, Snow Hawk," she said to the dog. She closed her eyes. Stories of people and their illnesses spun into her head, mocked her with medicines she did not have, until finally she retreated into the helpful tales mothers told small daughters. Sometimes those stories offered women the best advice.

Suddenly Aqamdax began to laugh. Snow Hawk whined and pressed her cold nose into Aqamdax's face. Aqamdax wrapped her arms around the dog, but Snow Hawk broke away, crouched with forelegs on the ground, rear end raised, tail wagging.

"A game?" Aqamdax said, and sat up to ruffle the dog's fur. "Yes, Snow Hawk, a game."

How foolish not to realize . . . But she had not been sick with her son, and her moon blood times had not been regular since his birth.

"Now you have two people to guard," she told Snow Hawk, "until Chakliux comes for us."

She slipped one hand under her parka, felt the soft hood she had made for her dead baby. Tears came to her eyes, and she began to cry—in sorrow for that little one who had died, in joy for the new baby she carried so close to her heart.

Sok squinted at the tear-shaped woods. The Cousin People called it the Hunters' Spring. Take More had once grudgingly led him to the place when they were hunting moose. Sok had laughed to himself about the old man's reluctance to share its location. Chakliux had already told Sok about the spring. Did Take More think Chakliux would keep hunting secrets from his own brother?

Sok shook his head. What would he do without that brother? He sighed, looked again at the thin gray trees. Suddenly he crouched, gripped his spear, ready to throw.

A wolf stood at the edge of the woods. No, not wolf; the animal's tail was curled almost to its back. A dog. Not as dangerous as a wolf—at least, more predictable—but still, he gripped his spear. Perhaps the animal had come with a hunter who had stopped at the spring, most likely one of the men from the Cousin River Village. Sok raised his voice, called out. The dog lowered its head and stared at him, then slowly wagged its tail.

Sok cupped his hands around his eyes, squinted. Snow Hawk? Yes, his own dog Snow Hawk. Aqamdax must have lent her to a hunter to use as a pack animal on a hunting trip. Or perhaps one of the men had decided to take Cries-loud hunting and the boy brought Snow Hawk with them. Sok broke into a run, his snowshoes slowing him, forcing an awkward gait.

"Cries-loud!" he called, his pulse jumping in the hope of seeing his son.

But there was no answer, and if they had brought Snow Hawk, why was the animal loose, without pack or travois harness?

Sok held out his hand, approached slowly. "Did you chew through your tether?" he asked, his voice low, soft. If the animal had been running loose, wild since he and Chakliux left the village, she would not yield easily. For Chakliux, perhaps, she would come. Not for Sok.

"Snow Hawk," he called softly. "Snow Hawk."

Snow Hawk lowered her tail. She snapped once at the air, then dropped to her belly. Sok reached up under his parka, brought out a piece of dried meat. He had not had the presence of mind to bring much food from Chakliux's tent. Each time he sorted through his pack, he was surprised at what he had brought—foolish things—extra blades, not yet knapped for use; large balls of babiche; a pack of caribou teeth. Little meat, no extra boots.

Suddenly Snow Hawk perked her ears, looked back into the trees. Before Sok could stop her, she bounded off toward the woods. He followed her. If she had come with hunters, he would probably find them at the spring. His own water was gone, the last swallow taken at dawn. Dry cold days, dim of light but clear of sky, always seemed to draw all the water from his body, leaving him parched, with lips cracked, eyes burning.

He came to other trails, all made by one person, someone with small feet. Surely not a boy. Would the Cousin Rivers have forced Cries-loud from the village after Sok and Chakliux had left? No, there were too many good people there to allow such a thing. Perhaps they were a woman's tracks. Yes, the toes turned in. How else did a woman walk when she was carrying a heavy load or pulling a travois? Most likely an old woman, then, one who had offered to leave the village so there would be more food for the children. But what fool had allowed her to take Snow Hawk, a golden-eye, pregnant with a litter and one of the best dogs in the village?

Then he knew. Ligige', of course, it was Ligige'. She was, after all, Near River, the most Near River of anyone except he himself, his sons and Yaa. And she had probably stolen Snow Hawk, especially if her leaving had been forced on her by others.

"Ligige'!" he shouted, then turned and called in all directions.

But the voice that answered him was not Ligige' 's. And it came so unexpectedly that he jumped, his snowshoes threatening his balance. He reached for an alder tree, grasped the thin bole to keep from falling into the snow.

"Sok? You are here? Where is my husband?"

He stared at Aqamdax for a moment before he could respond, and then he spoke only to say, "Where is Ligige'?"

"Ligige' is here?" Aqamdax asked, and in the foolishness of question upon question, Sok wondered if he were still in a dream, back in Chakliux's tent.

Snow Hawk jumped around them, making a dance in and out of the paths that cut through the trees, and Aqamdax scolded her, warned her away from a noose trap set in an animal trail. The pause gave Sok time to clear his mind. He pointed to Aqamdax's footprints and said, "I followed Snow Hawk here. When I saw your tracks, I thought perhaps some old woman had been driven from the village. I thought it might be Ligige'."

"They are my tracks," Aqamdax said. "Night Man forced me to leave." She frowned, and before he could ask her the many questions that came to him, she said, "My husband is with you?"

He shook his head. "I am alone."

"Where is Chakliux?" she cried out. Her voice was a wail, both demanding and denying, and he could not look at her.

"If one of us had to die," he said softly, "I do not understand why it was Chakliux. You know I would have given my life for him."

Slowly, Aqamdax sank to her knees. She curled herself into a ball, and Sok knelt beside her. He gathered her close, let his own cries echo hers until even Snow Hawk lifted her head and joined their mourning.

SIXTY

THE COUSIN RIVER VILLAGE
Ligige' brushed the snow from her stack of wood and kicked several pieces loose from the pile. Her thoughts were on a basket she was making, not a fishskin basket— the kind she had made since she was a child—but one of grass, in the way Aqamdax had been teaching her. Her stitches on one side were loose, and the basket was lopsided. Perhaps if she unraveled it back to where she had started her last weaver . . .

She picked up the chunks of wood that had scattered from her pile, groaned as she straightened, and started back into the lodge. Ghaden and Cries-loud were usually the ones who brought in the wood, but Sky Watcher had taken the boys on a morning hunt. She hoped they had good luck. Fresh meat in winter warmed a body as much as a hearth fire.

She stooped at the entrance tunnel, threw the wood inside piece by piece. Yaa would stack it there later after she finished scraping the caribou hide Ligige' had given her. The girl would need to escape the smoky lodge for a little while.

Ligige' rubbed her eyes. Winter hearth fires always left them red and weepy. Sometimes she walked the paths of the village just to get out of the smoke. She took a long breath. The air was clean but cold enough to make her cough.

Already, though spring was far away, the days seemed to be a little brighter, a little longer. Or perhaps it was only an old woman's wish, she thought.

As she ducked her head to enter the tunnel, something caught her eye, someone at the crest of one of the hills north of the village.

Sky Watcher already? A seed of fear lodged in her heart. Were the boys all right?

A trampled pattern of snowshoe tracks led from just beyond her lodge to the hills. She walked those tracks until the snow gave way and let her sink to her knees. She sat down and lifted her feet, crawled back toward her lodge, then stood again.

No, she thought with relief, it was not Sky Watcher. The man was too large and walked too heavily. Who, then? Perhaps a trader, or worse, someone who had been sent away from his own people for one reason or another. They did not need anyone like that here.

Best to tell the men. She started toward the hunters' lodge, made herself hurry over the frozen and slippery path. She scratched at the lodge's caribou hide doorflap, called out, and was answered by Take More. The old man's voice carried an edge of irritation.

"Come out here," Ligige' demanded, having no patience for his rudeness. When he was with other men, Take More acted as if he had the right to treat old women like slaves.

"What?" Take More demanded from inside the lodge. "What are you telling me? Who is it? Ligige'?"

"Yes," Ligige' said. "Someone is coming. A man. I saw him and now I have told you." She turned her back on the lodge, looked again toward the hills, pretended not to notice when Take More joined her.

"I am alone here," he said.

She grunted but said nothing. He was Cousin River; she was not. Perhaps he would recognize the one who was coming. But when the man topped the nearest hill, Ligige' knew who it was, and she whispered his name under her breath: "Sok."

* * *

The village, though small, looked good, the lodges strong, smoke spiraling up from their smoke holes. Only his lodge carried that appearance of neglect which seems to mark any shelter where people no longer live.

Several women were walking the village paths. He recognized Ligige' standing near the hunters' lodge. Someone was with her—Take More? Sok lifted one hand in greeting, felt the weight of what he had to tell them slow his steps. Then he thought of his sons, so that sorrow and joy suddenly lived together in his heart.

Take More had a blanket clasped around his shoulders as though he had come in haste from the hunters' lodge. He huddled near the entrance, but Ligige' came to meet Sok, and her first words were no surprise.

"Where is Chakliux?"

For some reason Sok could not answer her, but instead looked over her head, nodded a greeting to Take More and asked, "My sons?"

"They are well," Take More said, and Ligige' added, "Yellow Bird has the baby in her lodge. He is growing fast. Sky Watcher has taken Cries-loud and Ghaden hunting this morning."

Sok was disappointed that he would not see Cries-loud right away, but glad that Sky Watcher was acting the part of father.

"Chakliux?" Ligige' asked again, and Sok noticed that Take More, shivering, had turned to go inside the lodge.

"Wait, Uncle," Sok called to the man, then he turned to Ligige' and said, "My brother is not coming back."

Sok lowered his head and began to explain. When both Ligige' and Take More crowded close, he realized that he was mumbling his words and they could not hear what he was saying.

He lifted his head, started again. "We were together in his hunting tent for many days," he told them. "During that time my brother watched over me. He kept our fire strong. Each night my dead wife came with wind and storm and tried to take me, but Chakliux drove her away with his prayers and stories.

"I lived in a trance. I did not know day from night, and I heard my brother's words as if he spoke from a great distance. On the morning I came to myself, I found that the fire had died. The boiling bag was empty, and somehow my brother's spirit had been stolen."

Ligige' lifted her voice into a wail.

"I think it was my wife's revenge for his stories and prayers," Sok said to Take More. "I returned to the village to be sure she did not also steal my sons."

"They are safe, not stolen," Take More assured him, and led him into the hunters' lodge.

Ligige' stood outside, alone until her mourning cries drew the people from their hearth fires.

"Do you think they will bring his body back?" Dii asked.

It was night. All that day, she and Long Eyes had joined the women's mourning, but her husband had made excuses to remain in his mother's lodge.

After Sky Watcher returned with Ghaden and Criesloud, he came to see Night Man, and though they went together to the hunters' lodge, Night Man did not stay long.

Dii asked her question again, and her husband jerked as though her words had startled him from a dream. "Sky Watcher told me that he and First Eagle would go."

"Perhaps, if Sok's dead wife was the one who stole his brother's spirit, they should leave the body there. The wolves will have found him by now."

"Did you know . . ." Night Man began. He stopped.

Dii could see the anger in his face, could hear it in his voice. What was wrong now? He had hated Chakliux, he made no secret of that. He should be glad that Chakliux was dead.

"Take More's youngest wife told me something," he finally said.

Dii's heart froze in her chest. Take More's wife had told her also—good news that Aqamdax was not dead, that she was living at the hunters' spring.

"Take More's wife is foolish," Dii said. "Always telling people what is not true."

Night Man shrugged. He pointed with his chin toward his mother. "You fed her?" he asked. Long Eyes sat as though she did not hear them, her fingers moving without pause as she twisted sinew.

"She has eaten twice since this morning, and slept some."

Night Man grunted, then leaned against the woven willow backrest Dii had made him. She brought him a bowl of meat, but he waved it away and seemed to lose himself again in his own thoughts.

Dii picked up her sewing and punched her awl along the edges of a seam. She thought of Chakliux. She had known him as long as she could remember. He had been a good man, a hunter skilled with a spear in spite of his otter foot.

She thought of Chakliux's body, surely by now found by wolves and ravens. She raised her sewing closer to her eyes, tried to drive away images of death with thoughts of awls and sinew thread.

Suddenly Night Man laughed. Surprised, Dii looked up. Had she ever heard him laugh before? She looked at him, but he seemed to have forgotten she was in the lodge.

"Who will protect her?" he asked. His eyes were on the hearth, as though he were speaking to the flames. "Her husband is dead, and now for these few days the men . . ."

Suddenly he tipped back his head and shouted his laughter up into the top of their lodge.

Ligige' awoke to the sound of a woman calling. She glanced over at Ghaden and Cries-loud. They were asleep, exhausted by their hunt and then by the joy of Sok's return, the sorrow of Chakliux's death. Yaa raised up on one elbow, whispered, "Someone is outside."

Ligige' crawled from her bed and into the cold of the entrance tunnel. She pushed aside the outer doorflap.

"It is Dii," the woman said, and Ligige' scolded her for being out so late, for bringing night air into her lodge, but she beckoned Dii inside, and they huddled close to the hearth coals, Ligige' holding her hands above the warmth.

"I cannot stay," Dii said.

"No, you cannot," Ligige' told her. "Unless you want to sit alone while the rest of us sleep."

"My husband thinks that I went out to our cache to get meat."

"And instead you came here? Why?"

"Night Man knows Aqamdax is alive and that she is staying near the hunters' spring. He plans to go there in the morning."

Ligige' covered her mouth with her hands. "How did he find out?" she asked, her fingers muffling the words.

"Take More told his youngest wife. You know she cannot keep a secret."

Ligige' sat still for a moment, then reached out and clasped Dii's hands. "You said he plans to leave in the morning?" she asked.

Dii nodded.

"Slow him down as much as you can. I will get Take More to warn Aqamdax."

"You think he will go?"

"If he does not, I will," Ligige' said.

SIXTY-ONE

THE HUNTERS' SPRING

Aqamdax had been proud of her lodge, but now, as she sat with Ligige' and Take More, she saw it as if through the eyes of others. She saw how cramped it was, and the hoarfrost on the walls, the crooked lodge poles, the cold air, stale and without the welcoming smell of cooking meat. And she saw it through the eyes of what she was now—widow, not wife, her heart dark with sorrow.

"It is small," she said weakly, referring to the lodge.

But Ligige' said, "You have done well."

Aqamdax lowered her head, accepting the compliment, and allowed the kind words to lift a thin edge of her sadness.

They had brought Ligige' 's old dog with them, strapped packs of dried caribou meat to his back. Aqamdax had accepted the meat with gratitude, and now laid some out on grass mats, thankful she could offer a semblance of hospitality.

"So Sok arrived at the village and told you," she managed to say, her voice tight and small, like the voice of a child. "You understand the reason, then." She lifted a hand to her cheeks, black with soot, her hair cut short and ragged around her face. "Thank you for coming to share my sorrow."

Then she saw the look that passed between them, felt a quick catch of pain. "The children?" she asked, her voice dying on their names.

Ligige' held up one hand, palm out. "No one else has died. The children are strong. Yellow Bird's milk flows, and the baby is growing."

"We have come because of Night Man," Take More interrupted, then made Aqamdax wait as he crammed dried meat into his mouth. He spoke through the food, spraying it out with his words. "First Eagle and Sky Watcher went back for your husband's body," he said, then paused to chew.

Aqamdax sat very still, unaware that tears were flowing from her eyes until Ligige' leaned forward and wiped her cheeks with gnarled and callused fingers.

"I am glad they did," Aqamdax said, her throat so full of sorrow that the words were only a whisper.

"Someone told Night Man that you are here, and now that the hunters are gone, he thinks it is a good time to come and find you," Take More said. He swallowed, then added, "He has taken Dii as wife. Did I tell you that?"

"Yes," she said softly.

"He told Dii last night that he will kill you. He planned to leave this morning, but Dii is trying to delay him."

"You cannot stay here, Aqamdax," said Ligige'.

"Where should I go?" she asked. "Now that he knows I am alive, he will follow me."

"Perhaps snow will come and hide your trail," Take More said. "Or wind."

The weight of Aqamdax's sorrow pressed down upon her, and she struggled to think. She did not have enough time to prepare. She could not stay here. And with Chakliux's child in her belly . . .

She lay a hand over her stomach, saw Ligige' 's eyes on her.

The old woman tilted her head. "You do not . . ." she began. "You are not . . ."

Aqamdax raised her chin. "I carry my husband's child."

Ligige' leaned forward, put her elbows on her knees

and settled her forehead into the cradle of her hands. "Let me think," she said.

They sat in quietness, Aqamdax struggling to hold her thoughts above her fears. Snow Hawk whined and pressed herself against Aqamdax's side. Finally Ligige' looked up. She shook her head and blew out her breath as though she had just made a decision. Then she said, "Sometimes it is not a good thing to be an old woman, but this will be easier for me than to be left outside a village without food or fire when I am too old to be of any use."

Aqamdax frowned, tried to make sense of Ligige''s words. Then Ligige' pointed a finger at Take More and said, "Go back to the village. If Night Man has not left, do what you can to keep him away for yet another day."

"And what about you, old woman?" Take More asked.

"I and my dog will stay here with Aqamdax and that nephew of mine she carries in her belly. Do not worry. If you give us enough time, Night Man will not find her."

When Take More left, Ligige' walked with him into the woods, away from the lodge so Aqamdax would not hear her words. "If I do not return," she said to Take More, "tell Dii she must care for those children that live in my lodge."

"You think Night Man will let her take them in?"

"Tell her she does not need to worry about Night Man." Ligige' pressed a bony finger into his chest. "And you, old man, see that you find Dii a husband. Someone who will help her with those children. Someone who is a good hunter. Perhaps Sok, if he becomes strong again. Perhaps Sky Watcher or First Eagle." She chuckled. "Do not think to take her yourself," she told him. "You have enough trouble with the wives you have."

Then she went back to Aqamdax.

NORTH OF THE COUSIN RIVER VILLAGE

Chakliux had walked west for almost two days, slept in a snow cave he carved with his hands, and then, when he could not find Sok, returned to his hunting tent. He began to pack his clothing and bedding furs. He took enough food to last him three more days. He left the rest. There was always the chance that Sok would forsake his dead wife and go back to the Cousin village. If he stopped here to sleep, and came before wolves found the cache Chakliux had dug into the frozen ground under the tent, he would have more than enough food for the journey.

Chakliux pressed his fingers over his closed eyes. In spite of his wooden snow goggles, the glare of snow during the past few days of searching had left his head aching, his eyes red and swollen.

He had lived most of his life without knowing Sok, without realizing he had a brother. When he had first gone to the Near River Village to marry the shaman's daughter and thus bind the Near and Cousin River Villages in peace, Sok had been more enemy than ally. But now Chakliux wondered how he would live without the man he had come to love not only as brother but also as friend.

"Remember this," he said aloud to comfort himself, "you did what you could. Now you must take care of your wives and the children they give you. Do not forget, you also have Sok's sons to raise." He would tell Cries-loud and Carries Much what a good and honorable man their father had been. He would tell them how skilled Sok was with his spear, and he would teach them to hunt. Through them, some part of Sok would still live.

Chakliux strapped on his pack, fastened his snowshoes and began the journey to the Cousin River Village.

THE COUSIN RIVER VILLAGE

The night was clear, and the moon gave a cold light. Dii was tucked into her bedding furs, nearly asleep, when she heard someone scratch at the side of the lodge close to her head. She sat up, saw that Night Man was asleep, and crept to the entrance tunnel. She opened the outside door-flap and shivered as cold air flooded in.

"Who is it?" she called in a whisper, and was surprised to hear Take More's voice answer her.

He scooted into the tunnel, leaned close to say, "Is Night Man still here?"

"Yes," Dii answered. "Where is Ligige'?"

"She stayed with Aqamdax. To help her pack and leave the hunters' spring."

"My husband plans to go in the morning," Dii said. "Is there anything I can do?"

"Ligige' says to keep him in the village one more day."

Dii stared into the darkness. To keep Night Man in the village that day, she had pretended Long Eyes was sick. She had fussed over the old woman, begging her husband to stay, forcing tears to convince him that she thought his mother was near death. But by afternoon Long Eyes had been impatient with Dii's medicines and scrambled from her bed whenever she had the chance. Dii would have to think of another way to make her husband stay.

"It is a long walk from the hunters' spring to this village," Take More said, "especially for an old man with slow feet." Dii heard him laugh, a thin chuckle nearly hidden by the thick ruff of his parka hood. "As I walked, I thought of something that might work."

The next morning Twisted Stalk was the first to come to Dii's lodge. The scratch of her walking stick awoke Dii, who welcomed her, then hurriedly rekindled the hearth fire and set out food.

"I have come to thank your husband," Twisted Stalk said. "This morning when I went to my cache, I saw one of his packs there, full of meat. I could not believe that he would give me so much."

Her words were loud with joy, and they woke Night Man. When he saw the old woman in the lodge, he sat up with a start.

"My aunt has come to thank you, Husband," Dii said, and handed Night Man a bowl of broth.

"To thank me?" he said, his voice still rough with sleep. He looked down at the bowl in his hands, shook his head as though to help himself remember, and asked, "For what?"

"The pack of meat you left in my cache," Twisted Stalk said. "I know it is yours. The pack carries your mark. Two circles in red." She looked at Dii. "That is his mark, nae?" she asked.

"I did not leave meat—" Night Man began, but he was interrupted by curses and barking just outside the lodge. Take More burst through the inner doorflap. He was dragging Night Man's strongest dog.

"I have this one," he said, "but I am not sure where the others are. I had to catch my own first, but then I went after yours. Awl said someone tried to cut First Eagle's dogs loose, too. She thought they might be boys from the Near River Village. She heard them, but when she went outside, they ran. One looked like the son of a man who once owned her as slave. She said they were into the caches as well."

Night Man erupted from his bed with a roar, upsetting the bowl of broth into his blankets. Then Yellow Bird was calling from the entrance tunnel, a pair of fine fur mittens in her hands. "For Night Man," she said, her tears mingled with her thanks. "For the meat he left in my cache."

Then other old women were also crowding into the lodge, wrapping their gratitude around Night Man until he was tethered so tightly he could not move.

When they finally left, their gifts piled beside the hearth, Night Man, grumbling, went out to find his dogs. By dusk he had found all but one. He returned to the lodge, his face red with cold, his nose dripping and his leggings caked with snow. His first words were a snarl, so loud that even his old mother looked up from the sinew she was twisting and scolded him with a rush of gibberish, so that Dii had to set her teeth into her tongue to keep from laughing.

When Long Eyes ended her tirade, Dii threw her arms around her husband and began to sob, praising him for his generosity to the old women in the village, then scolding him for leaving his own wife and mother with so little meat for the winter.

Night Man tried to break into her ranting but finally gave up. He pulled off his outside parka and leggings, flung them into the women's side of the lodge and stomped over to his bedding mats. He refused food, lay down and turned his back on his wife, pulling a blanket over his head as he roared, "Let me sleep!"

SIXTY-TWO

THE HUNTERS' SPRING

Ligige' lifted her voice in a Near River song, one she particularly liked. Out of respect for the Cousin People, she had not sung it since leaving the Near River Village. She added wood to the fire, but still she was cold. She had not realized her stay at the hunters' spring would last more than a day. Take More had had better success than Ligige' thought he would in delaying Night Man's journey.

She had made Aqamdax take most of the supplies and also the tent skins, so Ligige' had only a crude lean-to of spruce branches, a woven mat for her doorflap, and a layer of boughs and dead grass as her floor. At least there was enough wood stacked to keep the fire going.

She shivered as she thought of what she must do and again sang the Near River song, but when the words did not chase away her fear, she began to speak to her dog as he lay beside her near the hearth. "I am an old woman," she told him. "How many more winters can I expect to live?"

Certainly it was worth an old woman's life to save Aqamdax and her baby. She hoped Aqamdax would find her way back to her own village. Surely Chakliux's son would

be a good Sea Hunter. After all, he would have some of
his father's otter blood.

Ligige' tried to imagine herself as a hunter on a sea so
vast that she lost all sight of land. But that, too, reminded
her of fear. She slipped the knife from her sleeve, grasped
it as tightly as she could, her fingers stiff and crooked in
their clasp around its handle.

"Chakliux," she said aloud into the smoke that rose to
sift through the spruce needle roof of her shelter, "do not
walk too quickly into that spirit world. It would be good
to have a little company on my journey."

Aqamdax stood at the top of a long ridge, and the panic
that had forced her into a night and day of walking suddenly ebbed. She bent to stroke Snow Hawk. The dog
answered her touch with a low rumbling growl. Aqamdax
glanced at the sky, tried to make out the position of the
sun under the gray clouds.

"We cannot stop yet," she said. "We must get to the
next ridge."

If Night Man were following them, he would walk faster than a woman with a dog pulling a travois, but he
would start from the Cousin River Village, and Ligige',
waiting at the hunters' spring, would surely give him
some story to delay his pursuit. There had been little snow
since Aqamdax had left, and what was already on the
ground had packed so hard that the wind could not lift it
to cover her trail. Her only hope was to travel far enough
so that Night Man finally decided to turn back.

How foolish he was to think she had killed Star. And
what of the other people in the village? Why was it so
easy for them to believe she was that evil? Or had their
fear of a killer who still lived beyond their justice blinded
them?

Surely some had considered that Red Leaf might yet be
alive, living close enough to kill again. Or had they realized, as Aqamdax did, that Red Leaf's killings, though
terrible and evil, had some form of logic about them?
What reason did Red Leaf have to kill Star? Why risk
being seen, being found?

More likely some outcast—a nuhu'anh—had done it. What reason, beyond that of his own madness, did a nuhu'anh need to kill?

As the daylight faded, Aqamdax stopped and made a night camp in a ridge of spruce. The trees grew so close that their branches were twined, providing a shelter that comforted her with its calm. She wished she were one of those trees, her arms stretched to the sky, her feet buried in the earth. But she was a woman, too small to reach the sun.

Her loneliness rose up within her, numbing her hands, blinding her eyes, and she buried her head in the fur at Snow Hawk's neck until the warmth of the dog's body pulled away some of her pain.

Aqamdax slept poorly that night, heard voices in the wind, woke with a start when her dreams were filled with the sound of a baby's cry. The morning brought snow. Not the howling snow of a storm, but wet, heavy flakes that weighed down the travois and melted into the fur of her parka.

She walked beside the dog, stopped often to break away the balls of ice that formed between the pads of Snow Hawk's feet. Aqamdax shivered each time she stopped, afraid that Night Man would catch her, her progress was so slow. She tried to keep her bearing by choosing landmarks—a tree, a ridge—as fixed points for her eyes, so that in the heavy fall of snow she would not begin to circle. Finally, looking ahead, she saw a darkness that was like a wall, thick and heavy, spreading side to side, as far as she could see. With a start she realized where she was, for what else could that darkness be but the black spruce that grew around the Grandfather Lake? Chakliux had once told her that a man walking could not circle that lake in less than ten days. It lay east a half day's walk from the Cousin River Village, but she was north of that village, and if she walked to the far northern side of the lake, she would be at least seven days away from the Cousin People.

Once there, she could make her winter camp. The trees

and brush would hide her. Through the ice, she could net the oil-rich blackfish, use them for food, burn them for light and heat. She could catch grayling and whitefish in her woven willow trap. Then, when summer came and her baby was born, she could find her way back to the sea, follow its shore to the villages of the First Men.

The wind blew harder. Aqamdax reached down and grasped the side of the travois, helped Snow Hawk pull it up from where it had settled into the snow, and together they walked to the Grandfather Lake.

THE HUNTERS' SPRING

The walls of her spruce shelter were close, so Ligige' kept the hearth fire only smoldering. Why risk that those brittle needles would catch and burn? She had caught a hare in one of the loop snares she had set near the spring. In the dying light, under a soft fall of snow, she sat outside her shelter, skinned and gutted the animal, then went inside and skewered it over the fire. The smell of it cooking made her stomach roll in hunger, and she warned away the dog as he inched closer to the roasting stick.

She had expected Night Man's arrival for so long that when he came, suddenly thrusting the doorflap aside, she did not startle, only laid her right hand carefully over her left sleeve, where she had hidden her knife, then invited him to sit down and eat.

He frowned and squinted at her, his lips drawn back from his teeth.

"Where is she?" he asked.

Ligige' shrugged. "She brought me this hare and went back out to her trapline. She wanted this cooked by the time she returned."

He moved as if to leave, but Ligige' spoke quickly, hoping to hold him with her words. "I knew you would come for her," she said. "I knew you would realize that she did not kill your sister." He turned to look at her, and she saw the surprise in his eyes. "Why take your pack?" she asked him. "Leave it here in the lodge. You will find her more quickly without its weight on your back."

He grunted at her, and she helped him with the straps.

He flexed his bad shoulder, and she said, "The hare is almost done. There is enough for you if you want some. Perhaps Aqamdax will bring another, and we will have a feast."

She took the roasting stick from the rocks she had used to wedge it in place and, licking her fingers, gingerly broke away a haunch, offered it to Night Man. She thought he was going to refuse, but he only opened the doorflap, looked out, then squatted down beside her, took the hare and began to tear at it with his teeth.

Ligige' pulled off a section of ribs, sucked at the thin covering of meat. When Night Man threw his bones to the dog, Ligige' picked up the skewer, held it out to him.

"More?" she asked, but he shook his head. "Why go?" she said. "Where else would she come but here?"

He ignored her, stepped outside, leaving the doorflap open so the wind swirled in to batter at the hearth coals until flames leapt up toward the spruce walls. Ligige' crept on hands and knees to the doorflap, jerked it from Night Man's grasp.

"Go, if you think you will find her any sooner," she said, "but why let the winter into my warm shelter?"

"I have no patience for your complaints, old woman," Night Man said. "Which direction did she go?"

"There, that way," said Ligige', ducking out from under the doorflap to point toward the trail that led to the spring.

He settled down on his heels, facing the trail, his back to the door, his spear on the ground at his side.

"Bring me more of that meat," he said.

Ligige' crawled back into the shelter, broke away a front quarter and took it to him. He grabbed it and, as she turned to go back inside, said, "Do not eat that other haunch, old woman, and do not save it for Aqamdax."

Ligige' muttered an insult under her breath, and suddenly Night Man was upon her. "You will treat me with respect," he shouted, and he pressed her face into the hard ice ridge that had formed under the doorflap. The force on her nose made her eyes tear.

He lowered his mouth to her ear. "You think I have come to tell Aqamdax she may return to the village? I have come to avenge my sister's death, and you, old woman, if you do not watch your mouth, will also be a part of my vengeance. Since Aqamdax was once my wife, perhaps I owe her a companion for her journey to the spirit world."

Ligige' collapsed under his weight. She could not breathe, and in her need for air, the sound of his words grew dim. But finally he released her, batting the back of her head with the heel of his hand as he stood. Her nose cracked against the ice, and she heard the sound of bone snapping. She drew in a shuddering breath, choked on the blood that was flowing down her throat. She sat up, cupped her face with both hands, and Night Man laughed.

Suddenly Ligige''s dog rushed from the lodge, knocked Night Man to the ground, sent his spear spinning.

Ligige' saw the dog's teeth snap at Night Man's neck, then heard his growls change to a high-pitched scream as Night Man plunged his knife to the hilt in the dog's chest.

Ligige' picked up Night Man's spear and gripped it in both hands. She lunged and the spearhead caught Night Man's parka, ripped through to his flesh, hit against his rib bones and stopped. Night Man roared, heaved the dog aside and fumbled at a knife sheath on his leg. Ligige' pulled back the spear, thrust it at his hands, cutting into both. Night Man scrambled away on all fours, then dove toward the dog. As he pulled his knife from the dog's chest, Ligige' raised the spear and, with all her strength, plunged it into the back of Night Man's neck, shoving it through until the earth, frozen and hard, stopped her.

Night Man shuddered, opened his mouth, but instead of curses he spewed out blood. Finally he collapsed and was still.

Ligige' dragged her dog into the spruce lodge. She sat with him draped over her lap, murmured comfort and praise long after he had bled his life into the mats and grasses of her lodge floor.

SIXTY-THREE

THE GRANDFATHER LAKE
The animal trail led through the woods to a clearing, the
spring floodplain of a narrow river that fed the lake. The
sun was setting, and the shadows of the trees ran together
into one darkness. A line of willows marked the edge of
the clearing, and Aqamdax noticed a rise at one side.

"There," she said to Snow Hawk, "a place to set our
lodge."

Snow Hawk's throat rumbled, and Aqamdax tensed,
pulled the spear from her pack. She sniffed the air for
bear or wolf, but there was only the cold, pungent smell
of forest and lake. She lay a hand on the dog's head,
hushed her with sounds of mother to child. Suddenly,
Snow Hawk bolted against her harness and snapped at her
own shoulders when the straps held her back. Then Aqamdax saw the fox.

The animal was smart enough to realize that the dog
could not come after it, and took several light steps toward
them, as if in a dare, before it turned and disappeared into
the trees. Aqamdax began to laugh. With a whine, Snow
Hawk sat down, raised her nose to the sky and howled.

"A good welcome for us," Aqamdax said, and guided
Snow Hawk to where she would set her shelter. She
cleared away the loose snow, then used the butt end of a

fallen branch to break through the crust until she reached bare ground. She set up her tent like a lean-to and made a fire at the open side with the kindling she carried under her parka. Then she gathered branches and split them with her knife to expose their dry centers, and fed them to the fire. She untied a bundle of dried meat from the travois, rubbed the meat with snow and set it near the fire to warm.

Snow Hawk lay down beside her, her head on her paws.

"We will live here," Aqamdax said. "There are fish in the lake and animals in the woods." She gave the dog a share of the meat, took a piece for herself. She let the smoke flavor carry her back to the days of their caribou hunt. In her mind, she saw Chakliux's face, then had to fight against the tears that suddenly burned her eyes.

She patted the small mound of her belly and spoke to the baby she cradled under her heart. "Have I told you the story about whales and their villages under the sea?" she asked.

Snow Hawk whined, and Aqamdax said, "The dog wants to hear it." Then Aqamdax pushed away her worries with the words she had learned long ago.

THE COUSIN RIVER VILLAGE

Three days after Night Man had left the village, Ligige' returned alone. Yaa, hearing someone in the entrance tunnel of the lodge, pulled aside the doorflap. When she saw Ligige', Yaa shouted out her joy and clasped the old woman in a hug that nearly knocked Ligige' down.

"Child! Enough!" Ligige' said.

Her voice sounded strange, and Yaa drew back, looked into Ligige' 's face. She caught her breath at the sight of Ligige' 's blackened eyes and swollen nose.

"Aunt, what happened to you?" Yaa asked.

Ligige' shook her head. "A branch fell," she said. "I was lucky. It might have done worse. What is a nose for an old woman like me? Even if it stays like this, it will not cost me a husband."

Yaa was not sure if Ligige' 's words were intended as a joke or if she was serious, so rather than risk laughing, she asked, "Do you want me to get your dog's packs? Do you need me to feed him?"

"The dog is dead," Ligige' said.

Her voice broke, and for a moment Yaa thought Ligige' might begin to cry, but then the old woman set a frown on her face and crawled past her into the lodge.

"The baby is with Yellow Bird," Yaa said.

"It is not the baby I worry about," Ligige' snapped. "Where are your brother and Cries-loud?"

"Out getting wood."

Ligige' stared at her, eyebrows raised. "You will be a good mother someday," she finally said. "Help me with my parka and roll out my bedding mats. Then go get Take More and Dii. Bring Sok as well. I need to talk to them."

"Did you see Aqamdax?" Yaa asked as she hung up Ligige' 's parka.

"I saw her."

"She is well?"

"She is well."

"And Night Man?"

"Aaa, child," Ligige' said, "you ask too many questions." She smoothed a blanket over her bedding mats and lay down.

Yaa went first to Sok, found him alone in Star's lodge, the hearth fire sputtering without enough wood to make it burn well. The bottom of the boiling bag was charred, the smell of burnt caribou hide thick in the air. She went out into the entrance tunnel—at least he had stacked up a good supply of wood—and brought back several sticks to feed the fire. Then she studied the boiling bag, considering what she could do.

It was too badly damaged for use, she decided, the hide too weakened to hold anything. She sorted through the supplies on the women's side of the lodge and found a new boiling bag, removed the ruined one and hung the new bag from the tripod.

Sok had lifted his head when she entered the lodge, but he said nothing to her, and as she worked, he continued to smooth a spear shaft, his eyes staring through her as though she were not there.

"It's better to keep the bag away from the fire," Yaa told him. "Just put hot rocks into it. It will last longer. But if you do set it over the hearth, you have to keep water in it, as high as the flames, or the bag will burn."

Sok suddenly seemed to notice her. He blinked, then rubbed his eyes with the balls of his thumbs.

"Ligige' is back," Yaa said to him.

She thought he almost smiled.

"She is alone, and her nose is broken." Yaa raised a hand to finger her own nose, short, but humped as her father's had been. She had admired her father's nose, was glad she had one like it, and wondered if hers would grow as large as his had been. "Her dog is dead."

Sok looked at Yaa as though he could not quite understand what she said.

"She went to bed, but she wants to talk to you," Yaa told him.

"Now?"

Yaa shrugged. "I think so. I have to get Take More and Dii. Then I can come back and make some soup for you, unless Dii wants me to stay with Long Eyes."

"No," he told her. "I eat and sleep at the hunters' lodge. I am here only a part of each day."

His words were slow, as though he thought about each one before saying it, but Yaa was not surprised. The old women said that he had only half his spirit since Snow-in-her-hair had died, and now with Chakliux dead . . . Yaa felt tears gather in her throat, and she cleared them away so they would not choke her.

She had lost many people in her life. First her father, then her mother, now Aqamdax and Chakliux. But no matter how many people died, she would not lose her spirit like Sok had. Not even part of it. She would stay strong. Otherwise, who would take care of Ghaden and Ligige'? Who would go on walks with Cries-loud and listen to him when he talked about his worries and dreams?

She left Sok, found Take More, then went to Dii's lodge. Dii met her in the entrance tunnel.

"Sok already came and told me," Dii said. "Will you stay with Long Eyes?"

Yaa crawled into Dii's lodge. The place was filled with the warm smell of meat and was cheerful with light from the hearth fire. Long Eyes sat as she usually did in a nest of bedding furs, a string of sinew dangling from her fingers. The caribou hide of her leggings was bare and dark over one thigh where she rubbed the sinew to twist it.

Yaa took off her parka and hung it from a peg, greeted Long Eyes, then teased away several strands of sinew from the chunk lying at Long Eyes's side. Yaa began to rub the strands between her palms, and thought of how well she had done, keeping Ligige' 's lodge while Ligige' was away.

The first day, she had burned some meat, but she had made the boys eat it anyway. She had kept the fire going and shook out the bedding furs, had almost finished a pair of boots for Ghaden.

Long Eyes began to mutter, a familiar rhythm that Yaa could not quite place. A song, she decided, something she should know. It battered at her mind like a riddle until she pushed it away with thoughts of Cries-loud.

I will be a good wife to him, she told herself, and as she worked, she began to smile.

"He killed my dog," Ligige' said, "and he would have killed Aqamdax. You think I could let him live?"

Sok stared at her. In his surprise, he could think of no response, but he realized that Ligige' had mistaken his silence for accusation.

"Aunt," he finally said, "you did what had to be done. I will keep his widow's cache full."

He nodded at Dii. Her face was pale, her eyes large.

"Where is the body?" Take More asked. Then, before Ligige' could answer, he said, "How did you kill him?"

"The body is there at the hunters' spring. I burned it in Aqamdax's shelter. Perhaps someone can go and get the bones."

"I will get them," Sok said. "Tomorrow, I will go, in the morning."

"Aqamdax?" Dii asked.

"I told her to travel to the Grandfather Lake," Ligige' said, "but who can say if she did?"

"Who can say if she is alive?" Take More said.

Ligige' hissed her disgust. "Aqamdax is alive!" she spat out.

"She needs to come back to this village," said Sok.

Dii shook her head. "Many of the old women still think she was the one who killed—"

"They are fools, those old women," Sok told her.

"It is easier for them to believe Aqamdax is the killer since she is Sea Hunter," said Dii, "than to believe someone from this village did it."

They spoke together for a long time, until finally Take More decided to go to the hunters' lodge and tell whoever was there what had happened to Night Man. "So," he said to Ligige' as he was leaving, "you did not yet tell us how you killed him."

"You see what he did to me," she said, raising her hands to her face. "Then he killed my dog." She shook her head at the memory. "I killed him with his own spear. That is how I killed him. A spear in his neck." Then she settled herself into her bedding furs. "Now go away," she said, "and let me sleep."

Ligige' slept through the day and into the night. She awoke to a sound at her lodge door, shook herself awake. Who was fool enough to come here in the night? By now the whole village knew what had happened. She was an old woman. Did they think she could live without sleep?

Surely there was no one who would seek revenge for Night Man's death. But the thought chilled her bones, and she wrapped herself in a hare fur robe, took her walking stick and used it to push aside the inner doorflap.

"Who is it?" she called.

She saw from the corners of her eyes that all three of the children were awake. Ghaden and Cries-loud had already left their beds, and Biter was crouched at Ghaden's feet, growling.

Ligige' cried out, dropped the stick, and rushed into the entrance tunnel.

"Aqamdax, it has to be," Yaa said and almost knocked the boys down as she ran across the lodge. Suddenly she was backing away, eyes huge, hands over her mouth.

As Ghaden turned to grab a weapon, Cries-loud shouted, "Chakliux!"

Then all three children were in Chakliux's arms, and he was smiling, in spite of the sorrow in his eyes.

"My brother," he said softly, mouthing the words as he looked down at Cries-loud, the boy with his head on Chakliux's shoulder.

"Sleeping in the hunters' lodge," Ligige' told him.

Chakliux's mouth dropped open. "He came back? He came back here . . . to the village?" He shouted out in laughter. "He is not hurt? He is . . ."

"He is sad," Ligige' said, "and worn out from his grieving, but when he sees you . . ."

Her words caught on a sob, and Yaa said to Chakliux, "Sok thought you were dead. He came and told everyone—" She stopped and, with her eyes suddenly wide, asked, "You aren't dead, are you, Chakliux?"

"I am alive, Yaa," he said quietly. Then he rubbed a hand over his face, and Ligige' saw how tired he was.

"I have food," she said, and scurried toward the hearth.

"No," said Chakliux, "I must go to my wives. I stopped at Aqamdax's lodge, but she was not there. I thought perhaps she had decided to live here with you while I was gone. I did not go yet to Star, but—" He saw the look in Ligige' 's eyes, stopped. "Aunt," he said softly, "where are my wives?"

SIXTY-FOUR

THE NEAR RIVER VILLAGE

K'os stood at the ridge that ringed the Near River Village and looked down on the well-made lodges. Woodpiles were stacked high, and banks of snow pressed against the lodge covers to protect against winter winds.

She heard a rill of laughter, and three boys ran out from between two caches, each brandishing a stick. Their game carried them through the village and earned them a scolding from one of the grandmothers at the cooking hearths. K'os smiled. How good to return to this place, not as Gull Beak's slave but as River Ice Dancer's widow. Silently she counted the lodges: five handfuls, another five handfuls; fifty, at least. And how many warriors in each? One, two? Sometimes more.

The walk had been difficult. Her lips had split and bled in the cold; her fingers were so bent and swollen that she could hardly fasten the travois straps. She needed a warm fire and some goosefoot and willow bark tea.

She called the dogs forward and led them to the elders' lodge. The battle between the Near River and Cousin People had cost almost all the old men in this village their lives. Only Sun Caller, that stutterer, and Fox Barking had survived, and, of course, Giving Meat, but his mind was less than that of a child. Surely by now Dii had killed

Fox Barking, and probably been killed in return by the Near Rivers. Pity. She had been an interesting companion.

K'os hoped that the middle-aged hunters of the village had taken their places as elders. Of those men, there were only a handful she had not pleasured when she was a slave. Wolf Head, River Ice Dancer's father, was one she had not yet taken to her bed, but he was her best chance for revenge. In his sorrow, she would win him to her cause. They would avenge River Ice Dancer's death at the Four Rivers Village, then, with their success giving them strength, would go and finish off the Cousin People.

K'os removed her snowshoes, tied them on the travois, and stepped into the entrance tunnel. She brushed the snow from her parka and leggings, pushed back her hood and used her walking stick to scratch at the inner door. She recognized Sun Caller's voice as he stuttered out a welcome.

K'os had spent much time considering a greeting that would establish her place in the village and put thoughts of revenge into the minds of the Near Rivers, but when she entered the lodge, she stood with her mouth open, her fine words forgotten. Ringing the hearth fire, each sitting in a place of honor, were the old women of the village— Vole and Blue Flower, Lazy Snow and Three Baskets. Two others sat on either side of Giving Meat, feeding him as though he were a child, one wiping his chin with a scrap of grass matting. Beside them was Sun Caller.

He nodded at her, opened his mouth to speak but could not get his first word past his tongue. He lifted his chin toward the woman at the back of the fire, the place given the chief elder. The hearth smoke was a cloud that blocked K'os's vision, and so she took a step to the side, then stopped in disbelief. The chief elder was Gull Beak.

THE GRANDFATHER LAKE

Aqamdax had worked long into the night setting up her tent, digging the fire pit and lining it with stones. She had arranged her packs and Snow Hawk's travois across the open side of the lean-to in the best way to protect against wind. She banked snow high on the sides of the tent walls.

Finally, she had allowed herself to sleep, but her dreams were full of her dead baby, living now somewhere in the Grandfather Lake, and when she awoke, she was not sure where she was.

She listened for Carries Much, his early-morning cries for milk, then she felt the soft emptiness of her breasts, and suddenly the blackness of her grief broke over her. She turned her head into her bedding furs and wept. Chakliux was dead. Her son was dead. Ghaden, Yaa, and Sok's sons were all lost to her. She cried first in sorrow, then in anger—at Night Man, at Sok and at Snow-in-her-hair, at Star and the one who had killed her, even at Chakliux for leaving the village to go with Sok. She cried until her throat was raw, and when she had used up all her tears, she lay still and spent, breathing hard, as though she had run a long way.

Then in her mind she heard the quiet voice of the old First Men storyteller Qung. The tale was one that Aqamdax knew well, about a young woman who had been sold as a slave by her brother, a woman who had found her way back to her people by walking the shores of the North Sea. Aqamdax began to repeat the words, first in a whisper, then more loudly. She sat up and began to pitch her voice differently for each of the people and animals in the story, sometimes bringing the words from her throat in the way Qung had taught her, so it seemed that they spoke from outside the tent, or from the hearth or a tree. How long since she had told stories in such a way?

She had been forbidden to do so in the Near River Village when the shaman decided her story voices were a threat to his own powers. And in the Cousin River Village, she had told her stories mostly to the children. Now, here at the Grandfather Lake, she was alone, telling stories with no one to listen.

Then suddenly she felt the smallest flutter, like a feather brushing inside of her belly. She held her breath. The baby? No, she told herself, it was too soon. Then she felt it again, the lightest touch, less than a breath of wind. She smiled and continued her story, twining her fingers over that little one who listened from beneath her heart.

THE COUSIN RIVER VILLAGE
Chakliux stood in the sacred woods and stared at the death scaffolding. She was there now, Star and that daughter they had made together. Star had not been a good wife, and his life would have been easier without her, but his mourning for her had somehow tangled itself into his remembrances of his first wife, Gguzaakk, a woman he had loved. And his sorrow at losing Star's little daughter seemed to renew his anguish at the loss of the son Gguzaakk had borne him, and that baby Night Man had killed.

Had his prayers and chants, his willingness to fight for Sok's life, not lifted the curse he had brought upon himself and Aqamdax? What good were those rituals, and even the stories he had learned as Dzuuggi, if they could not give a man the chance to live each day anew? Was there nothing stronger than those spirits that seemed to find joy in destroying a man's life?

"So then," he cried out, lifting his voice beyond the bones of the dead, shouting to be heard above the trees that protected Star's body, "if there is one out there, some spirit who is great enough to lift the curse I have brought upon myself and my family, then I ask your help in finding my wife Aqamdax."

He waited but felt nothing except the darkness of his despair, the fear that he had lost more than even those he now mourned. He made a chant for the dead and turned back toward the village. After a night of sleep, he would go look for Aqamdax, and he would not return until he found her or her bones.

He started back, cutting across a clearing he had skirted on his way to the death platform, leaving a trail marked by the webbed circles of his snowshoes. Then suddenly a flock of ptarmigan, their winter plumage as light as the snow, broke up through the crust of white and rose into the winter sky. Chakliux thought of a riddle he had learned as a child.

Look! What do I see? White hidden by white.

Then he asked himself, "Why do you think everything should be easy to understand? Have you forgotten that the gift of each riddle is its unraveling?"

And as he walked back to the village, he prayed for the vision to see what was hidden, for the wisdom to understand the riddles that bound his life to the earth and the prayers that would open his eyes to the truth.

THE NEAR RIVER VILLAGE

"I come as wife, not slave," K'os said.

Gull Beak raised her eyebrows. "Anaay told me he would take you as wife sometime during the caribou hunt. Where is he?"

But before K'os could answer, Blue Flower asked, "And that other wife he took, the Cousin woman, where is she?"

"I do not know," K'os told them, and tried to hide her confusion. Was Fox Barking still alive, then, or had Dii somehow been able to hide his death? K'os nearly smiled. Perhaps the girl was more cunning than she had thought. "I was one of those women who left the hunting camp and returned to my own people," she said. "There are men in this village who can tell you that." She lifted her chin at Sun Caller. "My son Chakliux bought me from Anaay."

Gull Beak snorted. "You think, then, that we would consider you no longer a slave? A Cousin woman owned by a Cousin man? You are less than a slave."

The other women murmured their agreement. Anger rose bitter in K'os's throat, and when she spoke again, her words seemed honed by the edges of her teeth. "Perhaps that is true," she said, "but there is something more. As I told you, I was wife. A man of this village paid a bride price for me."

"Who?" Gull Beak asked.

"River Ice Dancer," said K'os, and watched as the women looked at one another.

Sun Caller coughed, and Gull Beak's face was suddenly pinched and white.

"We left the Cousin River Village together, my husband and I," K'os said, "and we went to the Four Rivers Village. We had lived there only a little while when someone in the village killed him. I had taken medicine to a sick woman and stayed with her for the night. When I

returned to my lodge, my husband was dead, killed with
a knife. There are Four Rivers men who claim close ties
to the Cousin River People. I think one of them killed
him. I came here to find my husband's father, Wolf Head,
and plan vengeance on those who took my husband's
life."

The women began to murmur among themselves, and
Sun Caller stammered out a few words of polite concern,
but K'os lost patience with them. What group of women,
in making a decision, ever acted quickly? They could
spend days debating whether or not anyone in the village
should help her. So without giving Gull Beak a chance to
reply, K'os left and led her dogs to the fine strong lodge
where Wolf Head lived with his two wives.

SIXTY-FIVE

THE COUSIN RIVER VILLAGE
The sleep that claimed Chakliux was so quick and so deep
that when he heard the voice calling, he knew he was
living in his dreams. He sat up and saw Long Eyes standing beside his bed.

"Rekindle your hearth fire," she said to him, her voice
strong.

And because it was a dream, Chakliux did what she
asked, bringing the fire into a blaze so the flames lit Sok's
lodge.

"I was surprised you decided to sleep here," Long Eyes
said to him.

She settled herself beside the fire, sat straight, her
shoulders back, as though she were a young woman. He
saw that her eyes were clear, without the confusion that
had clouded them since her husband's death. But why
should he be surprised? He had asked that hidden things
be revealed. How better than in a dream?

"This is my wife's lodge," he said.

Long Eyes laughed. "But you are alone. She is not here,
nor is your brother."

"He sleeps in the hunters' lodge."

She nodded as if she knew, then said, "They say you
mourn my daughter."

462

"She was my wife. I mourn her and the child she carried."

"It was your child," Long Eyes said.

"Yes."

Though the lodge was warm, she still wore her parka, and like a mother with a baby, she had tied a band around it just under her breasts. "I would have carried that child on my back," Long Eyes said. She patted the band. "I made myself this belt to hold her in place." She reached into a pouch that hung from the band and pulled out a ball of sinew thread.

"I did not know your words could be so clear, Mother," Chakliux said.

She looked at him with narrowed eyes. "No one knows," she said. She twisted the thread around her fingers, made a web between her hands. It caught Chakliux's eyes, and he watched as she knotted the sinew into shapes: a tree, a circle.

"You are surprised?" she asked.

"I saw storytellers from the Walrus Hunter Village do that. They taught me."

She nodded. "That other wife of yours, the Sea Hunter woman, when she first came to my lodge as Night Man's wife, she had a bracelet made of knots. It was an otter. You think I did not notice that? When I saw it, I knew you had made it. Who else? Is there another otter anywhere in this village? Perhaps you did not know that my mother was Walrus, raised by those people before she was given as wife to my father. She taught me some things.

"When I was still a girl my father traded me to my husband for three yellow-eyed dogs. My father made a joke. He said I should change my name to Three Dogs. He was a foolish man, but I got a good husband, and four strong sons, then my daughter, Star." She held her hands apart, let Chakliux see the knot at the center of her web. "This, you see, is Star's child." She jerked her hands and suddenly the knot was gone. "Children die too easily," she said.

She looked at him and laughed. "Children die too easily, but I would have kept all mine, and my husband, if it were not for you."

"I did not kill your husband," said Chakliux. "It was River Jumper, and he was sent by K'os."

"I have heard your story. My daughter told me. She loved you, so she believed you. You remember my sons? Tikaani was the oldest. Perhaps you did not kill him, but you are to blame for that war between our villages. You were supposed to stop the fighting, remember? Then I had Caribou and Stalker, a year apart, those two. The old women said they would die. They said I would not have milk enough for both. But they grew to be strong, healthy boys. Do you claim you did not kill them? Now Night Man is dead. They think I do not know, but I hear their whispers. Four sons dead, a husband dead, and my daughter and her baby."

"I did not kill your daughter."

Long Eyes began to laugh.

Yaa drifted in and out of sleep. She was spending the night in Star's lodge, watching over Long Eyes. The old woman had a habit of wandering at night, but to Yaa's surprise, this night, Long Eyes had fallen asleep slumped over her work, the sinew thread she had been twisting still dangling from her fingers. Yaa had spread bedding furs beside the old woman and gently laid her down and covered her.

After Yaa finished sewing the last seam of Ghaden's boot, she rolled out her own bed. For a little while, sleep claimed her, but then the rhythm of a song wove itself through Yaa's dreams and woke her up.

What was it, that song? Yaa asked herself, then remembered that the last time she had stayed with Long Eyes the old woman had been singing it, muttering the words under her breath. The rhythm teased at the back of her mind, and finally Yaa recognized it—a song the women of the Near River Village sang. But Yaa had never heard a Cousin River woman sing it.

Who would have taught Long Eyes? Could she have learned it as a child?

Yaa began to hum the song, allowed its familiar words to lull her back toward dreams, but suddenly she was very much awake. How could Long Eyes have remembered that song when she could not even remember to eat? Something was not right.

Yaa sat up, looked at the old woman's bed. It was empty, the covers thrown back, and her parka was missing from its peg. Yaa scrambled from her bed, pulled on boots and parka and went out into the night calling Long Eyes's name.

She ran the paths of the village, saw no one. Her heart was like a stone in her chest, and she could not breathe. Chakliux and Ligige' had trusted her to watch Long Eyes. Now they would think she was worthless, a little girl who could not be given any responsibility. She held in her tears and turned toward Chakliux's lodge. He might be angry, but at least he would help her look.

Long Eyes stood and lifted her arms, tilted her head back to look at the top of the lodge. "You did not kill my daughter? Do you deny that you put that child in her belly? Do you say it was not yours?"

"It was mine," Chakliux said softly. He heard a sound behind him, and looked back to see Yaa on her knees, peering into the lodge from the entrance tunnel.

Suddenly he knew he was awake. Long Eyes had not come to him in a dream. Somehow she had slipped away from her lodge, from Yaa, who was supposed to watch her.

"If the baby was yours, then you killed her," Long Eyes said. She pulled the sinew from her fingers, let it drop into the hearth fire, watched as it curled and burned. Then she reached into her left sleeve, drew out a long-bladed obsidian knife.

"A sacred knife," she said, and held the blade point up, turned it so the fire lighted the facets of the knapped edge.

Chakliux did not want to draw Long Eyes's attention to Yaa by looking at her again, so he said, "A riddle."

"I am too much Walrus," said Long Eyes. "I have never been good with riddles."

"This one is easy," Chakliux told her. "Look! What do I see? A child remembers the sun."

Then Yaa was gone, and Chakliux hoped she had understood. Long Eyes shook her head. "It is too difficult for me, but see if you understand mine."

"Look! What do I see? Blood in the snow. Blood in a woman's bed."

When he gave no answer, she shrieked with laughter. "You do not understand?" she asked. "I thought you were so wise. How could I let your child live? He would carry your curse and kill as you have killed."

"But why not wait until the baby was born? Why kill Star, too?"

"Then there would be more babies. Star was young. She would have given you many children."

"She was your daughter," Chakliux said softly.

"She was your wife," Long Eyes answered. She licked her lips, moved her feet in a quick shuffling dance as though she were pleased with herself. "Do you know how easy it is to kill someone who thinks you are old and weak?" she asked. She raised the knife, twisted it and closed her eyes as though she was caught in the remembrance of Star's death. "The baby, when I cut it out, was a girl. I might not have killed it had I known. Your wife, she was so sure she carried a boy."

As she stood with her eyes closed, Chakliux moved quickly toward her, but suddenly she slashed out at him, nicked the palm of his right hand with the tip of her blade. He jumped back.

"You are like your Cousin mother," Long Eyes said. "She was more difficult to kill."

"My mother?"

"That one who died in her bed. Didn't you listen to my riddle? What better way to avenge my husband's death than to kill those you love?" She lifted her knife, plunged it into the air as though to show Chakliux what she had done. "She fought. But I was the one with the knife."

"And now you have decided to kill me," Chakliux said.

"I cannot kill you," Long Eyes told him, "but perhaps there are others in this village who will do so when they see what you did to an old woman who could not protect herself, one who could barely speak."

She raised the knife, and though Chakliux dove toward her, tried to knock it from her hands, she plunged the dark blade into her neck before he could reach her. She dropped to the floor, her hands cupped at her throat. She looked up, but Chakliux saw that her eyes were not on him. He turned. Sok and Take More were standing behind him.

Long Eyes moaned, closed her eyes and then was still. Sok took a blanket from Chakliux's bed and covered her.

Yaa peeked in from the entrance tunnel. "She is dead?" she asked.

"Yes," said Chakliux, and opened his arms to the girl. She ran to him and hid her face against his chest. "So you understood my riddle," he said.

"I remembered Sok's sun parkas," she told him. "And Take More was with him in the hunters' lodge."

"Long Eyes killed her own daughter?" Sok asked.

"And our mother," Chakliux told him.

"Then Red Leaf did not," said Sok. "And Aqamdax did not."

"No, and now there is no one left to seek vengeance."

THE NEAR RIVER VILLAGE

Wolf Head was a large man, his voice so loud that K'os heard him scolding his wives while she was still outside the lodge. She called out, waited until the younger wife opened the doorflap. The woman's eyes rounded with surprise when she saw K'os.

"You have come back?" she asked, then gasped as K'os pushed past her into the lodge.

She came in behind K'os, sputtering apologies to her husband. K'os pulled River Ice Dancer's amulet from the neck of her parka, held it so Wolf Head could see. His eyes moved from the amulet to her hair, cut short near her ears. Wolf Head stepped forward, clasped the amulet, then looked hard into K'os's eyes.

"You recognize it?" she asked.

"Yes," he said.

"I come in sorrow to tell you that your son is dead, killed by the Four Rivers People. They stole his dogs and travois, furs and meat, but I was able to escape from them and return to you with a few of his belongings."

Wolf Head looked at his wife. "What did she bring?" he asked.

"Two dogs, a travois," she said.

K'os saw the young woman glance at her sister-wife, River Ice Dancer's mother.

"My tears flow for you," K'os said, and the woman turned away. "The things they stole were the bride price your son paid for me. I will help you win revenge."

"What did he give for you?" Wolf Head asked.

"Eight dogs, six travois, pelts and meat and fish. The Four Rivers People stole all of it, but I was able to—"

"Be quiet. You have too many words for a woman." Wolf Head leaned close to his younger wife, whispered something, and she hurried from the lodge.

He was rude, but K'os had known that Wolf Head was a hard man and treated his wives poorly. She held back her anger, did not allow it to color her cheeks or edge her words.

"Six dogs, you say."

"Eight."

"Six travois."

"Yes."

He turned away from her and paced the length of the lodge. "Fox pelts?" he asked.

She nodded. "Fox and lynx, wolf, caribou hides," she told him.

K'os heard a noise at the lodge entrance, saw that the wife had returned. Gull Beak was with her.

"This slave says she was wife to that one who stole the dogs and travois from our village," Wolf Head said. "She claims he gave my fox pelts as part of her bride price. She has returned two of the dogs." Wolf Head drew his lips back in a smile. His teeth were long and yellow. "Treat her well," he said to Gull Beak. "Few slaves would be so loyal."

K'os let out her breath in a hiss. "I was wife to your son, River Ice Dancer," she cried.

"During the past moon someone stole my dogs and travois, my furs and much meat from my cache. You think *my* son would steal a bride price from his own father?" Wolf Head said. "Foolish woman. I have no son."

SIXTY-SIX

THE GRANDFATHER LAKE

Aqamdax's early-morning work was done, wood gathered, the dog fed. She banked more snow around her tent and added spruce boughs to the entrance tunnel she had made of bark and willow poles.

When she was finished, she untied Snow Hawk, took the dog with her to the lake. The ice that covered the shore rose in thick hard ridges, but when it reached the lake it smoothed into a wide white plain that spread as far as Aqamdax could see. She walked until she came to a place where the wind had swept away the snow and the ice was bare. She padded the palm of her mitten with a strip of caribou hide, then used a stone hand ax to begin another hole. She measured the width of the hole against her forearm to be sure it was wide enough to hold her fish trap. She worked until her hand was numb from pounding and her fingers would no longer grip the stone.

"Tomorrow we will finish it," she finally said to Snow Hawk.

The dog was curled near the hole, tail over nose, back against the wind. Aqamdax had food enough to last until she caught more fish. Three hares were buried in the snow at the floor of her entrance tunnel, and she still had some dried salmon, a little caribou meat, blackfish that she had caught in a net suspended between two holes in the lake ice. Snow Hawk still hunted for her own meat, and sometimes, like Biter, brought back part of a carcass—ptarmigan or hare—for Aqamdax.

Still, Aqamdax was often hungry, but who was not hungry in winter? She did not let herself think of the full caches at the Cousin River Village, or of the seal meat and oil her own people would have put away. Instead, as she walked back to her lodge, she thought of the grayling or pike she might catch tomorrow in her trap.

The sky, heavy with clouds, was darkening toward night, and the wind gripped Aqamdax like hands, pushed her as she walked, drew tears from the corners of her eyes. She wiped them from her face, then stopped short, reached down to grip the ruff of fur at Snow Hawk's neck. She crouched beside the dog, felt the animal tremble. Through the brush, she could see her lodge, its peak dark against the snow. Smoke spiraled from the top, more than should come from a fire banked before she went to the lake.

Night Man? she wondered. She shrugged her pack from her shoulders, pulled out her spear and crept closer. With her belly growing, she was more clumsy and did not throw the spear well. What chance did she have?

She crooned a song under her breath to calm herself and tried to think. Perhaps she should wait until night, get some of the meat she had hidden in the entrance tunnel and walk to the Near River Village. Eight, ten days might take her there. Perhaps some man would accept her as his wife, especially since she had Snow Hawk.

Yes, she would do that, but she would not wait for night. She could check the snare traps she had set in that direction. Surely she would have caught something. She had set so many. . . .

"We will go now," she said, whispering the words to Snow Hawk, but Snow Hawk suddenly jumped away and began to bark in quick joyous yips like a pup. Aqamdax stood, and when she saw the one who came from the tent, she could not move, could not speak. She waited as he ran to her, Snow Hawk jumping at his side.

"You are not dead," were her first words to him, and Chakliux, his laughter broken by tears, held her close and answered, "Nor are you."

"How did you find me?"

"Ligige' said she told you to go to the Grandfather Lake. I was afraid that your son would call you and you would go . . ."

He pushed back her hood and buried his face in the softness of her hair.

"But then you found my camp."

"I saw that your fire was banked and the coals were still alive. I saw that you had cached your meat, so I knew that you had decided to live."

He put his arm around her and walked her to the lodge. She knelt and crawled inside, waited as Chakliux followed her. He squatted beside the hearth and added more wood to the flames.

"You were right," Aqamdax said. "My son does call me." He looked at her with fear in his eyes, and she moved into the light of the fire, clasped his hands and set them over her belly. "Each night he calls," she told him, "but not from the lake."

She smiled as his eyes grew wide, as his laughter filled the walls of her lodge. Then he wrapped her into his arms and claimed her as wife with his tears.

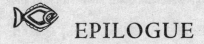 **EPILOGUE**

He was still only a boy, his arms and legs thin with much growing yet to do. But the old woman could see that he had changed. Though he was boy outside, inside he was more nearly a man. The People had celebrated their return to the winter village with a feast. The caribou hunt had been good, and the old and very young who had been left behind were content now with bellies full of caribou meat.

For the first time in many years, she sat with the other women in the storytelling lodge, her mind open for the storyteller's words. The boy sat down in the Dzuuggi's place and began to speak. His words carried full and strong. The old woman listened and felt the stories fill her anew with understanding.

Then the boy did something no Dzuuggi had been able to do for years, the skill lost in the years before he was born. He lifted his voice and brought it from the smokehole of the lodge, then from the doorflap and from the hearthfire, so it seemed as though each person was telling his own story in his own words.

And when he spoke about Chakliux, the boy took off his boots. The old woman heaved herself to her knees and lifted her head until she could see past those who sat in front of her.

" 'Ih!" she said in amazement.

The toes were webbed like otter toes; the foot was bent and ready to swim.

AUTHOR'S NOTES

Cry of the Wind is a study of war and war's most natural and tragic aftermath: revenge. Like its prequel, *Song of the River*, it weaves a story around the inhabitants of the Near River and Cousin River villages and is set in ancient Alaska.

Many of the characters and plot elements are based on Native mythologies, two of which perhaps need further explanation.

In traditional Native literature—which is, of course, oral literature—heroes and villains abound. Often the villains are very evil indeed and are used as foils for the heroes of the stories. Sometimes, especially for those of us who have grown up within the nebulous gray world of situational ethics, this stark dichotomy is difficult to understand.

Quite obviously, I have followed Native literary traditions in creating my villainess K'os and the villain Anaay. In an effort to make their behavior believable to modern readers, I have given them motivating factors and mind-sets that provide a psychological basis for their actions, but I would ask my readers to remember that they represent a long-standing tradition in North American Native literature: the classic, unredeemable antihero.

The second mythological tradition is that of the

nuhu'anh, known by many names, including windigo, witigo, outside man, and woodsman. Most groups of northern Native peoples tell legends about the windigo or nuhu'anh. In my studies, I have noticed that in areas with an extremely cold climate and limited winter food resources the legends take on more mystical and terrifying proportions than among those peoples who experience less winter starvation. The Aleut and some of the Athabascan peoples generally consider the nuhu'anh a nuisance more than a threat—someone whose behavior has mandated exclusion from his or her village. The nuhu'anh may kill to steal a wife or food but is seldom if ever cannibalistic, like the windigo/witigo of the Ojibwa or Cree.

Scientists have only recently begun to believe there is a physiological basis for windigo mythology. Research points toward the possibility that people who face extreme fat deprivation under bitter weather conditions may suffer delusions that lead them to believe other humans are food resources—animals that may be legitimately butchered. It is interesting to note that though Native stories offer many different ways to kill a windigo, one often cited is to pour hot fat down the windigo's throat.

I have had a number of requests from readers asking that I explain the concept of the "handful," which I use in the Storyteller Trilogy to denote counting. According to what I have been able to find through my research, most Native peoples of North America based their counting systems on five (rather than ten, as we do), thus the concept of the handful—five fingers.

For those who, like me, are mathematically disadvantaged, I offer this explanation in the hope that it will help. In a base five counting system, the sequence of numbers one to ten would be as follows: one, two, three, four, five, five plus one, five plus two, five plus three, five plus four, two fives. Eleven would be two fives plus one . . . and so on.

The reader may notice that in this trilogy, and in my previous trilogy (*Mother Earth, Father Sky*; *My Sister the Moon*; and *Brother Wind*), the First Men count by tens. The Unangan or Aleut people upon whom the First Men are patterned have (and this is very unusual for Native Americans) a base ten number system. Thus, in my novels I include two number systems, one used by the First Men and designated by "tens" and the other used by the Walrus Hunters and the River People and denoted by the term "handful."

One last explanation: some of my readers may wonder why the old woman Ligige' addresses the wolverine she inadvertently caught in her snare trap as a parka hood ruff (see chapter 48). Among the various Athabascan peoples, and in numerous other Native cultures, women traditionally do not say the names of animals considered to have unusual or sacred powers. Instead, they will use a euphemism. Thus, a woman talking about a black bear will say, "The black one," "The black place," "That humpback." This usage is intended to show the bear respect and to give spiritual protection to the speaker. In *Cry of the Wind*, Ligige' is following this practice when she addresses the wolverine as a parka hood ruff.

Thank you for joining me on another journey to ancient Alaska! I hope you will check out my website for information about upcoming books—www.sueharrison.com

Sue Harrison
Pickford, Michigan
February 1998

CHARACTER LIST

PEOPLE OF THE COUSIN RIVER VILLAGE

Elders (Men):   Take More

Elders (Women):   Day Woman (mother of
                              Chakliux and Sok)
                            Hollow Cup
                            Ligige' (aunt of Chakliux and
                              Sok)
                            Long Eyes (mother of Night
                              Man and Star)
                            Twisted Stalk (aunt of Dii)
                            Yellow Bird

Hunters: Chakliux (adopted son of
                              K'os; biological son of
                              Day Woman and Gull
                              Wing; brother to Sok)
                            First Eagle (Near River hus-
                              band of Awl)
                            Man Laughing
                            Night Man (son of Cloud
                              Finder and Long Eyes;
                              brother of Star)

Hunters (cont'd):

Sky Watcher (husband of
    Bird Caller)
Sok (son of Day Woman and
    Gull Wing; brother of
    Chakliux)

Wives and Young Women:

Aqamdax (half-sister of
    Ghaden; stepsister of Yaa)
Awl (wife of First Eagle)
Bird Caller (wife of Sky
    Watcher)
Dii (niece of Twisted Stalk)
Green Bird (sister of Squirrel
    and Black Stick)
Gguzaakk (deceased, wife of
    Chakliux)
Little Mouse
Owl Catcher
Red Leaf (wife of Sok;
    mother of Cries-loud and
    Sok's infant daughter)
Snow-in-her-hair (wife of
    Sok; mother of Carries
    Much)
Star (daughter of Cloud
    Finder and Long Eyes; sis-
    ter of Night Man; wife of
    Chakliux)

Children:

Angax (infant son of Aqam-
    dax and Night Man)
Black Stick (brother of
    Squirrel and Green Bird)
Carries Much (infant son of
    Sok and Snow-in-her-hair)
Cries-loud (son of Sok and
    Red Leaf)

Children (cont'd):   Ghaden (brother of Aqamdax; stepbrother of Yaa; adopted son of Chakliux and Star; son of Cen, the trader)

Squirrel (brother of Black Stick and Green Bird)

Yaa (stepsister of Aqamdax and Ghaden; adopted daughter of Chakliux and Star)

Dogs: Biter (male; Ghaden's)

Ligige' 's dog (male)

Snow Hawk (female; Sok's)

PEOPLE OF THE NEAR RIVER VILLAGE

Elders (Men):   Anaay (also called Fox Barking; stepfather of Chakliux and Sok; husband of Dii and Gull Beak; owner of K'os)

Blue-head Duck (deceased; former chief elder)

Giving Meat

Summer Face (deceased; father of Yaa)

Sun Caller (father of Least Weasel)

Tsaani (deceased; grandfather of Chakliux and Sok; brother of Ligige')

Wolf-and-Raven (deceased; former shaman; cousin of Ligige'; husband of Blue Flower)

Elders (Women):   Blue Flower (Wolf-and-Raven's widow)

Gull Beak (wife of Anaay)

Elders (Women) (cont'd):   Lazy Snow
    No Teeth
    Three Baskets
    Vole (widow of Blue-head
      Duck)

Hunters: Black Mouth (owner of K'os;
      husband of Two Fist)
    First Eagle (husband of Awl)
    Gull Wing (deceased; father
      of Sok and Chakliux,
      brother to Anaay)
    Least Weasel (son of Sun
      Caller)
    Many Words (husband of
      Owl Catcher)
    Muskrat Singer
    River Ice Dancer (son of
      Wolf Head)
    Third Tree
    Wolf Head (father of River
      Ice Dancer)

Wives and Young Women: Awl (Cousin River captive;
      wife of First Eagle)
    Cut Ear (Cousin River cap-
      tive)
    Daes (deceased; mother of
      Ghaden and Aqamdax;
      originally from the First
      Men Village)
    Dii (Cousin River captive;
      wife of Anaay)
    Green Bird (Cousin River
      captive)
    Happy Mouth (deceased;
      mother of Yaa)
    K'os (Cousin River captive;
      adoptive mother of Chak-
      liux; slave of Black Mouth
      and later of Anaay)

Wives and Young Women (cont'd):	Light Hair
	Owl Catcher (Cousin River captive; wife of Many Words)
	Red Leggings
	Stay Small (Cousin River captive)
	Talks-all-night
	Two Fist (wife of Black Mouth)
	Willow Leaf (Cousin River captive)
Children:	Best Fist (girl)
	Blue Necklace (girl)
	Daughter of Red Leggings

PEOPLE OF THE FOUR RIVERS VILLAGE

Elders (Men):	Brown Foot
	Tree Climber (husband of Sand Fly)
Elders (Women):	Near Mouse
	Sand Fly (wife of Tree Climber)
Hunters:	Brown Eye
	Cen (a trader; husband of Gheli)
	Eagle Catcher
	Fat Mink
	First Spear (chief hunter)
	Gives-dogs
	Jumps-too-far
	Willow Stick

Wives and Young Women:	Fern
	Gheli (also known as Red Leaf; wife of Cen)
	K'os (adoptive mother of Chakliux)
	White Lake
Children:	Daes (Gheli's infant daughter)
Dogs:	Tracker (male; Cen's)

GLOSSARY OF NATIVE
AMERICAN WORDS

AA, AAA (Aleut Athabascan) Interjection used to express surprise: "Oh!" (The double or triple *a* carries a long *a* sound.)

ANAAY (Ahtna Athabascan) That which moves, caribou or caribou herd. (The Athabascan vowel *a* is pronounced like the *u* in the English word *but*. The *n* is similar to the English *n,* and the *aa* takes on an *aw* sound. The *y* is like the *y* in the English word *you*. The accent falls on the *naay*.)

ANGAX (Aleut) Power. *Anga* is the root used in the Aleut word for "elder brother." (The *a*'s are short; because it falls before the letter *n*, the first a takes on more of a short *e* sound. The Aleut *n* is quite nasal; the *g* is a voiced velar fricative, quite guttural; and the final *x* is a voiceless velar fricative.)

AQAMDAX (Aleut) Cloudberry, *Rubus chamaemorus*. (See Pharmacognosia.) (The *a*'s are short. The Aleut *q* is like a harsh English *k*, the *m* like an English *m* and *d* much like the English *th*. The Aleut *x* is a voiceless velar fricative.)

BABICHE (English—probably anglicized from the Cree word *assababish*, a diminutive of *assabab*, "thread") Lacing made from rawhide.

CEN (Ahtna Athabascan) Tundra. (The *c* sounds like an English *k*. The *e* carries a short sound like the *e* in the English word *set*. The Ahtna *n* sounds like the English *n*.)

CET'AENI (Ahtna Athabascan) Creatures of ancient Ahtna legend. They are tailed and live in trees and caves. (The *c* sounds like an English *k*. The *e* carries a short sound like the *e* in the English word *set*. The *t'* is much like an English *t* followed by a glottal release. The diphthong *ae* is pronounced like the *a* in the English word *cat*. The *n* is much like the English *n*, and the final *i* has a short *i* sound as in the English word *sit*. The *t'aen* is accented.)

CHAKLIUX (Ahtna Athabascan, as recorded by Pinart in 1872) Sea otter. (The word is pronounced as it would be in English, with the final *x* a voiceless velar fricative.)

CHIGDAX (Aleut) A waterproof, watertight parka made of sea lion or bear intestines, esophagus of seal or sea lion, or the tongue skin of a whale. The hood had a drawstring, and the sleeves were tied at the wrists for sea travel. These knee-length garments were often decorated with feathers and bits of colored esophagus. (The Aleut *ch* is much like the English *ch*, the *g* like a guttural English *g*, and the *d* carries almost a *th* sound. The vowels are short. The *x* should be properly written as $\hat{x}$, and is a voiceless uvular fricative.)

CILT'OGHO (Ahtna Athabascan) A container hollowed out of birch and used to carry water. (The *c* sounds like an English *k*. The *i* has a short *i* sound as in the English word *sit*. The *l* is properly written *Ł* and has no corresponding sound in English. The tip of the tongue is held on the palate just behind the front teeth and breath released so as to push air off both sides of the tongue. The *t'* is much like an English *t* followed by a glottal release. The Ahtna *o* is like the *o* in the English word *for*. The Ahtna *gh* has no English equivalent. It closely resembles the French *r*. The *t'ogh* carries the accent.)

DAES (Ahtna Athabascan) Shallow, a shallow portion of a lake or stream. (The *d* is pronounced with the tongue tip touching the backs of the top front teeth. It carries almost a *t* sound. The diphthong *ae* has an *a* sound similar to that in the English word *hat*. The final *s* has almost an *sh* sound.)

DII (Ahtna Athabascan) One alone, on one's own. (The *d* is pronounced with the tongue tip touching the backs of the top front teeth. It carries almost a *t* sound. The double *i* carries a long *e* sound as in the English word *free*.)

DILK'AHOO (Koyukon Athabascan) Raven. (The *d* is pronounced with the tongue tip touching the backs of the top front teeth. It carries almost a *t* sound. The *i* has a short *i* sound as in the English word *sit*. The *l* is pronounced like the *l*'s in the English word *call*. The *k'* has no English equivalent. It is similar to the Aleut *x* and is pronounced in the back of the throat with a very harsh, guttural sound. The apostrophe denotes a glottal stop. The Athabascan vowel *a* is pronounced like the *u* in the English word *but*. The *h* is similar to the *h* in the English word *help*, and the *oo* takes on the long *o* sound as in the English word *rove*.)

DZUUGGI (Ahtna Athabascan) A favored child who receives special training, especially in oral traditions, from infancy. (The *dz* takes the sound of the final *ds* in the English word *leads*. The *uu* sounds like the *ui* in the English word *fruit*. The Ahtna double *gg* has no English equivalent. It is very guttural and pronounced with the back of the tongue held against the soft palate. The *i* has a short *i* sound as in the English word *sit*. The accent is on the first syllable.)

GGUZAAKK (Koyukon Athabascan) A thrush, *Hylocichla minima, H. ustulata* and *H. guttata*. These birds sing an intricately beautiful song that the Koyukon people traditionally believe to indicate the presence of an unknown person or spirit. (The double *gg* has no English equivalent. It is very guttural and pronounced with the back of the tongue held against the soft palate. The *u* sounds similar to the *oo* in the English word *book*. The *z* is similar in sound to *zh*, or like the *s* in *treasure*. The *aa* carries an *aw* sound. The *kk* is a very hard *c* sound.)

GHADEN (Ahtna Athabascan) Another person. (The Ahtna *gh* has no English equivalent. It closely resembles the French *r*. The *a* sounds like the English vowel *u* in the word *but*. The Ahtna *d* is pronounced with the tongue tip touching the backs of the top front teeth. It carries almost a *t* sound. The *e* carries a short sound like the *e* in the English word *set*. The Ahtna *n* sounds like the English *n*.)

GHELI (Ahtna Athabascan) True, good. (The Ahtna *gh* has no English equivalent. It closely resembles the French *r*. The *e* carries a short sound like the *e* in the English word *set*. The Ahtna *l* sounds like the *l*'s in the English word *call*. The *i* is like the *i* in the English word *sit*.)

'IH (Ahtna Athabascan) Exclamation of amazement made by a listener. (The apostrophe denotes an initial glottal stop. When a word begins with a vowel preceded by a glottal stop, it takes on a quick, crisp beginning with a burst of air forced quickly through the vocal cords to produce the vowel sound. The *i* takes on a short *i* sound as in the English word *sit*. The *h* is a voiceless glottal fricative.)

IITIKAALUX (Atkan Aleut) Cow parsnip, wild celery. See the pharmacognosia. (The *ii* is pronounced like a long *e*. The *t* and *l* are much like their corresponding English letters. The single *i* and *u* are short, and the *aa* carries a long *a* sound. The *k* is a guttural English *k*. The *x* is properly written as x̂, and is a voiceless uvular fricative. Accent on the penult.)

IQYAX (Aleut) A skin-covered, wooden-framed boat. A kayak. (The two vowels are short. The *q* is like a harsh English *k*, the *y* much like an English *y*, and the final *x* a voiceless velar fricative. Accent the first syllable.)

KOLDZE' NIHWDELNEN (Ahtna Athabascan) Nothing remained. (The *k* has no English equivalent. It is similar to the Aleut *x* and is pronounced in the back of the throat with a very harsh, guttural sound. The *o* carries a short sound similar to the *o* in the English word *for*. The *l*'s are pronounced like the *l*'s in the English word *call*. The Ahtna *dz* is pronounced like the *ds* in the English word *lads*. The *e*'s in both words carry a short sound like the *e* in the English word *set*, and the apostrophe denotes a glottal stop. The Athabascan *n* is similar to the English *n*. The *i* carries a short sound like the *i* in the English word *sit*. The *hw* is a voiceless labialized glottal fricative like the Athabascan *h*, but the lips should be rounded as in pronouncing the English word *hoe*. The *d* is pronounced with the tongue tip touching the backs of the top front teeth. It carries almost a *t* sound.)

K'OS (Ahtna Athabascan) Cloud. (The Ahtna *k* has no English equivalent. It is similar to the Aleut *x* and is pronounced in the back of the throat with a very harsh, guttural sound. The apostrophe denotes a glottal stop. The *o* carries a short sound similar to the *o* in the English word *for*. The Ahtna *s* is pronounced almost like an English *sh*.)

LIGIGE' (Ahtna Athabascan) The soapberry or dog berry, *Shepherdia canadensis*. (See Pharmacognosia.) (The *L* is properly written Ł, is voiceless, and has no corresponding sound in English. The tip of the tongue is held on the palate just behind the front teeth and breath released so as to push air off both sides of the tongue. The *i* has a short *i* sound like in the English word *sit*. The single *g* corresponds most closely to the English *k* and is pronounced in the back of the throat, with the final *e* pronounced like the *e* in *set*. The final apostrophe denotes a glottal stop. Accent on the final syllable.)

NAAX (Ahtna Athabascan) Command given to a dog— "Go!" or "Proceed!" (The Ahtna *n* sounds like the English *n*. The *aa* carries an *aw* sound. The Athabascan *x* is a voiceless velular fricative.)

NAE' (Ahtna Athabascan) Yes. (The Ahtna *n* sounds like an English *n*. The *ae* acts as a diphthong and takes on the *a* sound in the English word *fad*. The apostrophe represents a glottal stop.)

NUHU'ANH (Koyukon Athabascan) (The *n*'s sound like the English *n*. The *u*'s carry the sound of the *o*'s in the English word *cook*. The *h*'s are similar to the *h* in the English word *help*. The apostrophe denotes a glottal stop. The *a* sounds like the English vowel *u* in the word *but*.)

QUNG (Aleut) Hump, humpback. (The initial *q* is like a harsh English *k*. The *u* is short, and the digraph *ng* is nasal, pronounced much like the *ng* in the English word *gong*.)

SAEL (Ahtna Athabascan) Container made of bark. (The Ahtna *s* is pronounced almost like an English *sh*. The diphthong *ae* carries a sound similar to the *a* in *bat* or *at*. The *l* is properly written *Ł*, is voiceless, and has no corresponding sound in English. The tip of the tongue is held on the palate just behind the front teeth and breath released so as to push air off both sides of the tongue.)

SAX (Aleut) A long, hoodless parka made of feathered birdskins. (The *s* is pronounced like a slightly lisped English *s*; *a* carries a short vowel sound. The *x* is a voiceless velar fricative.)

SOK (Ahtna Athabascan) Raven call. (The Ahtna *s* is almost like the English *sh*. The Ahtna *o* is like the *o* in the English word *for*. The *k* is a guttural English *k*.)

TIKAANI (Ahtna Athabascan) Wolf. (The Ahtna *t* is much like the English *t*, and *i* has a short *i* sound as in the English word *sit*. The Ahtna *k* has no English equivalent. It is similar to the Aleut *x* and is pronounced in the back of the throat with a very harsh, guttural sound. The *aa* carries an *aw* sound, and the *n* is similar to the English *n*. The *kaan* receives the accent.)

TIKIYAASDE (Ahtna Athabascan) Menstruation hut. (The *t* is much like the English *t*. The *i* has a short *i* sound as in the English word *sit*. The Ahtna *k* has no English equivalent. It is similar to the Aleut *x* and is pronounced in the back of the throat with a very harsh, guttural sound. The Ahtna *y* is pronounced like the *y* in the English word *you*. The *aa* carries an *aw* sound; the Ahtna *s* is pronounced almost like an English *sh*. The Ahtna *d* is pronounced with the tongue tip touching the backs of the top front teeth. It carries almost a *t* sound. The *e* carries a short sound like the *e* in the English word *set*.)

TSAANI (Ahtna Athabascan) Grizzly bear, *Ursus arctos*. (*Ts* takes a sound similar to the *ts* in *sets*. The double *aa* carries an *aw* sound; the *n* is pronounced like the English *n* and the *i* has a short *i* sound as in the English word *sit*. The first syllable is accented.)

TUXAKUXTXIN HI (Aleut) Do you hear? (The *t*'s take on a nearly *th* sound [unaspirated postdental stop]. The first *u* carries a short *u* sound; the second carries a short *o* sound. The first and third *x*'s are voiceless velar fricatives; the second *x*, properly written as *x̂*, is a voiceless uvular fricative. The *a* is a short *a*. The *k* is a velar unaspirated stop. Both *i*'s carry the short *i* sound, and the *n*, because of the antecedent *i*, is a strong palatalized nasal. The *h* is nearly a glottal stop, merely an aspiration prior to the pronunciation of the vowel that follows.)

ULAX (Aleut) A semisubterranean dwelling raftered with driftwood and covered with thatching and sod. (Pronounced "oo-lax," with the accent on the first syllable. The *a* carries a short vowel sound, and the final x is a voiceless velar fricative. Plural: **ULAS** or **ULAM**.)

UNANGAX UTING (Aleut) I am Aleut. (The initial *u* takes on a *y* sound. The second *u* carries a short *u* sound. The first *n* is quite nasal, and the *ng*'s are voiced velar nasals, slightly stronger than the English *ng*. The *a*'s carry a short *a* sound. The *x*, properly written as *x̂*, is a voiceless uvular fricative. The *i* carries a short *i* sound.)

XOS COGH (Ahtna Athabascan) Devil's club, literally "big thistle" or "big thorn," *Echinopanax horridum*. (See Pharmacognosia.) (The *x* is a voiceless velar fricative. The Ahtna *o* is like the *o* in the English word *for*. The *s* is similar to the English *sh*, and the *c* sounds like an English *k*. The Ahtna *gh* has no English equivalent. It closely resembles the French *r*.)

YAA (Ahtna Athabascan) Sky. (The Ahtna *y* is pronounced like the *y* in the English word *you*. The *aa* carries an *aw* sound.)

YAYKAAS (Ahtna Athabascan) Literally, "flashing sky." The aurora borealis. (The Ahtna *y* is pronounced like the *y* in the English word *you*. The Ahtna *k* has no English equivalent. It is similar to the Aleut *x* and is pronounced in the back of the throat with a very harsh, guttural sound. The *a* is like the *u* in the English word *but*. The *aa* carries an *aw* sound, and the *s* is similar to the English *sh*. The last syllable receives the accent.)

YEHL (Tlingit) Raven. (A similar pronunciation to the English word *yell*.)

The words in this glossary are defined and listed according to their use in *Cry of the Wind*. Spellings, pronunciations and words in the Aleut language are used as per their standardization in the *Aleut Dictionary, Unangam Tunudgusii*, compiled by Knut Bergsland. Spellings, pronunciations and words in the Ahtna Athabascan language are used as per their standardization in the *Ahtna Athabascan Dictionary*, compiled and edited by James Kari. Both dictionaries are published by the Alaska Native Language Center, University of Alaska Fairbanks.

PHARMACOGNOSIA

Plants listed in this pharmacognosia are *not* cited in recommendation for use, but only as a supplement to the novel. Many poisonous plants resemble helpful plants, and even some of the most benign can be harmful if used in excess. The wisest way to harvest wild vegetation for use as medicine, food or dyes is in the company of an expert. Plants are listed in alphabetical order according to the names used in *Cry of the Wind*.

ALDER, *Alnus crispa*: A small tree with grayish bark. Medium green leaves have toothed edges, rounded bases and pointed tops. Flower clusters resemble miniature pinecones. The cambium or inner layer of bark is dried (fresh bark will irritate the stomach) and used to make tea said to reduce high fever. It is also used as an astringent and a gargle for sore throats. The bark is used to make brown dye.

AQAMDAX: See **Cloudberry**, below.

BALSAM POPLAR (cottonwood), *Populus balsamifera*: A tree of the willow family that grows from the Alaska panhandle region to the Arctic in moist, gravelly soils. It attains heights of up to seventy feet. Leaves are smooth, ovate and slightly toothed, a dark green above and pale underneath. The gray bark becomes thick and ridged as the tree ages. Spring catkins are rich in vitamin C. Like willow, balsam poplar inner bark contains salicin (aspirin), and steeped in hot water is a good gargle for sore throats. The bark, ground and applied to sores, is said to dry seepage. The root—steeped, not boiled—taken as a tea, was used by some Native peoples in an effort to prevent premature birth. The buds are used as an expectorant.

BANEBERRY, *Actaea rubra*: The baneberry is the only deadly toxic berry native to Alaska. It is a vigorous plant that grows in southeastern and coastal Alaska north to the Yukon River area. It attains heights of up to four feet, though two to three feet is normal. Leaves are elongate, dentate and compound; delicate white flowers grow in ball-like clusters. Berries are red or white with a characteristic black dot. Warning: All portions of the baneberry are poisonous, and ingestion will cause pain and bloody diarrhea. Death may result due to paralysis of the respiratory system and/or cardiac arrest. Do not even touch these plants!

BEARBERRY (ptarmigan berry), *Arctostaphylos alpina, Arctostaphylos rubra*: A low, ground-hugging shrub that forms thick mats. Berries are black (*A. alpina*) or red (*A. rubra*) and edible, but quite tasteless. *A. rubra* grows in lower altitudes. The foliage of both plants turns a brilliant scarlet in autumn.

BEDSTRAW: See **Goose Grass**, below.

CARIBOU LEAVES (wormwood, silverleaf), *Artemisia tilesii*: This perennial plant attains a height of two to three feet on a single stem. The hairy, lobed leaves are silver underneath and a darker green on top. A spike of small clustered flowers grows at the top of the stem in late summer. Fresh leaves are used to make a tea that is said to purify the blood and stop internal bleeding, and to wash cuts and sore eyes. The leaves are heated and layered over arthritic joints to ease pain. Caution: caribou leaves may be toxic in large doses.

CLOUDBERRY, *Rubus chamaemorus*: Not to be confused with the larger, shrublike salmonberry, *R. spectabilis,* this small plant grows to about six inches in height and bears a single white flower and a salmon-colored berry shaped like a raspberry. The green leaves are serrated and have five main lobes. The berries are edible but not as flavorful as raspberries, and are high in vitamin C. The juice from the berries is said to be a remedy for hives.

CRAMPBARK: See **Highbush Cranberry**, below.

DOG FENNEL (wild chamomile, pineapple weed), *Matricaria matricariodes*: This small (three- to twelve-inch) plant thrives in all but the northernmost part of Alaska. The leaves are delicate and feathery; rayless domed yellow flowers, usually less than a half inch across, emit a pineapple fragrance when crushed. A tea made of flowers (and foliage, if desired) is soothing and is said to release tension and promote sleep. Aleuts drank dog fennel tea to ease gas pains. Caution: in some individuals, large amounts of the tea may cause nausea or vomiting. Those with sensitive skin may notice minor skin irritation after picking or handling the herb.

FIREWEED (wild asparagus), *Epilobium angustifolium*: Fireweed grows throughout Alaska and northern North America. Plants grow upright to a height of three to five feet and end in a spikelike flower cluster. Each flower has four petals, which bloom from the bottom of the stalk up during midsummer to late summer. Colors vary from a deep and brilliant red-pink to nearly white. Leaves are willowlike: long and narrow, and medium green in color. Early spring shoots (high in vitamins A and C) may be harvested prior to development of the leaves without harm to the plant. (Harvesting the white stem below the soil level actually promotes plant growth.) The tip of the stem should be discarded due to the disagreeable taste; the rest can be steamed and eaten like asparagus. Leaves should be harvested before flowers bloom to add to soups as seasoning. Flowers are often used in salads and also make good jelly. Fireweed leaves steeped for tea are said to settle stomachaches. Salves made from roots are said to draw out infection.

GOOSEFOOT (lamb's quarter, pigweed), *Chenopodium album*: Soft goose-foot-shaped leaves grow in an alternating pattern from stems that average one to three feet in height (though these can grow to ten feet). If grown domestically, the plant can be difficult to contain due to effusive self-seeding. Greens, good in salads, are high in vitamins A and C, and the B complex. Tea decoctions are used as a wash for sores inside the mouth. Leaves are used as a poultice for wounds and rheumatism. Caution: plants contain oxalic acid and when eaten in extremely large amounts might cause kidney damage.

GOOSE GRASS (northern bedstraw), *Galium boreale*: The narrow leaves grow in groups of four under the fragrant white flower sprays. Young plants warmed (not boiled) in hot water and placed on external wounds are said to help clot the blood. The dried plant, made into a salve with softened fat, was used to treat external skin irritations. Teas (steeped, not boiled) made of young leaves, seeds or roots may be diuretic. Roots produce a purplish dye.

HIGHBUSH CRANBERRY (crampbark, mooseberry), *Viburnum edule*: This erect but scraggly bush grows throughout Alaska from the Alaska Peninsula to the Brooks Range. Its lobed leaves are shaped somewhat like maple leaves, grow opposite one another and are coarsely toothed. The average height of the highbush cranberry is about four to six feet, though they sometimes reach ten feet. Five-petaled white flowers grow in flat clusters and mature into flavorful but bitter red berries in August and September. (A frost sweetens the berries considerably.) Berries are high in vitamin C and make tasty jelly. The inner bark, boiled into tea, is used as a gargle for sore throats and colds. Highbush cranberry bark contains *glucoside viburnine*, a muscle relaxant. Bark made into tea decoctions is used to relieve menstrual and stomach cramps, and is said to be effective on infected skin abrasions.

IITIKAALUX (cow parsnip, wild celery), *Heracleum lanatum*: A thick-stemmed, hearty plant that grows to nine feet in height. The coarse, dark leaves have three main lobes with serrated edges. It is also known by the Russian name *poochki* or *putchki*. Stems and leaf stalks taste like a spicy celery but must be peeled before eating because the outer layer is a skin irritant. White flowers grow in inverted bowl-shaped clusters at the tops of the plants. Roots are also edible, and leaves were dried to flavor soups and stews. The root was chewed raw to ease sore throats and was heated and a section pushed into a painful tooth to deaden root pain. Caution: gloves should be worn when harvesting. Iitikaalux is similar in appearance to poisonous water hemlock.

LIGIGE' (soapberry or dog berry), *Shepherdia canadensis:* A shrub that grows to six feet in height with smooth, round-tipped, dark green leaves. The orange-colored berries ripen in July and are edible but bitter. They foam like soap when beaten.

LUNGWORT (chiming bells), *Mertensia paniculata*: Two- to three-foot plants sport hairy, elongated ovate leaves that grow opposite one another on the stem. Small groups of delicate, purplish, bell-like flowers cluster at the ends of short drooping stems. Flowers and leaves are said to be good added to teas. Leaves are better picked before the plants flower. The plant has supposedly been used to relieve asthma and other types of lung congestion.

MARSH MARIGOLD (cowslip, meadowbright), *Caltha palustris*: A short plant (about a foot tall) that thrives in marshy areas. Arching stems grow from a central cluster, and leaves are large (up to six or seven inches across), rounded and roughly kidney shaped. Each flower has five rounded petals and is bright yellow. They range throughout Alaska. The marsh marigold is used as an expectorant and is thought to loosen lung and bronchial mucus. Caution: marsh marigold contains *glucoside protoanemonin*, a toxin that can be destroyed by boiling. Greens should be used only after boiling twice. Daily use can cause damage to kidneys. Those with sensitive skin may experience a contact dermatitis after handling the plants. Please note that marsh marigold looks similar to wild calla, which is considered poisonous. Both plants grow in similar habitats.

NAGOONBERRY (wineberry), *Rubus arcticus, Rubus stellatus*: A ground-hugging berry plant that grows in wet, open areas. Leaves are trilobate and resemble strawberry leaves; red berries look like small raspberries. Blossoms are bright pink. The berries are delicious and high in vitamin C, but are difficult to find in large quantities. Leaves and roots are used to relieve diarrhea. Caution: use only fresh or very dry leaves. Wilted leaves are said to induce vomiting.

PLANTAIN (goosetongue, seashore plantain—not to be confused with broad-leaved plantain, an introduced plant), *Plantago maritima*: Pointed, narrow leaves grow from the plant base to a height of twelve inches. It grows along the southeastern Alaskan seacoast and is a favorite food of the Alaska brown bear. Leaves are good raw or cooked and are mashed to use as a salve for skin irritations. Caution: seashore plantain closely resembles poisonous arrowgrass, and they grow in the same general areas. Arrowgrass contains cyanide.

RASPBERRY, *Rubus idaeus*: A prickly shrub that grows up to six feet in height. Berries are prime, bright red and made up of many drupelets, each containing a single seed. Soft leaves have five to seven lobes, are pointed and have serrated edges. Flowers are white and contain five petals. Raspberry leaf tea is said to aid in the health of reproductive organs. Berries are high in vitamins B and C and a number of minerals, including calcium. Caution: wilted leaves are slightly toxic. Some people experience contact dermatitis after handling leaves or berries.

SALMONBERRY (not to be confused with *Rubus chamaemorus*; see **Cloudberry**, above), *Rubus spectabilis*: A woody biennial shrub that grows up to seven feet in height. Bright rose-purple flowers are five-petaled and mature into large raspberrylike berries, red or salmon pink in color. Berries are high in vitamin C. Bark and leaf infusions are used to treat stomach upset, and root teas are said to relieve diarrhea. Poultices of pounded bark are used to relieve toothache. Caution: wilted leaves are slightly toxic.

SPRUCE (white spruce), *Picea glauca*; (black spruce), *Picea mariana*: Evergreen trees with four-sided needles. Black spruce have a more scraggly appearance and generally grow on wetter, lower ground than white spruce. Needles are high in vitamin C and may be boiled into a relaxing tonic tea (carefully strained). Warmed pitch is used as a chest plaster said to help relieve congestion, and also may be used as makeshift "stitches" to close cuts.

SOUR DOCK (sorrel, curly dock, yellow dock), *Rumex crispus;* (arctic dock), *Rumex arcticus*: Leaves are shaped like spearheads, wavy at the edges, and fan out from the base of the plant. A central stalk grows to three or four feet in height and bears clusters of edible reddish seeds. Steamed leaves are said to remove warts. The root of these plants is crushed and used as a poultice for skin eruptions. Fresh leaves are abundant in vitamins A and C, but they also contain oxalic acid, so consumption should be moderate.

WILLOW, *Salix*: A narrow-leafed shrub or small tree with smooth gray, yellowish and/or brownish bark. There are presently more than thirty species of willow in Alaska. The leaves are a very good source of vitamin C, though in some varieties they taste quite bitter. The leaves and inner bark contain salicin, which acts like aspirin to deaden pain. Bark can be chipped and boiled to render a pain-relieving tea. Leaves can also be boiled for tea. Leaves are chewed and placed over insect bites to relieve itching. Roots and branches are used to make baskets and woven fish weirs.

XOS COGH (devil's club), *Echinopanax horridum*: A prickly, woody-stemmed plant that may reach heights of eight feet. Large leaves resemble maple leaves. Tea decoctions are said to help stabilize blood sugar and prevent cancer. The root, pounded and heated, can be used to treat skin abrasions and infections and insect bites. The plant's spines are considered a nemesis of hikers.

YELLOW DOCK: See **Sour Dock**, above.

YELLOW VIOLET, *Violaceae*: Small yellow five-petaled flowers are borne on stems that grow to approximately ten inches. Flowers carry irregular dark lines at the center of each petal. Serrated leaves are heart-shaped. Both leaves and flowers are edible. Leaves are a good source of vitamin C. Leaves were mixed with fat and used as a salve on skin contusions. Caution: leaves and flowers tend to have a laxative effect.

ACKNOWLEDGMENTS

Mere words cannot convey my gratitude, nor the debt I owe so many for their help, encouragement and willingness to share their expertise.

All those I cited in *Song of the River* again deserve my mention: our friends in Akutan, Anchorage, Atka, Beluga, Dutch Harbor, St. George, St. Paul and Unalaska. You will never know how much I have learned and continue to learn from all of you, and how much you mean to Neil and me. To those steadfast friends whose expertise has guided me since my first novel, *Mother Earth Father Sky*, again I say thank you: Dr. William Laughlin, Mike and Rayna Livingston, Dr. Ragan and Dorthea Callaway, and Mark and Forbes McDonald.

My sincere thanks to those who read this manuscript in its many versions: my husband, Neil; my daughter, Krystal; my parents, Pat and Bob McHaney; my sister Tish Walker; my friends Linda Hudson and Joe Claxton, astute readers all. I am fortunate to have friends and family like you, willing to help by wading through pages riddled with notes and typos and pleas for feedback!

My gratitude to our friends at Shobunsha and Tuttle-Mori in Japan, and our translators, Akio Namekata, Hiromi Kawashima and Atsuko Sakurauchi, who patiently introduced us to their beautiful and complex culture. A special mention to Mr. Hashida Yoshinori, who was so generous with his books and information about the prehistoric culture of the Japanese Islands and the Jomon People; and to Mr. Ohno and his wife, who so graciously allowed us to experience a wide variety of the bounty of Pacific Rim seafoods at their beautiful Tokyo home.

My sincere thanks also to my father, who was able to give me information about dislocated shoulders from his firsthand experience, and not once chided me for lack of sensitivity when my interest proved to be motivated as much by literary concerns as sympathy!

I am truly fortunate to have Rhoda Weyr as my agent. She is a gifted editor as well as a wise counselor and friend, always astute in both business and literary matters. My most sincere appreciation and heartfelt thanks go to my editor at Avon Books, Ann McKay Thoroman, and her very gifted staff.

Words always fail me when I seek to convey my thanks to my husband, Neil. I am grateful for his insight, his computer work on the map and his knowledge about wildlife and survival skills. He is gifted in so many areas where I am not, and always willing to advise when advice is needed and to listen without criticism when I want a sounding board. We convey our appreciation to our children, Krystal and Neil and Tonya; to our parents and friends; and to our extended families, always supporting, always encouraging. We are abundantly blessed.